Storm Before Sunrise

Storm Before Sunrise

June Wyndham Davies

PIATKUS

First published in Great Britain in 1993 by
Judy Piatkus (Publishers) Ltd of
5 Windmill Street, London W1P 1HF

**The moral right of the author
has been asserted**

*A catalogue record for this book is available
from the British Library*

ISBN 0-7499-0186-1

Phototypeset in 11/12pt Linotron Times by
Computerset, Harmondsworth, Middlesex
Printed and bound in Great Britain by
Biddles Ltd, Guildford & King's Lynn

For all the friends who
saw me through the tough times

The Waif

Cold. So cold. Even the glass was so frosted with it that it was like looking at the world through lace curtains. The pain in her feet had gone at last, but the numbness in her fingertips had spread up as far as her elbows.

Faces swam before her eyes. So many strange faces. She turned her head restlessly from side to side, but it was dark and she could not make out the narrow mattresses that crowded the dormitory. Where were the other orphans? Where was Matron? She called to Lizzie, but there was no answer.

She closed her eyes tightly to press back the panic that threatened to overwhelm her. She opened them again to see the anxious faces of the other passengers swimming in front of her eyes.

Jolting, swaying, lurching. And above all, the bone-chilling, mind-numbing cold. She could feel the snow, stinging her face. But that couldn't be, for no one would have been fool enough to open the window. She must be getting light-headed. How long was it since she had eaten? A day? Two? Perhaps even three?

The train was climbing again. The wheels toiled along the rails, grinding out their insistent chant: *So* cold, *so* cold, *going* to freeze, *going* to die.

Her head began to spin again with the compelling rhythm, and the blackness all around threatened to engulf her. Beyond the blackness, voices called to her, the voices of people long dead: poor consumptive Lizzie, Aggie, and the other orphans who had died in the scarlet fever, reached out

1

welcoming arms to her. Her exhausted body longed to go to them, but her spirit still fought them: she hadn't come this far to give in so easily! She struggled to overlay their faces with a vision of Sarah and Matron. What would *they* think if she gave in now?

The overcast grey mantle of the sky had changed to the cold navy of a freezing winter night when they pulled into the next station. 'Anyone for Hamilton?' called the porter cheerily at each window.

A stout man hurried to open the door and called him over. 'Think this young 'un's for here,' he called. 'But she don't seem quite right in the head. Keeps mutterin' summat foreign.'

'See your ticket, Miss. Miss?' The porter prised her fingers from the handle of the portmanteau with some difficulty; clenched in her frozen fingers was a crumpled scrap of paper.

He held it towards the flaring gas lamp and struggled to make out the letters. 'Edensville!' he exclaimed. 'But that's clear over the other side of the lake! What fool sent her this a-way?'

The stout man shook his head. 'Hand her over to the authorities, you should. For certain she shouldn't stay on board. We're afeared she'll do something reckless.'

The porter put down the portmanteau and helped her on to the platform. 'Don't you fret, sir. I'll take her to the station master.' He closed the door and deposited the girl and her bag on a bench.

'You sit down there and wait for me,' he said in a kindly voice, hurrying off to close up the doors. The guard waved his flag, the train steamed out, heading for points further west; the porter turned back to see his charge staggering down the platform, perilously close to the departing locomotive, towards the great drifts of snow which had been piled up through the winter to keep the lines clear.

'Not that way!' He hurried after her, grabbed her arm and dragged her through to the office.

After a hurried conference with his station master, it was decided to put her on the steamer to Edensville.

'Not our problem, Jeb,' said the station master, puffing contentedly on his pipe. 'Let 'em sort it out over there.'

2

The porter looked up from the bag. 'She don't seem to have a ticket . . .'

'Ed Payne'll take her on my say so. He can get his money back from this doctor in Edensville. Says she's being met there.'

'Should we give her something hot first? She looks all in.'

The station master consulted his pocket watch. 'No time,' he said firmly. 'Or you'll miss the last sailing – and we'll be stuck with her.'

'Thought you said you was being met?' demanded the mate, shouting above the noise as the crew and dockers unloaded the goods and human cargo the steamer had brought through the snowstorm across Lake Ontario on to the Edensville docks.

Like Captain Payne, he had not been too pleased to be handed the responsibility of a ticketless waif with no money, no friends, and bereft besides of most of her wits, but the captain and the station master had a good scheme going with the emigrant traffic across the lake border, from which he took his cut, and a free passage every now and then wouldn't hurt. Since it had become illegal to bring contract labour into the United States, a number of immigrants had come through this way.

'Put her under the awning where you can keep your eye on her,' the captain had instructed the mate. 'When we dock, we'll see if there's anyone to meet her. We'll get back the price of her passage then. And if not – if not, we'll have to hand her over to the Asylum.'

He had tried questioning the girl, but all she would answer was: 'I'm expected in Edensville. Doctor Carter will send to meet me,' and that in a voice so exhausted you could hardly make it out.

Now she repeated it in answer to the mate's question. 'I am to be met,' she whispered hoarsely. 'Doctor Carter. Edensville. I'm expected.'

He looked across the quayside through the falling snow to the yard in front of the shipping offices, where a number of carts and gigs were pulled up in line, their horses tied to the nearby hitching-rail, the drivers stamping their feet, their

3

collars turned up against the cold while the dockers transferred cargoes and luggage from the steamer. 'Any of you lot
for Doctor Carter?' he called hopefully.

'If that's Doctor Carter, Eden Springs,' said a thin wiry
little man, 'then Ellsky's the man you want. Estate manager
out that-away. Dines at the Albany when he's in town.'

'Let's hope he's there tonight,' said the mate with an
exasperated sigh. 'Hey, Jack!' He called the second mate
across and gave him his instructions. 'I'd take her over there
myself, but I can't leave this lot. I'd like to get shot of this 'un
afore she decides to go fer a swim or walks under a train!'

'What if this Ellsky ain't there?'

'Leave her at the station house. Police can decide what to
do with her.'

Like a sleepwalker she allowed herself to be drawn along
the wharves and across the tracks of the dock railway, in the
shadow of the huge grain silos. It seemed an age till they
reached the main square, and it was as much as she could do
to put one foot in front of the other.

The hotel on the main square was busy, carriages driving in
and out of the stableyard and horses hitched to the rail in
front. They crossed the foyer to a smoke-filled room, strong
with the smell of drink and ringing with unbearably loud
voices.

''Suse me, gents,' shouted the second mate. 'Anyone here
know Doctor Carter of Eden Springs?'

A man of middling height with a ruddy face and fair
moustache and beard stepped away from the bar.

'Doctor Carter died three months ago,' he said in a strongly
accented voice. 'His widow's gone to New York.'

He had not noticed the girl standing behind the second
mate until she began to laugh hysterically.

'Stop it!' said the sailor, shaking her. 'What ails you, girl?
Are you mad?'

'Don't you see how funny it is?' she laughed. 'Four thousand miles from the Home and then he's dead? No job! Don't
you see?'

She laughed again, despairingly this time. Then, with a low
moan, her eyes rolled up and she fell to the floor in a dead
faint.

The tall man looked up in irritation from the pile of papers. 'Yes?'

'Steward's here, sir,' said the maid, wiping her none too clean hands on her apron. 'Wants to see you.'

'Max here at this time of night?' He brushed an errant lock of dark hair out of his grey eyes. 'Well, show him in, girl!'

'Wants you down at the yard door, sir. Says he's got summ'un sick down there.'

He ground his teeth with impatience. 'Why the devil didn't you say so straight away, Nancy?' he demanded, pushing past her and taking the stairs two at a time.

'Max.' he nodded briefly to the fair-haired man who stood in the doorway, brushing snow from his tweed overcoat and stamping his booted feet, then turned his attention to the stiff body in the bottom of the cart. One glance was sufficient. 'Explanations later,' he commanded. 'Get her up to the surgery. We may still be in time.'

Half way down the corridor, the unconscious figure in his arms, he looked back over his shoulder to the faces peering anxiously around the door.

'Is Mrs Chobley here? No? You, what's your name?'

'Jessie, doctor,' whispered the little scullerymaid nervously.

'Jessie, I need quilts up in the surgery. Quickly. Understood?'

'Yes, sir!' With a smile of triumph at slovenly Nancy she shot back down the corridor to the linen room.

'Build up the fire, Max!' directed the doctor, laying the frozen figure on the leather couch in front of the fire and turning back one eyelid. 'She's very deeply chilled and we'll have to bring her temperature up slowly.' He started to strip off the sodden outer clothes. 'At a guess she's been like this for several days. Where did you find her?'

'You won't thank me for bringing her,' he said. 'She's another of the housemaids Mrs Carter sent for.'

'God save us, Max, she's already left me six! What the hell am I to do with another?'

Max shrugged. 'This one was hired in London.'

'She's come from *London*? In *this* weather? In these clothes?'

5

'Aye. Knowing Almeria, she would have sent just enough to cover the fare. Will she live?'

Kingsley shrugged. 'Where did you find her?'

'Seaman brought her to the Albany. Seems she turned up at the other side of the lake. Off a train. She'd come overland from Quebec.'

'What?'

'I don't understand it either. Child's from an orphanage, according to her papers; daresay they had no idea about North American winters. When I told her Carter was dead and Almeria gone to New York, she just collapsed. They were going to put her in the Infirmary, Adam. And –'

'And there's typhoid there.' He nodded his head. 'In this state, she wouldn't have stood a chance.' He put a cushion underneath the girl's head and the honey-coloured hair spilled out from under the shawl, spreading round the frozen face like a halo.

'Reminds me of one of Rossetti's painting,' said Max.

'Mmm. Or Millais. The drowned Ophelia springs to mind,' said Kingsley dryly. 'It's all that hair.' He stripped off another layer of frozen clothing. 'Good God, the child must have put on every item of clothing she had!' He rolled back the eyelid again. 'You did the right thing, bringing her here,' he said sombrely. 'Though God knows what I'll do with her – always assuming she lives that long.' He looked anxiously at the blue face.

'Ah, good girl, Jessie!' he said as the little scullerymaid staggered in under the weight of four feather quilts. 'Put them in front of the fire.'

He stripped off the rest of the frozen layers of clothes down to her chemise before swathing the body in a cocoon of warm quilts. The heavy, ugly boots proved more difficult and he swore vigorously as he tore a fingernail on the lacings.

As he chafed her frozen feet he fancied he heard a sound from between the blue lips.

'Rub her hands, Jessie! There's still some life there. Max, fetch the brandy!'

He turned the body on its side and saw with relief the blue shade begin to disappear from the lips.

'Fill some stone hot bottles, Jessie, and fetch a jug of warm water.'

6

He added another quilt from the pile by the fire, tucking a corner around her head but leaving her face free. By the time Jessie returned with the warm water, the girl's eyelids were beginning to flicker. He crossed to a cabinet on the wall, selected a small phial and held it up to the light to check it. He shook a few drops of yellow liquid into the water and added a small amount of brandy.

He crossed rapidly back to the sofa, flinging off his jacket and loosening his cravat as the heat of the built up fire struck him. Gently he raised the girl in his arms, running his finger round her mouth the check there were no blockages.

'Open your mouth,' he commanded. 'Open your mouth and drink this: it will warm you.' She didn't seem to hear, so he tipped the contents of the glass down her and she coughed and spluttered as the warm liquid caught the back of her throat.

Jessie plumped up the cushions and he laid her back against them.

'Keep rubbing those feet, Max,' he bade. 'When the feeling comes back she's not going to be too happy.'

'She won't die, will she, sir?' asked Jessie, round-eyed.

'No, child. We've caught her in time. You can run along to your bed now.'

'I'll stay if you've need of me, sir.'

'I think we're over the worst.'

'What about some coffee, sir, for you and Mr Ellsky? There's always a pot on the stove.'

'Excellent. And Jessie – you've been most efficient. Thank you.'

She blushed fierily, bobbed a curtsey and left.

As the medicine began to course its way through her veins, the girl on the sofa began to whimper.

'Only to be expected,' said the doctor in response to the look of alarm on Max's face. 'The feeling's coming back to her extremities and it'll be cursed painful.'

'Frostbite?'

He looked carefully at the fingers and then unwrapped the girl's feet.

'It's almost unbelievable, but she seems to have escaped that. Must be tougher than she looks. She'll pull through, but it's going to be a long night.' He looked up briefly from rubbing the girl's hands. 'There's nothing more you can do, Max. You'd better go home'

'If you're sure.'

'You've done your part in bringing her here. Now we just have to wait and see.'

'I'll see myself out.'

'Mind *you* don't get frozen on your way home. And if you're not too busy tomorrow, you can call by and see how your orphan of the storm is progressing.'

As the door closed behind Ellsky, he looked down at the still unconscious figure, whimpering and tossing restlessly in her cocoon of quilts. 'In God's name, child!' he murmured. 'What kind of a nightmare journey did you have to reduce you to this state!'

She woke in the early hours of the morning, wondering why the train had stopped. Then a voice spoke at her side and she remembered.

'How do you feel now?'

It wasn't the fair-haired man with the beard and the accent like Little Polack.

'Doctor Carter?' she said hesitantly.

'No. Doctor Carter died. I'm Doctor Kingsley. We met last night.'

That was the dark-haired man. But he had not looked like any doctor she'd ever known. Doctors – even Doctor Morel's medical students – wore frock coats and top hats, not a Norfolk jacket and tweeds.

She screwed up her eyes and peered into the darkness.

'Doctor Kingsley,' he said patiently. 'Don't you remember?'

'Will you light the lamp, if you please? I can't –'

'There's enough light from the fire,' he said, a frown furrowing his brow.

'Then why can't I see you? I could see you last night!' She sat up in a panic, thrusting the heavy blankets away. 'I can't see!' she whispered hoarsely. 'I can't see!' Her voice rose in panic to a scream and she pressed her hands tightly to her eyes.

8

'Let me look.' He took her wrists in a strong grip and drew them firmly but gently away. 'Let me look,' he insisted, and the strength in his voice quelled the note of rising hysteria in hers.

He held her wrists easily with one hand, noting as he did so the thinness of her arms. With his free hand he gently opened the cringing lids. She had the most extraordinarily deep moss-green eyes, long and slightly tilted at the upper edges, giving her a most exotic, almost oriental appearance, but they were clouded now, the whites reddened and the pupils contracted to a black pinpoint.

'Wait a moment. I want to try something.'

Shaking with fear and dread, she could only sit helplessly, listening to the door opening. She thought he was leaving her, but then, with the acute hearing which comes with the dulling of another sense, she heard his footsteps crossing back to the couch and sensed him close behind her. A cool hand touched her cheek and turned her towards the centre of the room, away from the firelight and towards the threatening blackness.

A light flared to one side of her.

'Did you see that?'

'Yes – but only for a moment.'

He struck another Vesta on the silver case and held it to the other side.

'And this?'

She nodded.

'Follow it.'

She followed the small arc of light.

'Snow blindness. The effects are purely temporary.' He tossed the dead matches into the hearth. 'You little fool, did no one tell you not to look at the snow all day? Look, don't cry.' The girl, head cushioned on her folded arms, was sobbing helplessly. 'I told you – it's temporary! A week, maybe less.'

But she was beyond comfort, beyond reassurance, sobbing helplessly as the pent-up miseries of the last week over-whelmed her.

He put his arms around her and held her until the wracking sobs died away.

9

'Better now?' He reached across her and drew a white linen handkerchief from the pocket of his jacket, flung over the back of the couch.'

She mopped her eyes, blew her nose and looked up, straining to make out his face, her bottom lip trembling.

'It – it really will pass? You're not just saying it to. . . .'

'I never deceive my patients,' he said, gazing down at her pale oval face, and a part of his mind separate from the analytical eye of the doctor saw behind the reddened eyes and the damp, fair tangled hair the beauty of the high cheek bones and the pale forehead, the tilted green eyes framed by the long soft lashes, and the lustre of the skin. But the swollen eyelids were drooping now, her exhaustion, mental and physical, total.

He laid her back against the cushions on the couch and dripped a few drops of brown liquid into the unseeing eyes. 'There. That will help. It will be some days before your vision is back to normal. But don't rub them or I'll have to tie your hands and you won't like that.'

She shook her head vigorously, remembering how she and Matron had had to do this to the little children in the Home when chickenpox had broken out with exceptional virulence; prospective employers did not like scarred servants, even skivvies and bootboys they would see no more than twice a year.

He turned away and busied himself with something warming over the flames. 'When did you last eat?' he asked curtly.

'I'm not sure,' she said unsteadily. 'After Quebec. Before Montreal, I think. I shared the last of the bread with Irina and her baby.'

'Had you no money?' he asked angrily.

She shrugged. 'The Trustees gave me a shilling. It was gone before I left England.'

'Here.' He placed a cup of broth in her hands and guided it to her lips. She drank it down greedily and held out the cup for more.

The journey had started out more like a triumphal progress.

Matron had been delighted to find the post with the Carters for the girl. 'She'll see things differently in a new country,

10

away from Sarah Thomsett and her outlandish idea,' she confided to Mrs Evans. 'Less inclined to see going into service as such a burden.'

The farewells had been prolonged and tearful; Matron had shaken her hand and spoken to her bracingly; Mrs Evans had hugged her and the little children had kissed her goodbye with tears in their eyes. And Sarah . . . She bit her lip as she remembered the sight of Sarah: her face set and bitter, she had barely managed to bid her a civil farewell. The words Sarah had hurled at her that dreadful, never-to-be-forgotten day still rang in her head. She had not known the meaning of half of them, but the venom behind them was unmistakable. In all the weary months while they waited for the tickets to come through Sarah had refused to speak to her. It was all so unfair.

She wouldn't let anyone come to the railway station with her; she knew the extended leave-takings would have broken her rigid self-control.

She sat in the dingy third-class railway carriage, watching the last soot-stained houses of the London suburbs fall away. It was the first time she had ever been alone in her life, and she was so frightened. All she had ever known – Matron, Mrs Evans, Sarah and the orphans, even Sarah's brother John – she was leaving behind to go to a strange country, to strange people, to do work she knew she would hate. It was all she could do not to burst into tears. Resolutely she suppressed her sniffs and clutched the shabby portmanteau tightly to her. In it were all her worldly possessions: her best skirt, a blouse from Mrs Evans, some spare stockings and underclothing hastily collected by Matron, a Bible from the Trustees of the Orphanage, a pen and some writing paper and the treasured book with *her* story in it.

The carriage was empty but for a couple of commercial travellers. One of them tried to strike up a conversation with her, but Sarah's words were still echoing in her head and she dared not so much as smile for fear that he would see what a wicked girl she was. Anyway, she knew he was looking down his nose at her old-fashioned jacket and bonnet; meeting with no encouragement he settled his feet on his heated foot-warmer and buried himself in his trade journal.

11

It was already dark when she changed trains in Crewe and she spent one of her precious hoard of pennies to buy some apples from a pasty-faced urchin; reaching Liverpool at last, she climbed wearily out of the train, her back and legs stiff from bracing themselves against the jolting.

A friendly station master directed her to the tram for the Pier Head – and there were a few more of her precious pennies gone. Sarah had bought her tickets with the passage money Mrs Carter had sent – London to Liverpool, Liverpool to Quebec, Quebec to Hamilton – but she had only the shilling Matron had given her to cover any other expenses.

She was the only passenger to alight at the Pier Head and as she watched the glow of the tram lamp disappear into the darkness, she felt so alone, it was all she could do not to sit down and howl.

It began to snow as she turned into the Dock Road, past the great ocean liners still loading passengers and supplies by the uncertain light of storm lanterns, and she knew a great heart-wrenching longing to be back in the old warehouse by the Thames, tucking the little ones into bed, telling them a bedtime story. The docks seemed to go on for miles and she had left all signs of life and bustle behind before, cold, tired and miserable, she at last found the *York*, a much older and smaller vessel than those she had passed earlier. She changed the portmanteau from one aching arm to the other and began to trudge wearily up the gangplank.

A seaman emerged from the shadows and touched his cap in a sketchy salute.

'I have a ticket for the sailing to Quebec,' she said wearily.

'Sorry, missie. We don't take on no more passengers till mornin'.'

'But I must! There's nowhere else I – Oh, please!'

'Sorry, missie. Don't take on no passengers without the orfficers – and they're all out on the town. Night before we sails, see.' He shrugged and turned away. 'Board at first light – we sails on the a'ternoon tide.'

'But where can I go?'

The seaman shrugged, indifferent to her plight. 'Dunno. Cunard hostel might've taken you, even though you ain't sailing with them nor you ain't paid the supplement, but they don't take no one this late.' Not that this one looked like a prostitute, whose exclusion the rules had been formed to ensure, but he knew the wardens wouldn't bend them, not for anyone.

She staggered down the gangplank, shoulders slumped in defeat. There were miserably few pennies left in her purse and she had no idea where to start looking for shelter for the night.

While she had been arguing with the seaman on the *York*, the other ships had finished loading and closed up for the night; the dim light from their deck lanterns flickered, barely reaching the barrels and boxes piled high on the wharves. With a shiver she realised that she was alone on the dockside.

She looked at the warehouses, redolent of tobacco, coffee and tarred rope – not unlike the Orphanage buildings, after all! She put out a tentative hand and pushed a door aside. She stood for a moment, then as she peered into the darkness of the great cavernous hall, shapes began to rise from the floor and detach themselves from the walls. 'Jesus, Patrick,' wheezed a voice close to her feet. 'Looks like our luck's in after all.'

She whirled and fled, her heart racing, her feet stumbling and slipping on the uneven floor. Outside the snow was still falling steadily and the cobblestones were treacherous beneath her ill-fitting boots, but she dared not stop until she was sure she was far enough away to be safe from pursuit. At last she slithered to a halt and stood a moment, pressed against a dripping wall, while she fought to get her breath back and still the rising panic that threatened to choke her.

A noise behind her lent wings to her feet and she ran again, not stopping until only the echo of her own footsteps bounced back from the dank, dripping walls. Though she didn't dare go into another warehouse, she peered into every niche or doorway she passed on the Dock Road. But every archway or corner which might provide even the most illusory shelter was already filled with at least one pathetic bundle or rag- or newspaper-wrapped humanity.

At the far end of the Dock Road, the clanging of the bell heralded the last run of the tram from the main station. She summoned up her last reserves of strength and just caught it.

'You look as though you've seen a ghost!' said the conductor, and before she had time to think, she'd poured out all her troubles to him.

He swore under his breath. 'Shouldn't be allowed, young 'uns like you left to yerself in a strange place.' He scratched his head. 'Somewhere cheap an' decent, y'say? Don't always go together, they don't.'

For once her luck was in: the conductor's widowed sister, living in a scruffy two up, two down, back to back on the Waterloo Road, took her in, fed her some watery soup and let her sleep on the sofa for the night for her last pennies.

The next morning the dockside was crowded once more with seething masses of humanity, some making their way up the gangplanks, others having come to see their loved ones off. Many of the emigrants were Irish, many of them looking in worse case than her, having just stepped off the packet boat from Cork and now hurrying to the steamboats for the second stage of their journey to the American continent.

She pushed her way through the heaving crowds and along the quayside to the *York*. This time she was able to board at once. The decks were alive with activity, but one of the petty officers, supervising the loading of cargo, broke off to direct her to her berth. Cabin 49, he told her, one of the second class after cabins, beneath the poop. She breathed a sigh of relief. Cabin passengers, however lowly, were fed, so Mrs Brand, the landlady, had informed her in a ripe Liverpool accent, while steerage were expected to provide for themselves.

'Disgrace, sending a wain like you across the world by yerself, and you no more fit to look after yerself than a babe!' she had exclaimed. 'Whatever are yer to do if ye're in steerage, eh? I'd give yer some carryin' out meself if I could, but with all the bairns t'feed, there's none to spare. And then 'twouldn't have been that hard to put yer with a family, surely to God!' She shook her head. 'Fellas is on the look out fer ones like you, wi' none to protect 'em. More couplin' goes on in steerage than in a rabbit warren, and it ain't all the passengers neither! Take me advice, now, gel. Fix yerself onto a family, soon as yer can. And you ger' any trouble from the sailors, just tell 'em yer da's waitin' on yer.'

At the bend of a corridor, ill lit by a flickering lantern, she realised she was lost. Just then a petty officer came down the

14

steps and, heart in her mouth, she asked him the way to the cabin. 'All by yourself, are you, dear?' he said, gazing boldly into her face.

'No. I – I–'

With a knowing leer he put his hand across the corridor, casually barring her way.

She took a deep breath and, imagining she was declaiming one of Sarah's Shakespearean speeches, managed to suppress the tremor in her voice. 'If you please, my family is waiting for me,' she said, trying not to let the panic show. 'They will be growing anxious.'

Reluctantly he withdrew his arm and gave her the necessary directions.

At last she found the cabin; she opened the door and her heart sank into her boots as she surveyed it. It was a dark and poky hole with three sets of double bunks and two single, a table and two benches, all bolted to the floor. The thought of being shut up for weeks with seven strangers – some of them, judging by the crowd she had pressed through on the quayside, possibly lousy and stinking like the slum children when they first came to the Orphanage – made her skin creep. Matron had fought a ceaseless battle against 'crawlers' and she had been a willing ally. She chose the single bunk furthest away from the rest.

The crossing was a nightmare. In her cabin there were three other Orphanage girls from Salford going into service in Quebec, and a family from Hungary, consisting of a sickly mother, five daughters ranging in age from two to sixteen, sleeping head to toe, and their grandmother, who looked to be at least ninety but was not yet sixty. Their menfolk, father and two sons, were in a cabin on the next corridor, which ran parallel to theirs.

Eleven sharing a cabin for eight was bad enough as the *York* chugged down the Mersey, but once they crossed the bar into Liverpool Bay and met the strong winds gusting up the Irish Sea, many of the occupants began to look very unwell indeed; for them, the arrival of the slopping cauldron of grey stew was the last straw.

For her it was a reminder of the Orphanage and the gristly stew they had had on meat days. When she was small she'd

15

always contrived to slip her portion to the insatiable Lizzie. Today, hungry as she was, she still couldn't face it, so she just chewed on a hunk of dry dark bread. Years of scrimping in the Orphanage had given her an abhorrence of waste, so when the others didn't stir she went out into the corridor looking for an officer.

'A-many in steerage as'll welcome it,' said the purser bluntly, relieving her of the cauldron. 'So they're all sea-sick, are they? Well, Magyars, what else can you expect? Land-folk they are, every one of 'em, 'cos they don't have no navy, see? But us English, natural sailors, once we gets our stom-icks settled. Even in weather like this.'

'Dry bread and tea you want to stick to,' said the big Negro cook over his shoulder. 'In two days you'll be able to eat anythin'.'

She hadn't believed him, but his prophecy had prove accurate; even when the wind howled outside the portholes and the waves pounded against the hatch covers and sucked back into the scuppers, she was able to keep on her feet while the rest of the cabin occupants lay groaning and retching in their berths. For the wretched steerage passengers it must be even worse, she thought grimly: six hundred crammed into a space intended for two hundred, and even more at the mercy of the elements than the cabin passengers.

Less than a day out of Liverpool she found that any thought she might have had of seeking shelter with the Vilaghy family had been stood on its head. Instead she found herself looking after them, in particular the mother, who was very unwell indeed. For the first couple of days she found herself nursing every waking hour, but when on the third day the storm subsided, the woman slipped into an uneasy sleep and she took the opportunity to slip out on deck for some fresh air.

The sky was still grey and overcast, and there was a chill wind that cut through the thin layers of her inadequate clothes, but after the stench of the cabin it was as welcome to her as a balmy spring day and she breathed in great lungfuls of the cold salty spray-drenched air.

She found Mr Vilaghy, the sick woman's husband, sitting at his ease on the deck, his back propped against one of the lifeboats, contentedly puffing on a pipe.

16

He was a man of middling height who had once been fit but was now running to fat; his white skin had a permanent damp sheen on it, like something that had lived too long underground. He seemed quite unperturbed by his wife's suffering, and in no rush to see her nurse return to her care. He was a university professor, he told her, a radical on the run from Franz Josef's police. He started to tell her of his adventures, with a great deal of boasting and, she suspected, a deal of embellishment, but she excused herself as rapidly as she could.

'Ah, well.' He sighed theatrically. 'If you must go . . . It is so good to find someone with whom one can have intelligent converse,' he said, bowing with a flourish.

She nodded curtly and hurried away. It seemed unlikely that anyone in Cabin 49 would have time for 'intelligent converse' in the next few days; besides, there was a strange intense look in his pale eyes as he spoke to her that made her uneasy.

On the third night out from Liverpool, Mrs Vilaghy took a turn for the worse and all the tender care in the world could not save her. On the fourth night she died, not of the seasickness, the overworked ship's surgeon diagnosed, but of a condition she had already had when she set out.

'You'll tell her husband?' she said to the surgeon.

He shook his head. 'Have to leave that to you,' he said. 'I've got two confinements in steerage, besides all the usual sickness.' He rose from his knees and stretched his aching limbs. 'Cover her up,' he said brusquely. 'I'll send a couple of seamen to take her to the carpenter's shop.'

The children lay shocked and wide-eyed in their bunks as she drew the sheet over their mother's face. The old woman was sleeping, her breathing steadier now than it had been since they left Liverpool. She hadn't the heart to wake her up just to tell her her daughter had died.

The three girls from Salford lay listless in their bunks, their faces grey and pinched with the after effects of the sickness; no help to be had there.

She waited until the sailors had come to take away the woman's body and comforted the weeping children as best she could. She wanted nothing more than to subside on the

17

bench, rest her head on the table and sleep for evermore, but she knew she would not rest until she had told Mr Vilaghy the sad news.

With a sigh she turned to Sadie, the least comatose of the three Northern girls.

'Keep an eye on the little ones,' she said briskly. 'If the baby starts vomiting again, turn her on her side.' Summoning up her last reserves of strength she left the cabin and headed for the decks.

Unnoticed by her the sun had come out and those who were still on their feet had taken the opportunity to get some fresh air. Many were still confined to their cabins, or lying in steerage, breathing the stench of vomit and diarrhoea, but on the crowded deck there was an almost carnival atmosphere.

By the lifeboats, where Vilaghy was often to be found playing cards with a group of single men from steerage, a man sat on an upturned box playing a squeezebox, while several groups danced around him, clapping their hands and stamping their feet in time to the music. On the upper decks, groups of handsomely dressed men and women strolled about, or hung over the rails, shouting encouragement to the dancers. She walked round as far as she could, but there was no sign of Vilaghy.

She turned back and went down once more to the cabins. She hesitated a moment outside her own door; all she wanted to do was lie down and sleep, but she knew she would not rest until the husband had been told. Reluctantly she went down the next corridor and knocked on the door of his cabin.

From within there was a heavy thud, followed by a shuffling, and then the cabin door slid open and Vilaghy stood in the doorway. Over their heads the squeezebox player moved into a lively Irish jig.

'Dear lady!' he exclaimed. 'You come to talk? At last, some intelligent converse!'

'I'm afraid not, Mr Vilaghy,' she said. She hesitated. Death had been no stranger at the Orphanage, but then there had been no family to tell, no next-of-kin to console. She took a deep breath. 'I'm sorry, Mr Vilaghy. Your wife has died.'

Vilaghy gave a kind of groan and held out his hand. Without thinking, she reached out to take it in sympathy. His

18

fingers closed over hers and with a jerk he pulled her over the threshhold. With a rush of fear, she heard the door close behind her as he grabbed at her.

For all his flabby flesh, he was surprisingly strong. One arm held her pinned to his side with comparative ease while his other, damp and cold, was insinuating its way between the buttons of her high-necked blouse. She tried to kick out at him, but hampered by her skirts, made little impact.

After the initial shock she found her tongue and began to yell, but it was unlikely anyone would hear her above the noise from the boat deck and she soon realised that she would need all her strength to fight him off. His grip tightened painfully; his face was only inches from hers, shining moistly in the weak ray of sunshine that crept in through the porthole. A blast of fetid breath caught her in the face and she recoiled far enough to be able to free one had and strike out blindly at his face. She felt a brief moment of triumph as her hand connected with his cheek and instinctively she curled her fingers into claws and raked them down the side of his face. But it was only a short respite. With a snarl he turned on her, twisting her arm viciously until she lost her balance, then throwing her to the floor. She fell in a tangle of skirts, crying out in pain, but her voice was muffled by the cloth and she was so caught in the folds that she was effectively trapped even before he threw his body on top of hers, pinning her to the rough floor.

She could hear him panting, feel the weight of his body on hers as he dragged her on to her back and tore at her skirts and petticoats, pushing them up until the long folds flapped over her face. And above them the squeezebox played a jig and the feet stamped on the deck, beating out a mad counterpoint to the desperate silent struggle below. She felt a rush of nausea as his hand brushed her naked skin above her garter and something – his other hand? – pressed into her stomach as he wrestled with the buttons on his trousers, his eagerness making him clumsy.

She made one last convulsive attempt to throw him off, succeeding for a moment in freeing her face from the folds of clinging material. Above his heavy breathing she heard the sound of footsteps clattering down the companionway, and screeched as though her lungs would burst.

19

Vilaghy drew back his hand to strike her, but it never connected. It was as if time had been suspended, her attacker frozen in his pose. There was a shaking of the boards, a deal of loud cursing, and then Vilaghy was no longer on top of her but flying through the cabin, to fetch up painfully against the iron-framed bunk. In his place stood a large man with a full red beard.

'I told you before – don't bring your doxies back to my cabin!' roared the newcomer as Vilaghy slid down the bunk and ended in a heap on the floor. He turned on her. 'You want to do jig-jig, you keep your customers up on the boat deck – or down in steerage, where you belong, you hear me?'

'I don't know what you're talking about!' she said furiously, scrambling to her feet, swearing vigorously under her breath, words learnt long ago, in another language, of whose meaning she had no notion. Her face scarlet, she hastened to rearrange her skirts. 'I only came to tell him his wife had died!' she said, stung with the unfairness of it all.

For a very brief moment she saw the same look flare in the bearded man's face as she had seen in Vilaghy's. A sob of panic rose in her throat and she stepped back in terror, but then the bearded man blinked rapidly and it was gone.

'You stupid bitch!' he said in vibrant tones. 'Don't you know better than to come to a man's cabin if you ain't goin' to . . .'

'Don't you call me names!' Rage and nausea fought for supremacy within her.

'Well, I guess you just could be as innocent as you seem. If y'are so, then in that case, ma'am, I apologise for my language.' The red-bearded man scratched his jaw thoughtfully. 'They say as how grief takes people different ways,' he said with a wry grin at Vilaghy, slumped on the floor clutching his head. 'But that jest about takes the biscuit!'

She hurried back to her cabin, heart sick, and threw herself into her bunk, turning her face to the wall and refusing to speak to anyone for hours. She wanted to weep, but the tears would not come. She cried silently, deep inside. Sarah had been right, she thought tragically. She was all those things she had called her. First John Thomsett and now . . .

20

She must be right. Why else would Vilaghy have done what he had done. What *had* he done? She burnt with shame as she recalled his hands groping around in her undergarments. Matron had said – in the only piece of advice she had ever given the girls – that if you let a man touch you under your clothes you were a fallen woman.

She bit her hand to hold back the scream that knifed its way up from her stomach to her throat. Oh God! she begged. Please don't let me have a baby! I'll be good. I'll be obedient. Always. I'll go for a servant and forget all about the teaching, I swear it! Only please – don't let me be a fallen woman!

Only the very weak died on the Atlantic crossing now, unlike the dreadful days in mid-century when burials at sea were a daily occurrence. At the brief funeral service, the officer, hearing how she had nursed the woman in her last illness, insisted that she be placed with the family. She didn't like to argue.

'Better this way,' said Vilaghy with an ostentatious sigh. 'We would not come through the immigration with her, I think. They say the officials on Ellis Island are very strict.' She looked pointedly away from him, refusing to be drawn. 'A pity it was not the old one, though,' he said, with a vicious glare at his mother-in-law, held up by two of the daughters. 'No work left in her.'

Before his wife's weighted body was on the ocean bed, Vilaghy had asked her to marry him.

'No, thank you,' she said, forced to politeness by the presence of the officers nearby. 'I have a position to go to.'

'You were made to be mother, not drudge!' he declaimed theatrically.

'Rather a paid drudge than your unpaid one!' she snapped back.

Fortunately for her, the purser, who remembered her from the first day, saw her discomfiture and came to her rescue. He escorted her safely back to her cabin, but Vilaghy was persistent. She took to jamming a piece of wood under the handle at night and when she went to the sluice room each night – courtesy of the purser – to wash herself from head to toe in icy brackish water, she always took her train tickets with her, tucked into the stocking top, under her garter.

21

Ten days out from Liverpool they spied land – a speedy crossing considering how far south they had come to avoid the icebergs. Despite the bitter cold, the emigrants poured on to the deck, exchanging the fetid and unwholesome atmosphere of the hold for gulps of bitter cold air. Sometimes there were so many on the lower deck that it was almost impossible to move. She looked enviously at the upper deck where the small number of first-class passengers strolled around their wide and airy promenade. For two days they chugged up the Gaspé Passage, past ice-floes as big as islands, up the Saint Lawrence through a dazzling landscape which stretched away as far as the eye could see. Impossible to see where sea ended and land began; nothing but blinding white ice, shrieking seagulls, the howling wind and the cold.

The cold was like nothing she had ever before experienced, not even in the depth of winter at the Wapping Home, where they had crawled from bed, noses blue and toes numb, to break the ice on the water jugs. This cold did more than numb the toes: it penetrated to the bones and froze the blood.

After the agonisingly slow progress through immigration at Quebec, she trudged through the thick snow to the railroad station. The platform was packed: excited and agitated groups of Poles, Italians, Ukrainians and Hungarians hung out of windows or jammed doorways, chattering volubly or bidding tearful farewells to those of their friends and families staying on in Quebec. She pushed her way through with difficulty, hanging on grimly to her portmanteau, almost empty now, for she was wearing every stitch of clothing she possessed in a vain attempt to keep out the bitter cold. The purser had given her some bread and salt beef: it was all she had to last her for however long the journey took. He had also arranged to hold Vilaghy back for the next train, to give her a chance to get away from him. With a sigh of relief she found a few inches of board between two vociferous families who continued to argue across her, occasionally almost coming to blows. She was too tired to care.

She had hardly slept on board the *York*, so busy had she been tending the sick occupants of Cabin 49, and now as the train set off across the snow-covered plain, she slept, despite the hardness of the slatted wooden seat.

She woke a few hours later and took herself to the noisome privy at the end of the carriage; she returned to find a burly Italian sprawled across her seat and that of a young Polish woman with a baby who had squeezed in alongside her.

'Excuse me, that's my seat,' she said as firmly as she could.

He looked her up and down with an insolent stare and stayed where he was. He would not move and they could not make him. They had to sit on the dirty floor and brace themselves against the jolting as best they could.

The train chugged on through the night, the dim flicker of the lamps at either end of the carriage casting an eerie glow over the faces of the sleeping occupants.

The failures and rejects of Europe. How many of us, she wondered, will be any more successful over here? This bleak land will show no mercy to the sick and the incompetent. She looked out of the unshuttered windows at the inhospitable landscape, eerily white in the moonlight, and shivered.

She rubbed her stinging eyes and turned her attention to the baby, stirring now between them. A handsome child, a ready smile in his deep brown eyes. Was he the future of this frozen land?

And what of *her* future? She shivered as a blast of freezing air whistled under the door and cut through her layers of clothing as if they were muslin.

At the end of the second day, Irina and her baby reached their destination; she watched sadly through the frosted window as a tall fair-haired man ran down the platform and swept them up in a bear hug. It seemed everyone had someone to meet them. Some threw themselves into the arms of their relatives, others climbed into gigs, reunited families set off towards the town. Before she realised what was happening, she was alone in the carriage.

She let her tired eyes close as the train drew out of the station, but they had only gone a little way down the track when they stopped again.

'Come along there, missie!' called the guard impatiently, holding the door open. 'Out you get.'

'But I'm going on to Hamilton!'

'Not on this train you ain't! Turns round here and goes back to Quebec, this 'un. Should have got out in the main station. Don't know how I missed you.'

23

'How will I get to Hamilton?'

'Train leaves first thing in the morning.'

'Can't I stay here?'

'What? On this train? Nah! Going back up track to take on cordwood and water.'

'But what will I do tonight?'

He scratched his head. 'Same as everyone else, I guess. Walk into town and bed down.'

She stood alone on the cold, windswept platform of the junction station and cursed silently as the train disappeared back down the track. If only she'd known, she could have begged Irina and her husband for a bed for the night. Now, even if she could walk into town, there was no money left for a bed. Her only choice was to look for a shed or outhouse – and hope no one else had the same idea. As she remembered the warehouse on the Liverpool docks, she shivered with fear. And even if she did find somewhere to sleep, she was so bone tired from the night on the train floor that there was a strong chance she would not wake in time to catch tomorrow's train.

Her eyes filled with tears of frustration. She might just as well lie down here in the snow and die! No one would care. Perhaps no one would even notice. If it snowed again in the night she would just lie buried under the gentle, welcoming drifts until spring – if spring ever came to this cold, harsh landscape.

She heard a clang behind her. Someone was locking up the linesman's shack. Her eye wandered to the thin plume of smoke still rising from the chimney. Why walk all the way back to town to look for outhouses when there were plenty of buildings here! All thoughts of death and dying were forgotten as she slipped round the corner of the building, heart beating furiously, and waited for the linesman to leave.

Ten minutes later he trotted down the banks on a broken-down old horse, the snow which had just begun to fall again muffling its ragged hoofbeats. As they disappeared around the bend in the lane, picking their way towards the lights which were just visible through the veil of snow, she darted out and stood a moment, heart hammering, in the shadow of the buildings.

The windows were either locked or frozen into place but through the frosted panes she could see the stove glowing warmly. There was nothing for it: she would have to break in. It was wrong, she knew, but her spirit was up now and she was damned if she would lie down and die!

She drew out the pin that held her braids on the top of her head and bent over the lock, sending up a little prayer of thanks to Tommy, who had taught her this trick among many others in return for her teaching him his letters. In seconds the lock clicked open and the door moved outwards on squeaky hinges.

She crossed the room to the welcoming warmth of the stove. Opening the little door at the side, she poked in a couple of sticks on top of the dying embers and shivered ecstatically as the heat from the flickering flames began to penetrate the frozen layers of clothes.

It was a sparse room, with nothing but a table and bench built into the alcove by the stove. A pot on the side of the stove contained dregs of coffee and another water. She mixed them together and heated them through, burning her tongue in her eagerness to take in the hot liquid. Then she put a little more wood on the stove, wrapped herself up in her shawl and lay down on the bench to sleep. Something rustled in the pile of wood beneath the bench, but she was too exhausted to care. North American rats would surely be no worse than the English ones. Besides, the choice was already made: nothing would persuade her to leave this haven of warmth before she had to.

She'd intended to be up early, but the blissful warmth proved too much and only the sound of the linesman leading his horse into the adjacent stable woke her.

She slipped out of the door, the lock clicking into place behind her, and hid behind the woodshed just in time. She watched the man unlock the door and walk in unsuspecting. The fire had died in the night: with luck he would never know she had been there.

She slipped back on board the train while the driver was exchanging greetings with the linesman and lighting the first pipe of the day; she ducked down below the window so that no one would spot her. Back at the main station, people were crowding the platform four and five deep and as the train drew in with a deal of fussing and hissing they pushed and shoved their way on, jostling for the seats in the middle away from the worst of the draughts.

Rows of icicles had formed overnight while the train had been in the sidings, and they hung down from the edge of the roof. She tried to guess which would be the first to break off with the force of the wind and the snow which was flung back by the plough at the front as the train gathered speed. It helped to take her mind off the gnawing pain in her stomach and the cold which pervaded her body, seeming to freeze the blood and stop it reaching her fogged brain. Within minutes, the warmth of the line station had evaporated as if it had never been and it became a matter of great importance, greater than life itself, to guess correctly which icicle would be the next to snap off and fly, dagger-sharp, to the rear of the train. The sounds of the wheels on the tracks bid her *choose* the right one, *choose* the right one. When all the icicles were gone and only the bare white landscape remained, she slumped back in the corner in despair.

Her eyes were burning; she wanted nothing but to sleep, and sleep eluded her. She stared out of the window as if hypnotised and thought again how pleasant it would be to lie down beneath that soft, white, welcoming mantle; she would be sure to sleep then.

The sounds of the wheels on the track changed their tune as the train began to climb up the gradient.

So cold, *so* cold, *going* to freeze, *going* to die, they chanted, until she clapped her hands to her ears to try to shut out the insistent rhythm.

The train chugged on, but she no longer saw the scenery through which they passed. She did not see the awesome splendour of the huge lake, capped with frozen waves, when they dropped down below Missisauga; she did not see the little settlements perched on bluffs or nestling in the plain between railroad and lake: she saw only the beckoning faces of the dead.

He woke in the cold light of dawn to find himself being regarded by a pair of over large tilted green eyes peeping over the top of the mound of blankets, like a chick taking a wary look out of the nest.

26

He unwound himself from the chair and laid a cool hand on her brow.

'Fever's abating,' he said approvingly. 'And your eyes?'

'Just . . . shapes. No more,' she said, fear in her voice.

'That's what I'd have expected.' He sat beside her and took her pulse. 'Best place for you, young lady, is bed. Cup of tea, some more drops, then we'll take you up.

Nancy brought the breakfast tray to the doctor's study, muttering angrily under her breath. Word had gone around that the ragged invalid was no more than a housemaid and Nancy did not see why she should wait on her. She'd have spoken her mind, if Mrs Chobley hadn't followed her in, and she had to make do with a scowl as she put the tray down.

'Sit down, Mrs Chobley,' said her master pleasantly, taking the cup of tea she had poured and putting it carefully in the girl's hands. 'How are your feet today?'

'Much better, sir, thank you. Wonderful how they've improved since I started resting them up like you told me.'

'Good.' He sat at his desk and twisted a pen between his fingers. 'We'll have to keep this one, I'm afraid. She couldn't stand the journey back – and I doubt there's much for her to go back to. Her eyes are bad – snow blindness – so she'll have to rest.'

'Mr Ellsky said as how she'd travelled all the way from Quebec! Whatever did she come in that way for? With New York barely a day away . . .'

He shrugged. 'It may have been Mrs Carter's plan to get round the Contract Labour law.'

'The what law?'

'Contract Labour, Mrs Chobley. You may not contract to bring in immigrants to fill a position that can be filled by someone already here.'

'Doubt *she* would have let that worry her. Brought in all her ladies' maids from England, she did. To my certain knowledge.'

'Quite. I think it was more likely just a straightforward misunderstanding.' He opened a drawer in his desk and drew out a crumpled scrap of paper.

At the head of it someone had scrawled, in an atrocious hand:

Eden Springs Lake
Ontario N

'What's that blot after the *N* supposed to be?' she demanded. '*Y? NY? New York State?*'

'I guess so. But it could as easily be mistaken for a *W*. You can see how blotched it is.'

'*W! NW!* That'd give you north west!'

'Eden Springs Lake, Ontario Northwest. Easy to see how someone who doesn't know could think we were in Canada.'

'Poor lamb! What a mix-up! And that journey – all to no purpose.'

'Mix up!' he exclaimed furiously. 'If Max hadn't happened to be in Edensville, she would almost certainly have died!' He took a turn about the room and went on more calmly: 'She must rest for a few days, then we'll see how she shapes up. Give her a bath and burn her clothes; they're sure to be lousy.'

There was a crash as the tea cup fell on the floor.

'How dare you call me lousy!' She leapt up from the couch, grabbing distractedly at the slipping blankets. 'I bathed every day on that ship in icy salt water! I'm as clean as any of you!'

The doctor was at her side in a moment. He picked her up effortlessly in strong arms and tossed her, blankets and all, back on to the couch.

'You just lie quiet, young lady, before you make yourself ill again!' He pressed her back against the cushions, a dark featureless shape looming above her, half-seen, half-imagined. 'You'll have a bath if you want to stay here. If Mrs Chobley finds any trace of infestation you'll be scrubbed with carbolic and your clothes burnt. Otherwise you will be sent back to England again. Agreed?'

She stuck her lower lip out mutinously and muttered something that sounded suspiciously like a curse.

'Agreed?' he repeated.

'Don't have much bloody choice, do I?'

She lay back and savoured the crisp lavender-scented sheets and the solitude. Not since that half-remembered magic world before the Orphanage had she slept anywhere but a dormitory. She closed her eyes against the fading light that streamed through the window, framed with faded chintz curtains that matched the washed out bedspread.

The door rattled and Nancy crashed in with a tray, her face sour and her eyes vicious.

'Here. Mrs Chobley says you're to eat all this. 'S a fraud, if you ask me. I mean, look at you. Nothing wrong with you. Just skiving. Well, I don't say I wouldn't 've done the same in your shoes. Beats washin' pots and pans in the scullery.'

'I'm not skiving!' said the girl indignantly.

'All the same, you Londoners. Think you're so much better than the rest. The housekeeper warned Madam when she was so set on sending for you.'

She giggled at the thought that a girl from the Wapping Home for Waifs and Strays might consider herself better than anyone else.

'You can laugh!' snapped Nancy. 'But Doctor Kingsley says there's gonna be changes round here, and you'll laugh the other side of your face when you're in the scullery with your dainty hands gone red and I'm parlourmaid.'

Sarah's parlourmaid Ellen had been clean, neat and polite. Unless standards in this strange country were very much lower, she could not imagine coarse, ill-mannered Nancy fitting into this category.

Tucked up beneath a downy quilt she slept long, but not dreamlessly. She was back in the Home for Waifs and Strays in the old warehouse close by Wapping Docks. Not a handsome building, but it held so many memories for her. It was, after all, the only home she had known since that dread, half-remembered day which had begun with her throwing the candlestick at the bad lady and ended when the man had drawn up outside the grim building and handed her over as an 'orphling'. She would never forget that, but the bruised seven-year-old mind had carefully blanked out the years that went before. Only the music had stayed in her head. Music and beautiful dresses and Mary – stout, comfortable Mary in the rocking chair, knitting by the flickering firelight.

It had taken her some time to settle in, a frightened child whose world had suddenly been turned upside down, and the other girls in the dormitory had at first not taken to her. Too many prying questions and she would rattle off a stream of awful queer words. Matron reckoned it was French mostly, but other times it was something else.

'It's real maddening,' said Aggie. 'She could be screaming summat terrible at us and we wouldn't know it. And even when it *is* English, it's all posh and breakjaw.'

Allowed to take lessons with the boys' classes on the other side of the yard, she soon overtook them all and by the time she was ten was already helping the smaller ones to read and write.

Milly they called her, for Matron did not hold with fancy names for orphans – and certainly not such an outlandish one as this child claimed to possess. She had a Biblical list for nameless foundlings and as one left at fourteen to go out into service, so the next foundling abandoned on the doorstep was given their predecessor's name. The new arrival was fortunate to be allowed to keep even a shadow of her former name; at seven years old she was in no fit state to argue with them, so Milly she remained, among the Marthas and Hephzibahs, the Josiahs, Jobs and Ezekiels.

She was confined to her room for three days, the curtains drawn against the bright dazzle of the glistening snow outside. For three days she submitted to the boredom of lying on her bed, her eyes closed for as long as she could bear, the monotony broken only by the visits of Mrs Chobley, who heaved her bulk up the stairs at least twice a day to check on the girl's progress.

'Though Gawd only knows what would have happened to you if you'd arrived while the old doctor was alive!' she exclaimed. 'He'd not have taken the trouble Doctor Kingsley's taken, that's for sure. And his wife – soon as she'd heard there was aught amiss with your eyes, she'd have dismissed you before you'd had time to thaw! But don't you fret yourself. You eat my good meals and we'll soon have some flesh on those bones!'

She was a plump cheerful woman who had come out many years before with her first husband in one of the first big waves of emigration.

'Proper Cockney was my Albert,' she sighed reminiscently. 'Came out on account of his health, but it was too late. Had consumption, he did, and he was dead within the year. I could have stayed in New York but I fancied a bit of country life. I' moved on upstate. Only stopped when they ran out of railway, for it didn't go no further then, gel,' she explained. 'Not till they opened up the prairies. Then we joined up with Chicago and now they tell me you can go right across America to Californey – if you was mad enough to want to. But there. Now, I'd better be getting back to my kitchen. I've left one of them silly lasses in charge.' She surged out of her chair and down the stairs, leaving behind her a strong odour of cheap violet scent.

Most of the rest of the large staff took no notice of the new arrival, used as they were to the coming and going of staff under Mrs Carter's wayward rule.

Except Jessie. She took a proprietorial interest in 'her' patient and often stopped to chat when she carried a tray up. Although completely uneducated and rather too ready to take anyone else's opinion as gospel truth, she was a sweet-natured girl.

'See, Nancy, she's on the turn, like, because Mrs Jameson's going. Mrs Jameson's the housekeeper and Nancy always sucked up to her. But the Doctor, he don't need so many people to look after him, so he's letting some of them go.' She giggled. 'And Mrs Chobley won't take none of Nancy's nonsense. She said so.'

'It's a very big staff to look after one man!'

'The other doctor, he had big ideas, see. Butler and valet and lots of grooms and that. And the Missus, see, she liked to have new faces around her all the time, so any time as she got bored with one parlourmaid, she'd send off to England for another. Wouldn't 'ave no furriners in the 'ouse, she wouldn't: allus had to be from England.'

'And what about the parlourmaid she already had?'

'If she was lucky she went to maid one of the mistress's daughters,' explained Jessie. ''Less she weren't no good or the daughter didn't like her. Then she was let go.'

'Where?'

'Dunno,' she said with a shrug. 'She didn't like them to stay round, 'cos it looked bad on her, see? So, 'nless they left the area, she wouldn't give 'em no character.'

31

She said it dispassionately, as if it were the most natural thing in the world, but the very thought made the blood run cold. To lose a job 'without a character' was the worst thing that could happen to anyone in service; without a reference it was nigh impossible to find another post.

One girl had come back to the Orphanage after being turned off without a character for thieving. Matron had taken her in for a while, but no one had wanted her when there were so many to choose from, all eager to find a good post. She had gone when the next foundling was left on the doorstep and had soon, in Mrs Evans's words, gone to the bad.

And Mrs Carter would turn a girl out, when she had done nothing wrong, just because she had grown bored with her face. No one would abandon a lap dog for such a petty reason!

Occasionally Hetty the parlourmaid would bring up the tray. She was a little older than the other maids and walking out with the son of a farmer on the other side of Eden Springs. She had a pretty face, as befitted a parlourmaid, but there was no spirit or expression in it. 'Blank as a bowl o' milk,' as Aggie would have said. She tried to strike up conversation with her, but soon gave up the effort.

Nancy was the least welcome visitor: aware that the girl's sight was still troubling her, she took great pleasure in moving the tray just out of her reach, or taking any particularly tasty morsel and eating it in front of her.

On the third day, the invalid was sitting in a chair by the window while Jessie plumped up her pillows and Nancy sat admiring herself in the mirror. She rummaged in the drawers and picked out a small flagon.

'What d'you reckon this is?' she said, taking out the stopper and sniffing at it 'Love potion. Or –'

'With any luck it'll be poison,' snapped the invalid.

'You'll be sorry you was so sharp with me when I'm parlourmaid. Won't get any share of the cakes I lift.'

'There's plenty of food here.' She shrugged. 'I don't need to pinch.'

'Quite right! And the day you get up off your fat backside, Nancy, and do some real work, that'll be the day to start talking of parlourmaids,' snapped Cook, bustling in to catch Nancy with her hand in the drawer. '*And* the day you learn to keep your fingers out of other folk's concerns.' She looked at the girl in the chair. 'You look worn to a thread, gel. You lie down or the doctor'll be scolding me for letting you up too soon.'

'Oh, *she* must have a rest, *she* mustn't do too much. *She* . . . bet she's never done a stroke of work in her life!'

'That's enough!' Mrs Chobley could be firm when it was needed. 'He was as good to you, every bit, when you jammed you hand in the ice-house door!'

The doctor came upstairs morning and evening to put drops in her eyes and check on her progress. He'd been relieved to hear from Mrs Chobley that there was no infestation: just as well when he remembered how he had held her and comforted her when she broke down. Lice were the least of the horrors the immigrants could carry, as the typhoid in the Infirmary had shown.

Towards the end of the first week he came back from Edensville early and found her seated in the chair, a warm shawl round her shoulders.

'And who gave you permission to be out of bed?' he demanded.

'Mrs Chobley,' she answered. 'At least,' her spirit rose to the older woman's defence, 'she said I couldn't see Mr Ellsky in my bedroom, so of course I had to get up.'

He raised his eyebrows in enquiry.

'Well, I hadn't thanked him for fetching me here. I expect I'd have died if he hadn't, wouldn't I?'

'Undoubtedly.'

She put her head on one side and looked at her employer with interest. It was the first time she had really been able to make him out without straining her eyes.

His was an interesting face, she decided. A strong face, all hard planes, with not a curve in sight, except on those rare occasions when he smiled. His grey eyes watched her now with some amusement as she surveyed him, until at last he grew restless under her scrutiny and he ran his fingers through the silky dark hair that flopped over his forehead.

'Did I thank you?' she asked with a puzzled frown. 'I can't remember.'

33

'Several times,' he said with a smile. 'But doctors don't expect thanks. And of course, I had a vested interest in saving you.'

Like a table that's been attacked by dry rot, she thought savagely. One of the assets of your estate, part of the fixtures and fittings! She bit back the words of gratitude.

'Anyway,' she said with a brightness she did not feel, 'Mrs Chobley would not allow Mr Ellsky to come up, so I went down to see him.'

'Very proper. But now back into bed!' he commanded. As he turned away to open his bag, she hurriedly slipped the book she'd been reading down the side of the chair.

'What's that?' he demanded. '*Peg's Romance*?' That was the kind of rubbish the maids all read – those who could read.

'No.'

At least it showed her eyes hadn't suffered any permanent damage.

He took her pulse, then took out his stethoscope. 'I want to listen to your chest,' he told her. Malnutrition and consump- tion often showed the same symptoms.

She shifted uncomfortably in the bed, but thankfully he only laid the stethoscope against the flannel of Mrs Chobley's fourth best nightgown to listen to her breathing.

'Much better. Now, we'll just put some more drops in . . .'

'If you please, sir?'

He raised a questioning eyebrow at her.

'Please may I get up tomorrow? I'm feeling much better, truly I am.'

'You are so anxious to start work, Milly?' he frowned. Most girls in her position would have spun it out as long as possible.

'Yes sir. And my name isn't Milly.' She forced herself to add: 'If you please.'

'In your papers it says . . .'

'They never could pronounce my name.' Only Sarah, shown the name by an excited child in a book of French fairy stories, had ever used it. 'And I was too young then to argue.'

'But not now, one gathers,' he observed dryly. 'Well, what do you call yourself?'

'My name is Melisande Stevens – sir.'

His eyebrows rose. 'I suppose it adds a certain cachet to have a housemaid with such an exotic name.' He turned back

34

to his bag and missed the look of impotent fury on her.
'Well, Melisande, you may get up tomorrow and stay up
long as you can manage. I suppose gossiping with the maid
won't exhaust you. As for work – we'll see how you go on at
the start of next week.' He picked up his bag. 'I'll have the
indentures drawn up and you can make your mark on them
next week.'

'I'm perfectly capable of signing my name properly.' He
raised his eyebrows. 'And reading. And accounting. Sir.'

'Whoever brought you up in that Orphanage had more
elegance of mind than practical sense,' he said as he went out
of the door. 'What use did they think such training would be
in service?'

His words were an unconscious echo of Matron's and tears
pricked the back of Melisande's eyelids. Oh, Sarah! she
thought. We had such high hopes, such vaunting ambitions!
And all for what? I shall end up a scullerymaid after all!

Sarah Thomsett had come into Melisande's life soon after
Lizzie had been transferred to an Orphanage in the Vale of
Health near Hampstead, where the waters were thought to
help consumptives.

'Life must go on!' Matron had said bracingly as Melisande
moped around the Orphanage, missing her friend dreadfully. ·
And Melisande had earned herself a week's punishment by
blurting out a string of curses and swear words which Jem and
the irrepressible Aggie had taught her and of whose meaning
she had not the remotest idea.

Sarah had taught most of her life in a girls' boarding school
in Essex until an unexpected modest inheritance had freed
her from a life of genteel drudgery. However, housekeeping
for herself and her brother in the modest house in Elms
Square, where the prosperous Wapping merchants had lived
in the seventeenth and eighteenth centuries, did not fill either
her time or her mind and so she had offered her services to a
grateful Orphanage.

For Sarah the young girl, so eager to learn, had been the
challenge she needed. Her spirit had leapt at the chance
presented to her in, of all places, the Wapping Home for
Waifs and Strays, of taking a girl with a sharp mind and a

35

talent for learning, and moulding her. Her own dreams had been shattered by a peevish father and a weak brother, but an orphan had no ties to hold her back.

She had first come across 'Milly' in the sewing room where she was making over worn Holland aprons to fit the younger girls. A dark-eyed boy sat at her feet cutting the bad bits out of potatoes.

He held up the knife and looked enquiringly at the girl.

'Knife,' she said, and he repeated it.

'Potato,' she said, pointing.

'Po-ti-to,' said the boy.

'Ivan is trimming the potatoes. I am sewing.' She pointed to herself, then swore fluently as she jabbed her finger with the needle.

The girl lived up to Sarah's expectations. At mathematics she was as gifted as at history, her interest in far-off lands as great as her fascination with the written word. She never mastered drawing or water colours, but that was dismissed as a minor detail. Otherwise she could not learn enough. It was as if the years of marking time had only sharpened her appetite for knowledge.

They conversed daily in French and Sarah brought in newspapers to discuss with the older children. They spoke of Japan and Mikados, massacring Turks, the Union Pacific railroad, encroaching Russians and the North West frontier. The world was more exciting than Milly had ever realised.

Matron thoroughly disapproved, even when the episode with Little Polack revealed her charge's gift for languages. But although she always insisted the child should be treated no differently, she hadn't sent her into service with the others . at fourteen and gradually, as Sarah became more and more embroiled in her brother's chaotic business affairs, Milly took over the teaching of the younger Orphanage children and on Doctor Morel's death began to help Matron with the administration of the Home.

She had thought her life would never alter, that it would go on from year to year unchanging. Until the day the man with the gold-rimmed spectacles and bushy side-whiskers came to sit at the back of the echoing schoolroom that looked across the cobbled yard and down to the bustling docks, and turned all her dreams to ashes.

Melisande sank wearily back against the pillows and sighed. It wasn't that she was afraid of hard work, and she had seen enough of it at the Home to know that there was very little she could not turn her hand to. There had been very little respite from everyday toil for the inhabitants of the Orphanage: food had to be prepared from the most unpromising ingredients, clothes fashioned and refashioned from garments turned and returned until they literally fell into shreds, and the old warehouse buildings had to be swept and scrubbed daily in the endless battle against lice, fleas and disease. She had done all that willingly, because it was for people she cared for, those who had taken her in and given her a home when no one else cared whether she lived or died. But to be a skivvy for such an arrogant man, who spoke as if he owned her . . . it was more than her spirit could bear.

When she was feeling a little stronger, Mrs Chobley showed Melisande round the house, so that she could familiarise herself with the layout.

Springs House was a handsome cobblestone structure, the oldest building in Eden Springs, dating from the mid-eighteenth century when the town had been laid out on the site of an earlier settlement wiped out during the Indian wars. The estate had earlier belonged to the Edens, one of the old families who had divided up the Upper Hudson Valley between them; through war and invasion, it had retained most of its land, although the house was no longer at the centre of the estate, but situated to one side of the elegant Square at the heart of the town.

Famous as the site of one of the major skirmishes of the War of 1812, Eden Springs had once rivalled Saratoga as a spa for weary New Yorkers, many of whom had stopped there for a few nights en route to the splendours of Niagara, but with the growth of Edensville down on the lake the little town had become a desirable retreat for the ironmasters and shippers and in becoming less exclusive it had lost the battle to attract the rich and fashionable travellers.

The house was built of local materials in the Queen Anne style with stable and kitchen wings on either side; the Historical Society of Eden Springs still pointed with pride to the bullet holes in the stable wing where the factor and his men had held out against a British invasion force in 1812. Inside, a handsome staircase swept down into the wide hall and a narrower one at the rear led to the servants' quarters. The front rooms on the right of the ground floor served as estate offices for the steward, Max Ellsky, who had held the property together while his previous employer, Doctor Carter, had extracted every last cent to indulge his wife and daughters. To the left as one entered the imposing front door was the doctor's study; a side door led from this into the dispensary and consulting rooms, which could also be entered from outside. Upstairs were a number of handsome reception rooms, which the doctor rarely used.

'He only uses the drawing room and Hetty looks after that – no need for you to go in there. It's still full of Mrs Carter's ornaments and so forth: too many breakables to let you loose on yet awhile.'

Everywhere there were paintings, some of them old landscapes, the varnish so aged that it was hard to see what the subject was; over the stairs hung more modern ones, with models in medieval robes with clouds of frizzy pale hair.

'Them's by them funny London painters,' said Mrs Chobley with scant approval. 'The ones that sound like Eyetalians.'

'Dante Gabriel Rossetti,' said Doctor Kingsley, coming up the stairs behind them. 'And this is by Millais. Two of the pre-Raphaelite artists. And you shouldn't judge a painting by the lifestyle of the artist, Mrs Chobley. All artists are allowed to be somewhat Bohemian.'

'I like this one,' said the new maid, looking at the Rossetti painting. She tilted her head on one side. 'Strange. I feel as if I had seen it before.'

Every time you look in your mirror, he thought, but didn't say it.

'Looks a lot like you, gel,' Mrs Chobley said. 'That pale face and all. Mind you, you don't have a neck like that. Lucky for you.'

'Goitres,' said the doctor.

'Beg your pardon?'

He smiled. 'Goitres, Mrs Chobley. Iodine deficiency. All those staring eyes and outward curving throats. Unless Mr

Rossetti's models moved to live by the sea, I fear they would not long have outlasted the paintings.'

'Well, that's all very interesting, sir, but we must get on. . . .' She looked around her. 'Drat. Now the girl's wandered off . . .'

At the back of the house, built out over a huge ballroom, was a library with more books in it than Melisande had ever seen; she had been drawn back to it as though by a powerful magnet. Wandering through, she had found a small staircase leading off it, to a room a little like a study. On these walls hung pictures of a quite different nature: paintings by Gérôme of Arab women reclining semi-naked by a Turkish bath or in the harem; paintings by Alma Tadema of scantily clad women in an approximation of Roman or Greek garb, some in chains, some stepping into or coming out of a bath. Over by the window was an older painting, heavily varnished, showing the scene of the Elders spying on Susannah in *her* bath.

'What do you think you're doing here, gel?' demanded Mrs Chobley, puffing valiantly up the stairs.

'I came back to look at the library.'

'Well, the library's fine, but don't let me find you in here again,' she said, looking round her in distaste. 'This here's the master's room and –'

'Doctor Kingsley's?'

'No. The old master, Doctor Carter.' She ushered her out of the room and locked the door with a key on the bunch at her waist. 'I suppose I should crate these up and send them on to New York with the rest of his things. But dear only knows what Mrs Carter'd say if she opened a packing case and saw all them.'

Melisande wrinkled her nose. She hadn't liked the feeling in that room. Somehow it brought back memories of John Thomsett: she was quite sure he would have like those paintings.

She was still not entirely recovered when she made her first appearance in the kitchen, but she was beginning to grow bored. Besides, she told herself, she could not put off the evil moment forever: if she had to be a servant, then the sooner she came to terms with it the better.

39

She dressed herself in the black dress and starched white apron that Jessie had brought up to her, and made her way downstairs. At the sound of her steps Jessie looked up from the hearth in the doctor's study, where she was starting the fire. 'I don't know where Cook wants to start you,' she said. 'Hetty's in the dining room. Give a hand in there.'

But Hetty, setting out the chafing dishes on the side board in the dining room, did not need her help, and sent her back to the kitchen for orders.

Nancy was standing by the huge tiled stove, laughing heartily at something Olsen, the sharp-faced stable hand, had just said to her. She looked up as the new girl came in.

'Look what the cat dragged in!' she mocked. 'Grantin' us the honour of your company, are you? I s'pose your ladyship got nothin' better to do!'

Melisande resisted the temptation to answer in kind. 'I'm looking for Mrs Chobley,' she said.

'Well, she ain't in here,' said Nancy, turning back to the stove, trying not to notice that Olsen was looking the new girl up and down with an insolent leer.

As Mel looked into the pantry and the still room, Olsen's expression suddenly changed to a most unpleasant grin. He jerked his head at Nancy, caught her by the arm and dragged her across to the door, where she would have a clear view of the back hall. He placed his finger over her lips and winked at her conspiratorially.

He crossed back to the stove and started to pour the hot water from the boiler at the side of the stove into two cans. 'Right then, Stevens,' he said briskly. 'First duties, take these cans upstairs.'

'But I –'

'Hurry up,' he said, coming up close behind her and setting the cans at her feet. 'He's waiting.'

'But –'

'Second door on the left at the top,' said Nancy, polishing a mark off a pane in the kitchen door with studied insouciance. 'Get a move on, or his breakfast will be ready before he is.'

Melisande bit her lip. She was beginning to realise just how ignorant she was. While the other orphans had all been trained from very early on in the running of a household, all her time with Sarah had been spent on other pursuits, for she had never believed she would end up in service.

Nancy looked at her scornfully. 'See?' she said to Olsen. 'Another skiver. Told you so.'

Melisande compressed her lips angrily and went to pick up the heavy cans. 'I leave them outside the second door on the left?'

'Take them in, you fool,' said Nancy. 'No good to him outside the door.'

Her eyes widened. 'I'll knock, then . . .'

'Don't know nothin', do you?' sighed Nancy, crossing to take a skillet off the rack.

'Don't knock,' said Olsen, rolling his eyes impatiently. 'Only hired-in servants knock.'

She recalled Sarah once saying much the same. 'But –'

'Oh, get on with it!' snapped Nancy, banging the skillet down on the oven.

She'd carried heavier loads, but she was weaker than she had realised. Not that she would admit that to Nancy and Olsen, of course. The back stairs were not steep, but the heavy men's boots she wore could not get a grip on the highly polished boards of the top landing and she swore as some of the hot water slopped over the top of the cans.

Setting her load down outside the door, she straightened her apron, took a deep breath and turned the handle.

As the door swung open, she picked up the cans and started into the room. But one step was all she took. Across the room, in front of the ornate marble washstand, half turned to the door, stood a broad-shouldered, slim-hipped, tanned and muscular figure, quite naked. Her jaw dropped and her eyes widened.

Grey eyes held green for a horrified second, then Doctor Kingsley whirled away and snatched desperately at a large white linen towel which he held in front of his lower torso. With a gasp, Melisande dropped the cans from nerveless fingers, turned, almost tripping over her own feet in her agitation, and fled. The reverberations of the falling cans faded away, and she raced down the stairs, pursued by the doctor's low, fluent swearing and the gurgling of the hot water as it spilled out of the cans. She did not stop until she reached her bedroom. She flung herself into bed, wet boots and all, pulled the quilts up around her ears and lay there shaking.

She would have liked to stay there all day, but Jessie arrived soon after with instructions for her to report to the housekeeper's room.

'It's Mrs Chobley as wants to see you, though,' said Jessie conscientiously. 'Mrs Jameson's not back from Rochester yet, o'course. She says you're to get yourself down there sharpish, mind,' she went on, when Melisande made no sign of moving. 'I'd shift meself, if I were you. Don't do to get on the wrong side of Cook, it don't.'

She'd expected to be hauled over the coals, for the mess she'd made, if for nothing else, but Cook was quite off-hand about the whole affair.

'Don't take too much heed, gel,' she said when the girl, scarlet-faced, reported to the housekeeper's room. To her relief there was no sign of Nancy or Olsen belowstairs. 'There's always some ribbing for new girls, though they went too far this time, and so they know.' She set a plate of eggs down in front of the new maid. 'They usually have enough sense to keep it within limits.' She sighed. 'I don't know what new-fangled ideas they have in London, but I don't hold with girls going near the men's rooms. Not dressing-rooms even, let alone . . . Here it's the valet's place to take anything up to the master's room.'

'But the doctor hasn't got a valet . . . !'

'And if so be there isn't a valet,' said Cook, as if she hadn't spoken, 'then it's Olsen takes it. Be it water, wood or a tray. You stay below stairs where I can keep an eye on you. Besides, the doctor says you're not to do too much till you're a bit stronger.' She looked at the girl with a frown between her eyes. 'I don't know. I wouldn't have thought you were daft enough to do anything that lout Olsen told you to.'

'I didn't know . . .'

'Course you didn't. But in future you takes your orders from me direct. Or the doctor, of course.'

'The doctor? I'll never be able to look the doctor in the face again,' she said with a shudder.

She never knew what Cook and the doctor said to Nancy and Olsen; she did not see them again that day. But as ill-luck

42

would have it, she seemed to come across her employer every time she turned around. Wherever Cook sent her, whether to dust the hall with Hetty, or to replace the heavy silver chafing dishes on the sideboard, Doctor Kingsley always seemed to walk in a moment later.

He had known that their next encounter might be slightly awkward. He himself had been far from unaffected by the incident, which had annoyed him: as a doctor, he ought to have been able to deal with such matters without embarrassment. He had a light-hearted remark ready to dispel any awkwardness, but the girl could not bring herself to look him in the eye and as soon as he entered the room, she scuttled out of it. The third time she did it, he lost his patience.

'Anyone would think you had never seen a naked man before!' he snapped, standing in the doorway and blocking her exit.

She never had, for after the age of eight, Matron had always kept the boys and girls strictly apart, but she doubted he would believe her. She cast her eyes down, quite unable to look him in the face.

'You were hardly brought up in a convent!' he went on angrily. 'For goodness' sake girl! I didn't know there was room for prudery in the East End slums. Heaven knows how you would have managed if you had gone as a maid of all work.'

'Matron would not have permitted it, sir,' she said in a small voice. Unlike many less particular establishments, Matron had always refused to send her girls where they would be the only maid in the household, and she had never permitted the pretty ones to go into predominantly male or bachelor households.

'It was a shock for both of us,' he said as he stepped aside to let her pass. 'But it's over and done with. Put it out of your mind. I'm sure you have far more pressing matters to deal with.'

Such as her try out as cook maid, she thought miserably. The household didn't really need another general maid, but with so many people in the household – below, rather than above stairs – Cook needed an assistant. She sighed. It was being brought home to her how very unfitted she was for work

43

in a gentleman's residence. She could not prepare the simplest meal, she had no notion how to begin cleaning a room with carpets and elegant furniture. Ask her to scrub out and disinfect a dormitory, or provide porridge for forty or mutton and vegetable broth for eighty, from nothing but butcher's bones and trimmings and vegetables too old and bruised to sell, and she could have done it with no difficulty. Trained by Matron and Sarah, she could have taken their places without a second thought, but she was beginning to realised she was little use for anything else.

A few days later she was hurrying down the stairs, dressed in a neat black skirt and blouse with a crisp white apron over the top of it, when she heard voices in the hall. She stopped in her tracks. She shouldn't have been on the front stairs at all, but she'd lingered over long in the library where she'd been sent to dust. Enchanted by the handsome, book-lined room, she'd pulled out the library steps and climbed up to pull out a leather-bound volume here, a binder of journals there, and had quite forgotten the time. She was about to turn back when she heard her name spoken and paused on the landing to listen.

'She's a very good girl, sir,' said Mrs Chobley. 'A real hard worker. She do get a bit uppity with Nancy and Olsen – you know how it is, there's always a bit of teasing for the new girls, though I try to keep it within bounds.'

'And her health?'

'Much better sir. Though I won't let her do anything too strenuous.'

'Perhaps she could help Hetty?' suggested Mr Ellsky.

'She seems quite bright,' agreed the doctor. 'And clean.'

She gritted her teeth. Matron had been right: listeners heard no good of themselves. With a defiant toss of her head she carried on down the main stairs into the hall before turning towards the kitchen. She should have curtsied to her employer, of course, like a good subservient domestic, but she was too angry for more than a slight inclination of the head. She tried to walk down the corridor with dignity, and cursed under her breath as her boot rubbed the blister on her heel for the fortieth time that day.

'She'd never do for a parlourmaid,' came the doctor's decisive tones. 'Walks like an old lady with the gout.'

She turned in the doorway, eyes flashing.

'If you had to wear boots that didn't fit, you'd walk like a cripple too!'she said furiously.

'I beg your pardon?' he said, icily angry.

'Mel!' Mrs Chobley was appalled. 'Doctor Kingsley's not accustomed to being spoken to like that by his servants!'

'And I'm not accustomed to being discussed like a sick horse!' she shouted, turning angrily on her heel and slamming away through the baize door.

Mrs Chobley found her a few moments later in the still room, her hot forehead pressed to the cold glass.

'Thank Gawd it's Nancy's afternoon out!' she exclaimed. 'Her and Olsen, they been looking to get at you all week. Now you give them something like this – on a plate, that's what it is!'

Melisande turned and pulled away and Mrs Chobley looked at her, baffled. She'd expected tears, not this furious silence, and she didn't know what to say.

There was a heavy fall of footsteps on the stairs, too heavy for Jessie's, and Doctor Kingsley glanced round the door.

'Mrs Chobley – coffee and brandy to my office, please. And if she's calmed down, send the girl too.'

Cook nodded and turned away to prepare the coffee.

'Come on, gel,' she said as she laid out the tray. 'Get it over and done with. You apologise properly, I'm sure he'll give you another chance.'

'I won't apologise! I wasn't in the wrong. He was!'

'He pays our wages, gel. Him as pays the wages ain't never in the wrong.'

'Rubbish!' But behind her bravado she was shaking in her uncomfortable boots. She blew her nose defiantly and tucked her hair back behind her ears. 'Give me the tray.'

'No. Jessie'll take that. Give it a few moments and then you follow.'

'Afraid I might throw it at him?' she asked caustically.

'Don't know what you might do when your dander's up and that's a fact!'

45

Outside the study door she smoothed her skirt down nervously with damp hands. For today at least she would force herself to play the servant.

Max Ellky was there, but she could not bring herself to return his smile. She stood in front of the doctor's desk with demurely folded hands, but the expected words of censure did not materialise.

'Sit down, girl!' he said harshly. 'And take those damned boots off!'

'But I –'

'Come along! I haven't got all day!'

'But – aren't you going to dismiss me?' she blurted.

'No. Though if you speak like that again, I shall be sorely tempted.'

When her boots were off he knelt to look at her feet and his lips thinned in anger at the sight of the blisters, some red raw, on her heels and toes.

'You should have said.'

She shrugged. 'They've always been like that, ever since I can remember.'

'These are most ill-fitting. Men's boots, by the look of them.'

'Men's boots don't wear out so fast. And they are cheaper. But they don't ever seem to match my feet.' She thought she heard him curse, but his head was bent and she could not be sure. 'I had a good pair once . . . ' Once, almost longer ago than she could remember, Sarah had bought her a pair of ladies' boots, soft and well-fitting, but Matron had disapproved of any one orphan being treated better than another; they had been returned to the shop, and Sarah forbidden to replace them.

'Might we have some?' suggested Mr Ellsky softly.

'Mmm. Wait there,' he commanded her.

When he returned he held a pair of leather side-lacing ladies' boots and a pair of soft slippers. 'Wear the slippers until the blisters have healed. And here.' He handed her a small jar. 'Some salve. It will speed the healing.'

'Thank you.' She slipped her feet into the blissful softness of the slippers, took the little pot and the boots, and limped gingerly to the door.

'Remember,' he said as she paused at the door, 'I expect good manners from my servants.'

'Then please set us a good example,' she answered quietly, 'and don't discuss us as though we were pieces of furniture.'

'It's all very well for you to laugh, Max,' he said in exasperation as the door closed behind her, 'but if all the servants are going to insult me and get away with it, they'll be running the house and doing as they please!'

'But she was right, Adam.' He leant back in his chair and pensively blew a cloud of smoke from his pipe. 'Strange girl. More to her than meets the eye.'

'I know what you mean. I always feel as though I should be rushing to open the door for her. But if she's to stay here she must learn to keep her tongue between her teeth.'

Melisande limped down to the kitchen where Mrs Chobley was putting a huge roast in the range.

'Look what I've got!' she said triumphantly. 'New boots and slippers!'

'Not turned off?'

'No. Nor told off.'

'Well, I'm blowed! I'd have sworn he'd have given you a good earful after what you'd said!'

'No. How could he?' asked the girl coolly. 'He knew I was in the right.' She bent down to try on the boots. Upstairs the front door slammed as the doctor went off to his appointment. 'Lucky he found the right size, wasn't it?'

'Come out of his box, they have. He gets all his lady patients to give him their cast-offs for all them poor souls in Edensville what lives in the slums round the docks.'

'Well, here's one poor soul who's exceedingly grateful!' she said with a laugh.

Later that afternoon she slipped back upstairs to the library, hoping to find a trade directory there of the sort that Sarah had had, before she had become too poor to avail herself of the many and varied services advertised within its scarlet covers. If she could find the direction of an employment agency in Edensville, then she would not feel quite so lost when she went there, as she was now quite determined to do.

47

Someone had left the door on the central wall ajar; she didn't want any of the household to find her rummaging where she had no right to be, so she crossed the room to close it.

She peeped around the door and was so intrigued by what she saw that instead of closing the door, she stepped through it.

The room was splendidly proportioned, light and airy with beautifully carved cornices and ceiling. Two sets of floor to ceiling double windows opened on to a balcony which over-looked the splendour of the formal gardens at the rear. Each window had two sets of panes, one opening inward, the other out, with a space in between which accounted for the fact that the deep cold outside never seemed to infiltrate the house.

She had never seen a beautiful room so hideously spoilt. The furniture was heavy, the sofas – too many of them – were over-stuffed, draped in purple and crimson velvets with a profusion of tassels and fringing. Crimson velvet curtains hung at the window, their over-elaborate drapings all but destroying the delicate symmetry of the frames. And some-one – Mrs Carter, she wondered savagely? – had covered the upper half of the exquisite panelling with dark olive-green flocked wallpaper.

Her progress around the room was impeded by a great number of small tables and whatnots, crowded with cluttering ornaments and daguerreotypes for which Mrs Carter had yet to send.

There was a bay thrown out to one side of the room and in it she could just make out a familiar shape, shrouded of course in yet more purple velvet. With a painfully thudding heart she drew back the fringed cover and ran her fingers over the silky, gleaming satinwood. Then, like a sleepwalker, she raised the lid and seated herself at the keys. And as she ran her fingers hesitantly over them, she knew again the liberation she had first experienced that dark and dismal day at Sarah Thom-sett's house.

She was permitted to go to Miss Thomsett's comfortable house in Elms Square every Saturday afternoon. Ostensibly she went to help with the housework just as the others were hired out as part of their future training as skivvies or boot-boys. But in reality little housework was done and the time was usually filled with extra tuition.

On one of her earliest visits, with the rain pouring down outside, she was permitted to help polish the drawing-room furniture and she recalled that shiver of ecstasy she had felt when beneath a heavily tasselled crimson cloth she had found – a piano.

Miss Thomsett was briefly out of the room. She sat on the stool and opened the lid. Tentatively she picked out a few notes with stiff fingers and then she closed her eyes and heard that half-forgotten voice speaking to her through the mists of memory.

'Relax the fingers, my darling. Let the music take you . . .'

Her fingers moved gaily across the keys, playing first a favourite Beethoven study piece whose name she had long since forgotten, then a Russian folk song, then, hauntingly, a Chopin nocturne.

She turned, startled, as applause rang out from the door-way. She looked up and saw Miss Thomsett's brother John, eyes sparkling, slightly drunk even at this early hour.

'Bravo! A girl of many talents! Where did you learn to play like that?'

'I – I don't know,' she faltered. 'I'm sorry – I should have asked permission. . . .'

'Nonsense!' That was Sarah, bustling up behind him. 'If you play that well, of course you must carry on. Practise here as often as you can.' She handed her a polishing cloth. 'The very thing, since you do not sketch. Young ladies always wish to be taught one accomplishment or the other.' She began to polish the wooden surround of the piano seat with vigour.

'I say!' protested John Thomsett. 'You're not going to turn the poor girl into another drudge, are you? Girl's far too young to turn into a blue-stocking. Probably far too pretty as well,' he said with a roguish wink, 'but it's devilish hard to see under all that armour they dress 'em in over there.'

'You must not take too much notice of my brother, Milly,' said Miss Thomsett after he had gone out. 'Wherever you go to teach there will be men like him, brothers or sometimes even fathers of your charges who will try to draw you from your line of duty. But to them it is all a game and you must not allow yourself to be distracted from your purpose.'

She tried to imagine a young man trying to distract Miss Thomsett from her purpose but could not. Not that Sarah was not pretty: even in her forties she had attractive eyes, pretty soft brown hair and a skin that glowed as she polished a sheen into the lid of the piano. No, it was not her looks but her attitude. There was no warmth. She was . . . well . . . *rigid* to people.

But what little warmth there was she gave to Milly although she never permitted her to forget the destiny she had planned for her. Every Saturday afternoon was strictly planned: first a little light housework, then piano practice which Sarah regulated, although she herself played rather stiltedly; then reading and discussion of the books she sent to the Orphanage for Milly to read at any spare moments in her crowded week. In one of them, she had found the old story of Melisande. She had excitedly pointed out to Sarah her christened name, which Sarah never afterwards omitted to use. Only after the work was done would come the moment the young girl looked forward to all week: tea time.

It was not because of the food that she took such delight in the ceremony, although the delicate sandwiches and cakes made a welcome change from the thick grey meal porridge she would otherwise have eaten at the Orphanage: it was the dainty cups they drank from, the beautiful little silver cake stand, the lace-edged tablecloth and silver cutlery. At such times the curtain across her memory would lift a little and she would hear the sound of music and laughter and those elusive voices.

'Look at the girl,' John Thomsett teased her one day. 'Such good taste she has. Ah, you won't end up in a dames' board school, my dear; I see you in a beautiful house with elegant furniture, servants to wait on you . . .'

'Don't tease the child!' snapped Sarah. 'Melisande must teach! It's that or go into service.'

'But no rich man with any sense would leave such a refined beauty in the *kitchens*!' he said, rolling his eyes wickedly.

'Come. Melisande! Miss Thomsett drew herself up, every inch of her expressing disapproval. 'Time for more pianoforte practice before you return.'

Time that had made of her an excellent, if unpolished, pianist. For a wild few weeks, she had even hoped to make a living giving piano lessons to daughters of the middle classes, until the day she learnt she was not fit even to teach the children of Wapping their letters.

Kingsley walked back to his house, his highly polished boots crunching on the crystalline snow of the sidewalk. He had finished his business early, for his mind was not altogether on the matter in hand. Was it just because he had saved her life that he did not relish the thought of the Orphanage girl scrubbing floors and heaving buckets of coal up the stairs? Of course, she could easily be trained as a parlourmaid – she was impossibly well-spoken for a servant – but then he would see a great deal more of her than if she stayed in the scullery and he could not fathom whether that would be welcome or not.

He stopped by the stables to check on the progress of one of the horses. Coming in from the yard he caught a glimpse through the kitchen door of Mrs Chobley and some of the maids gossiping over a pot of tea and a plate of scones.

He was halfway up the stairs before he heard the sound of the piano. The children across the Square had been learning to play for some time, but he had not thought either of them up to that standard. He stopped in his tracks as he realised that the music was not coming from the Frintons, but from inside the house. Only Max ever played the instrument in the drawing room and he did not play Chopin nocturnes!

He walked quietly up the stairs, stepping over the tread that always creaked. The door to the drawing room was locked from the inside. As he stood there, irresolute, the pianist hit a wrong note and stopped abruptly.

As the playing began again, he made his way to the adjoining room, opened the door on to the balcony and stepped out quietly. As he reached the drawing room windows, the pianist stopped again at the same point and he pressed himself back against the wall. As the player returned to the opening bars he stepped forward and pressed his face to the glass. The pianist had her back to the window but he had no difficulty identifying the new maid. Her fingers sped over the keys and she was obviously lost in the music, quite oblivious to anything else. Then she hit the same wrong note, crashed her hands down discordantly on the keys, buried her head in her arms and wept bitterly.

The night sky was black with a stark white half moon sailing across it. She sat in the basket chair by the window, struggling to keep awake. The maids had come up the stairs in twos and threes and now only Mrs Chobley remained downstairs in the kitchen. At last she heard her shuffling slowly up the stairs, breathing heavily. Nearly an hour later she heard the study door close and then the soft 'plop' of the oil lamps as the doctor went round the house closing up for the night. She crept to the door and listened to his footsteps disappearing up the front stairs to his chamber.

Silence.

She would wait half an hour before she moved, she decided. She sat back in the chair again, curtains drawn back so that the bright moon would keep her from falling asleep.

She woke with a start as the long case clock at the bottom of the stairs struck four. In a few hours Jessie would be rising to light the kitchen fires and take Cook her cup of tea! In a panic she began to collect her things together, becoming entangled in her shawl as she did so. She took a deep breath, forcing herself to calm down before she brought the entire household down on her.

At last the thudding of her heart slowed down to a gentle banging. She cast a last farewell glance around the room which had proved such a brief safe haven, picked up her battered portmanteau and set off down the stairs.

She paused at the door of the doctor's study, turned the handle and tiptoed into the room. By the glow of the banked down fire she groped her way across to the door to the dispensary. It took her a while to find what she was looking for, but it was worth the delay. In the charity box she found a knitted spencer, as well as a thick cloak warm enough to keep her from the worst of the weather while she made her way to Edensville.

Returning to the doctor's office she dipped the pen into the inkwell and on a clean sheet of paper she wrote:

Dear Doctor Kingsley,

I have taken one cloak and one spencer from your charity box. I shall pay for them as soon as possible. Thank you for your care and shelter.

She debated a moment how she should sign herself. 'Yours sincerely' would be much too familiar but 'Your faithful servant' seemed a trifle inappropriate under the circumstances. In the end she signed herself with a flourish: M.. Stevens.

The key was on the inside of the dispensary door; as she slid it open she was met by an icy blast. She wrapped the large cloak around her with a grateful sigh. The side gate creaked as she opened it and a dog barked suddenly and furiously across the Square, causing her heart to thump against her ribs once more, but no one stirred in Springs House.

Olsen had told her there was an old road that ran through the woods all the way down to Edensville, but she decided after some hesitation to stay on the coach road; it wasn't that she believed his tales of wolves and bears in the forest, but she knew that in the dark she would never find the forest path.

She had covered about a mile when she paused in the shelter of a clump of pines to catch her breath. The wind had got up and was blasting icily in her face, and her nose was beginning to lose all feeling. She put down her portmanteau and bent to rip a wide strip off the bottom of her petticoat which she wound round her nose and mouth. She was on her way again very quickly, for to linger too long would soon slow down her circulation and leave her at the mercy of the cold.

Her progress was slow, for the cloak, although warm, was heavy and trailed ponderously behind her. She stopped again and fished out of the portmanteau the old hand-knitted shawl which she tied around her waist outside the cloak, blousing the heavy material over the makeshift belt to draw it up and away from her heels. Now she could clutch her bag inside the warmth of the cloak, and after a while her freezing hands could begin to thaw out.

A couple of miles away from Eden Springs, the road began to run downhill between fir-covered hills that afforded a little shelter, and with the wind at her back she made much swifter progress, arriving on the bluff above Edensville just as dawn broke, grey and threatening more snow from an overcast sky.

Down by the docks the smoke was already rising from the factories and warehouses that lay under a crusting of dirty snow and dripping icicles along the muddy shore. All along the harbour inlet, in the muddy turning basins and unloading slips, grain ships from Chicago and ore carriers from Lake Superior were being unloaded into barges for the Erie Canal or railroad trucks for the line that ran alongside the Canal through the Mohawk River gap and down through the Hudson Valley to New York. Beyond the grain elevators low clouds drove in from the west on an icy wind.

Hooters and sirens sounded, bells tolled, and men, women and lanky youths spilled out of huddled tenements and alleys to hurry past the pawnshops and the flophouses, the saloons and the pie shops to the canning factories, the steel mills and the lumber yards, their feet crunching on the thick clean snow that had been laid on the streets overnight. Resolutely she turned her back on the docks and made for the centre of town.

The snow was upon her almost before she realised it, carried on a shrieking wind that howled and eddied around her, covering her from head to toe in white flakes and obscuring her view.

At the head of Main Street the tramps slept, arms suspended on the window bars of the power house, toasting themselves alternately front and back, seemingly oblivious to the blizzard raging down between the six storey office buildings. Further on, the shop lads were opening shutters, brushing the snow that had drifted up heavily against the doors during the night onto the heaps that rose between the roadway and the pavement, and exchanging banter with the newspaper men and sandwich board men warming themselves over the cellar gratings.

Wearily she trudged past the gothic pile of City Hall, covered in a flattering mantle of snow and icicles, to the square where the stalls in the covered market were being set up. Washington Street, she decided, had the most elegant shops. She would start at the top and work her way down. Nervously she smoothed a hand over her braids and set off. Lost in thought she did not hear the bell clanging in the distance.

She had just stepped out into the road when one of the newspaper men shot out and grabbed her arm with a yell of

54

warning. He tried to drag her back on to the pavement, but they fell in an undignified tangle of arms and legs into the pile of snow by the gutter.

She was about to open her mouth and protest most vigorously his treatment of her when she heard the clanging of a bell, the hiss of runners and the ground began to vibrate beneath her feet. She cringed back into the snow as, like a vision of hell, a huge horse plough rattled and banged its way past them, drawn by five spans of heavy horses, bigger than any she had ever seen, their heads wrapped in a cloud of steam through which she could see the red lanterns flickering. As they lay there, the plough streamed jets of snow over them.

'Let's get out of 'ere,' said the newsman, dragging her to her feet. They were just in time to escape a layer of sand as the sand-shaker chop-chop-thudded its way along behind.

The newsman would have none of her thanks. 'Could see you was a stranger, the way you was lookin' in the shops,' he said, returning to straighten up his placards with their stark headlines of the sinking of the battleship *Maine* in Havana harbour. 'Want to be careful. Snow muffles the sounds, see. And it's mostly sledges what does the deliveries round 'ere while the snow's thick.'

She promised to be more careful, thanked him once more, dusted down her cloak and went on her way. The first shop she came to was a draper's, its windows elegantly set out with ribbons, wraps, buttons and trimmings under flaring gas jets. Nervously she smoothed her braids; taking her courage in her hands she tried the door, which opened under the slight pressure of her hand.

A thin gentleman, dressed entirely in black, came forward. 'Good morning, miss, and what may we fetch you so early in the morning?'

His voice was almost as stiff as the cloth of his suit; he reminded her of the undertaker's assistant who used to come to the Orphanage. But he'd called her miss: she must look respectable, at least from a distance.

'I'm seeking employment as a shop assistant.' As an afterthought she added 'sir.' His eyebrows shot up: he was not accustomed to making such a mistake! 'No vacancies,' he said curtly.

'Might you take on more assistants in the spring, sir?'

'I haven't taken on staff for over a year,' he said, more gently. 'My daughters assist in the shop, my dear. It's the only way a shop like mine can make a profit these days.'

It was the same story at every shop she called at. With the rapid growth of the last few years, and the influx of immigrants which had turned the modest lakeside town into the gateway to the west, big stores from Chicago and Toronto had opened branches in Edensville and the smaller family stores now found themselves up against competition which they were ill-equipped to fight. They had been forced to cut down on their staff; daughters were removed from genteel ladies' academies or dragged away from the busy social life of 'At Homes' and subscription dances to serve behind the counter, which most of them did with a very ill will.

'Try the dressmakers, young lady,' suggested one shopkeeper helpfully. 'My wife says they can't get enough seamstresses, not now the canning factory's started taking on women.'

She thanked him with a smile and left the shop with a lighter step. A seamstress, she thought, would be just the thing! After all, she had done all the alterations for the Orphanage girls for many years and turned and altered Sarah's cast-offs to fit her. Sarah would willingly have clothed her entirely out of her own pocket in those early, prosperous days, but Matron had forbidden it, deeming it unfair she should have any more than the next girl. But Matron had complimented her on her neat, tiny stitching and allowed her to devote herself to sewing while the other girls knitted the rough shawls and wraps, for Melisande's knitting had long been a standing joke in the girl's dormitory. 'Lace knitting' they had called it: more holes than surround.

She followed the man's directions, crossing the road carefully, avoiding the occasional horse-drawn sledge careering down the centre of the road, making the early morning deliveries before the customers were out and about; with their lanterns flickering in the half light and the horses' hooves muffled by the overnight fall of snow, the hiss of the sled runners was often the only warning to the unfortunate pedestrian.

She stopped in Rochester Street and asked directions to the first address on the list.

'If it's dressmakers you want,' said the woman, 'you're standing right outside one.'

An omen, though Melisande, took a deep breath and knocked on the door. A slatternly girl in a torn dress answered the door.

'Yes? What d'yer want?'

'To see Madame Czestowa.' She read the name off the battered plate beside the door.

'Who is it?' a voice screeched harshly from within.

'Girl here wants ter see yer!'

'Bring her in the, yer lazy trollop,' shrieked the same voice, and as Melisande backed away in some trepidation, the girl reached out a thin claw-like hand and pulled her in.

She would have liked to turn tail and flee, but this was no time for timidity: she needed work and would have to take it wherever it offered.

She followed the girl down a rickety flight of stairs to a gloomy basement workroom where a lady of indeterminate age sat at a bench sewing a fall of lace on to a dress of palest blue. Around the room hung a quantity of dresses, some frilled, some flounced, in all the colours of the rainbow.

'Pretty, aren't they, my dear?' The woman twisted round in her seat to watch Melisande's expression as she looked at all the dresses. 'Like to wear them, would you?'

'Me? Oh no, Madame. But I could sew them. I'm very handy with –'

'Take your cloak off, girl, and let me have a proper look at you,' interrupted Madame in a voice that tried hard to be genteel. She might indeed be Madam Czestowa, but only if she had married into the name, for her accent was pure East · End of London.

'Now turn around. Hmmm. Good proportions, but much too thin.'

'But I want to sew clothes, not wear them!'

'Don't need a sewing hand just now, but I know just the place for you. Teresa! Get your shawl and take this young lady up to Missus Mason's. Quick, now, before the streets gets busy.' She set aside her work. 'What's a pretty thing like you doin' lookin' for a sewing job, eh?'

57

She shrugged. 'I need the work. One of the shopkeepers gave me a list.' She peered at it with a frown. 'Mason's . . . I can't see them.'

'Don't bother with those others, dearie. I know they haven't any places, not a one. But Missus Mason is always busy, always looking for new hands. You trust me.' She stood up and led Melisande back up the stairs. 'Over from the old country, are you?'

She nodded.

'Got no family? No friends who'd look after you?'

'No. No one.' She felt more alone than ever.

'Never mind, dearie.' She patted her on the shoulder. 'Missus Mason looks after her girls real well, she does.'

The snow had stopped and the streets had come to life while she'd been at Madame Czestowa's. There were people opening shutters, sweeping doorsteps, exchanging remarks with their neighbours and going about their business. The taciturn Theresa led the way through streets that became progressively shabbier as they walked back towards the lake, though the building they eventually stopped at was not quite as dilapidated as the others. Some attempt had been made to patch up the peeling paintwork: the storm shutters had been painted a rather bilious shade of bluey-green, while the door was a stark red, which in its shabby surroundings shone forth with twice the brilliance it would otherwise have had. She didn't think much of Mrs Mason's taste.

Teresa hammered on the door and after a moment Melisande realised that they were being regarded, unnervingly, by a disembodied eye visible through a small hole in the centre panel of the door.

The door was opened by an extremely ugly man; he must once have been a boxer, for his nose was flattened and twisted to one side, his ears were no mor than fleshy stumps and the skin round his eyes so badly scarred that one eye was practically invisible.

Teresa gave her a shove between the shoulder blades and propelled her into the hall. 'Missus Mason!' she called. 'Madame Czestowa's sent you a new girl.'

A curtain moved aside at the end of the hall and a woman in her fifties swept into the hall, wearing a dress of puce silk deeply scooped to display an ample bosom. Feathers dyed to match her dress nodded from an over-elaborate coiffure and she moved in a cloud of sickeningly sweet perfume which seemed to permeate the house. The girl's eyes widened as she took in Missus Mason's full glory, then, at the edge of her vision, just before the curtain fell, she caught a glimpse of two girls in the back room, dressed in nothing but clinging shifts.

She could have cried with rage at her gullibility: in her desperation to find work she'd let herself be tricked into a brothel as bad as any of the stews around Wapping.

Her first instinct was to run, but the man was still behind her and she knew she was no match for him. And the hideous old woman with the heavily painted face was surging down the hall towards her like a galleon in full sail.

'The little girl isn't shy, is she?' she purred throatily. 'Help her in, George.'

As the man took his arm off the door, she saw her chance. With a soft moan she turned to him and appeared about to swoon in his arms. While everyone was still frozen into inaction, she twisted her knee up and drove it into George's groin. The man doubled up and fell, groaning, across the width of the hall, and with one fluid movement Melisande snatched up her bag and slipped past him.

She knew she had only a small advantage and made the most of it, slithering precariously around a corner as she sped back to the more respectable area of town. They would not bother to follow her too far, she told herself stoutly. There were plenty of other girls and in her own estimation she was nothing special as far as looks went.

As she ran through the streets, she sent up a prayer of thanks to Little Polack, wherever he might be now; the trick which had so often saved Ivan from the bullies had today saved her from an even worse fate.

Her heart was still thudding painfully, as much from fright as from the furious pace of her escape, when she rounded a corner and ran straight into a little knot of people standing together.

Parcels and umbrellas, handbags and portmanteaux went flying in all directions and the girl, unable to keep her footing on the hard, compacted snow, went flying with them. Amid

59

all the exclamations and protests, she heard only one friendly voice as an elderly gentleman bent down to offer his hand.

'I'm terribly sorry!' she gasped as she clambered back on her feet, disentangling herself from a particularly vicious black umbrella.

'It's a plot, that's what it is!' exclaimed one of the women, dressed, like all the others, in unrelieved black and heavily veiled. 'A plot by the Episcopalians to disrupt our services!'

'I think not, Miriam,' remonstrated the elderly man gently. 'Just a young lady in some distress.'

'I'm so sorry.' She picked a bag up from the pavement and held it out hopefully. 'But – I had to get away!' she said incoherently. 'They weren't dressmakers at all . . . There wasn't a job. It was all a trick!'

'A job?' echoed another member of the little group. 'Dressmakers?'

'I was looking for employment as a seamstress . . .'

'God moves in a mysterious way,' said the woman, who had a curiously creaky voice, like a door that has long needed oil for its hinges. 'I have been short of a sewing hand since Louisa's family left for Chicago. You have experience, girl?'

'Yes.' It was not a lie, but she would not tell her that the experience was all in the Orphanage!

'But the Fellowship, Agnes!' exclaimed another woman, as stout as her friend was thin. 'We may only associate within the Fellowship!'

'Three months I have waited for a seamstress from the Fellowship!' snapped Agnes. 'Our sisters in Quebec and Albany have failed to send a single apprentice. I have a good cutter, that is true, but I am reduced to taking on little cripples who cannot even sew. This girl is in need of salvation! Are we not bid save our brethren who have not seen the Light from the Darkness of the Devil? She has the look of the damned about her: even Brother Ezekiel cannot resist her lure.'

The others, male and female, turned their reproachful glance on the elderly man who had come to the girl's aid and he quickly dropped his hand from her elbow.

But Melisande didn't care. All she grasped was that here at last was the job she had been looking for, with a respectable employer, offering her independence and a safe haven from the Mrs Masons of this world.

60

Adam Kingsley was about to sit down to breakfast when he received an urgent call to a nearby house where a servant, carrying cans of hot water up the backstairs to the bedrooms, had slipped on the highly polished surface and not only broken her leg but scalded herself in the process. He cast a regretful look at the chafing dishes of eggs, bacon and kidneys on the side board, snatched a muffin from the tray and hurried to his dispensary to fetch his bag.

It was nearly noon before he returned to the house, tired, hungry and more than a little irritable. Bishop had taken some persuasion not to send his housemaid into the Infirmary, but he had at last allowed his wife to talk him into allowing the girl to be nursed at home.

Mrs Bishop was eager to be accepted into Eden Springs society and she had soon realised that the resident of Springs House carried a deal of influence in the little town. Her husband owned a shipping line in Edensville which made a good living carrying immigrants up through the Lakes to Michigan or on to Canada, but though the Bishops had more money than some of the old Springs families put together, that was no guarantee of acceptance.

Kingsley was perfectly aware of the reasons for the Bishops' change of face over the housemaid; he had no illusions it was done for Christian charity. With a sigh he made a mental note to introduce Mrs Bishop to some of the Eden Springs matrons: there was no end to the responsibilities he had inherited when he took over Carter's practice. Sometimes he daydreamed about what life would have been like if he had travelled a littler further and found himself a quiet country practice.

After a moment his face lightened: he would introduce Mrs Bishop to Mrs Patterson, then at least somebody would benefit from all the social nonsense.

Still, not a bad morning's work. Many employers, faced with diverting servants to wait on the invalid, would have packed the unfortunate wench off to take her chances in Edensville Infirmary. It was a sound building, equipped to the finest standards of the time by the City Fathers some thirty years before, but although the typhoid outbreak was now under control, to send anyone there at the moment could still be to sign a death warrant.

Damn McCorquodale! thought Kingsley savagely. If only he'd listened they could have had new water supplies from unpolluted sources piped into Edensville last year, when the immigrants first began to pour in in their thousands to work in the new steel and ironworks. But McCorquodale had over-ruled them, and as he was the senior surgeon, the City Fathers had listened to him.

Of course in the long run Adam and his colleagues had been proved right, but there was scant comfort in that when the poor and the sick had died in their hundreds. Perhaps he should have made more of a fuss, but at the time he had only been Carter's junior partner and dependent on McCorquodale for the premises for his free dispensary in Edensville, a dispensary that was all the poorer immigrants had. Like the new girl. If she had been sent to the public hospital, sick and underfed as she was, she would not have survived more than a few days, and though every life must always be important to him, the thought of pretty, rebellious Milly quietly fading away affected him far more deeply. Strange how in such a short time she'd made such an impact on the household. Even Max had taken to coming over to the house regularly, offending Mrs Chobley's propriety by his attentions.

'Being as how we usually only see him once a week at most and he's here most ever day, well, the maids are talking. And however strange they brought her up in that Orphanage, she's to be your housemaid and that kind of thing under my roof I cannot allow. Nancy's already got her knife into the girl and I'd not like to give them a reason to put her in bad, not for a big clock I wouldn't. It's Mister Max as should know better, and one of us is going to have to tell him . . .'

It was never easy to stop Mrs Chobley when she was in full flight, but when he could get a word in edgeways, Adam promised to see to the matter. Once the girl got down to work properly, that should put an end to it.

It was half way through the afternoon before he found time to see Mrs Chobley to discuss the evening's menu. It was a matter that he did not usually concern himself with, having every confidence in her notions of nutrition, economy and style, but that evening he was entertaining the Pattersons to dinner – not a prospect that attracted, for he considered the mother a grasping hypocrite and her son a bully, with an unsavoury reputation where women were concerned. But they owned, beside most of the shipyards and the new canning factory, a sizeable number of empty properties in Harbourside, down by the docks; if only he could induce Mrs' Patterson to lease two of them to him for the two projects he had in mind, then he would be independent of McCorquodale and could set about lobbying for the new water supplies.

He cast his eye over the menu for the evening.

'Very good, Mrs Chobley,' he said with a warm smile. 'I knew I could rely on you.'

'And the wine, sir? Being as how the butler always used to deal with the wine . . .'

'I'll see to that. I'll go down to the cellars now, while I remember. And if you could send the new girl to my study in about half an hour, she can sign her indentures.'

Mrs Chobley looked a little worried.

'She hasn't come down today, sir. I had meant to go up and see to her, but with all the cooking for this evening, I just haven't found the time.'

'But she's well past the point of a relapse. What ails her?'

'Probably scared at the prospect of a bit of hard work,' sneered Nancy.

Before Cook had a chance to reprimand her, the doctor turned a contemptuous glare on her.

'I allow my servants a great deal of freedom, Nancy,' he said levelly, 'but insolence I will not tolerate.'

He had been thinking of letting one of the maids go – six was far too many for a household of one man – and he rather felt the unpleasant and unpleasing Nancy would head the list. But he was a just man and no servant would leave his roof without another post to go to.

'Did she say what ailed her?' he asked Mrs Chobley.

'Nancy?'

She looked down at the floor. 'I didn't . . . I mean, I knocked and told her to get up. She didn't say nothing, so I just left the tray outside.'

Kingsley exchanged a look of deep foreboding with his cook then rushed along the hall to the stairs. He took them two at a time and flung the door open with a conviction that to knock first would be pointless. As the door swung wide, he knew with a sickening certainty that the room was empty.

He never knew how he managed to get through the formal dinner that evening. He had concocted an excuse to cover Max's absence and sent him to ride out to the outlying farms and cottages on the estate to see if the girl had passed that way. He had wanted to go himself, but to offend Mrs Patterson would risk all the work he had put in on the free dispensary and abandon his responsibility to a much greater. number. As it was he'd spent the late afternoon on the road to Edensville, searching for her.

The Pattersons arrived, sleigh bells jingling, in a great flurry of snow, and his heart sank at the sight. It was a gentle fall, but that would be just as dangerous to an ill-clad girl, perhaps worse because it was so insidious, a creeping cold which had you in its grip before you realised it.

As course succeeded course, he ate with an indifference that would have appalled Mrs Chobley, could she but have seen him. He carried out his duties as a host with the same automatic reaction, but the Pattersons were all so fond of the sound of their own voices that they didn't notice it. He responded to Sophia's less than subtle attempts at flirtation so absent-mindedly that her mother was moved to hope. Ever since Almeria Carter had let slip some interesting details of the new doctor's family connections, she had fixed her sights on him for her daughter.

As their carriage disappeared at last around the curve in the drive, Adam turned on his heel and went swiftly to his study. Max had just arrived and his snow-caked boots were steaming gently in front of the fire.

'Don't get up.' He waved his steward impatiently back to his seat, strode across to the desk and poured a generous measure into each of two crystal glasses. 'You look frozen. Drink that down, it will help you thaw out. Any sign?'

'Nothing. I've sent Olsen in to Mrs Randall with a note, but I told him to stay over if the weather was too bad. We don't want another lost in the snow.'

'Serve him right if he did! He and Nancy have been tormenting and teasing her ever since she got here. They're probably the reason she left!'

'She's not that poor-spirited.'

'I know.' He passed his hand tiredly through his hair. 'Then why? Why leave the only place she knew, in a strange country, in the depth of winter?'

'Perhaps she wasn't as friendless as she'd have us believe. Certainly she must have found shelter, otherwise –'

'Otherwise we'd have found her body? Yes, I'd thought of that.' He paced up and down the room. 'You could be right, of course. An attractive girl like that . . . But if you're wrong? We can't just abandon her.'

'She would seem to have abandoned us,' said Max gruffly. 'But, yes, you're right. We keep looking for the next day or two; if we haven't found her by then, it will be too late anyway.'

They fell silent, occupied with a vision of a small, huddled body under a gentle, deadly mantle of snow. Adam picked up the decanter and refilled their glasses.

'There's no more we can do tonight. I've sent a good description to Beatrice Randall.'

'We'll just have to wait till we hear from her.'

It was almost two weeks later, when they'd give up all hope of finding her, that one of his patients, a widow with seven children to clothe, found the note which Melisande had left in the charity box. By that time, the trail of the girl in the cloak had gone cold and no one looking for pretty, rosy-cheeked, fair-haired Miss Stevens would have wasted a glance on the thin, wan Miss Smith who emerged from Madame Chantal's gloomy basement workroom only to go to the Prayer House, her hair covered by an old-fashioned black bonnet and her eyes wary behind a heavy veil.

As the weeks went by, Melisande began to regret the ease with which she'd let herself be taken over by Madame Chantal. At first she had seen the tall house in the fashionable thoroughfare as a haven, a refuge from the more unpleasant side of life she had so narrowly escaped, but she soon realised how deceptive appearances could be.

The *modiste*, a New Yorker born and bred, who had adopted the name to give an air of spurious Parisian chic to her salon, lived in an elegant town house with three floors served by a wide curving staircase with a beautifully carved balustrade; above them was a floor of attic rooms where the sewing hands slept. The elegance of the salon, however, stopped short at the display and fitting rooms. The silken drapes and delicate furniture offered for the comfort of the fashionable ladies who patronised Madame Chantal found no counterpart in the rest of the house: all but the attic and basement were kept firmly locked, the boards bare, the windows uncurtained. The warmth of the salon never penetrated to the attics or the freezing basement where Anna, the supervisor, and the other sewing hands huddled round oil lamps for warmth while their numb fingers, in fingerless mittens, turned lengths of cloth into the exquisite creations designed by Madame for the rich ladies of Edensville.

Madame always dressed elegantly for the salon but the minute the shutters went up she would retire to her bare room and emerge in drab, unadorned black. Even in her own quarters she rarely lit a fire and her evening meal was little better than the miserable food she doled out so reluctantly to her workers. Every cent she could scrimp went on the Fellowship. To Melisande it was like a return to life in the Orphanage, except that the cold was so much worse.

To Anna, the sour pattern cutter, neither deprivation nor treat ever seemed to make much difference, but the other apprentices had the voracious appetites of growing girls and were always hungry. Shortly before Melisande's arrival Natasha, the lame Russian girl, had crept down in the still watches of the night from her attic bedroom and, desperate with cold and hunger, had gorged herself on the remains of some fatty pork. The effect of such richness on the underfed girl had been as inevitable as it was unpleasant and Madame, finding her retching uncontrollably, had gone for her with the switch. Natasha recounted this in her broken English with a matter-of-fact acceptance which Melisande found more chilling than the punishment. For days she could not sit down, which made her usually mediocre stitching even more untidy, for which she received a regular tongue-lashing from

Madame that matched anything Melisande had ever heard in Wapping.

Madame had no cause for dissatisfaction with the new girl's work, for she sewed a neat seam, but her fury knew no bounds when she came up to the attic one day to find her sharing her dinner with Natasha.

'I said the little cripple was not to be fed!' she screeched. 'So you think you know better than *me*?'

Melisande looked up from her plate. 'I've seen too many sicken and die for lack of food,' she said with a calmness she did not feel. 'While I have food, no one shall go hungry.'

'You defy me?'

'No, Madame. I hope it won't come to that.' She was shaking in her shoes as she said it, for it was not pleasant to be desperate for employment and the memory of the house on Lake Street, the sound and the smell of it, came flooding back to remind her of the alternative. 'Natasha does her best. But her sewing will hardly improve if she's faint with hunger.'

'Highty-tighty, miss!' snapped the older woman. 'Then you will take responsibility for her. See to it that she doesn't shirk her work, or it will be your wages that will be docked.'

There was no more talk of starvation or whipping and Natasha began to lose the hunted look she had borne so long. Melisande shielded her from the worst of Madame's anger and even helped her improve her plain stitching, for she had always found encouragement a better teacher than fear. Although Natasha spoke a fairly broad Russian dialect, they were able to converse together, which annoyed Anna, against whom they soon formed a protective alliance.

Speaking Russian to Natasha stirred up once more some of the old memories; she could hear a man's voice speaking to her, but however hard she tried she could not conjure up the face. The curtain refused obstinately to lift.

Natasha reminded her of Little Polack. He was probably captain of his own ship by now, sailing the seven seas. Oh, how she envied him! He'd been an undersized but wiry lad of about ten who had been fetched to the Home in a high fever after an accident in the docks; no one on the boys' side had understood him and he had understood none of them; no one had known quite what to do with him until the day he was sent to Smithfield with Melisande.

As his contribution to charitable works, an act which raised him a notch or two up the social ladder in his neighbourhood, Mr Josiah Dewsbury, who had risen from slaughterhouse hand to Purveyor of Meat to the Nobility, had offered to provide the Home with meat two days a week. The Trustees had taken up the offer with alacrity and sent an orphan with a hand cart to collect pork on Wednesdays and beef on Sundays.

Melisande had hated dinner on those days. The fat pork, in which you could distinguish barely a trace of meat, always stuck in her throat and the gristly lumps of beef were tough for children raised on broths and porridge. She'd always passed most of hers to Lizzie, who'd wolfed it down, for woe betide anyone who left anything on the plate. With the little they had at the Orphanage 'Waste not, want not' was the watchword.

Pulling the handcart to Smithfield was her least favourite task: the smells and sounds of the slaughterhouse nauseated her and the bleating and lowing of the animals as they were led to their death in the shambles echoed in her ears for hours afterwards. Other children, scrubbing floors and dollying laundry, would willingly have gone in her stead, but Matron made no allowance for preferences. Last time it was her turn she had pleaded sickness which had passed off suspiciously rapidly when someone else took her place. To cry wolf twice would draw Matron's wrath upon her.

Doctor Morel had been visiting the Home and came as far as the market with them, feeling that an imbecile boy was no protection for a young girl out on the streets alone, even if she was very obviously from the foundlings' home, in her grey serge and Holland apron. Milly was already an attractive child, her pretty face fine-boned with a straight nose, the exotically slanted mossy green eyes fringed enchantingly with long lashes just a shade or two darker than hair the colour of warm honey. Her figure was beginning, much to her discomfiture, to develop, and even in the ugly uniform and heavy boots, people would always turn to give her a second glance.

Morel drew out his pocket watch and compared it to the clock which hung above Dewsbury's premises.

'Two of the clock now,' he said. 'I shall return at three. THREE O'CLOCK,' he repeated to little Polack, in that alarmingly loud voice which Englishmen reserve for foreigners and half-wits. As they hurried round to the back door, she though she heard little Polack mutter '*Ijiot!*' under his breath.

The apprentices greeted Milly with enthusiasm, teasing and flirting, their hands dripping with blood from the carcasses they were cutting up. Now, if ever, she felt the need of Doctor Morel's protection, but he was across the road at Bart's, his old hospital. The more she blushed, the more the apprentices teased, and the bolder among them began to make even more suggestive remarks and comment on her budding figure. When she refused to respond to their banter, they began to wave trotters at her, then an ear, then two of them tossed a bull's eye back and forth over her head. 'This'll see you through to next week!' shouted one with a raucous laugh, tossing it up against the tiled wall beside her where it slid glassily down, leaving a smear of blood behind. 'Come on, darling,' said a skinny dark-haired youth, reaching out a bloody hand to grab her. 'Give us a kiss!'

Little Polack stepped between them. 'Wait outside,' he said in his own tongue. 'I will stay with the handcart. I will call you when we are ready.'

Without thought she answered him in the same language and was out on the street breathing great lungfuls of the blessed fresh air before she realised what had happened.

She had never thought of herself as foreign, but in those distant half-remembered days she had switched without thought from one language to another. English to Mary, French to the beautiful lady and – At little Polack's words she had seen a tall bearded man standing with one hand casually leaning on a grand piano. But further than that her mind would not go.

Doctor Morel had been very excited at the new discovery and proposed to Matron that a child who could speak three languages deserved a wider education than that offered in the Orphanage.

'Out of the question, I'm afraid,' said Matron with a sigh. 'We feed and clothe them, make sure they can read and write. That's all we can hope to do.'

'But in a few years' time there'll be a great need for educated girls!' he exclaimed. 'Only last week one of my·

colleagues purchased a typewriting machine for his assistant. We could train her as a clerk. And you want to send her out as a skivvy! It's a crying shame!'

'There are no funds for extras.' repeated Matron firmly. 'It's a waste, we all agree, but she is not the only child we have to care for.'

'One of our patrons –'

'If a patron makes an extra contribution, it must be shared out!' she snapped. 'We don't even have enough boots to go round this winter! Can I send the rest barefoot so that Milly can have extra teaching?'

And that was how it remained – until Sarah came to Wapping.

It was fortunate that Melisande was not scared of hard work, for that she had in plenty in Edensville and as February slipped unnoticed into March and she sewed on in the cold basement workroom, the long days and the poor food brought back the look of fine drawn frailty to her face. The long hours of toil were broken only by the Fellowship's meetings.

They met in a huge, unheated barn of a place, built originally for a much larger congregation, its stone walls unfaced, the pews rough-hewn and unfinished. The men in the congregation were separated from the women by a wooden wall down the centre; the seven Elders of the Fellowship were set back from their flock on a raised dais behind a board and rail structure and the preacher of the day hovered, black-clad, above them all in a tall pulpit. Like a vulture, thought Melisande, recalling the picture in one of Sarah's books. The Fellowship preached equality before the Lord, but some were clearly more equal than others – and closer to Heaven than the uncomfortable pew where she sat.

The Elders took upon themselves not only the running of the service, but also the supervision of the daily lives of their flock and often, before the sermon, one or other of them would leap to his feet, point accusingly at someone in the body of the chapel and proceed to denounce him or her for some dereliction or oversight. Those sitting by the unfortunate on whom the attention was focused, even their own family, would shift ever so slightly away from the victim, avoiding his or her eye, withdrawing black skirts and capes lest they obtrude too closely to the sinner. She wondered they had any congregation left at all.

By dint of singing her favourite hymns to herself in her head, Melisande managed to close her ears to the threats of doom and damnation being hurled at the congregation by the preacher of the day and still maintain a semblance of attention that would satisfy Madame; she suspected that the rest of the apprentices did much the same – even Anna. Most of the congregation were elderly, for Madame's sect was dedicated to a life of celibacy and was dependent on converts such as the sewing hands if they were not to die out. The sect believed in adult baptism by total immersion and after Anna had told her that the dais on which the Elders sat formed the cover of the baptism pool, Melisande was never again able to take them as seriously, for one corner of her mind was always imagining what would happen if someone accidentally knocked the lever and tipped them, beards, sanctity and all, into the water.

There was a great deal of leaping up and down in the Service, and not only from the Elders, for the sect believed in bearing witness loudly and publicly. Sometimes members of the congregation would jump to their feet and start speaking in tongues; at one morning meeting, as a young and charismatic preacher was addressing them, a woman in the pew in front of them leaped to her feet, crying out ecstatically, and began to rend her clothes. Madame was appalled. *That* preacher would not be invited to Edensville again, she pronounced.

As in the Orphanage, Sunday observance was in word rather than action and they spent most of their time between services in the workroom, cutting out the next week's work.

At first, after the fright in Lake Street, the lack of free time did not worry Melisande, but as the tips of the grass began to poke through the snow into the wintry sunlight, and Edensville society put away the richly decorated sleighs and harnessed the horses instead to their splendid carriages, she felt the blood stir in her veins once more. When Madame Chantal produced the indentures for her to sign, she was amazed to find herself suggesting that they first discuss terms.

71

'Terms?' shrieked Madame. 'What terms?'

'Pay and time off,' said Melisande crisply.

'But you are an apprentice . . . ' Madame's voice tailed off.

'Nonsense!' Melisande wondered if the spring air had somehow got into her blood. 'You know as well as I that I served my apprenticeship years ago in the Orphanage. I sew better than any of the other girls here. I should think about three-quarters of Anna's pay, would you agree?'

Madame named a sum much nearer Natasha's meagre wages, but Melisande knew she was worth more. She shook her head, not trusting herself to speak.

At last they reached an acceptable compromise. 'Payable at the year's end,' said Madame.

'At the end of every month, if you please. I have some debts to pay.'

'Debts! Debts?' Madame cried in a strangled voice. 'Who goeth a borrowing, goeth a sorrowing!'

'Nevertheless –'

'Quarterly,' offered Madame.

'Monthly,' said Melisande firmly. 'Or, I regret, I shall have to seek employment elsewhere.' She knew Madame would have liked to turn her out on her ear, but now that the canning factory was employing women, good seamstresses were hard to come by. And the spring balls would be starting soon. 'And if you could let me know which afternoon I may have free. . . .?'

'You are far too young and heedless to be let out alone! It is my Christian duty to protect you from the evils of this world.'

'I would be perfectly happy to take one of the other girls.' Preferably Natasha, she thought.

Madame promised to consider the matter.

She fished the last greasy pan from the greasy bowl and stretched her aching back. She had not sufficiently appreciated the kitchen at Springs House, she told herself, carrying the bowl up the worn back steps out into the sunlight where she poured the contents into the drain which emptied into the cesspit behind the noisome little shack which was the only sanitation in the entire dwelling. There was no bath, not even a battered old hip bath such as they had used in Wapping, nothing but a small tin bowl, cold water and harsh soap, grudgingly doled out, despite Madame's insistence that cleanliness was next to Godliness. Some of the apprentices, in the bitter weather, did not pay the attention they should have to this part of their routine but Melisande, brought up in fear of sickness and disease, never failed to have a thorough scrub in the most icy weather.

Work done, she hurried to her attic bedroom. She brushed her hair vigorously, wound it into a neat bun and put on her only presentable clothes, the ones she had worn to the interview in London on the day of the Jubilee picnic. How they had all conspired together to make sure that she did not disgrace them! Matron had found her a sober navy skirt with three rows of silk braiding round the hem, Mrs Evans had produced a high-necked cream blouse with mother-of-pearl buttons for which she had long grown too stout, and Sarah had added a little cameo brooch. Only nine months, but it seemed a lifetime ago.

How different her life would have been if they had not decided to send the Orphanage children to the local school.

She'd hurried round to Sarah's house to blurt out the news of the school inspector's visit.

'He said I'd done well under the circumstances,' she said dispiritedly, ' but the children needed a full day and better facilities. They're to go to the new school by St Mark's! Oh Sarah,' she wailed, 'now I shall have to go for a skivvy after all!'

'Not if I can help it!' exclaimed Sarah, drawing herself erect. 'What! Waste a brain like yours in a kitchen?' She sent Melisande to splash her tear-stained face with water and set out the pens and blotters on the table – the big old cylinder desk with its intriguing pigeon holes and slides and secret drawers had gone, like so much else, to the auction rooms to pay off bad investments and John Thomsett's gambling debts.

'Who are we going to write to?'

'To whom are we going to write?' corrected Sarah gently. 'You will write to the School Board and the Parish and the School Inspector, and you will apply for the post at St Mark's.'

'They won't have me.'

'They'll be mad if they do not. How much easier the transition from Orphanage to school with you there . . .'

'But the Rector –'

'He is not the only one with any say in the matter.'

With a great deal of thought and chewing of pens they arrived at a letter designed to convince the recipients of the suitability of the undersigned to be entrusted with the education of the children of Wapping.

The undersigned.

For the first time it was brought home to her that she had no name.

'What do other orphans do?' she asked in a small voice.

'Take the name of the place they live or the first house where they go into service.'

'Melisande Wapping!' she said dramatically. 'Miss Melisande St Mark's!' she giggled. 'Oh, Sarah, they sound awful!'

'You could use mine,' she suggested.

But her name was also John's name and for reasons she could not have explained she did not want to take his name. 'Melisande Thomsett'. Not wishing to hurt Sarah's feelings, she overemphasised the *d* and *t* sounds to make it sound clumsy.

It was Thomsett himself, coming home in a rare mood of sobriety, who rescued her.

'Nonsense,' he said decisively. 'She must have her own name. Think!' he urged Melisande. 'Your father . . . surely you can remember something about him?'

'He was Russian. Melisande Russian?' she suggested.

'Oh, no!' Sarah was appalled. 'Suppose we went to war with them again!'

She sank her head in her hands, willing herself to remember. The misty veil lifted a little and she could see a tall figure, bearded, leaning against the piano. A woman's voice called: 'Stefan! Stefan!' She tried to hold on to that voice, to look beyond the moment, but it slipped away and the black curtain fell into place once more.

'Stefan. That's all I can remember,' she said sadly.

'Father's name Stefan,' said Thomsett. 'That's Stephen, isn't it? Put an *s* on it, if you like.

So she signed herself, with a flourish:

74

Ever your obedient servant,
Melisande Stevens

She received just the one reply. Mr Mackenzie of Her Majesty's Inspectorate of Schools had persuaded the Governors to interview Miss Stevens on Saturday, 27th June at 3 p.m. 'In view of the excellent work I had the pleasure of seeing at the Orphanage last week'.

'It's the day of the Jubilee picnic,' she said inconsequentially. The Orphanage, its children having been deemed too ragged to help line the route for the old Queen's Diamond Jubilee, planned to make use of the general holiday and take the children on a picnic.

'What's a Jubilee picnic compared to a career?' said Sarah bracingly. She drew out her gold watch. 'Off you go, child. Matron will be waiting for you.'

It was Ellen's afternoon out and so she fetched her own cloak. Halfway down the hall she heard the raised voices.

'You are setting fair to ruin that girl's life,' said Sarah's brother. She heard the clink of glass as he unstoppered the brandy decanter. 'Why will you not let her face up to the realities of life?'

She shouldn't have listened, but it was, after all, her life they were discussing.

'Nonsense! She deserves that post!' snapped Sarah. 'She's probably the best educated applicant.'

'What the Hell has that to do with it!' He banged the glass down and slopped it. 'She might be the greatest genius since da Vinci, but all they will see is a penniless waif with no formal schooling and no public examinations. Face the truth, woman! Stop trying to live your life through her!'

'What do you think would have happened to her if I had not seen her talents?' said Sarah angrily.

'She'd have gone as a shop girl, perhaps. She wouldn't have stayed there long.'

'No! She'd have fallen prey to such a one as you. I know all about that shop girl you had in keeping before you drank all our money away!'

'So you knew about Kitty? Well, it was no secret. You see, I have red blood in my veins, as Kitty did. Aye, and as Milly

75

has, for all you bundle her up in those ghastly clothes and hide her hair. It shows in the eyes, y'see.'

Melisande shivered, drew her cloak around her and slid silently out of the door.

She was up early to help pack the food for the Jubilee picnic. The children were to set off at eleven, when Mr Evans the milkman had finished his rounds. He and his son, who had a round in the next parish, would strip their carts of the fittings and hooped canopies to fit them all in, and drive them out to Epping.

'I'll be praying for you,' said stout Mrs Evans, her cheeks rosy as she hacked away at the loaves. 'A waste, someone as clever as you to go into service – though mind, it's what I did. Not that I stayed there long once Mr Evans came a-calling,' she said with a chuckle.

Sarah had given her sixpence for the omnibus.

'But I can walk! It's not far to Westminster.'

'And arrive with your skirt six inches deep in London dust?'

It was the first time she'd travelled in the omnibus and she was in two minds about it: sitting sideways as it rattled over the cobbles made her feel slightly unwell – though that might have been a combination of nerves, and fear that the child bouncing on its mother's knee in the next seat and clutching a very sticky sweet might mark her costume.

Alighting from the omnibus in the broad square, she looked round her open-mouthed. St Margaret's, the Abbey, the new Houses of Parliament, the clock tower pointing up like a finger above the bridge . . . she could identify them all from Sarah's albums of prints and photographs, but she hadn't expected them to be so huge.

Smart carriages driven by liveried coachmen bowled along, the horses adding to the layer of muck that clung to the streets even in this more salubrious district of London. Inside she caught glimpses of elegant ladies, hair piled high beneath fashionable broad-brimmed picture hats, and gentlemen in smart morning coats and tall hats. The streets outside the Parliament buildings and the approaches to Westminster Bridge were regularly swept, but with the constant passage of carriages and hackney cabs, there was still work for the

ragged crossing sweepers who darted out in front of gentlemen in tall beaver hats to clear them a path through the mud
and ordure. Looking at the handsome buildings around the
Square and the smart carriages with their high-stepping
horses and elegant occupants, it was hard to believe that this
was part of the same city she lived in. Only the river, broad
and brown, joined Westminster with the squalor of Wapping,
indifferent alike to the richness of one and the poverty of the
other as it flowed on to the sea.

She stood a moment drinking it in; awed by the size and the
splendour of it all, she sank into a reverie. She didn't see the
hackney cab draw up in front of her, nor the man who alighted
from it.

'New in town, are you m'dear?' he asked with a knowing
smile, looking her up and down with an openness that
brought a flush to her cheeks. 'Would you like me to show you
all the sights?' Above them the huge bell struck the three-
quarters and brought her out of her reverie with a jolt.

'I have an appointment,' she said with all the hauteur she
could muster, drawing her skirts back as if to avoid con-
tamination, quite in the manner of Miss Widgery, the Minister's sister. The man, anticipating shy country tones, was
taken aback, and while surprise held him rooted to the spot,
she side-stepped around him and fled.

SCHOOL BOARDS AND SCHOOLS INSPECTORATE read the
brass plaque on the narrow Georgian town house in Great
Peter Street. She took a deep breath and pulled the bell.

After an agonising delay in a spartanly furnished outer
room, Mr Mackenzie the Inspector came to fetch her in to the
Board. He showed her to a chair in the centre of the room,
facing a long mahogany table, behind which sat seven elderly
men, each surveying her over gold-rimmed glasses or pince-
nez. Seven wise men, she thought irreverently, and had to
bite her lip to stop herself giggling.

Mr Mackenzie sat at the end of the table and opened the
proceedings by giving her a glowing report. Then the inquisition started.

'I must say at once, Miss Stevens, that you look far too
young for a post of this responsibility,' said Mr Arbuthnot,
the headmaster.

'I am eighteen, sir.'

'At what . . . at what . . . er . . . establishment did you . . . er . . . receive your education?' said a venerable gentleman who made her think of the dormouse in Alice in Wonderland.

'At the school where I now teach, sir.'

'No, no, Miss Stevens,' said another, barely troubling to conceal his irritation. 'We know you are at present teaching at the Wapping Home, but at which College did you yourself receive your training?'

Mr Mackenzie stepped in. 'Miss Stevens was pupil and teacher at the Orphanage School, Sir James.'

'What?' roared Sir James, shaking the windows. 'Are we to entrust a *foundling* with the moral welfare of the children of Saint Mark's? Unheard of!'

She gritted her teeth. 'Your pardon, sir,' she said softly, 'but I have been entrusted with their moral welfare for some years now.'

'Of the orphans, Miss Stevens, yes,' said Mr Arbuthnot. 'But they would form only a small part of each class; absorbed, as you might say, by the greater numbers of the offspring of the upright citizens of Wapping.'

She had difficulty biting back the retort that sprang to her lips.

'You are a regular churchgoer?' demanded another man.

'Yes, sir.'

'At Saint Mark's?'

'Sir.'

'And I understand you have some musical skills?'

'Yes, sir. I play the piano and –'

'And the organ. And yet the Rector has never seen fit to ask you to play at service?'

Impossible to answer. Matron and the Reverend Thomas Widgery had been at loggerheads for years. The Minister barely tolerated the orphans' presence, fearful they might frighten off his more prosperous parishioners. Miss Widgery, the organist, had cuffed her soundly when she found her one day after Bible class sitting at the organ. And Ivan – Little Polack – had avenged his friend by spreading Miss Widgery's seat with wet varnish the following Sunday.

She knew as she left the room that she had not got the post.

'Preposterous!' exclaimed Sir James before the door was even closed. 'Can't have the likes of her teaching in a church school . . .'

'No telling who her parents were –'

'Probably born in sin –'

She had a sudden memory of the candlelit rooms, the tall bearded man and the beautiful lady in the silk dress, and ached to tell them it was not so. But it would serve no purpose.

'I'm so sorry, my dear,' said Mr Mackenzie, following her out of the room and closing the door behind him with a snap.

She forced herself to smile, despite the pain in her heart. 'You did your best.'

'What will you do now?'

'Go for a skivvy,' she said bitterly, fighting back the tears.

'May I give you a piece of advice? *In loco parentis*, as it were. Put today out of your mind and get on with your life. I would hope the Trustees may be able to find you work in a shop, or even an office. But if you do have to go as a housemaid, do it whole-heartedly and before you know where you are, you'll have worked up to housekeeper. To keep harking back to the might have been will only serve to unsettle you.'

She walked past the Abbey without even looking up. She would have liked to walk back to Wapping, putting off her return, deferring for as long as possible the moment when she must set her hopes aside and set out on a life in service, but the borrowed shoes pinched her feet too much. She somehow found her way to the omnibus stop and climbed on board the right one, but the journey passed in a daze; she hadn't the heart to look at the sights. Unable to face the empty echoing Orphanage, she left the omnibus one stop early, at Elms Square.

She went in through the kitchen, declining the offer of a cup of tea from Ellen. Upstairs she drew a book from the shelf, opened it and then peevishly snapped it shut again. She paced the room a few times, impatient for Sarah's return, then found herself drawn, inevitably, to the piano, one of the few precious items not sent to the auction rooms. She worked her way through her new piece, but for once her troubled spirit failed to find solace in the serenity and haunting beauty of Chopin's genius.

'Beautiful.' The voice startled her; she had thought herself alone. 'But only as beautiful as the beauty who plays it.' John Thomsett stood in the doorway, a hectic flush on his cheeks and a beatific smile on his face.

'I – Sarah – she – she must have been delayed.' She stood up nervously and closed the instrument. 'Would you tell her I called?'

'Don't go, my dear.' Carefully he closed the door behind him. As he crossed to her side she smelt the fumes on his breath. 'Not a little girl any more, are you?' he purred, catching her hands as she tried to fold away the music. 'And just as beautiful as I expected.'

It was difficult to pull her hands away without an undignified struggle.

'All this finery is for the interview, I suppose?'

She nodded nervously. 'If you please, Mr Thomsett, I must be getting back.' She was beginning to feel strangely breathless and there was a churning sensation in the pit of her stomach. 'Please, sir! Matron will –'

'There had to be some reason for my sister to let you out of children's clothes!' he said, as if she had not spoken. 'But the picture's not complete yet.' And before she could stop him, he pulled off the bandeau which held her hair so carefully in its neat bun and tumbled the long golden tresses around her face. He drew in his breath sharply. 'I knew it would be worth waiting for!'

He stared at her curtain of hair, mesmerised, until she jerked herself away from his questing hand; the sudden movement seemed to galvanise him and he pulled her fiercely to him with a strength that astounded and terrified her.

He bent down towards her. 'You are too beautiful to be a drudge,' he muttered against her throat. 'Come to me, child. I'll look after you. I'll make you happy.'

She wanted to cry out, but her breath seemed to have stopped in her throat and then, too late, his mouth was on hers.

He had waited for a long time for this. He wanted to kiss her greedily, forcing her lips apart and crushing her body against his, but only for a moment. Then some instinct of common sense took over; he remembered that she was young and ignorant. He began to kiss her as he had once kissed Kitty.

His mouth began to move over hers more gently, fleeting butterfly kisses that aroused strange new feelings in her, feelings that were not entirely displeasing.

The feel of his arms around her was oddly comforting; no one had touched her like this, held her close, in eleven long years. One hand came up to cup her face and the other began to stroke her unbound hair, adding to the giddy feelings that permeated her whole body. At last he raised his head to smile mockingly down at her. 'Who knows?' he murmured. 'With you I might even reform.'

It was wrong, she knew. She had to stop him. Breathless, she opened her mouth to speak, but the words were never uttered. The door swung back on its hinges and Sarah hurtled into the room.

'John, how could you!' she cried.

He looked at his sister as if he would like to murder her. 'I do what I want in my own house!' he yelled furiously. Releasing his grip abruptly he stormed out of the room and up the stairs.

'How could you betray me like this, Melisande,' said Sarah furiously, before the girl had time to speak.

'How could I – ? I did *nothing*! ' she protested.

'To go behind my back in this way!' she cried. 'To bite the hand that fed you!' She raised her eyes imploringly to Heaven. 'To think I have nurtured a viper in my bosom all these years.'

'Sarah! I didn't! I –'

'No gentleman would behave so without encouragement!' screeched Sarah, who seemed to Melisande's horrified eyes to be working herself up into hysterics. 'Oh, I warned you about your bold behaviour! If you conduct yourself like a whore, then a whore you will become! You deserve everything that happens to you. I thought you were different! But I should have known . . .'

'Oh, Sarah,' she said brokenly. 'How could you even think that I –' Melisande dashed her hand angrily across her bruised lips and rushed past her, down the hall and out of the door. Sarah's shrill voice pursued her, screeching harsh words, words she had never heard before.

She hurtled down the steps and across the road, almost under the wheels of a dray, and ran, heart pounding in her throat, through the narrow streets, not stopping until she reached the Orphanage, strangely quiet in the early evening sunshine. The children had not yet returned from the picnic and the factories outside the high wall were deserted for the holiday, their chimneys still and dead.

She paused at the gate and leant against the wall to catch her breath and beat down the waves of fear and panic, mixed with anger, that threatened to overwhelm her. She looked at the dark four-square building which had been home to her for as long as she could remember and which she would soon have to leave. Without the heavy pall of yellowish grey smoke which normally belched out of the tall factory chimneys and hung above it, the old warehouse looked quite different. The evening sun shone out of a blue sky and sparkled on its many windows. There was even a dusty starling chirping on the high wall between the two sides where she and Tom and Ivan and Aggie had so often met.

She closed her eyes to imprint it all on her memory. It would have to last her forever.

Her heart sank in her boots as she came down the stairs and saw the black-clad woman at her employer's side.

'Miss Greville will accompany you today, Smith,' said Madame, in tones that dared her to argue. 'I trust you will give her no cause for complaint.'

She looked sideways at Miss Greville, who was drawing her veil down over her face, and thought she looked more nervous than forbidding.

Madame held out a veiled bonnet. 'But that's not mine!' she protested. 'Mine's smarter than that!'

She should have known better. She drew down on herself a long lecture on the evils of pride and vanity and it was nearly twenty minutes before she and her guardian could get out of the door: twenty minutes in which she bethought her of the doctor and his steward and the horrors of the house in Lake

Street and decided there was much to be said in favour of veils.

The air was still crisp but the sun was shining, its warmth encouraging the green buds on the lilac trees and lighting up the tips of the early flowers pushing up through the thawing ground. In gardens and window-boxes, round the bases of the trees lining the main thoroughfares and in the flower beds in the town parks, the delicate white of the snowdrops set off the more robust gold and purple of the crocuses while pale wind-flowers turned their faces gratefully to the sun. Spring came earlier in the broad strip of land between the lake and the hills; the wind which had blown so bitterly in the depth of winter was moderated by its passage across the waters of the Great Lakes, and warmed to a more spring-like temperature.

Miss Greville was hard pushed to keep up with the girl's long strides, but she puffed along valiantly, occasionally pausing to point out the residences of some of Madame's customers, as she had been instructed.

'I shall start to send her with deliveries,' Madame had said to her fellow worshipper. 'Faster than the cripple, and of course more acceptable to the clients. You can make sure she knows her way around.'

It was still too chilly to sit on the park benches, but they paused at the bandstand in the centre of the park, where a family of enterprising Italians set up tea rooms.

'When I was a young girl, there used always to be a German band playing here, on all but the most bitter of days,' Miss Greville reminisced. 'My parents used to bring us over for the day.'

'I thought the Fellowship frowned on music?'

'Music can be so cheering. I recall the stirring hymns we used to sing in church.' Her gaze grew misty. 'My parents were not in the Fellowship, d'you see? Such happy days . . . We lived in Owenstown. Such a busy town it was then, before Edensville took all the industry. But after my parents died, my sister, poor soul, fell in love with an Edensville man and when he joined the Fellowship, she followed him. Then the Fellowship took this idea of spiritual and celibate love, d'you see? And that was the end of poor Florence and her Horace.'

'And you?'

83

'When Florence took a notion in her head, it was easier to go along with her. I did think of leaving when she died, but I no longer had any friends – or even acquaintances – outside the Fellowship.' She sighed. 'I'm really too old to start all over again.' They walked around the bandstand once more. 'You remind me a little of poor Florence. She was beautiful and spirited, like you. But once the Fellowship got their hold on her, all that joy of living – as if it had never been, d'you see?' She shook her head as if to clear away the sad memories.

'You needn't worry about them getting a hold on me,' said Melisande firmly. 'Attending the meetings is almost a condition of employment, and I need the job, but I haven't signed any indentures –'

'I am relieved to hear it.'

' – because I don't intend to stay there for ever.'

As they passed the tea rooms the door opened and a warm smell of tea, coffee and chocolate drifted out on the crisp air. Melisande stopped and took a deep breath, a blissful look on her face.

'What a fool I was to argue with her!' she exclaimed at last. 'I quite forgot to ask her for my money!'

Miss Greville pursed her lips in a prim little smile, took her young charge firmly by the arm and steered her through the doors. A waitress with laughing black eyes showed them to a table, daintily set with a crisp linen cloth and sparkling cutlery.

'Oh, but I – I didn't mean . . . You must think me very rude to –'

'I have the money, you have not!' said Miss Greville briskly, forestalling any further protests. 'Believe me, my dear, young company is a delight to me: I get so heartily sick of all the doom and gloom of those old fools in the Fellowship, d'you see?'

The last of the snow finally melted away and the sunshine took on a more golden hue. The German band returned to the park; the shutters were taken down from the basement windows and the apprentices sat in narrow shafts of dancing sunlight, warming their winter-chilled bones. Edensville society put away its furs and boots and began to pay calls further afield. Invitations were sent out to balls and breakfasts to mark daughters' debuts and sons' coming of age and society felt a need to renew its wardrobe.

Once Melisande began to find her way around the town, she was sent on errands to collect trimmings from gloomy warehouses down by the docks, where the sun never seemed completely to penetrate the thick clouds of smoke which hung like a pall over the grimy factories and mill chimneys, or to deliver exquisite ball dresses, clouds of diaphanous silk and gauze, and walking costumes trimmed with froggings and Russian braid to elegant town houses where superior ladies' maids relieved her of the boxes. These expeditions were a freedom and a fascination for her. She often lingered, wide-eyed, looking into the store windows along Washington and Hamilton Street, or sat unnoticed in lofty entrance halls watching the comings and goings, listening eagerly to the discussions of fashions, politics and society gossip that formed the mainstay of society above as well as below stairs.

She had thought Springs House large, but some of these residences were much larger. Watching the gaggles of maids coming and going through the green baize doors in the Mayor's house she began to understand something of Natasha's desire to go into service. For herself, independent and with a burning ambition to better herself, it would not do, but for Natasha, the company would outweigh the hardest work.

Not if you worked for Mrs Patterson, though. No one seemed to smile in her house, from the family to the parlour-maid. And Natasha has seen enough harshness and rejection in her short life. For a while she had been useful, keeping the babies away from the fire and the cooking pot, looking after the infants while the adults worked in the fields, but when there were no more children, she became, with her lame leg, a burden; her parents, en route to the rich prairie lands beyond the Upper Lakes, had sold her as apprentice to Madame Chantal.

On one of her free afternoons with Miss Greville, Melisande came across the public library. Miss Greville would not go in, for fear of being seen by anyone from the Fellowship who held all books apart from the Bible to be tools of the

85

Devil, so Melisande took to visiting it briefly on her way home from Madame's errands and perusing the newspapers, full of grim predictions of war with Spain, in the hope of finding another position.

She confided her plans to Miss Greville as they walked across the market one day, her mouth watering at the delights on offer on the stalls. She begged her not to give a hint to anyone in the sewing room. 'Particularly Anna. She'd go running to Madame with it. I can't understand why she toadies to her so much. I don't think she's any more enamoured of the Fellowship than the rest of us: it's all a sham.'

'Chantal is not young: nearly sixty. She has no family to whom she could leave the business. Anna has been with her for years. When Madame dies, she will probably leave it all to her.'

'I suppose she'll have earned it, but she hasn't the eye for fashion Madame has,' said Melisande. 'Oh, look!' Her eye had been caught by a poster and she dragged Miss Greville across to inspect it. 'Concert in the City Hall,' she read. 'Afternoon recitals.' Oh, Miss Greville, may we go next Wednesday? I could pay for myself now Madame's paid me, and oh, you've no idea how much I would enjoy it. We could –'

'My dear!' said Miss Greville. 'It's quite out of the question. The Fellowship does not approve of music.'

'But we listen to the band in the park!'

'That is quite different. If we are walking and the band happens to be playing . . . But to go to a public hall – I absolutely could not contemplate it!'

Fear of being seen and her presence relayed by some means unspecified back to the Fellowship was a prospect that turned the older woman's knees to water and caused her hands to tremble violently. She remembered the occasions when members of the Fellowship had transgressed the unwritten rules, and the public humiliation they had undergone at the Meetings, and she knew she had not the spirit to withstand them.

I'll just have to leave her out of my calculations, decided Melisande cheerfully. She did not refer to the subject again, which Matron would have seen as a warning sign. Instead, on the way back from a delivery, she bought herself a ticket for the Saturday evening concert with some of her wages.

Standing in the hallway of the Pattersons' house on Saturday morning, waiting for the housekeeper, she fingered the stiff square of card in her pocket and smiled in anticipation of the treat in store.

She often wondered why Madame went to so much trouble for the Pattersons. It wasn't as if they did her much credit. Both mother and daughter had very poor taste, Mrs Patterson insisting on the fashionable puces and crimsons which exaggerated her already high colour until she looked as if she were in danger of going off in an apoplexy – a not unlikely event, given her alarmingly uncertain temper. Her daughter, while not plain, had no great claim to beauty; she wore pale colours more suited to a girl of seventeen which did nothing for a rather pasty complexion, and too much over ornate jewellery which only drew attention to her deficiencies.

But Madame, making one of her rare house visits, never allowed herself to forget that the Pattersons were the biggest landowners in town; they could do her business a great deal of good.

'Here you are. This is the one she wants.' The housekeeper handed her a bale of apple green silk which had been presented to the family by a grateful businessman, returning from a voyage to the Orient. It would make Miss Sophia look sallow, but her mother was determined to use it. Crossing the upper hall, lost in a dream of the Orient, wishing she was a man and could stand at the wheel of a clipper and sail the seven seas like Little Polack, Melisande did not see the figure hurrying towards the stairs until she collided with him.

Arms full of silk, she had no hand free to stop herself falling as her heel snagged in her hem. She was relieved to feel wiry arms catching her and setting her back on her feet and told herself that the hand that brushed her breast did so only by accident.

'Th-thank you, sir,' she stammered, kicking the hem of her skirt impatiently aside.

The man she had bumped into was in his mid-thirties, stocky, with pomaded locks and a pointed Imperial, in the style of Napoleon III. He held her a moment longer than was necessary, staring at her with a close scrutiny she was beginning to find offensive. Her eyes narrowed behind the thick veil and she returned the stare with a defiant lift of her chin.

'It is customary for servants to curtsey,' he drawled

She could hardly restrain a crow of delight. 'Sir, in our Fellowship we bow only to God.' Madame's words. She could only hope Madame would back her on that. If instead she chose to report her to the Elders for insolence, then she'd never get to the concert!

As she bent to pick up the billows of silk his hand shot out and caught her wrist in a painful grip that made her gasp. 'Put back your veil, my dear,' he purred in her ear. 'I'll swear there's a pretty face behind it that shouldn't be hidden.' He tightened his grip and pulled her into an alcove; she swore under her breath as the silk fell back on the floor again. She struggled to pull away from him, but he was stronger than he looked. And intrigued. Since it was known he paid well for his pleasures, he was not accustomed to meet with opposition.

'Don't be shy!' he said throatily. 'I'm a great connoisseur of beautiful faces.'

With his free hand he grasped the heavy veiling and began to raise it. He had just caught a brief glimpse of her face, its pallor overlaid by a flame of fury, when Madame Chantal appeared in the doorway, demanding to know what had happened to the silk. Mrs Patterson, close on her heels, was not best pleased to see her son, red-faced and furious, involved in an unseemly struggle with the dressmaker's assistant.

Madame was enraged and Melisande was stunned to find that the anger was directed as much at her as at Mr Jeremiah Patterson. Perhaps Sarah had been right, she thought sadly. ·Perhaps it was her fault that men thought they could treat her so. She remembered the unseemly haste with which Matron and Sarah had found her the post and sent her off to America after the unhappy scene with John Thomsett.

'Perhaps I was at fault, letting her visit so frequently,' she had overheard Sarah say to Mrs Evans. 'But I never thought she would behave so badly.'

'But surely Mr Thomsett, being so much older . . . ' protested Mrs Evans.

'It was for her to draw the line!' said Sarah shrilly. 'I daresay she hoped to compromise him. But he is a gentleman and she is, after all, only a – a –'

Melisande flung aside her pen and emerged from the alcove where she had been listening, unobserved. 'I am not a bastard!' she had said angrily.

'The word would never pass my lips!' said Sarah, a flush on her cheeks at the very suggestion. 'A foundling. Let us say, a foundling.'

Melisande sighed. She would never in her wildest nightmares have contemplated marriage with John Thomsett, but it had hurt to be told she was not good enough even for a drunken sot like him. And that she was responsible for leading him on. It all seemed so very unfair.

Madame Chantal spent the better part of the rest of the day lecturing her on the impropriety of men in general and the need for virtuous women to keep themselves away from these devils in human clothing.

'But I –'

'But me no buts, miss!' exclaimed Madame shrilly, two spots of colour livid on her cheeks. And Melisande, remembering the concert, deemed it wisest to bite her tongue, bow her head and say no more.

By the end of the day she had finished all the work Madame had set out. To her delight, Anna had been invited to join Madame and her friends from the Fellowship for an evening meeting at the house, an honour which caused Anna's sour face to lighten for the first time since the new hand had joined.

Melisande prepared a hash of liver for herself and the other apprentices, then washed the dishes and left the two younger girls stacking them away neatly. She hoped Natasha would not need to be involved in any way, but she had to have her story ready in case Madame should come to look for her; they had gone over it carefully up in the attic bedroom they shared.

She checked that she had her handkerchief in her pocket, the remains of the dollar she had persuaded Madame to part with last week – 'To replace my chemise, ma'am, it's past repair' – tied tightly in one corner with her ticket of admission. She toyed with the idea of changing back into her own clothes, but decided in the end she would be less distinctive in the old black bombazine dress Madame had provided to wear in the workroom. She tied the bonnet and veil inside the cloak she'd taken from Doctor Kingsley's charity box, tied a piece of rope from the lumber room around it and lowered it carefully out of the window until it came to rest in the leafy heart of an old tree in the back yard which was just about to burst into flower.

As she passed Madame's rooms, she heard the soft voices, murmuring in prayer. With a deep breath she lifted the latch of the back door and let herself out. She headed up the area steps directly for the privy where, through the hole in the door, she kept careful watch on the back of the house. After a while a light appeared in Madame's window and the curtains were drawn. She slipped, silent as a wraith, out of the privy, pausing only to retrieve her bundle from the tree, then past the cesspool to the wall at the rear of the garden. This presented little challenge to one who had often scaled the fifteen-foot wall in the Orphanage yard and sat atop it with Tom and Aggie, and in a few moments Melisande was in the alley that ran behind the garden.

She arrived at the concert hall just as the audience was beginning to file in. A doorman, clad in splendid scarlet livery, held the door open for her. She stepped inside and stopped in her tracks, overwhelmed by the fairy-tale splendour of the interior. Everywhere was creamy marble, gilt and crystal: the walls were covered with the most splendid frescoes and on either side of the foyer, elegant staircases with marble balustrading swept up in tiers to the circles and gallery. Overhead electric lights flickered, reflecting a myriad tiny points of light from crystal chandeliers. She thought there could be no more splendid building in the world!

Ladies in elegant dresses and gentlemen in sober tailcoats and white bow ties and waistcoats swept ahead of her to take their seats in the circle and in the tiered boxes around the raised stage; Melisande slipped quietly into the hall, trying not to draw attention to herself as she searched for her seat, one of the cheapest in the house as the view of the stage was partly obscured by one of the lofty pillars which supported the circle.

Around the hall young ladies soberly dressed in black with white lace bands were selling programmes and refreshment tickets. She enquired of the nearest attendant, rather timidly, the price of a programme, but decided reluctantly that it would be better to save the money for another ticket.

She looked around her, admiring all the crimson and gold draperies and seats; it reminded her of a picture she had once seen in one of Sarah's journals of the Albert Hall in London, built by the Queen in memory of her dead husband. That too had been a splendid building and she had often read wistfully of the magnificent concerts there. Why had Sarah never taken her?

Gradually the chatter of the audience died away, to be replaced by an air of hushed expectancy. There was a rustle among the ushers at the back of the semi-circular platform and the orchestra began to file on stage: violinists, horn and trumpet players, a short man carrying a double bass which dwarfed him, and, wonders of wonders, a *lady* who crossed the stage to sit behind the vast set of drums and cymbals.

When the orchestra had assembled, a tall young man came on to the stage, to tumultuous applause, bowed and took his seat with the rest of the violinists. She wondered why he was applauded when the rest were not; not wishing to draw attention to herself, she just did as everyone else did, applauding once more as an elderly man with flowing white locks strode with great dignity to the podium at the front of the stage where he bowed solemnly several times. When the applause died down, he turned to the orchestra, rapped sharply on the podium twice and the orchestra began to play.

The music began with a strident fanfare from the brass section, full of a foreboding sense of doom and hopeless despair that sent shivers down her spine. She sat engrossed, overwhelmed by the splendour of the music and the skill of the players. The music rose to a climax, then the fanfare sounded again, in a variation of the opening, and the pure notes fell into a perfect silence. So carried away was she that at first she was hardly aware that the music had stopped. She caught her breath and was just about to applaud the magicians on the platform when she realised, just in time, that no one else was clapping; there was only the rustle of silks as ladies shifted slightly in their seats.

The conductor raised his baton and the magic began again. This time there was joy mixed with the sorrow and when the theme faded sadly away, from clarinet to oboe, to flute and violins, to cellos, to bassoons, Melisande was no longer sitting

91

on the hard wooden seats, she was floating in the dome of the concert hall, at one with the music, hearing it, feeling it, touching it, tasting it.

The audience broke into enthusiastic applause, but Melisande sat stunned, exhausted, overwhelmed. So taken was she by the magic of these mortals, presently taking their bows before filing off at the back of the stage, that she failed to notice a man in the front of the circle, observing her intently through a pair of opera glasses.

The audience were rising from their seats, but as she rose and regretfully drew her shabby cloak around her, she realised they were not leaving, but only circulating, exchanging bows with acquaintances while the programme sellers carried champagne or teatrays up to the boxes.

Further down the row from her a tall gentleman with old-fashioned Dundreary side-whiskers rose in stately fashion and led his family out to the foyer to take refreshment, his wife and six daughters following in his wake like a string of ducklings. Watching them go, she saw that they had left a programme behind. It lay temptingly close to her and, heart beating fast in case they came back and caught her, she slid along the seats until she was next to it. Everyone around seemed to be absorbed in their own conversations, discussing the rival merits of this orchestra and the one that had visited some months previously. 'Of course it cannot compare with the first Edensville performance,' said a man in front of her. 'But then Tschaikowsky himself was in the audience.'

She reached out for the programme with shaking hands, then promptly dropped it as a voice spoke in her ear.

'Here!' said the programme seller she had approached earlier. 'Didn't mean to make you jump! Just, I got one programme left over,' she went on in friendly tone. 'I checked it in so it won't get docked from me takings. I saw you was a bit disappointed, like, thought you might like it.' She thrust the last programme into her hands.

'S'alright,' she said as Melisande tried to thank her. 'Saw straight off you was interested in the music, not here on the strut, like.'

'Strut?'

'Looking for the promising touches.' She saw she was still looking puzzled. 'The pick up. On the town.'

'Ah!' Now she understood. 'No, I'm not.'

'I thought not. 'Course, the Music Hall's a better place for that, although some of the young swells there are that forward you wouldn't believe . . . Only it was that daft veil, see. All the dolly-mops wears 'em. Thinks it makes 'em look mysterious.'

'It goes with my employment, I fear. My employer belongs to a strict sect.'

'You don't say! So why ain't you selling?'

'Why ain't – aren't I selling what?'

'Programmes. And teas. That'd get you in free.'

Another girl hurried past with a tray for a family in a stage-side box. 'Better hurry and get your trays out, Molly,' she said, 'or Mrs James'll have your guts for garters.'

'Got to fly,' giggled Molly. 'But they're always needing more sellers. Course, you got to take your share of the public meetings. Sometimes the speakers are real ranters, other times they'll send you to sleep faster than a knock on the head. The rest of it's good. We're on the New York circuit, we are. They try out the best here. Even Wallack's comes here before the New York run. Look, I'll take you to him afterwards, shall I?'

With that she was gone. Melisande saw her soon after, carrying a laden tray up to a group of fashionable young people in the circle. She sat back and read the programme, contemplating with a delightful glow of inner warmth the prospect of being able, in the future, to come to the recitals and concerts without having to pay for the privilege from her hard-earned money!

The second half of the concert was, she saw from the programme, also by Tschaikowsky: ballet music written for the Imperial Russian Ballet's performance of 'Romeo and Juliet'. Melisande knew the play well: Sarah Thomsett had made her learn and recite speeches from a number of Shakespeare's plays in the drive to eliminate all traces of foreign intonation and East London harshness from her pupil's speech.

When the last haunting notes died away, after the orchestra and conductor had taken their bows and encores, Melisande sat on, lapping up the last of the atmosphere until Molly, true to her word, came to find her; chattering volubly, she escorted her up a narrow stairway to a small office where the other programme sellers were paying in their money under the watchful eye of a sandy haired man in his early thirties.

'So this is your young lady, Molly!' he said, rising with a smile and offering his hand. 'I understand, Miss – er –'

'Smith.' She gave the name that she had given to Madame, the first one that had come into her mind.

'Miss Smith. You'd like to sell programmes.'

'Indeed. I –'

'We're always losing our best workers, Miss Smith,' he said with a grin. 'They earn so much here, it goes to their heads and they go off and marry their young men. Speaking of whom, Molly, he's waiting downstairs for you.'

Everyone laughed. It was clearly a standing joke among them.

'That veil is surely unnerving, my dear,' he said, turning back to the new girl. 'Is it essential?'

'My employer insists on it. And I can't risk losing my position. . . .' Her voice trailed off as he frowned.

'Well, it's not our place to interfere with anyone's religious principles,' he said at last. 'It does seem a pity such a pretty young girl . . . Ahem. That is to say, one assumes . . . one can hardly tell . . .'

One or two of the girls began to giggle and she lifted the veil to put him out of his embarrassment, smiling up at him hopefully from beneath the brim of the old-fashioned bonnet, whereupon he promptly offered her the job, at what seemed to her a princely sum, for as many of the wide range of concerts, recitals and public meetings as she could attend.

'Her little face lit up,' he told his wife, a somewhat fierce-looking young woman who ran the box office. 'Rather fancy I've done a good deed.'

'More to the point, you've found a replacement for Molly,' she said practically. 'As for the rest, we'll see how she turns out.'

Melisande floated out of the hall on a cloud of joy. To be paid for the privilege of attending the concerts seemed to her an unbelievable stroke of luck. With the extra earnings, she could even begin to look around for lodgings. And if she no longer needed a living-in job she could widen her scope. She almost danced across the main square, so absorbed in her plans that she failed to notice the man who had been watching her from the circle slipping out of the shadows and following her.

She stopped in front of a pie and ale shop, her mouth watering at the smell of fresh-baked pastry wafting out on the still night air; she fingered the coins in her pocket, imagining Natasha's face at the sight of a crisp, oozing pie.

'Come in for a drink, dearie,' said a voice behind her, making her jump. She turned to find a burly docker looking down at her, a suggestive leer on his broad face.

She shook her head, every nerve in her body screaming to her to run away, her feet as firmly fixed to the ground as if they'd been glued.

A second docker emerged from the doorway. 'Leave be, Jo,' he said firmly as his mate made a move towards her. 'Could be worse-looking than your old woman, else why would she be wearing a veil? Me, I likes to see what I'm gettin'.'

Hysterical laughter bubbled up in her throat and she turned away in panic, almost knocking over a man in a grey overcoat who had come hurrying up behind her. She ran away as fast as she could; half way down the road she stopped in a doorway and peered back. The dockers were still standing outside the pie shop, making no effort to follow her, but she still could not bring herself to go back that way. Instead she doubled back to the main square and took another, less direct route back to Madame Chantal's. Almost there, she saw a hot pie stand on a corner.

Carefully she counted out the coins for two small pies which the vendor wrapped in a paper for her. She tucked the pies into her capacious pocket and drew the cloak closer about her.

The cloak.

She remembered the letter she'd left in the charity box and knew that, before she spent another penny, she must pay for the clothes she'd taken. No use to say the doctor wouldn't notice the loss, she told herself severely: they weren't his clothes. She had robbed the poor, and to pretend otherwise was a specious argument, as Matron or Miss Thomsett would not hesitate to point out. When she'd paid off her debts, that would be time enough to think about looking for lodgings, and not before.

As she was about to cross the road, a carriage drew up on the other side. The driver leaned down to ask directions from someone; with a shock she saw that it was a man in a grey overcoat, just like the one outside the pie shop. Panic returned, threatening to overwhelm her, but this time it was a panic which lent wings to her heels; she ducked down a side alley while he was giving directions and did not stop running until she had lost sight of him and the carriage.

At last, heart pounding, she reached the safety of the back alley at the rear of the garden. There was neither sight nor sound of pursuit and with a shaky laugh she almost persuaded herself that she had imagined it all. Even so, she was over the wall, through the garden and up the stairs past the prayer meeting before she had time to think any more on it, and she didn't stop until she was safe and sound in the attic bedroom.

While they wolfed down the pies, she told Natasha about the concert, striving to convey to her some of the magic of the evening. She did not mention the man. It was always possible that she had been mistaken; either way, best not to worry Natasha.

The brief escape from her hard and colourless existence had invigorated her and the memory of those few magical hours made it easier to cope with the hard work and the monotony of the workroom. While her fingers flew obediently over the material, cutting and stitching diligently, careful to give Madame no cause for complaint, she lived only for the next concert.

'No more airs or setting herself up, no more pert remarks! I do believe this recalcitrant child of the ungodly is being brought to the ways of the righteous,' Madame told Miss Greville as they waited for 'Smith' to fetch her cloak and bonnet one Wednesday afternoon.

Miss Greville searched her conscience and decided not to mention the purchase of writing materials from the counter clerk, nor the burly farmer, in from the country, whom Smith, pleading ignorance of the system, had persuaded to hand in the letter for her. If the girl was looking for a better position, who was she to stand in her way?

'Max! Max!' The doctor's voice echoed down the corridor, causing Hetty almost to drop the tray of muffins she was carrying into the dining room for the doctor's breakfast.

Ellsky came swiftly out of the estate office, pipe in his hand, a look of mild surprise on his bluff face.

'Here. Read this.' Kingsley thrust a letter at him. 'Posted yesterday in Edensville.'

Dear Doctor Kingsley,
I enclose part payment for the cloak and spencer, as I am, I regret, unable to return them to you. I shall send the rest of the money at the earliest opportunity.
                             Yours, Melisande Stevens.
P.S. Please tell Mrs Chobley not to worry.

'Tell Mrs Chobley not to worry,' mimicked the doctor, running his fingers distractedly through his hair. 'And the rest of us can go hang, eh, Max?'

'Miss Prebble will see you now,' said a plump vacuous female, her voice a gentle lament.

Melisande took a deep breath and walked into the office, head up and a pleasant smile on her face. Miss Prebble, a desiccated lady of uncertain years, bade her a brusque good afternoon and motioned her to a seat opposite the little desk where she sat, pen in hand.

She made a show of consulting her note. 'I see from your application that you wish to register as –'

' – as a governess, ma'am, or companion.'

'Experience?'

'I taught children in London, ma'am.' She hoped she wouldn't ask where.

'I have very few vacancies for governesses, Miss Smith,' said Miss Prebble, looking at her searchingly over her gold-rimmed spectacles. 'You have recommendations from previous employers?'

'Miss Sarah Thomsett would be pleased to give me a reference.' As instructed by Matron, she had sent just one letter to London, telling of her safe arrival at Springs House, but she was confident that Sarah would help her with a reference, even though they had parted so bitterly. She wondered what her mentor would make of the situation she had got herself into now.

'Schools and colleges attended?'

'No, I'm afraid I –'

'No certificates?'

Melisande shook her head.

'I see.' She perused the details Melisande had provided. 'You claim proficiency in a number of foreign languages?' she observed.

'French and Russian I know well, ma'am.' Mostly from newspapers and learned journals. Sarah had scoured the second hand bookshops for improving works: together they had read French books on politics, a Russian book on required etiquette at the court of Tsar Alexander. 'And some German too.' She knew more about coffee growing in German East Africa than anyone could ever wish to know. Even now she could close her eyes and see the illustrations – including the one of bare-breasted native women that Sarah had failed to cut out and been so shocked to come across in a translation lesson.

Miss Prebble waved her to silence. 'I have recently placed a young lady as clerk with a trading company that might be just the thing. Of course, I should need examples of your work – translations would do.' She sighed. 'Without certificates you would be well advised to reconsider, Miss Smith. I could place you as a housemaid in no time. Or nursery maid? We have more vacancies there than we can possibly fill.'

'I fear that would not suit me, ma'am,' she said decisively. 'Though I have a friend who has looked after children all her life.'

'My dear Miss Smith, bring her to see me without delay!'

'She – she is lame,' she said, 'although very active.' Pointless to smuggle her out of the house and risk Madame's wrath if Miss Prebble then refused to consider her.

'Then of course we could not consider her for the best families. They can afford to be selective. English?'

'She speaks good English, although Russian is her first language.'

'Bring her to see me,' said Miss Prebble. 'I will see what I can do.' As she said to her companion Miss Smart later that evening: 'With so many posts to fill, one cannot afford to dismiss an applicant simply because of a lame leg.' Immigrants, so long the source of servants, no longer stayed in Edensville as a matter of course, except to overwinter. So many had been tempted out west where the new prairie land was opening up that one could no longer pick and choose.

'Saturday. Two o'clock sharp. As for yourself, Miss Smith, I will keep your details on my books. Let me have those examples.'

'I will get them to you as soon as possible,' she promised. She had absolutely no idea how she would do it, but do it she would.

'How may we get in touch with you, if the occasion arises? At your present place of employment'

'Oh, no! Pray do not! I will call by each Wednesday and – and – you may write to me care of Mr James at the City Hall.'

One hurdle dealt with. She hurried back to the bandstand with a light step and a sparkle in her eyes. A young man strolling nearby flashed her a smile and tipped his hat to her.

'Miss Smith! My dear, your veil!' hissed Miss Greville in panic. 'What if one of the Fellowship were to see you?'

With a scowl Melisande flicked the veil back over her face and to the young man it was as if the sun had gone behind a black cloud.

'Miss Greville,' she said urgently, drawing her away from the bandstand, 'what do you know about the position of the apprentices? At least – no, now I come to think of it, she never gave her indentures, she wasn't good enough.'

Miss Greville threw her a despairing look. 'My dear, who?'

'Natasha. Madame calls her the little cripple. She works in the sewing room with me, but she is no good at all at it. And when I went to the agency this afternoon –'

'Agency?' Miss Greville said weakly, halting in the middle of the path.

'To look for another post. They didn't have much for me, but I may have found the perfect post for Natasha. Her idea of paradise would be to work with children in a household full of other female servants.'

'Not yours, though?'

'No.'

'Glad to hear it,' said Miss Greville with an unaccustomed flash of humour. 'I would not envy anyone who employed you in such a capacity!'

'It would not suit me at all,' she agreed. 'But I try to remember that not everyone feels the same as I do.'

'And you say you have found a position for this girl?'

'I hope so. And if they take her – Madame can't stop her, can she? Legally, I mean.'

'If the girl has not signed indentures, then legally she may apply for another post.' Her eyes twinkled. 'Though I would not care to persuade Chantal of that, d'you see?'

That evening, Melisande slipped away to the City Hall for the mid-week concert. The escape was a little riskier this time, as she was required to be at the hall rather earlier in order to set out the trays and sell the programmes. Following the same routine as before, she arrived in plenty of time and was admitted through a small side door.

She attracted a few curious glances as the audience came in, but Americans were accustomed to seeing a motley selection of religions and sects in their midst; by and large they were tolerant of their peculiarities. She was kept busy until the concert started when she made her way to a seat with a clear view of the stage, quite unaware that she was being watched.

The work, even in the interval, was not too arduous for one who had worked in the Orphanage laundry, and the concert, by a visiting choir and orchestra from New York, was a delight. At the end of the evening she checked in her money satchel to Mr James and received from him a handful of coins which she tied tightly in the corner of her handkerchief.

Leaving City Hall to cross the market square, she passed a shadowed doorway and barely smothered a scream as an arm came out and barred her way.

'Miss Stevens?' A solid figure stepped into her path. 'May I?' He put out his hand and put back the veil. 'Ah! I thought it was you!'

She let out a sigh of sheer relief. 'Mr Ellsky! My goodness, you gave me a fright!'

'I am pleased to see you are well,' he growled.

'You don't sound very pleased.'

'You left in such a hurry there was no time to say goodbye.' She could think of nothing to say.

'You could at least have left word with Mrs Chobley!' he said angrily. 'She was sick with worry!'

'I didn't think –'

'Why?' He grabbed her arm. 'Why did you go?'

'You wouldn't understand,' she said tiredly. Close by, the clock struck the quarter. 'Please.' She tried to pull her arm away. 'I have to –'

'Your man waiting for you, is he?' he said with a sneer.

In the light from the nearby gas lamp he saw the colour drain from her face.

'I'm sorry. I shouldn't have said that.'

'Think what you like!' she said in a voice low and vibrant with fury. 'Just leave me alone.' She snatched her arm away from him and turned on her heel.

He hurried after her. 'At least let me see you safely home. It's late and –'

'No! You'll ruin everything for me!' she snapped, drawing the veil back over her face.

'You shouldn't be walking the streets alone at this time of night. Even in that veil . . . why *are* you wearing that veil? Please –' He was puffing in his attempts to keep up with her. 'Miss Stevens, please. You know I mean you no harm . . .'

In her heart she knew that she had nothing to fear from him. Besides, it struck her that if she did run away, she could not be certain that he would not raise a hue and cry. She slowed down as her initial anger evaporated.

'The veil is a condition of service. Like the maid's lace cap,' she said with a wry smile.

'What?'

'I work as a seamstress,' she explained patiently. 'My employer belongs to a religious sect which –'

'And you'd rather do that than work at Springs House?' he said in disbelief.

'I don't expect you to understand,' she said with a shrug. 'Thank you for your concern, Mr Ellsky. And goodbye.'

'I shall escort you to your door,' he said doggedly.

'And tell Doctor Kingsley where I am? No, I thank you! I have no desire to be dragged back to Springs House!'

'If that was my intention, I could have told him two weeks ago when I first saw you!'

'Oh!' She stopped dead in her tracks. 'And you recognised me?'

He nodded.

'Oh!'

'I'd have spoken to you then, but I lost you.' He stepped in front of her and blocked her way. 'Can you give me any good reason why I should not tell him where you are?'

'Yes. Because if you do, I'll run away again.' She looked him straight in the eye. 'When I left Springs House and came here looking for work, I was nearly tricked into a brothel. Another time I may not be so fortunate. Would you like that on your conscience?'

'You need not run away because of me,' he said softly. 'Do you think I saved your life just to throw it away again?'

'But –'

'Do any of us have so many friends that we can afford to turn our backs on one?' he said coolly. 'I imagine your employer is not aware that you are out,' he continued, taking her arm. 'Do you not think we should be getting you back before she misses you?'

And suddenly it seemed to her eminently desirable to count Max Ellsky a friend.

At one o'clock on Saturday, after a hurried lunch, while Madame was busy with a client, Melisande announced that she and Natasha were off to make a delivery in town.

'It does not need two of you,' protested Anna.

'Natasha is in need of some fresh air,' she replied coolly, handing the girl her bonnet.

She was becoming a practised liar; she shuddered to think what Sarah would make of her now. 'Never think you get away with a lie or an evasion, child,' she had often said. 'God sees all – and the Recording Angel has it all to your account.'

She hoped the Recording Angel would understand why she was doing what she was doing – and give her perhaps only half a black mark?

102

'The stitching's well ahead of schedule,' she said blithely to Anna, 'so now seems a suitable time.'

'Madame will hear of your insolence, Smith!' warned Anna. But the two girls had already gone.

The interview at Miss Prebble's was short and swift.

'I have a request for staff for a family in the timber shipping trade,' she said, nimble fingers riffling through the cards in a box. 'Russians.' She drew out a card and copied out the address. 'I hold out no promises, of course, but you would seem eminently suitable, young lady.'

Melisande felt a warm glow of happiness inside as she watched Natasha's eyes widen and her face break into a rare smile; no one had ever called her eminently suitable before, only imbecile or cripple.

The house Miss Prebble sent them to was a tall thin building on a side street off Pennsylvania Avenue, between the Gothic splendour of Trinity Episcopalian and the Catholic cathedral being built by the German and Polish Catholics. They presented themselves at the kitchen door, put back their veils and asked to see the housekeeper. She was a dumpy little woman with black hair in a thick plait, and piercing black eyes that scanned them both from head to foot. Apparently she liked what she saw; she invited them in and within minutes discovered that Natasha hailed from the same part of the far-flung Russian Empire as she did. The happy circumstance of them both speaking Russian meant the two girls were made very welcome; they were invited to sit at the vast kitchen table and the children's nurse was summoned to take tea with them, served from a large copper samovar.

After the initial nervous introductions, Melisande tried to stay in the background, watching in fascination as Natasha began to emerge from her shell, deferring to the nurse, but putting forward her own opinions when they were asked for with a sound good sense that would have astounded anyone who had seen her reduced to a quivering idiot by Madame Chantal over a badly sewn seam.

'So. How soon can the little Natasha come to us?' demanded the plump nurse, who already seemed to regard Natasha with the same warmth she devoted to her young charges.

'It depends on Madame,' Melisande began. Then, as the light went out in Natasha's bright eyes, she knew she could not take her back to the workroom, to face Madame's wrath and her vicious tongue again.

'She could start straight away,' she said boldly.

'Could I?' Then Natasha's excited face fell. 'No. I couldn't leave you to face her,' she said miserably.

'Nonsense. I can deal with her. No arguments,' she said firmly. 'I'll bring your things round this evening on the way to City Hall.'

Brave words, but as she bade a radiant Natasha farewell and went up the area steps into the sunlight, her heart sank into her boots.

Smartly dressed in dress jacket and braided trousers of fine vicuna with a matching horseshoe-fronted waistcoat, Max Ellsky bowled along the road from Eden Springs. His attention was not entirely on his driving as he racked his brains to think of some way to help the girl with the green eyes who was beginning to haunt his dreams.

As yet, he had been unable to come up with any solution; for a single man to help a girl in her situation to find a post would imply that he had some moral obligation towards her; unprotected as she was by any family, the inference would be that he had cast her off, a slur which would cling to her and destroy her reputation for the rest of her life.

He wanted to help her; he wanted to see her happy. Above all, he wanted to stop worrying about her: it was beginning to affect his work.

When he arrived at the concert, she was already busy selling programmes. Reluctantly he took his seat in the circle, only to find that his view of the parterre was blocked by a woman in a large hat in which economy and fashion had combined to hideous results, the démodé hour-glass crown having been updated with a trimming of small colourful birds whose glass eyes stared unnervingly at him throughout the performance.

He caught only fleeting glimpses of her in the interval, crossing the foyer and hurrying up and down the staircase with refreshments. She was coming down the staircase, just as the first bell sounded, when he saw a man grab her arm. Anger sprang up in him as he recognised Jeremiah Patterson, not known for his chivalrous approach to women, especially those he deemed outside his own social class. With a suppressed oath Max put his glass on the table and began to cross the foyer, but before he was a quarter of the way across, and just as Patterson put his hand out to draw her veil away from her face, Mr James stepped out of the shadows and between Patterson and the girl, who took the opportunity to slip away. Max returned to his wine with a guilty stab of relief that he had not had to reveal himself and his concerns in front of everyone. It occurred to him as he picked up his glass that it was the first time he had ever rushed impetuously into something without first weighing up the pros and cons of his intended actions.

He was waiting for her in the same spot when she came out.

'Oh, I'm glad you're here, Mr Ellsky,' she said with a sigh of relief. 'I really do need your help.'

She had known that it would not be easy to tell Madame Chantal about Natasha, but she had not realised just how bad it would be.

There had been a terrible row when Madame refused to allow her to take Natasha's miserable belongings to her; when Melisande steadfastly declined to tell her where Natasha was, the dressmaker had tried to take the switch to her, only to have it torn from her grip and snapped in two.

'You are confined to your room!' screeched Madame. 'Bread and a jug of water! We shall pray for you to see the error of your ways!'

'Nonsense!' said Melisande briskly. 'You cannot keep me in. Natasha is expecting me; her new employers will come looking for me if I do not turn up! Would you like me to tell them how you treat your employees? I wonder what Society would say about that? Where would your commissions be then?'

'Society will hardly listen to you! You do not go where Society goes!'

'There is an open meeting at the City Hall next week, about the new water supply. Even the lowliest slum dweller can stand up and be heard, they tell me.'

'Doctor Kingsley and his godless radicals? I do not know how they reconcile it with their consciences, stirring up the working people to think they know what's best for them!' Two livid spots of colour burned on her cheeks. 'I forbid you to have anything to do with them!'

She felt her eyes widen and hoped that the shock she felt at the mention of the doctor's name did not show on her face. 'I know nothing of Doctor Kingsley,' she said with an affected indifference, 'but a great many Edensville ladies serve on the committees – I've seen their names . . .'

'All eager to play Lady Bountiful!' she sneered.

'. . . and after I've had my say, which of them would dare to commission from you again?'

Like all bullies, Madame collapsed at the first hint of firm opposition. She would have liked to turn the girl out on her ear, but she was a good worker, and these days hard to replace. And sufficiently determined to carry out her threats. Society ladies preferred to turn a blind eye to the conditions under which their dresses, hats and trimmings were made, but once it was drawn to their attention, they would, she was quite sure, pronounce themselves horrified and withdraw their custom forthwith.

'I'm sure no one could criticise my care for my girls,' she said huffily. 'Everything I ever do for my girls I do out of· Christian kindness. For is it not our duty to set the footsteps of the young on the path to righteousness?'

'Imagine if they heard some of your girls had no free time,' mused Melisande.

'The Devil finds work for idle hands –'

'Not mine,' said Melisande firmly. 'I have a great deal to do in my free time – which I propose in future will be taken on Wednesday and Sunday, one half day from noon and one full. And on Saturdays I shall finish at five.'

She would not go into a restaurant with Max, but she permitted him to buy her a pie and coffee at the pie-stand.

'Rather beneath your dignity, but it's better than being seen in a restaurant with a veiled woman.'

'Doesn't she feed you?' he demanded, watching her sink her teeth with relish into the hot pie.

106

'Only as much as she has to,' she replied, wiping flakes of crisp pastry from her lips.

'Then why go back there?'

'I'm not ready to leave yet. I am laying my plans, but there are still a few things to be done.' Like finding some books, she thought wryly, producing some translations for Miss Prebble, hoping she would have better fortune persuading a family that she was fit to care for their children than she had had in London. 'But if you could come and collect Natasha's bag . . . Madame won't argue with you.'

Far from it: Madame Chantal fawned over Mr Ellsky in the most nauseating manner, even tucking a shawl into Natasha's bag: 'The poor child feels the cold so.'

'Till next Saturday,' Max murmured under his breath. Then, as Madame handed over the battered canvas bag, he tipped his hat and left.

Wednesday dawned fair and warm, though not too hot yet to make walking uncomfortable. Much like a fine spring day in England, she thought, turning her face to the gentle breeze blowing in off the lake. She was beginning to regret the bonnet and veil, but the ease with which Max had identified her, even with the veil, had been a little worrying, so she kept them on until she was well clear of the last houses. When she had climbed the bluff above town she took them off and sat awhile in the shade of a huge pine tree, munching on a piece of bread she had saved from breakfast, watching the ships, like tiny dragonflies, plying the far Canadian shore. Over to her left, mist hung over the great waterfalls at Niagara and to her right, beyond the haze of smoke that lay over Edensville, Lake Ontario stretched to the horizon.

She brushed the grass from her skirt, folded her shawl, tied it to her bag and set off to find the old path that led away from the lake and through the forest to Eden Springs; it was the original corduroy road cut by the early settlers through the thickness of the virgin forest, but replaced in more prosperous times by the newer, wide stone road. Olsen had told her blood-curdling tales of how the original settlement had been burned by the Indians, its inhabitants massacred and scalped. 'And they still haunt the forest, moaning and shrieking,' Nancy had added with great relish.

She would just have to take her chance with the ghosts, she thought, for she had no wish to meet Mr Ellsky — or even worse, Doctor Kingsley – on the carriage road.

The forest had already begun to reclaim the old track, each year's growth obliterating more and more of the log road which had connected the early settlement with the lake. She put Olsen's tales resolutely out of her mind. High up on a branch a bird was singing and she found her spirits rising too.

What if she couldn't find a post as governess? Perhaps she'd stay with Madame, give Anna a run for her money, even become a modiste herself! She giggled at the thought.

The early morning mists had faded in the sun, leaving behind drops of moisture which hung from the branches like so many crystals from a chandelier. The thrushes sang in the lofty white oaks and sparrows cheeped chirpily in the thickets of birch. She might almost think herself in Epping Forest again, on one of the Orphanage picnics: a carefree child with no thought of apprenticeships or indentures to trouble her. She swung along in an easy stride, singing softly.

After about half an hour the landscape changed. It had grown gradually darker, for the sun did not penetrate the closely packed stands of red and white pine; the song died on her lips as her mind strayed back to the days in the Home and herself reading the tale of Red Riding Hood to a circle of open-mouthed, wide-eyed children. *'Oh, Grandma! What big eyes you've got!'*

Olsen had told her there were still wild animals in the forest.

She began to hurry, unable to shake off the feeling that she was being watched. *'Oh! Grandma! What big teeth you've got!'* chorused the children.

She took to her heels, running as fast as she could until she reached a clearing where she paused, panting, leaning against the bole of a vast sugar maple, berating herself for her folly. What did Olsen know? she demanded of herself angrily.

She walked on a little further, trying to regain her earlier poise. Then a twig snapped in the stillness behind her and she broke into a run, not stopping until she burst out of the forest on to the new road, where she sat under a tree until her heart stopped pounding and the violent stitch in her side had subsided.

She was glad when the spire of the church at Eden Springs came into sight at last; she stopped to put on her shawl and bonnet and draw down the veil again.

The stableyard was deserted. She had deliberately planned to come on Wednesday, for on Wednesday neither Olsen nor Nancy would be at Springs House. As she turned into the kitchen garden she smelt the delightful smell of fresh bread baking and stood a moment among the herbs, savouring it.

Her first work in the Orphanage had been in the bakery, where the older girls had taught her to turn dusty, sometimes mouldy flour into acceptable loaves. It was there she had first come across Jem, who heaved the sacks for the girls and whiled away their few idle moments by telling them of his life before he had been 'taken in'. He had had a varied career, at one stage working as a 'chive' for a terror of an old woman who made a living begging for herself and her 'poor crippled grandson'. He could twist his limbs into the most amazing positions and would propel himself along on his hands at an alarming rate up and down the centre of the bakehouse with his legs crooked up beneath him. When the old woman had died, he'd become a prater's lad.

'Prater'd set up his booth on a street corner, see, and start his prayer meeting. After the hymn, I'd go into a trance or have a fit, whichever'd suit the audience. I'd tell 'em I'd been a sinner, but now I'd seen the light and I wouldn't sin nor swear no more. If there'd been a missionary in town, that allus went well. 'Cos I'm quite dark, see, so I'd black up a bit and be a heathen and swear I wouldn't worship no more idols and graven images. Brought in the most money, that did.'

'Sounds more interesting than in here,' said hungry Lizzie. 'Why did you give it up?'

'No future in it,' said Jem with a shrug. 'The old 'un got murdered for her money, only time she ever had any. And the prater took the long drop in Newgate. Stuck a knife in a man what caught him pickin' pockets. An' they never gave me no shares, anyways; never even fed me regular like here. An' she used to beat me when she was drunk. Broke my arm once, the old lady did.'

That was when she first began to realise that what was to her poverty and misery was to these others shelter and

109

security. The Home might not be like anything she had known, but the alternative was starvation and death in the gutter.

Melisande put back her veil and stood a moment in the kitchen doorway. On the table stood hot crusty loaves and rolls, freshly made muffins and cakes, while on the side unbaked loaves had been set to prove. Mrs Chobley stood at the stove, stirring the contents of a large tureen. Humming gently to herself, she lay down the ladle and turned. As she saw the figure standing in the doorway, her eyes widened and her jaw dropped open.

'Mel, girl! It isn't you, is it?' She surged across the room to envelop her in a violet-scented hug. 'Gawd, we was glad to get that letter, girl! Till then we thought you was dead for sure!' she said, dabbing her eyes hastily with the corner of her apron.

'I'm sorry,' said Mel guiltily. 'I should have left word. I didn't think –'

'Sit down, let me look at you.' She shook her head. 'Well, there wasn't much of you before, but there's even less of you now. Don't they feed you?'

Within minutes, she was slicing vigorously at a large ham, piling up a plate with more food than the girl could possibly manage.

'Won't Mrs Jameson mind?' she said, looking wide-eyed at the feast before her.

'You are behind the times, my girl!' said Mrs Chobley, puffing out her chest. 'I'm running this house now. Cook-Housekeeper, that's me!' She's gone – that's why it's so quiet here!'

Mrs Chobley sat across the table, hand folded over her ample bosom as Mel ate her way hungrily through an impromptu feast of ham, cheese, fresh crusty bread and delicious golden home-churned butter, with early saladings from the estate's succession houses.

'I thought perhaps she was just away on holiday,' said Mel through a mouthful of food.

'Not unless you calls retirement a general holiday, which it may be, though I hopes I never comes to it. Drive me mad, that would, sitting round all day with nothing to do. Because

110

that's what he's done for Mrs Jameson – ah, and Mr Veasey, too. Butler as was. Retired them on a pension, which he didn't have to do when all's said and done, for they were the Carter's people, not his. And never a stroke of work did he get out of either of them. And half the others have gone too. Called us all into the dining room, few days after you went. Everyone, right down to the scullerymaid, after morning prayers – and we don't have them no more either. He reckons we can say our own if we're so minded. And he says as how one man don't need all the servants a family of five needs – though Gawd knows there weren't that many families of five needed all the servants the Carters had. Well, you can imagine how quiet it went. Springs House is a soft posting and they none of 'em wanted to lose it.'

'I can imagine.'

'He's kept Olsen, but he's groom and gardener. After all, Doctor drives himself most places and that Olsen used to laze round half the day. We've just the three maids: Hetty, Nancy and young Jessie.'

'How do you keep the house going on so few?'

'The sensible way. Women from the village what comes in and does the cleaning. Hetty and Nancy does the dusting and polishing. Jessie turns her hand to whatever's needed, and since all them other girls have gone – ah, and the footman and 'specially the butler and the housekeeper with their big notions of their own importance – there ain't half so much running around to be done. And the cooking too! You wouldn't believe it, but three-quarters of the cooking in this kitchen never went above stairs, it didn't, just went to feed all them others down here! And the peace, you wouldn't believe! No argufying over who takes the head of the table and who has the prime cuts! Tell you what, though, Mel,' she said with one of her swift changes of subject, 'why don't you come back, eh? Bet the doctor would take you on again. Why you had to leave I don't know!'

She tried to explain to Cook why she had felt it necessary to leave Springs House, but she knew she wouldn't understand; there were so many, like Natasha, who would have thought this a wonderful place to work.

'I can understand as 'ow you might prefer to be a teacher, though, I dunno, they allus seems a bit betwixt and between

111

to me, like as though they don't belong nowhere, nor upstairs nor downstairs, if you follow me. But what I can't see is 'ow working for this Madame Chantal, what sounds a right barbarian to me, is better than working for the doctor. Meself, I'd rather know where I stand. I gives 'im good service and 'e feeds me and keeps a roof over me 'ead in return. Seems like a good bargain to me. So tell me about this little girl you sent for a nursery maid.'

She began to describe, with a great deal of embellishment and a touch of self-mocking humour, the interview with Miss Prebble and the confrontation with Madame, leaving out only Max's intervention. Cook rocked with laughter. 'And the Russian family have lent me some books, so I can make translations to show Miss Prebble, but I still need to find some French books.'

'Bless you, child, did you never think of the doctor's library?' asked Cook, looking at her over the rim of her tea cup. 'Plenty of foreign books up there.'

'But there isn't time,' she said regretfully. 'I'll have to leave again soon if I'm to get back before dark.'

'Take 'em with you. Do 'em at your leisure – assuming that woman gives you any!'

'I couldn't take his books!' she protested. 'He doesn't even know I'm here!'

'He doesn't even know half the books are here, either. But I know there's French books upstairs – from the people that lived here before the Carters came. Seems to me it makes sense. All you're doing is borrowing them. No danger of bumping into him – he's not here today.' Her face creased into a wide smile. 'You're a funny one, Mel, you are. You must have paupered yourself sending him money he don't need for them cast-offs and now you'd give up the chance of the job you ran away to find rather than borrow books he won't even notice have gone! Don't be so soft, gel. Go and find what you want while I brew you up a fresh cuppa. Then you'd best be on your way, or this old Frenchie'll be confining you to quarters!'

When Mel came downstairs she was delighted to find Jessie in the kitchen.

'Jessie! I hoped I'd see you before I went!' The young girl was so taken aback that she was rendered temporarily speechless.

'It's not a ghost, you silly wench!' said Cook. 'It's Mel!'

'Oh, Mel! I thought for sure you were either frozen to death or gone to the bad!' Brought up herself on the knife-edge between poor but respectable, and poor but no hope, Jessie knew what the choices were for a friendless, homeless girl.

'Safe and sound!' Melisande assured her. They chatted a little more over a cup of tea, then it was time for her to set off. She swore them both to secrecy, which Cook agreed to with a reluctant: 'Well, when all's said and done, he already knows you're safe.'

Her basket was very heavy on the journey back, weighed down with the books she had borrowed, last week's newspapers with their prophecies of impending war between the United States and Spain, and the cold ham and cake that Cook had pressed on her. She would spend all her free time over the next week or two making a perfect translation and writing it up. She only hoped her Russian would prove sufficient for Lemontov: she suspected his speech would be rather more high-flown than Natasha's – or Little Polack's.

Just before she emerged from the forest, the sun went down and the stars began to show against a deep turquoise sky. Away to her left an animal howled and a shiver ran up her spine. She wrapped her shawl closer around her and quickened her pace. Walking down the bluff was not as easy as walking up it, for the path was steeply sloping and on several occasions she nearly lost her footing.

At Madame Chantal's she went straight to her room. She had intended to start on the work, but it had been a long walk and she had barely enough strength left to undress and wash away the dust before she fell into bed.

No one would have called Natasha a good seamstress, but at least she had been another pair of hands to fetch and carry and do some of the plain seaming. Now, short-handed, and with customers all wanting fittings for the balls and dinners of the Season, none of them had any time to spare and even Madame found herself cutting out.

113

By the time she finished in the workroom, Melisande would quite happily have tumbled straight into bed, but she forced herself to stay awake long enough to do a little more of her translation. There were times when her tired brain told her she was mad, told her to leave it till they were not so busy: after all there had been no word from Miss Prebble's agency. But always a small insistent voice within would remind her that the books were not hers, and that she had promised to return them at the end of the month. Besides, if word came from Miss Prebble, she had better be sure to be ready.

'Never put off till tomorrow what you can do today,' Matron had often said to a rebellious Milly. Sarah had said the same thing, although, being Sarah, she had gone to Shakespeare for her quotation.

'Procrastination is the thief of time.' Who had said that? Othello? Hamlet? Lady Macbeth? Her tired mind refused to remember. Whoever it was had undoubtedly come to a miserable end for not heeding his own words, and she would not risk following in his footsteps. She never got to bed until well after midnight and was up again before dawn; consequently she fell foul of Madame when her tired eyes made her slower than usual over her seaming.

In the middle of the week Anna had to attend at the Patterson house for a further fitting for Miss Sophia's new ball gown and took 'Smith' with her. In vain did she protest that Madame had forbidden her to return there.

'Whose fault is it we're short-handed?' demanded Anna snappishly. 'I have to have someone to carry the boxes.'

Melisande was in the upper hall, carrying the slippers and gloves Mrs Patterson's dresser had dyed to match the apple green silk, when Jeremiah Patterson saw her.

'The shrinking maiden again!' he exclaimed, catching her wrist and pulling her to him. 'Where is your bold protector now, eh?' He licked his lips as he gazed down into her face.

His arm was around her waist and he pressed his face closer to hers with a smile of gloating anticipation. 'And now we'll see what's beneath the veil, won't we?'

She struggled, swearing a stream of oaths, in various languages, that went ill with the nun-like costume, but his strength was greater than hers. He succeeded in drawing back

114

the veil and smiled evilly when he saw the green eyes darken with fear, but as he towered over her, his moist mouth descending towards hers, Anna erupted out of the boudoir. The wooden measuring rule was still in her hand and she brought it down on Patterson's unprotected head with great vigour.

Wrenching herself from his arms, Melisande saw the look of shock on his face and a laugh, as much nervous as exultant, escaped her. His expression changed to one of vicious fury and she knew she had made an implacable enemy.

But even that unpleasantness was pushed to the back of her mind by the events of the following day.

Anna came to her door, an unlikely event in itself. Hastily she put aside the book she had been working from.

'Madame wants to see you in her room,' said the girl, her customary sourness overlaid with gloating pleasure. 'There's a man to see you and she's absolutely livid.'

Not Max, surely? But she knew no other men. Unless the doctor had found out where she was? Her heart lurched sickeningly.

It was Mr James from the City Hall, doggedly standing his ground against Madame's displeasure.

He crossed to her side as she entered. 'I've brought a letter for you, Miss – ah . . . ' He blinked rapidly. 'A private letter, which you're under no obligation to show to anyone else,' he said fiercely, scowling at Madame Chantal.

'Th-thank you.' She flashed him a smile. 'I hope it has not put you to too much trouble?'

He did not linger, being given no encouragement to do so.

'If you have need of me at any time, young lady, you have only to let me know.'

His gesture of support gave her the courage to outface Madame and take herself and her letter up to her room before opening it.

The words leaped out of the page at her:

Mr Topping interviewing for position. Has agreed to see you nineteenth inst. at half-past nine promptly. Take examples of work. 109 Lower Wharf Street.
Araminta Prebble

115

An opportunity at last! Her mind reeled. She would have to arrange to change her free day. But if she did that, when would she be able to return the books? And how, if the post was out of town? She tried to imagine what Mr Topping might look like and what he would be seeking in a governess. Of course there might be any number of applicants for the post. She was still thinking about it when she fell asleep.

Max was waiting outside City Hall for her when she arrived the following evening.

'I hope you will permit me to pay for your ticket,' he said cheerfully. 'Then you will not need to sell programmes.'

She shook her head vigorously. 'Mr Ellsky, I *like* selling programmes. I cherish the independence it gives me. If you are poor, people can always tell you what to do. What I'll earn this evening isn't just dollars and cents to me: it's a week's lodging or half a ticket to New York.'

And tonight's earnings were particularly important. Behind in her work, and with the interview coming up, she had reluctantly had to miss the public meeting earlier that week – and payments for attending at public meetings were at a higher rate. According to Mr James, it had been a humdinger of a meeting, and Doctor Kingsley had raised Cain about the water supply. She wondered whether she had misjudged her erstwhile employer: she would have liked to hear him speak. But if Mr Ellsky had recognised her so easily, so might Kingsley have done.

'I could make up the difference,' said Max, breaking in on her thoughts. 'Consider it payment for the pleasure of your company.'

He knew as soon as he spoke that he had made a *faux pas*.

'I may be naive,' she said, snatching her hand from his arm, 'but I am not completely stupid! I do not sell my company – or anything else!'

'I – I meant no harm by it,' he said stiffly.

In her heart she knew it, and was prepared to forgive him.

There were no curtains at the high dormer window and the warm sun on her face woke her early on her free day. She tripped lightly down the stairs, singing softly to herself as she

116

pumped up water in to the tin basin to wash in. Passing Anna on the second landing, she returned her scowl with a cheerful grin.

It was fortunate that Madame had paid her before Natasha's escape and the episode of the letter – she might otherwise have had a pretext for withholding the money. In town Melisande bought some paper, a pen-holder and nib and a small bottle of the cheapest ink. She would be able to copy up her work tonight when she returned from Eden Springs. As for tomorrow – she would just have to slip away early. Madame would be furious, but if she was offered the job, she wouldn't care about Madame's rage. And if not – she'd just have to deal with that when she came to it.

The weather was much warmer now: great palls of ochre-coloured dust hung over the streets long after the horses whose hooves had raised them had disappeared. On the trees the leaves hung motionless and limp in the remorseless heat. Looking back from the bluff she saw Edensville lying beneath a layer of smoke and dust; above the Lake hung a shimmering heat haze that blotted out the shoreline and the horizon.

It was just after noon when she arrived at Springs House and she knew at once that it had been a mistake.

The kitchen was full. Over to one side women were chopping and sifting. In the cool-room she could see a vast array of syllabubs, flummeries and blancmanges, while in the kitchen Jessie and another girl were taking raised pies out of the ovens and scattering herbs over joints of beef and mutton.

'Mel!' Cook swept over to wrap her in a violet-scented embrace. 'Oh, it is good to see you gel. But I didn't expect you till next week – and here we all are at sixes and sevens!'

'I hadn't realised you would be so busy!'

Nor me, gel, or I'd have thought twice about letting the other servants go. But there, the women do their best. And when we're done, at least they goes back home and leaves me in peace. It's that dratted woman, of course.'

'Who?'

'Not that it's every day he opens a free dispensary, but why she couldn't have celebrated it in her own house, beats me. Though it's my opinion,' she muttered ominously, 'that she ain't one bit interested in his dispensary. No, what she wants

117

to celebrate is him taking an interest in that gawky lass of hers.' She drew a chair out from the table and chivvied her visitor in to it. 'But I swear and vow, Mel, if the day ever dawns when he lets hisself be talked into marrying the wench, that's the day I pack my bags and go.'

'Who?' she repeated.

'That Patterson woman, of course. Who else? Not that I'm amiss to having a mistress about the place. Even Almeria Carter knew better than to hold a party and disappear for the day!'

'Doctor Kingsley is not here?'

'That's what I'm telling you! And why? Because there's a pesky meeting at the Infirmary and he feels he ought to be there. Even though it means he'll turn up no more than half an hour before his guests!'

'You don't need me underfoot. I'll go – '

'I'll not have you going all that way back without a good meal inside you. And you'll need some new books. You run along up to the library now, while Mrs Jefferson and me makes us all something.'

'I think I had better not take any others,' she said reluctantly. 'I have an interview tomorrow and if they offer me the post, I may have to travel out of town.'

'If ifs and ands were pots and pans we'd have no need of tinkers,' said Cook sapiently. 'You don't build your hopes up too high, gel, 'less you gets disappointed. And if you miss this one, what are you going to do whiles you wait for the next one? Waste your time, that's what, when you could be learning something what would help you. Life's too short to waste it, gel.' She turned to call instructions across to one of the women about greasing the pans. 'If learnin's what will get you what you want,' she said, turning back again, 'then you set to it! And if so be you get this post, you just leave them books at the receiving office; I'll pick them up next time I'm in town.' She surged to her feet. 'Now Mrs Jefferson, we'll see to that ragoût . . .'

Melisande did not linger in the library. On a dusty top shelf she found some French plays and selected the first volume, with plays by Moliere. On the shelf below she found a ponderous tome: *Discourses on travels in America, by a*

Gentleman Traveller, with maps appended. It was dated 1869, but there was nothing more recent and she was conscious of the gaps in her knowledge of her adopted country's history. With the third book she had had all too brief an acquaintance at Sarah's, just before the library had been sold to pay off John Thomsett's gambling debts: *Palgrave's Treasury*, 'a selection of the best original lyrical pieces and songs in our language, by writers not living' according to the modest Mr Palgrave.

Downstairs she found Cook in the cool-room, putting the finishing touches to a confection of iced oranges surrounded by a pile of ice. 'There,' she said, with a sigh of satisfaction. 'Mrs Bowlby, you can put that back in the ice-box again.'

Mel reached out and touched an orange that lay on the marble, revelling in the waxy feel of it. 'I had an orange once,' she said, smiling as she remembered the strange sensation of the fruit in her mouth. 'Sarah gave it to me on Christmas Day.'

'And you shall have one again, Mel,' said Mrs Chobley, patting her arm. 'Only not that one. I need it for my sauce.'

The hired women had stopped to snatch a bite in the kitchen and the maids had laid the table in the housekeeper's room with a tempting array of cakes and scones.

'Sit down, gel,' said Mrs Chobley, slicing through the crust of a large savoury pie. 'Mrs Jefferson!' she called. 'Hetty, go and tell Mrs Jefferson we're stopping for a bite.'

Hetty hurried back out to the kitchen, returning a few moments later with the information that Mrs Jefferson was watching a sauce she couldn't leave.

'I'll make sure she has her tea later,' said Cook comfortably, and Melisande wondered why Mrs Jefferson was honoured with a place at Mrs Chobley's table while the rest of the hired women ate in the kitchen.

'Jessie will be joining us shortly,' said Cook. 'Aye, and Nancy too. Tell her nothing but that you're visiting me. For if she can do you a bad turn she will, though she'd hesitate to cross me.'

The presence of Nancy quite took the edge off Melisande's appetite. She avoided answering most of her questions, and ignored her barbed suggestions as to her mode of living, but when the maid left to set up the table for dinner, she gave Mel a look of sheer enmity, and the scones and cream turned to dust in her mouth.

'That Nancy don't like nobody much these days,' said Mrs Chobley with a shrug. 'Best have nothing to do with her. Now leave them dishes, gel. The women will do all them. Best be on your way.'

She took up her basket, gave Mrs Chobley a swift hug and opened the door. While they had been eating the sky had darkened to a livid purplish-grey. A violent flash of lightning crackled over the stables, followed by a rumble of thunder, and a curtain of rain fell from a lowering sky and swept across the yard.

'Just a summer storm,' said Cook comfortably. 'It'll soon pass, but you'd best hold on a little longer.'

Melisande swore softly under her breath. She'd hoped to be back early in order to start copying out her work. 'I won't come back in, I'm holding you up. I'll just wait in the porch till it stops.'

But the rain showed no sign of abating and she knew she would have to set out soon, rain or no rain. She drew her shawl over her head, took a deep breath and dashed out across the stable yard. Head down, she ran for the gate that led from the kitchen garden to the shrubbery at the side of the house. As she wrestled with the latch, which seemed to have taken on a malevolent life of its own, a sudden bolt of lightning crashed to earth nearby, making her jump in terror. At last the latch gave beneath her hand and she shot through – straight into the rough grip of a cloaked figure on the other side.

The shock of the collision knocked the breath from her and before she could speak a strong hand grabbed her wrist, dragged her round to the verandah that ran along the side of the house and pushed her in through the storm door that opened onto it.

She struggled in vain. 'Let me go!' she panted, when she had caught her breath. 'Please – let me go. I've got to get back to Edensville!'

The hood of the mackintosh cape fell back from her captor's face. 'You're not going anywhere!' said Doctor

Kingsley, wresting the basket from beneath her sodden shawl. 'You needn't think you can come into my house and help yourself to my possessions!' He hauled her across to his study and as he pushed her through the door, she thought she caught a glimpse of Nancy and Olsen grinning in the shadows.

He slammed the door behind him and pushed her none too gently on to the nearest chair.

'What now?' he asked grimly, towering above her. 'We await your accomplice, I suppose.'

'My accomplice?' she repeated in a faint voice. 'I don't understand . . .'

'You missed your vocation, Miss Stevens,' he said with a harsh laugh, 'You should have gone on stage: you are a consummate actress.'

'But I –'

'Clearly you did not walk here. I assume your accomplice is waiting hard by with a cart.'

'I *did* walk here, I tell you!'

'I've been up and down that road all day and I saw no one on foot.' He tipped the basket out on the desk. The volume of American history fell on the new pen holder and snapped it in two. 'Did not your accomplice tell you that books fetch very little? Silver would have been much better. Though Nancy tells me she interrupted you in mid-search. No doubt the silver would have followed.'

Her jaw fell open, but she was too shocked to speak.

'French books too,' he said scornfully. 'I don't suppose you realised . . .'

'You think I stole them?' she gasped at last.

'It was fortunate that Nancy saw you creeping about the house. Fortunate that I arrived home in time to catch you. The question is –'

'It's a lie!' she cried, green eyes stormy in a pale face. 'Ask Mrs Chobley!' she demanded.

'Mrs Chobley?' he sneered. 'I'm surprised you even remember her name!'

'Of course I do! I came to see her and –' She was reluctant to get the older woman into trouble. 'Please, you only have to ask her!'

'I should hand you over to the authorities now – but I think I prefer to wait and catch your accomplice. Did you train for

121

this in London, or have you just started in this line of business?'

'You are insulting, Doctor Kingsley!' she exclaimed, springing up from the chair and looking straight at him, though he was a full head taller than she. 'I do not need to steal! I am a seamstress. I –'

'A seamstress?' he said in disbelief.

'Yes! I work for a respectable dressmaker. She belongs to a strict religious sect. Look!' She picked up the bonnet and veil which had fallen out of the basket with the books. 'I've worked for her ever since I left Springs House.'

'What an excellent disguise! And, by the way, she does *not* employ you.'

'But I –'

'I do. When Doctor Carter and his wife paid for your tickets, the Matron at the Home indentured you to work for three months to pay your passage. It is the usual arrangement. When I bought the house and practice, I bought your commitment too.'

'Like a piece of furniture!' This expression of her status offended her as nothing had before, not even being unjustly accused of being a thief, and the temper so often deprecated by Matron came boiling to the surface.

'You do *not* own me!' she yelled. 'No one owns me!' She caught hold of the nearest thing to hand, the volume of Molière plays, and hurled it at him in a blind fury.

He ducked swiftly and it missed him by a hair's breadth. He recovered his balance and in two strides was at her side. He caught her wrist as she lifted the second book to throw. As the book fell heavily to the floor he tightened his grip and drew her inexorably to him until they stood only inches apart and she could see her rage reflected in his face. He held her for what seemed an eternity, hard grey eyes looking angrily down into tempestuous green eyes, until a knock fell on the front door, closely followed by the hubbub of voices in the hall.

He swore softly and thrust her away from him so suddenly that her knees, which had begun to tremble as they always did in the aftermath of one of her explosions of temper, gave way beneath her and she would have fallen if she had not grasped at the desk for support.

'Damn!' He cursed some more under his breath. 'My guests!'

He bit his lip in momentary indecision, torn between his duty as a host and his determination not to let her slip through his fingers once more.

'Let me go!' she begged. 'Please. I must –'

'You will stay here,' he said through clenched teeth, 'until I get the truth out of you!'

She took an unsteady step towards him, her hand outstretched. 'I have told you the truth,' she whispered. 'You have only to ask Cook.'

'You think me very gullible, do you not?' He looked her up and down, not a glimmer of warmth in his eyes. 'But I am not to be won over again by sweet words and soft answers!'

He crossed to the door, his eyes hardening as he looked back at her. 'I'm sure you'll have another heart-rending story ready for me when I return.'

She heard the key turn in the lock and sank down on the floor, her shoulders drooping in misery.

The long case clock in the hall struck nine. She had not thought he meant to leave her for so very long. The study still held some of the heat of the day but outside the storm raged on, moving round in a circle, first to the east, then the south, until it arrived overhead, the thunder vibrating through the house. Her clothes had dried clammy on her skin and now she began to shiver.

Was he planning to keep her here all night? If she was still there in the morning Mrs Chobley would be swift to tell the doctor the truth about her, but if she was still there in the morning it would be too late. Tomorrow was the interview and neither Mr Topping nor Miss Prebble would be likely to give her a second chance.

Panic began to set in. She tried the door to the hall, as much for something to do as in any hope that it might open. Then she groped her way in the fading light towards the rear door, through which the patients came to sit in the waiting room. That too was firmly locked. The only other door led into the little dispensary and that, she knew, had no windows. She tried all the casements too, but they were firmly locked and

123

she could not shift them. As she tried the last one, there was a violent flash of lightning and she recoiled from the window with a frightened gasp; as she turned aside, she thought she saw a thin strip of light under the dispensary door.

Turning the handle, she stepped hesitantly inside. The room was in total darkness and she scolded herself for her foolishness; she had been dazzled by the lightning, that was all. She turned to leave, then stopped as an idea struck her. Taking care to move slowly, lest she knock over one of the many bottles with which the room was littered, she crossed to the middle of the room and stood there quietly, face upturned. After a moment she imagined she could discern a faint lightening of the gloom.

With the next flash of lightning her patience was rewarded: in the centre of the ceiling was a fair-sized skylight. She groped her way back to the door and found the steps which were used for reaching the upper shelves of the high glass-fronted cupboards which lined the walls of the room. She dragged the steps cautiously into the centre of the room and tried to open them, swearing under her breath as they stuck.

In the hall the clock struck ten and her heart sank. Madame locked the house at ten-thirty sharp. Even if she ran all the way she would never get back in time – and in the dark she dare not risk the shorter path through the forest. How would she get her good clothes – and most important of all, her work? As panic set in she tried to force the steps apart and trapped her hand painfully in the hinge. The sharp pain and the feel of the blood running down her wrist threatened to overset her completely. She forced herself to take a deep breath and count to ten.

When the next flash of lightning came she was poised at the top of the steps. By its light she climbed gingerly over on to the top of the cupboard, just beneath the skylight, and crouched there, hardly daring to breathe for fear of oversetting it.

The storm was moving further away and she had to wait a little longer for the next flash to reach out from her precarious perch and grope for the catch to the skylight. At last it gave way under her hand and she pushed the pane back until it rested on its hinges, halfway down towards the roof. She hauled herself out and slid down the gently sloping roof until she came to the cast iron drainpipe. As she shinned down it the gash in her hand began to well again, but she forced herself to ignore it.

The rain was still falling in torrents and within minutes she was soaked to the skin. The humble little attic in Edensville which had once seemed a prison and a place of misery, now seemed to beckon to her like a lighted inn window to a lost and lonely traveller.

She plodded determinedly along the road and tried to think of a way to get into the house. And then she remembered Anna who always, no matter what the weather, insisted on. leaving her bedroom window ajar – a legacy of her apprentice days when she had worked and slept in a windowless cellar. If only she could reach the window . . . if the tree were only strong enough to hold her . . . then she could climb on to the low roof and across the parapet to the window. She had done more dangerous things with Tom and Aggie and to much less purpose.

She had gone barely a mile when she heard the sound of a horse and cart. Her first instinct was to hide, but common sense reasserted itself before it was too late: the doctor and his guests would still be at the dinner table – and they wouldn't be travelling in a cart.

She stepped out into the road and waved at the oncoming driver. It was the postman, called out to deliver an urgent telegram. He took her up, offering her a rather malodorous horse blanket to keep the worst of the rain out. She spun him a yarn of having missed her pre-arranged ride home and, his command of English being rather poor, they soon lapsed into a companionable silence.

It was easier than she'd thought to climb in and collect her belongings. Anna stirred as she passed through her room, so rather than risk disturbing her again, she tiptoed down the stairs, her clothes and papers in the portmanteau under her arm, slid back the heavy bolts on the front door and slipped away into the night.

The scullerymaid at the Tschenchenyov house wakened Melisande from an uneasy sleep just after dawn. She rose stiffly

125

from the rocking chair, feeling as though she'd only just dozed off. By seven, washed and dressed in her navy braided skirt and Mrs Evans's cream blouse, with Sarah's cameo neatly pinned on the high neck, she was sitting at the kitchen table with the rest of the indoor servants, making a hearty breakfast.

The housekeeper brushed away her thanks with a chuckle.

'Like the drown-ed rat, she was,' she told the others. 'We turn her away, she be all melted by morning!'

'But what will you do if you don't get this post?' demanded Natasha anxiously.

'Then I shall have to go to Madame Chantal and tell her I couldn't get back because of the storm.' She bit her lip. Another one for the Recording Angel. She wondered what Sarah and Matron would make of her now, finding a lie to suit any need.

Head held high she stepped boldly out, wearing her clothes as proudly as if they were the silks and satins she made for · others. 'Repining never altered the world, my dear,' Sarah had said, as she parted with yet another treasured possession to pay some gambling debt or wine merchant's bill.

It was strange to see the world directly instead of through the hideous black veil, and she smiled sunnily as she walked down to the main square. Edensville, offered its first sight of Melisande Stevens, was as enthusiastic about her as she about it on this bright May day and her progress was attended by several whistles from the cheekier errand boys and raising of eyebrows and felt bowlers by young clerks on their way to offices.

She would not allow herself to remember that other time when she had set off so enthusiastically to an interview. That had been under a duller sky, before her world had begun to fall apart. But she was still the same foundling girl as she had been then, with the same hopes – and the same handicaps.

She had looked up Wharf Street in a directory in the Public Library; it lay in the commercial centre of the city, not far from the industrial belt that ran alongside the inlet of Lake Ontario around which Edensville had grown. She found the industrial area without difficult – all she had to do was follow her nose. She picked her way along the raised edge of the potholed roads, avoiding the mud and manure that lay thickly in the middle; fortunately the early morning sun had dried up the worst of the puddles. Evil-smelling smoke belched forth from the chimneys of the mills and the factories; sinister dark water pumped into the harbour, turning it an unpleasant shade of brown. The stench was even worse outside the canning factory, where a shambling crowd of men, women and adolescents, some barely more than children, still stood around in the hope of being set on. Most of them were very poorly dressed, though some of the women had thrown brightly coloured shawls over their drab rags. One man, his toes showing through broken boots, nudged his neighbour and said something in a foreign language. She didn't understand the words, but when they sniggered at her openly, she felt the colour rise in her cheeks.

Past the canning factory she turned up a side alley to emerge at last in the commercial district upwind of the manufacturing area, above the new docks. Everything here was cleaner and bore a more prosperous air than the area she had just left. She stopped briefly to check her appearance in a shop window and tucked a few strands of hair back into place.

The main commercial road ran parallel with the shore line, edged with counting houses and shipping offices. Below her the shore was lined with quays and wharves: barges and lighters tied up, discharging one cargo into a warehouse, taking on another; the smell of salt and tar was strong in the air. Ropes creaked on stanchions, cranes and gantries rose and fell and seamen and dockworkers yelled orders at each other.

She enquired the time of a portly gentleman in a heavy Inverness cape who had just emerged from the timber shipper's on the corner; he told her it lacked seven minutes to half after nine and directed her to a tall dirt-blackened building at the end of the street.

It had been erected in 1815, which made it one of the earliest buildings in Edensville, dating from the rebuilding after the British had razed it to the ground in 1812. With a last nervous twitch of her skirts and a deep breath, she stepped inside.

The doorman, sitting in his little cubbyhole by the main entrance, directed her up three flights of stairs to an outer office, which commanded an excellent view of the main harbour. She gave her name to the clerk who disappeared into the inner office. Putting her portmanteau on the floor by the desk, she crossed the room and gazed out.

Below the window the dockers were unloading a ship from France. Though the harbour was so much wider than the Thames alongside which she had spent her early years, the familiar smells and sounds reminded her of Wapping. She thought of Matron and Sarah and Mrs Evans and her hand went surreptitiously to the little cameo. If they were here they would have wished her good luck, so she wished herself luck on their behalf.

'If you would come this way, Miss?' said the clerk.

She picked up her portmanteau and walked into the inner office.

'Miss Smith,' the clerk announced sonorously.

'This is indeed a surprise,' said Doctor Kinglsey.

As if in a dream she heard the door close behind the clerk.

'Sit down, Miss Stevens,' said the doctor.

Her legs seemed to have become detached from her body and would not do her will. A shaft of sunlight slanted across the room; transfixed, she watched the dust motes dancing in the golden light.

'Sit down!' he snapped.

She came back to the present with a start and the portmanteau slipped from her nerveless fingers.

With a muffled curse, he rose from his seat, came around the desk, picked up the bag and handed it to her. 'Sit down,' he said, more gently.

She perched nervously on the edge of the chair he had held out for her. When he had seated himself once more behind the desk she opened her mouth to speak but no sound came out of her dry throat.

'What the devil are you doing here, Miss Stevens?' he demanded harshly.

'I – I – the interview. Mr Topping –'

'Mr Topping is interviewing teachers, not housemaids!'

'I came – I –' She took a deep breath. 'Miss Prebble sent me.'

His eyebrows flew up in surprise and this time he was the one at a loss for words.

'My name's on the list. Miss Smith.' She dropped her eyes before his unnerving gaze. 'I shouldn't have come,' she muttered, 'only it said –' She bit her lip. 'I'd better go.' She rose to her feet, still clutching the portmanteau.

'Go where?'

She shrugged. 'Back to the workroom, I suppose. Madame Chantal –'

'Sit down,' he said tiredly. 'Since you are on Mr Topping's list – albeit under false flags – I had better fulfil my duties and interview you.' She made no move to resume her seat. 'Dammit, girl, sit down!' he roared. 'Stop bobbing up and down!'

She sat down again quickly, eyes widened in surprise. 'Your duties?' she ventured cautiously.

He inclined his head. 'As chairman of the Board of Trustees of Harbourside School.' She closed her eyes in despair. 'Perhaps you would tell me how you persuaded Miss Prebble to describe you as *an experienced teacher*?' he demanded, leafing through the papers in front of him.

She gathered her wits together with an effort. 'I – I taught at the Orphanage,' she stammered. 'Until the children were sent to the new school – St Mark's.'

He looked at her through narrowed eyes. 'Indeed!' he said slowly. 'You never told me.'

'You never asked.'

'If you had a teaching post in London, then why come out here as a housemaid?'

'I have no formal qualifications. St Mark's would not take me. Because I was from the Orphanage.'

'Did Miss Prebble tell you that this is an experiment only – nothing to do with the city schools – working with immigrant children?'

She shook her head. 'Miss Prebble told me nothing of the · post.'

'Reluctant to put you off, I daresay.' He looked down at the papers again, then gave her a long considering look. 'You have informed your present employer of your application?'

'No. She would not have permitted me –'

129

'Your employer in the eyes of the law, Miss Stevens, is the owner of Springs House.'

'But you don't want me.'

'You must understand, Miss Stevens, that I wear my trustee's hat to ask you these questions. You must not confuse the trustee with the employer of the housemaid.'

She subsided, seething, into her chair. He was playing cat and mouse with her and she did not like it.

He leaned back in his chair, at his ease, and contemplated her across the polished expanse of desk. 'Will your present employer be able to give you references?'

'Able, yes,' she said through gritted teeth. 'But there is no certainty that he would be willing to do so.'

'A pity.' He made a brief note on the paper before him. 'And – er – how much notice would you have to give?'

'I – I don't know. I'm not –'

'Putting on my other hat, I have to tell you, Miss Stevens, that the contract signed on your behalf requires you to give three months' notice.'

'And how soon does the board wish to appoint –'

' – the new teacher? Within the month.' He saw her shoulders slump. 'The Harbourside school will not be run as a normal school. No breaks for school holidays. The pupils will constantly be coming and going as their parents move on west.'

He rose from his desk and crossed the room to open the door. She watched him warily.

'However, since there appear to be no other applicants awaiting interview, the Board will consider your application.' He sat back behind his desk and stretched his long tweed-clad legs out in front of him. 'You have examples of your work, I understand? Miss Prebble was informed that abilities were needed in languages other than English.'

She reached into her portmanteau and drew out the papers. 'I have brought some translations I made. Molière and Lermontov translated into English and Sir Walter Scott into French and Russian. I regret I cannot furnish the originals.' She looked him in the eye as she handed them across the desk. 'I might have been suspected of stealing them, you see.'

He met her look straight on, a gleam in his eyes.

130

After a moment he dropped his gaze briefly to the papers she had handed over. 'I must fetch someone else to check the Russian,' he said.

He went to the door once more and she heard him talking in a low voice to Mr Topping.

'Do stop clutching that bag in front of you!' he said irritably as he turned back into the room.

She made a conscious effort to relax, but in vain. If she did not get this post – and chances seemed very slim – would he drag her back into service at Springs House?

A footstep sounded on the stairs and Max Ellsky came in. At the sight of Melisande, his heavy face lit up with a smile.

'You found her, Adam! Where was she?'

'You mistake the matter, Max,' said the doctor dryly. 'She found me.' At the sight of the estate manager's puzzled frown he gave a short, humourless laugh. 'May I present to you Miss Smith, applicant for the post of schoolteacher to the immigrant children.'

Ellsky's jaw dropped as he struggled to find words. Before he could ask the questions on his mind, the doctor handed him the sheaf of papers. 'If you will cast your eye over these, Max, I will endeavour to deal with the French, while Miss Smith-Stevens fills in this application.'

'I regret they are in pencil,' she muttered.

'It is not important,' said Ellsky bracingly.

'I did not know you were Russian,' she said.

'My father's name was Lichterokowski,' he answered with a half-smile. 'Over here they always wrote his name 'L-sky'. After a while, it seemed easiest to adopt it.'

'The application, if you please, Miss Stevens!'

That did not take long. Father's name, mother's name, dates of birth, place of birth, places of education, certificates . . . An endless stream of questions she could not answer. Languages or no languages, what committee would accept an applicant who could not even fill in her own application?

At last Doctor Kingsley laid aside the papers and picked up the form.

'You do not know your date of birth?' he demanded with a frown.

She shook her head.

131

'No birth certificate?'

Again she shook her head, eyes downcast.

'How old do you estimate yourself to be?'

'Nineteen – almost twenty.' She could not meet his eye. 'They reckoned I was seven when I was left there. That was on the thirteenth of July – twelve years ago last July.'

'Date of birth thirteenth July, eighteen hundred and seventy-eight,' he muttered, writing it down.

'Father's name – blank. You did not know your father?' Without waiting for her to answer he went on: 'Stevens is your mother's surname?'

'I *did* know my father!' she burst out. 'His name was Stefan! Not everyone in an Orphanage is a bastard!'

The doctor's face went perfectly white and with a muttered oath he turned sharply away to the window, crumpling the paper in a clenched fist.

'Miss Stevens!' said Ellsky reprovingly. 'Doctor Kingsley is trying to help you!'

'He hasn't exactly been encouraging so far, has he?' snapped Melisande.

'I haven't, have I?' The doctor turned away from the window, his face once more unreadable. He drew his gold watch from his waistcoat pocket and consulted it. 'I dine with the trustees at the Edensville Club in less than an hour. I cannot possibly present your application in this state.'

'You said you knew your father?' said Ellsky softly.

'Stefan. He was tall. He had a black beard and –' She pressed the heels of her hands against her eyes until lights flashed before her, but this time there was to be no lifting of the curtain, no glimpse beyond the misty veil created by the terrified seven year old.

'It's no use.' She looked up at them, pleading for their understanding. 'I've tried before, but there's only Stefan – and – and Mary . . .'

'Mary? Your mother?' When had he knelt down beside her and taken her hand? He did not know. Only that here was a mind bruised as his had once been, and he had to help.

'No!' she said decisively. 'Not Mary! No!'

'Can you be so sure?'

'Yes! My mother was . . . was . . .' Her voice rose, the emotion raw as an open wound.

132

'Yes?'

'I don't know.' Her voice was flat once more. 'But not like Mary.'

He turned away from the haunting look of loss on her face and made a show of shuffling the papers to give her time to recover her composure.

'Your father's name was Stefan?' he said at last. She nodded silently. 'That could be either German or Russian. But you speak Russian.' He looked across to Ellsky who nodded in confirmation. 'So we have a birthplace for him.' He took up the pen and wrote in *St Petersburg*.

'Father's name Stefan Stefanovitch,' added Ellsky, entering into the spirit of it.

'And she learnt her French from her mother,' suggested the doctor.

'Seems likely.' Ellsky pulled up a chair and sat alongside her. 'Marie? Jeanne? Thérèse? Hélène?' he suggested.

She shook her head dumbly.

'None of them strikes a chord? Very well then, Hélène it shall be. Place of birth: France. Age? Young? Old?'

'I – I can't remember. Older than you when she –'

Kingsley indulged in a little mental arithmetic and wrote down some dates.

'And when you taught at the Orphanage – a pupil-teacher, I imagine?'

'No one ever called me that.'

'No matter. It looks better than a blank and it is only to stretch the facts a little.'

By the time Kingsley had finished, the form looked quite respectable. She tried to stammer out her thanks but he brushed them aside.

'You are quite certain you wish to apply for this post?' She nodded. 'It is no sinecure, believe me.'

'Perhaps you should explain precisely what is involved,' said Ellsky.

'You know, of course, that we already have both public and private schools in Edensville?' She nodded again. 'But too many of the immigrant children are slipping through the net. Sometimes the families are only here for the winter, or while they wait for a land grant from us, or from the Canadians; too often they won't register the children because full-time schooling would stop them taking piecework in the factories or the workshops. Too often the children's earnings are all that stands between the family and starvation. And yet they are intensely ambitious for their children to succeed where they have failed.'

'But without decent English, or French if they cross to Canada, there is not much hope of that,' interposed Ellsky gravely. 'So Doctor Kingsley has revived the old Committee for the Welfare of Immigrants.'

'And they have agreed to set up a school in Harbourside to give the children basic tuition while they are here.'

'Only part of the time, which will enable them still to supplement the family income.'

Kingsley consulted his watch again. 'I must go. Max, look after her. We don't want to have to start searching for her again.'

'You – you looked for me?'

'It is becoming an annoying habit,' growled the doctor.

'The first time you ran away there was the snow,' said Ellsky. 'And last night –'

'We found you gone and blood all over the skylight.' Kingsley crossed to her side and drew off the borrowed glove she had drawn over Natasha's bandaging.

'I – I didn't think anyone would care.'

'About a foolish girl by herself at night in a strange country? You have a very odd idea of us.' He picked up his hat and gloves and crossed to the door. Hand on the knob he turned back to her. 'By the way, how did you get out to Springs House? I know that Franz gave you a ride back, but no one seems to have seen you on the road out there.'

'I followed the old road through the forest.'

He nodded, as if he had already known the answer. 'You know, of course,' he said casually, ' that there are still bears and timber wolves in that forest?'

As she sat in the dining room of the Albany Hotel, mouth watering at the delicious smells wafting from the tables around her, she remembered the other time she had been here, when she had arrived, frozen and starving, only to find that the Carters had moved to New York, abandoning her even before she arrived. Even if she did not get the appointment, she thought, at least she had not starved. At least she had survived and she was beginning to feel that survival had a lot to recommend it.

She raised her eyes to Ellsky, who was putting away a prodigious amount of food on the other side of the table.

'Do you think I stand a chance of this post, Mr Ellsky?' she asked.

'I don't know,' he admitted frankly. 'If he wishes, Kingsley could persuade the trustees to almost anything. Even Mrs Patterson. But there might be others under consideration, who were not required to submit themselves for interview. It didn't help that –'

'– that I offended him with what I said about bastards,' she said, with devastating candour.

Ellsky choked on a mouthful of food and looked anxiously about him at the crowded tables. 'Miss Stevens, I beg of you!'

'But why should he have –'

'Young ladies should not speak of such things,' he said repressively, and it was clear that she would get no more from him.

It was as she slid her spoon into a deliciously creamy gooseberry snow that the answer came to her; she wondered how she could have been so stupid as not to see it before.

She had been in Matron's office, writing out for the Board of Guardians the annual admissions and departures lists. It was the year of the scarlet fever outbreak: despite the best efforts of Doctor Morel and his medical students, they had lost almost a quarter of the orphans. Where she usually listed departures of the fourteen year olds into trades, apprenticeships or service, that year she had found herself writing up cause of death and place of burial.

Agnes Strand: died of fever, age 13, buried St Mark's, Wapping
Jem Smith: died of fever, age 12, buried St Mark's, Wapping
Ezekiel and Josiah, twins: died of fever, age 7, buried St Bartholomew's, Smithfield

135

Her friends, comrades in adversity, consigned to a pauper's grave; she had found it hard to concentrate on the neatness of her hand.

'If it weren't for the medical students, we would have lost so many more,' said Sarah bracingly.

Matron had turned on the other woman a look of the utmost scorn. 'If it weren't for the medical students,' she said in her driest tones, rapping her knuckles against the admissions book, 'we wouldn't have so many inmates in the first place.'

Emmie, scrubbing the floor nearby, had suppressed her giggles with difficulty and Milly had later demanded an explanation of her.

'Medical students got a reputation for it,' said Emmie with a knowing wink. She had been twelve when she came into the Orphanage after the death of her mother who had worked in an alehouse on the river front; unlike the girls who had grown up, sheltered, in the Orphanage, her knowledge of life was wide.

'A reputation for what?' asked Melisande, bemused.

'Don't you know *nothing*?' demanded Emmie. 'Skirts. Girls,' she elaborated impatiently. 'Medical students are mad for 'em. Put 'em in the family way and then, when her family goes lookin' for 'im, 'e's finished 'is studies and upped sticks.'

It was the obvious explanation.

By the time they emerged from the Albany, the morning sun had disappeared; they returned to the harbour under a grey and overcast sky. The lake was almost black, except where the wind was whipping the tops of the waves foaming white.

Kingsley was standing on the steps consulting his watch. His steward hitched his wagon alongside the doctor's buggy, handed her down and disappeared into the building.

Down at the wharf below them, stevedores were unloading cargo from a heavy squat ship.

Melisande closed her eyes and smiled as she breathed in the mixture of timber, tar and an elusive hint of spice. She opened her eyes to find the doctor looking at her with a hard, speculative gaze. 'Reminds me of Wapping,' she explained. 'I often took the little ones down to see the ships unloading. We

136

used to make up stories about the ships, guess where they had come from, where they were going.'

'You were happy there?' he demanded, brows arched in surprise.

'Happy? No. Never that. But they did their best – and not all the memories are bad.'

Ellsky came hurrying down the stairs with a bundle of papers. 'I will say goodbye to you now, Miss Stevens. I have more business in town.'

She shook his hand and watched with a dry throat as he disappeared round the corner.

'If you please, Miss Stevens?'

She realised that the doctor was waiting to hand her up into his buggy and, without thought, allowed him to do so. In silence he climbed up beside her and took the reins.

As they bowled along the dock road, he reached beneath the seat and pulled out a thick plaid carriage rug.

'Put that over your knees. How you managed not to catch pneumonia running round in nothing but that shawl I'll never know.'

'You are taking me back to Madame Chantal's?' she said in a small voice as he turned into the main street.

'No.' He looped the rein expertly to guide the horse round the corner. 'Back to Springs House.'

Her shoulders slumped. Back to Springs House. Back to being a housemaid again. All that effort – for nothing.

'To work off my contract,' she said miserably.

'I do not think I have need of such a pert and disobedient housemaid,' he said, looking down at her with a grin. 'Nor can I spare the time to chase round New York State to fetch you back again every time someone says a word amiss.'

'Then why am I going to Eden Springs?' she asked in confusion.

'Because the trustees would only give you the position if they did not have to house you.'

'You mean – they'll let me teach?'

'Yes.' He'd taken his eyes off the road and was watching her intently.

She pressed her hands tightly together in her lap. 'Oh!' She lifted her eyes to him, glowing radiantly. 'Oh, thank you!'

'I wonder if you realise what you have let yourself in for?' he asked. 'Although it's only half the week, it will be extremely hard work. Only two breaks, for Christmas and harvest time. The children often speak no English – and they are from very rough backgrounds.'

'But no rougher than Wapping Docks! And as for hard work, it cannot be as bad as slaving sixteen hours a day for Madame Chantal. Or being a housemaid.'

'I did not realise I was such a harsh master.'

'I – I did not mean to compare you with her, truly I didn't. It's just that I – I don't think that I have the temperament for a housemaid.'

'I'll vouch for that!' he snapped. 'You are altogether too impertinent and full of your own importance.'

'If I were not so grateful for your help, I could say the same about you!'

'Touché!' he said grimly.

The horse turned off down the valley road, which ran between high pine-clad banks. She found her eye drawn to the dark green depths of the gloomy forest.

'Are there really wolves in there?' she asked nervously.

'Oh, yes. Large tracts of the north of the state are still wild. I would not venture into the heart of the forest without a gun.' She shivered. 'You really should not stray into these places alone.'

'How was I to know?'

'You had only to ask. If I had known you were contemplating so rash a course of action –'

'You would have locked me up, as you did last night.'

She thought he ground his teeth, but it might have been the low rumble of thunder that rolled down from the mountains as they pulled up the incline out of the narrow valley.

'There's a waterproof cape under the seat,' he said, as large cold drops of rain began to drive in on them.

He drew the horses to a halt, looped the reins over the board and reached behind him to pull the hood up.

From under the seat she drew out something resembling a boat cloak. 'Give it here,' he commanded. 'It will drown you.' He flung the cape over his broad shoulders and lifted a corner for her to sit under. She edged nervously beneath it. As her leg brushed against his, she jumped, her heart thumping in her throat.

'Still nervous about wolves?' he asked sarcastically.

'No,' she croaked, her mouth dry.

'You're surely not nervous of me?'

'Of course not.' She swallowed hard, trying to put out of her mind the memory of him the day she had taken the water cans up to his room.

'Then move over. I've no wish to be soaked.'

She licked her dry lips and slid across the seat until they were almost touching. He rearranged the cape until they were both covered, clicked his tongue at the horse and picked up the reins once more.

She glanced at him but he was staring ahead, his eyes fixed on the road.

'Doctor Kingsley?'

'Yes?'

'How – how did you persuade the trustees to take on a foundling?' she asked.

'Simple. I did not tell them. Let them think you've just arrived. None of them will know any different.'

'Mr Ellsky says Mrs Patterson is a trustee?'

'Yes.'

'I have met her,' she said. He cursed softly. 'I was wearing my veil,' she said anxiously. 'Though I doubt if she would have noticed me anyway. She is one of those who regards the servants as so many pieces of furniture.'

'As you once accused me of doing.'

They drove on a few more moments in silence until he drew the horses up in the stableyard. 'Can you get down without my assistance?' he asked brusquely, lifting the cape for her to slide out.

She jumped down agilely and almost danced into the house.

'Gawd! Look what the cat dragged in!' The harsh, unwelcoming voice stopped her in her tracks. 'Thought you'd be in the town jail by now,' crowed Nancy. 'Reported you to the police, has he?'

'No.'

'Blimey! Not keeping you on here, is he?'

'I suggest you ask him,' she said with a shrug.

'Ai suggest yew arsk him,' mimicked Nancy. 'Quait the little madam today, ain't we?'

'That'll do, that'll do!' said Cook, bustling out of the kitchen. 'Nancy! Get back to your work! And as for you, Mel, I should think a hot bath is what you need. Explanations can come later.'

The Schoolma'am

On Friday, Melisande drove into Edensville with Mrs Chobley to purchase clothes more suited to her position. Since Mrs Chobley's ideas as to what was suitable were as strict as Matron's, only the plainest of clothes were purchased: one navy wool skirt, one brown corduroy, and two crisp cotton blouses, one high-necked and one with a severe Puritan collar.

She had been rather nervous about going back to town, for fear she might meet someone who would connect her with Madame Chantal, but the establishments they visited were at the other end of the main street. Besides, said Mrs Chobley repressively, the doctor had sorted out all that nonsense.

Back at Springs House Melisande took her purchases up to her new room, on a side corridor, away from the main part of the house, not far from Mrs Chobley's quarters. It was light and airy and the tall windows looked out across the gardens to the orchard; she could just see the chimneys of the farm steward's house beyond the blossoming trees.

Singing softly to herself, she set her new possessions out on her bed and looked at them in some awe. In all her life she had never had so much to call her own.

She spent a happy afternoon and evening curled up in the armchair by the window, devouring books from the library; consequently she slept a little later than usual and hurried to dress and present herself in the kitchen. But here a surprise awaited her: under no circumstances, said Mrs Chobley, would she be permitted to help with the housework. It would not be proper.

141

'You're the schoolma'am, Mel, not the kitchen maid,' said the housekeeper firmly, 'and you're a guest in this house.'

'But what shall I do when I'm not teaching?'

'Whatever you please, you're your own mistress now.' Cook turned back to the range. And then, sternly: 'Come and go as you please during the day, but you don't go into the main part of the house in the evenings, not unless the doctor invites you to dine with him.'

Melisande was so delighted not to find herself scrubbing in the scullery that she was content to go along with any conditions anyone might care to impose.

Max Ellsky was aghast.

'What are you thinking, Adam?' he exclaimed. 'Do not you realise how people will talk?'

'I thought you were in favour of giving Miss Stevens the post?'

'Yes, but –'

'Well, I gave her the post. And having given her the post, I then had to find her somewhere to live.'

'At Carfax farm. It's where you put all the others.'

'I suppose you'd put her in the bachelor's barn?' demanded Adam, lips twitching.

'Ah! Perhaps not. But in town, surely? In a boarding house or –'

'Sharing a table with travelling salesmen and theatricals? How long do you think it would be before she ran off with a travelling theatre troupe?' he said cynically. 'You know very well she's no more fit to take care of herself than a new-born babe! She's fallen into scrape after scrape since she got here.'

'Then a respectable family . . .'

Kingsley shrugged. 'That would not cost much less than a boarding house and the trustees have made no provision for paying for her keep. The committee, I know, expected any number of elderly spinsters to come forward and offer themselves for the position – complete, of course, with independent means and a family home in the neighbourhood. But no one with talent *and* means is likely to take on such a thankless task when there are so many other better posts in public and private schools.'

142

'You make it sound so reasonable. But not everyone will see it that way.'

'I know that. Many people will be prepared to criticise the course of action I've taken, but I was unwilling to let the whole idea fail simply because no one local had applied for the post.'

'The Board could have paid for lodgings,' objected Max.

'Only at the expense of the money set aside for the new Harbourside dispensary! Folly, when I am perfectly able to accommodate any number of teachers in Springs House.'

Now that the library was at her disposal she found there was no longer the same urgency to bury herself in a book in every spare moment; besides, her eyes were still rather sensitive from the long hours sewing in the basement workroom. And she had plenty of ideas in her head for the first few getting-to-know-you days at the school. But she was not accustomed to sitting still, doing nothing: anyone who sat down in the Orphanage was liable to be handed mending, sewing, or a bucket of potatoes to be scrubbed and trimmed, and old habits die hard.

Fortunately for her peace of mind, Mr Ellsky turned up at the house in his buggy to take her on a tour of the estate. 'A drive in the fresh air will put the roses back in your cheeks,' he said heartily.

She ran up to her room to collect her shawl; as she came through the door to the stableyard she saw Mrs Chobley outside, talking to the farm manager in some agitation. What she was saying Mel couldn't hear, but she was wagging her finger at him and Mr Ellsky had turned quite red.

Eden Springs was situated some miles to the south of the great expanse of Lake Ontario, at the foot of the Eden Hills. The lush green plain between the lake and the mountains had its own climate, conducive to the growing of all kinds of crops, particularly fruit, which ripened early in the soft damp winds that blew in from the west, picking up moisture from the lake surface and dropping it in gentle rains over the fertile plain.

As they bowled down country lanes, skirting wide fields of unripe corn and wheat and acres of trees heavy with young golden pears and green apples, Ellsky took great pleasure in

143

explaining to her all about the farm and the way it was run. His broad, ruddy face came to life as he explained to her about the choice of crops, the rotation, the harvest they had achieved last year and the plans he had for the future. His father had been steward to the Forestiers, who had owned Springs House before the Carters, and between them, father and son, they had taken advantage of the fertile soil and gentle climate of the area to grow a wide variety of fruit and vegetables: with the doctor's enthusiastic support, Ellsky was determined to make Springs House produce renowned throughout the region.

'Do you have animals?' she asked.

'We have a mixed farm over at Carfax: hogs, cattle, sheep, chickens. Mrs Carter would never have animals near the house and as Samuel Jefferson runs Carfax so well, that was one area we were content to leave unchanged.'

After a few miles he turned the horse off the country lane and up a steep incline. From here the smoking sprawl of Edensville was hidden by the shoulder of rock to their right. She had never seen such a magnificent prospect: spread out before them, as far as the eye could see, was verdant, almost untouched countryside where the valley meandered down to the blue waters of the lake.

She caught her breath. 'Imagine!' she exclaimed. 'This is how it must have looked to the first white man. Toiling up through the hills and then breaking out of the trees and seeing the distant waters of the lake sparkling in the sunlight . . . It must have been an awesome spectacle!'

He cleared his throat and made what might have been a grunt of agreement.

'I wonder what his first thoughts were?'

'I imagine he was working out how long it would take to clear the land,' said Ellsky.

That was a little too prosaic for Melisande, but she was beginning to realise that the farm manager was not given to flights of fancy.

'Tell me about London,' he said as they set off back down the valley. 'Such a huge city! Such splendid buildings! I have often regretted that we did not stop there on our journey to America.'

What could she tell him? She could describe in detail the Wapping Home for Waifs and Strays and perhaps half a dozen streets between it and Elms Square. 'I don't really know London,' she said. 'Not the London you mean. I only went there once.'

She shook her head. Today the sun was shining brightly on the distant waters of the lake, the air was clear and sparkling and her spirits were high; she had no desire to spoil the moment with sad memories. It was all too close, too raw.

'I should have liked to visit New York,' she said. 'I read about it but – is it true that the buildings are so high they block out the sun? Is there really a huge statue there that rises from the waves?' She drew him out, persuading him to tell her of his life, his childhood before the family moved to Eden Springs, his dreams and ambitions. She laughed, she smiled and she joked, succeeding even in making her serious companion break into a grin that lightened his round face. He was still chuckling at something she had said when they drew into the stableyard and Kingsley, rubbing his horse down in one of the stables, saw them and felt a strange stab of envy in his heart.

He chastised himself for a fool, but the emotion was one he found hard to shake off and it was still with him after dinner that evening.

He dined alone; when he rose from the table he poured himself a brandy which he took with him into his study. He had intended to sort some papers relating to the Infirmary, but for once in his life he found it difficult to settle to his work.

Fortunate that the girl got on so well with his farm manager, he told himself: Max could take her off his hands, leaving him free to get on with his work and his projects without worrying about her. He knew Max was looking for a wife – well, maybe he would look in Miss Stevens's direction – although, as a successful farm bailiff, and a well-established figure in Eden Springs society, he could look higher than a poor orphan girl from London. He had a sudden image of the pair of them arm in arm; he shifted uncomfortably in his chair and poured himself another brandy. Unlike Max, he had no intention of changing the habits of a lifetime. The only time he had let a woman disturb his life . . . He shook his head and tried to put the picture of Cecilia out of his mind – it had been a long time ago, and himself no more than a green and raw boy. Much as it had hurt, it had been nothing compared to the day when the woman who above all others should have cherished him, had laid his life in ruins at his feet.

He passed his hand wearily across his eyes and turned back to the piles of papers on his desk. He sorted out a great deal of business that night, business which under Doctor Carter's tender care had been neglected, important papers which had been left to gather dust in a cupboard; when at last he left his study the level of the brandy in the decanter had fallen considerably. He made his way, rather unsteadily, up to his room, where he soon fell into a deep, dream-filled sleep.

In the far wing, Cook lay snoring gently in a vast feather bed; down the corridor Melisande lay wide awake, turning over a variety of problems in her mind, none of them in any way connected to her teaching.

Mrs Chobley had informed her that she was to take afternoon tea with the doctor on Sunday; it would be the first time they had spoken since he had driven her home from the interview.

Driving around the estate with the steward, she had realised how difficult it would be for them to conceal the fact that they had been meeting in Edensville. Not only difficult but improper, she decided. Doctor Kingsley deserved better than lies or evasions; besides, if the truth were to come out by accident, it might lead to strained relations between the doctor and his estate manager. Mr Ellsky would regard it as a matter of honour to keep the secret, so it rested with her to tell the truth.

At four o'clock precisely she presented herself outside the drawing-room door, dressed demurely in the new navy wool skirt and Mrs Evans's old blouse which, despite its age, still had more fashion in it, with its pin-tucks and pearl buttons, than either of the blouses Cook had selected for her.

She took a deep breath and raised her hand to knock, but before she could do so, the door opened.

'Come in, Miss Stevens,' said the doctor. 'There is no need for you to knock. You live here.'

Their eyes caught and held, and she knew that he too was remembering that morning when she had not knocked.

She felt again that rush of feeling that took possession of her body and threatened to betray her even as the colour rose in waves, suffusing her face. She wanted to turn and run, but she knew that she must force herself to stay. She took a deep breath; with an effort she dragged her eyes away from him and the spell was broken.

He crossed the room and held the chair out for her. 'You are finding your way around?' he asked as she arranged her skirts – so much more voluminous than any she had had before.

She looked up at him in surprise. 'You forget, doctor, I already – oh!'

'Precisely.' He leant against the mantelpiece and gave her a sardonic grin. 'Let's begin again, shall we? Are you finding you way around?'

'Thank you, yes. Mrs Chobley is looking after me well, making sure I – Doctor Kingsley!'

'What is it?' He looked at her sharply, alerted by the distress in her voice.

The words came out in a rush. 'Mr Ellsky will not tell you, I know, but –'

'What will he not tell me?' He gave her an encouraging smile.

'That he – that I – that we – met – in Edensville.'

The smile was wiped from his face. 'Indeed?' he said coldly. 'No doubt Mr Ellsky will explain why he saw fit to keep me in the dark.'

'Please do not be vexed with him, sir. I am to blame. I – I made him promise not to tell you.'

'But why?' He ran his fingers through his hair. 'From what Mrs Chobley told me, you did not exactly run away to a life of ease, did you? Was life here so bad that –'

'No. It wasn't that.'

'Could you not at least have let me know you were safe?'

'I feared you would have made me come back here to be a housemaid and –'

'And you were so much happier sewing in a basement?' he said scornfully.

147

'I was independent!' she exclaimed hotly. 'Not owned or disposed of by a contract signed by others like – like a parcel of land!' She saw the look on his face and sighed. 'I don't really expect you to understand.'

A muscle twitched in his cheek and he turned away angrily, crossing to the window to look out on to the shrubbery. After a moment he turned and looked back at her. 'And what did you say to Ellsky that persuaded him to forget his duty to me?'

She bit her lip. She had not realised how much trouble she was storing up for Max Ellsky. And yet what else could she have done?

She took a deep breath. 'Something very unpleasant happened to me when I first ran away to Edensville and I said if he told you where I was, I would run away again and if – if the same thing happened again, he could blame himself for it.'

'Poor Max!' He had crossed back to the fireplace and stood scowling down at her. 'I must tell you, Miss Stevens, you have all the makings of an unscrupulous blackmailer.'

'But I –'

'And you still have not told me what it was.'

To her relief there was a step in the corridor outside and Max Ellsky came in to join them, his face looking ruddier than ever above the starched collar. He took her hand and bowed formally over it, which made her feel rather strange, before taking a seat opposite her.

'Miss Stevens was just telling me about your acquaintance-ship in Edensville,' said Kingsley, dashing any hope she might have had that the subject had been forgotten.

'I am glad.' said Ellsky. 'It is what we should have done, but –'

'– but Miss Stevens thought it better not,' the doctor finished for him. 'She was about to explain to me just what threat she held over your head.'

'Oh, please, I'd rather not.'

'I think you must,' said Kingsley, in a tone that brooked no argument.

She swallowed hard. 'There was a house – Mrs Mason's. Madame Czestowa said – they said Mrs Mason needed seam-stresses.' Her hands writhed in her lap as she relived that moment of terror. 'Her girl took me there, but it was – not a dressmaker's.'

148

The doctor closed his eyes in anguish, as if to shut out what he knew was coming. 'A brothel?' he exclaimed.

'Yes,' she whispered.

'Places like that are just waiting for idiots like you. I suppose you just went round knocking on doors and –'

'No!' she said hotly. 'I had a list, but –'

'But Madame Czestowa sent you there. Little fool! If they had taken you in, life as a housemaid would have seemed like paradise!'

'I know.' She dropped her eyes from his angry gaze.

He crossed the room to the window, where he stood with his back to them, fiddling with the drapes. 'I hope you do not intend to treat this position as you treated the first,' he said over his shoulder at last. 'There will be no second chance.'

'Of course not,' she said impatiently. 'I will be doing what I always wanted to do.'

'Teaching immigrant children?' said Ellsky. 'I would find that a terrifying prospect!'

The door opened and Hetty came in with the tea tray. She hovered uncertainly in the middle of the room.

The doctor turned back into the room. 'Miss Stevens will pour,' he said, and set the tea table before her.

Melisande looked up at him nervously, but there was neither help nor sympathy to be found in the hard grey eyes. He was putting her to the test, of that she was certain. Was he trying to show her how unsuited she was to move in his circle?

Wide-eyed, Hetty placed the huge tray, with its bewildering array of silver pots and delicate china, plates of little cakes and slices of wafer thin bread and butter, on the table. She turned up the spirit lamp under the kettle and left the room.

Melisande opened the caddy and checked the various compartments as she had often seen Sarah Thomsett do.

'Which do you prefer, Doctor Kingsley?' she asked with a calm she did not feel. 'China, Orange Pekoe, Earl Grey or Ceylon?'

'Thank you, Miss Stevens, we will have Orange Pekoe.' The expression of surprise on his face gave her a warm inner glow.

'Milk, Mr Ellsky?' she asked brightly. 'Will you have cake or bread and butter?'

Kingsley watched with an amused smile on his lips as she dispensed tea in her best society manner, as though she had been doing it all her life.

'Have you made your plans for tomorrow's teaching?' he asked as he took his tea from her hand.

She shrugged. 'Until I see what I have to work with, there is little point in planning,' she said.

'I have arranged for slates and slate pencils,' he said. 'And of course a chalk board. You may help yourself to any books you need from the library, though I doubt many of the children will read English.'

'It remains to be seen how many of them can read and write in their *own* languages!' she said with a wry smile.

'You seem very unconcerned,' said Ellsky, who had been watching her, as much on tenterhooks as one of his bulk and placid nature could ever be, ready to intervene if she needed help.

'I have taught before,' she reminded him gently. 'In the Orphanage we had all sorts of children. I believe I shall be able to adapt to whatever awaits me. I'm looking forward to the challenge.'

Kingsley set his cup back on the tray. 'I have arranged for someone to drive you into town,' he said. 'If you could be ready a little before half-past eight?'

She inclined her head and turned back to refill Mr Ellsky's cup. The talk turned to estate matters and the deteriorating situation in Cuba and she listened with interest.

She stayed until the little clock on the mantel struck five and then she took her leave. Ellsky hastened to open the door for her and she smiled up at him as she passed.

'She acts as though she had been socialising in polite company all her life,' said Adam as the door closed behind her.

'She looked none too happy when you landed her with the tea tray!'

'But she coped. I thought she would. As she said herself, she is adaptable. Though I shudder to think how close she came to disaster in town. And at least there's something I can do about that!' he ended grimly.

Olsen rode into town that evening with two letters for the authorities, and the next morning Mrs Mason and Mrs

150

Czestowa, together with their protectors, found themselves escorted to the railroad station and on to the westbound train; it would not be conducive to their future well-being, they were advised, to reappear in New York state for the next ten or twenty years.

Melisande was all fingers and thumbs as she prepared herself for her first day's work. She had pressed one of her new blouses the previous evening, ignoring barbed remarks from Nancy about those who grew too big for their boots. Now, looking at herself gravely in the mirror, she twisted her waist-length hair up on to the top of her head in an attempt to look older, more severe. She picked up Sarah's cameo brooch and pinned it at her throat but decided it looked too smart for a slum schoolteacher, so pinned it to the inside of her pocket, where she could touch it for luck. She laughed at herself for her superstition, but she touched it anyway.

She ate a hurried breakfast in the housekeeper's room, her head full of schemes for the day's work, her stomach knotting in anticipation, part excited, part fearful, and presented herself far too early in the stableyard, a basket full of books over her arm and her shawl around her shoulders. She wondered nervously who was to drive her into town: she hoped it would not be Olsen, full of spite and unpleasantness. The morning was too lovely to be spoilt so: the sky blue with fluffy white clouds and the sun shining brightly on the orchards and the rolling acres of half ripe corn that stretched away to the sparkling waters of the lake beyond.

She closed her eyes, basking in the warmth of the sun. She had waited a long time to be so happy and warm and content.

A thrush began to sing in the orchard and, smiling, she whistled back to it as Big Tom had taught her so many years ago, before he had left the Orphanage for the frantic work of the printing-press. Lips pursed, she trilled up and down, matching the bird note for note in his joyful song. After a minute she became aware of someone watching her and broke off abruptly, startling the bird, which flew off with a shrill call of alarm.

Doctor Kingsley, dressed simply in a Norfolk jacket and tweed trousers – he rarely wore the traditional doctor's frock coat and top hat, which he feared would frighten his poorer patients away – was standing in the middle of the yard, watching her attentively.

'An unusual accomplishment for a young lady,' he said with a gentle smile.

She grinned broadly. 'Oh, I wouldn't want to be ladylike all the time,' she said mischievously.

Olsen led the gig round and the doctor took the reins and reached down a hand to help her up.

'Nervous?' he asked as the horses drew out of the stableyard through the arch and set off down the street.

'A little,' she admitted. 'Though it shouldn't be too different from teaching the children at the Orphanage.'

'Some of them will be twelve or thirteen,' he warned. 'Some may even be older.'

'So was Big Tom, and I coped with him.'

'Big Tom?'

'He was the boy who taught me to whistle. Well, he taught me all sorts of things.' He raised his eyebrows. 'Sailor's knots, things like that. I taught him to read.'

'Did he teach you to knit?' he asked. 'That shawl has more holes in it than stitches!'

'Oh, I cannot knit at all!' she said with a chuckle. 'Matron despaired of me, so I was taught to sew instead. I do that quite well,' she said defensively. 'Even Madame Chantal said so.'

'I wasn't being critical. You can't be good at everything. You have many talents, as well as a charming face.'

Damn! he thought. Why did I say that? Altogether too personal!

'Cook tells me you have no coat,' he went on in a studiously indifferent voice. 'There's one the Carter girls left behind which might suit. Behind the seat.'

She reached behind her and gasped as a dark blue double-breasted covert coat tumbled on to the seat. 'Oh, it's beautiful! Th-thank you,' she stammered.

'It's only a coat,' he protested. It wasn't even new. 'What would the students do if you caught a chill!'

'Only a coat!' she echoed. 'I've never seen anything so – so –'

152

'Here!' He pulled the horses into the side of the road. 'If you try to put it on while we're moving, you'll have us in the ditch!'

He looped up the reins, took the coat from her and held it while she slipped her arms into the sleeves, stroking her hand on the soft folds of fine wool.

'Lift your head up,' he said, fastening the buttons under her chin. She smiled trustingly up at him, a soft smile on her lips. The buttons fastened, his hands came to rest on her shoulders and as he looked deep into her eyes, a strange half-smile twisted his mouth. Then, abruptly, he pushed her back into her seat and snatched up the reins.

He clicked his tongue at the horses and, as they picked up their pace, he bit his lip in annoyance. After all these years, was there still something of his father's folly in him?

They drove on for a moment in silence, then he glanced at her out of the corner of his eye. This was an important day for her, he reminded himself. He must not spoil it.

He cleared his throat. 'There is a purse in the pocket with an advance from the trustees,' he said. He watched her plunge her hand into the folds of the coat and smiled when her eyes widened as she felt the coins through the thin suede. 'I suggest you go to the milliner's on King Street when you have finished and choose a hat to go with the coat. Be guided by Madame Brisarde: she has a good eye.'

'I don't need a hat,' she said sunnily. 'I cannot remember when I last wore one – apart from that dreadful bonnet and veil.'

'You must now. No lady goes bareheaded.'

'But I am not a lady. I am only a servant.'

'You are, at the moment, neither one nor the other,' he said harshly. 'But you will strive at least to present the appearance of a lady.'

She bit her lip.

'The working classes are very demanding of appearances,' he said more gently. 'If they do not respect you, they will not send their children. And we will have yet another generation who cannot speak English.'

'I – I will try, sir. It will be difficult.'

'I know. But I will be there to help.' And that was a damned fool thing to say. The more detached he stayed from the girl

153

the better. If only she could have set up house by herself . . .
But that was not possible. Apart from the cost, she was no
more fit to look after herself than a kitten.

He turned the corner down to the docks rather faster than
usual, clipping the kerb as he did so. 'And another thing,' he
said, giving vent to his anger. 'Unless you wish me to start
calling you ma'am, would you stop calling me sir!'

There was quite a crowd outside the single-storey warehouse at the corner of Dock and Quincey Street which the
trustees were renting from Mrs Patterson. She looked across
the street at the ragged children, some without shoes, at the
mothers with drawn and haggard faces, shawls pulled close
round thin shoulders, and swallowed hard.

'They've all come to see what the new teacher looks like.'
He paused, but she said nothing. 'Do you wish me to come in
with you?' he offered reluctantly.

'No. Thank you, but – I must make my own way. As you
say, appearances are everything.'

'You'll do,' he said reassuringly, resisting the temptation to
pat her hand. He drew up just beyond the warehouse, handed
her down and watched her make her way through the crowds,
head high and shoulders back. He sent up a silent prayer that
he had done the right thing for the trustees in taking her on.

Melisande forced herself to smile as she approached the
crowd, forced herself to ignore the curious looks and pretend
not to hear the whispered comments. She turned the large key
in the warehouse door, and as she straightened up and tried to
push it open, she heard a raucous voice behind her saying
something derogatory, obviously assuming she would not
understand.

She turned and looked the speaker, a lanky youth of about
fourteen, straight in the eye.

'The door is sticking,' she said in Russian. The boy's
bulbous eyes seemed to protrude even further in his surprise,
and a buzz of excited comments went round the crowd.
'Would you help me push it open?'

She was enveloped in a crowd of children all wanting to
help; under the weight of their bodies, the door at last gave
way, catapulting them all into the warehouse.

154

Melisande staggered, regained her balance, and looked around her with a sinking sensation in her stomach.

The warehouse had been used for fruit and vegetable storage and had not been swept before being closed up. What little light came in through the grime-covered windows picked out the rotting stalks and leaves that littered the floor. The smell had an almost physical force, stopping them all in their tracks; close by they heard the scuffling of unseen creatures as they scuttled away from the bright sunlight spilling in from the street.

A small child with a strong resemblance to the pop-eyed youth started to cry. Melisande had to suppress a strong desire not to burst into tears herself, or at the very least, to · run down the street after the doctor.

Her shoulders slumped as she surveyed the pile of old tables and chairs which had been thrown in heap just inside the loading bays. After a moment she pulled herself together and bent down and held out her hand to the little child, grimy thumb stuck in her mouth as she snivelled. 'We shall need some strong people to sort this out, shan't we?' she said to her. 'Will you help me find them?'

'Me, miss. I'm strong!' shouted one of the boys in the doorway, before turning to translate to the others, who promptly echoed his words. They spoke a variety of languages; some of them spoke broken English, but the gestures were unmistakable.

'I'm much stronger than him!' said another.

'My Yev strongest of all!' said a little bent woman, pushing forward the youth with the bulbous eyes.

'Hah! Load o'runts the lot of 'em!' exclaimed a strapping girl with an almost incomprehensible Scots accent. 'Me and ma mother'd have this place clean in no time. I'll fetch her. She's no workin' the day.'

With no shortage of volunteers, she soon had the work under way. It was not exactly what she had planned, but with the English speakers split up and scattered among the groups, she felt sure it would not be time wasted.

At five o'clock that evening Kingsley was waiting for her with the buggy outside Madame Brisarde's millinery emporium. If

155

it had not been for the coat he was not sure he would have recognised her in the slim graceful figure who tripped elegantly down the steps and smiled up at him from beneath a most enchanting flat-crowned hat with a jaunty up-turned brim.

An elderly gentleman, emerging from the bank adjoining the milliner's, hurried forward, tipping his hat, and handed her solicitously into the buggy.

'And since when have you been incapable of climbing into a buggy by yourself?' demanded the doctor, as the elderly gentleman departed, giving him a frosty look.

'Oh, it's so much more difficult in a hat, you know,' she said sunnily. 'Besides,' she went on with a mischievous smile, 'you said I had to become a lady and a lady would never dream of jumping up unassisted.'

'Your pardon, madam,' he said through clenched teeth. 'I had not thought my lesson would be taken to heart so thoroughly – and so speedily!'

'I expect you just forgot you ought to get down and hand · me in,' she said, settling her basket under the seat.

He did not trust himself to answer.

As they drew out of town, he looked at her consideringly out of the corner of his eye. It wasn't just the new coat and hat which had brought about the change, he realised: it was more than that. There was a new confidence about her which reflected in the way she walked, the way she talked, even the way she sat alongside him in the carriage.

'And how was your first day?' he said, returning his gaze to the road as he negotiated a sharp bend to turn onto the road to the Springs.

'Excellent!' She gave a little wriggle of excitement. 'The children are very willing to learn. There's one half Scots girl – Heaven knows what the other half is! – and a few others who speak quite passable English or have at least a smattering, so I've given them a group each, mixed languages, to work with.'

Looking down at the animated face beneath the feather-trimmed hat, listening with interest as she spoke of her day, he saw that the nervousness and hesitation of the morning had gone like early mist in the sunlight, as if it had never been.

As for Melisande, she was in a seventh heaven, almost hugging herself in delight. It had all gone so well: the children seemed to like her and she knew they had all learnt something useful today. The future spread before her, exciting and at the same time challenging.

'Is the warehouse comfortable?' he asked as he drew out of town.

'You have not seen it?'

He shook his head.

'It was just as they left it when they moved out. The floor was knee deep in rotting vegetables and the windows inches thick in muck. This morning we had to open the windows to read, so it was a little cold. Though I imagine the children are accustomed to that.'

'Damnation! Mrs Patterson told me it was suitable.'

She shrugged. 'She probably thinks it is suitable for dirty slum children,' she said calmly.

'I forgot you had met Mrs Patterson.'

'I hardly think 'met' is the right word,' she said wryly. 'I went to her house when I was working for Madame. As I told you, I was wearing my veil. Not that Mrs Patterson would remember me, anyway.'

He bit his lip. 'It is true that Mrs Patterson is somewhat lacking in the spirit of Christian charity,' he said carefully, 'but since she owns all the vacant buildings in the docks area – and many of the occupied ones – I am dependent on her continued goodwill for my dispensary, as well as the school. I cannot afford to offend her.'

She nodded. 'You mean I may tell you what I think, but I must not tell her?'

'Quite. But we must do something about that warehouse.'

She looked guiltily up at him. 'I hope you won't be vexed but . . .'

He looked at her suspiciously. 'When people say things like that, I know I'm about to be exceedingly vexed. Go on,' he said with resignation. 'Tell me the worst.'

'I've already arranged to clean the warehouse. In fact, it's half done.'

'What?'

'How had you thought to do it? That is, did you intend to pay?'

'I imagine the trustees would engage someone to clean it out and make it fit.'

157

'Would you mind *very* much paying the people who have already done it?'

'Already . . . who?'

'A group of mothers. Quite a number turned up at the school this morning. To look me over, I imagine.'

'I thought most of them went out to work.'

'They cannot all be set on at the canning factory on any one day. And of course some are at home with babies. They had almost finished when I left. They only stopped briefly to eat. Oh. . . .' Her voice tailed off and she looked down at her feet.

'Go on,' he said with a sigh. 'Tell me what they ate.'

'The children all ate the food the trustees had sent, then there was some left and I can't abide waste, and they had worked so hard that –'

'I can see my idea of setting up the school and leaving it to run itself was but a vain dream,' he said with a chuckle. 'You are getting me in deeper and deeper. But, yes, I will pay the mothers. And, no, I am not cross that you fed them.'

She heaved a sigh of relief. 'Thank you, sir,' she said.

'Madam, you are welcome,' he replied gravely.

They covered the last mile in silence and then, as they drove into Eden Springs, she looked up at him and said: 'If the mothers took turns to clean the school, would the trustees pay them?'

He shrugged. 'It's not something you should concern yourself about, Miss Stevens. If I were you, I would concentrate on the children, or you will find you have bitten off more than you can chew.'

As the buggy passed beneath the arch to the stableyard, the doctor looped the reins over the board and came round to help her down, but Ellsky, emerging from the stables, was there before him.

'The world is conspiring to prevent me behaving like a gentleman today,' muttered Kingsley, turning back to his horses with a long suffering sigh.

Max looked enquiringly at Melisande, but she only giggled.

As the days went by, she settled into her role of schoolmistress so completely that it was hard to believe that she had

158

ever done anything else. She looked forward eagerly to the twice-weekly trip into Edensville; occasionally Max Ellsky drove her in, but usually it was Doctor Kingsley. He shared the running of the Harbourside dispensary with two other young doctors, one from Edensville and one from Owenstown, and it seemed sensible for him to organise his days to coincide with those when the school opened. His presence enlivened the journey for her: he was knowledgeable about many things which interested her, and if he was in an agreeable mood, could be both witty and charming.

The language problems were to prove the least of the challenges that Melisande had to cope with in the running of the Harbourside school. She was faced with a variety of children, all shapes and sizes and ages, from a variety of backgrounds. There were the children of earlier immigrants, those who had been left behind, beached on the scum-slicked shores of Harbourside while their more successful fellow-immigrants moved on to brighter lands or better areas; they lived side by side with those fresh off the boats, for whom the land of opportunity was still a beacon, bright and welcoming. Others were birds of passage, merely marking time in Edensville, waiting for land grants from one of the states in the west, or Canadian grants in the new prairie lands just being opened up. From Edensville, close to the junction of the two lakes, and at the crossroads between America and Canada, it would be possible to make a quick dash in either direction.

Unlike London, where fresh waves of immigrants, absorbed over the years, had seemed to her youthful eyes to pull together in their poverty, immigrants in Edensville tended to live in racial groupings, clustering together with those who shared a common origin, a district or even a village, or else a common language or religion. The immigrants were despised by the resident Americans – themselves children or grandchildren of immigrants – and each group of immigrants in its turn looked down on the one that followed. The English, Scots and Welsh immigrants looked down on the Germans and the Irish, the Germans and Irish looked down on the Poles and Lithuanians, the Poles and Lithuanians despised the Russians and Greeks. There were even divisions within

159

divisions: Irish Protestants looked down on Irish Catholics, Orthodox Russians looked down on Russian Jews. Nor was a mutual religion any guarantee: Irish Catholics looked down on the Italians, and both scorned the Ruthenian Catholics, with their married priests. It seemed each immigrant could only enhance his own standing by setting someone else below him.

But some things they had in common, whether they would or no. The dark and crowded dockside streets beyond the school were the poorest in town; here there was no piped water, the sewage ran in open drains which overflowed in the heavy rains, and here the scavengers who kept the centre of Edensville clean and sparkling were hardly ever seen. While those with a public conscience agitated to improve the conditions in Harbourside, the immigrants saw the problem differently: 'It was a pleasant enough place to live before the others came,' was a common complaint.

By what means the doctor and his committee had persuaded the immigrants to bury their differences and send their children to the new school she did not know, but every school day, rain or shine, she would arrive to find a crowd of children aged from six to sixteen waiting outside the school. In the early days it was often an unruly crowd; one youth would jostle another, or be held to have insulted someone's sister, and all too quickly racial insults would be exchanged, lines drawn and sides taken. But Melisande would have none of this. Anyone caught fighting or name calling was sent to sit with the infants, and a morning of sitting with lanky limbs cramped at a small table with the little ones would cause the strongest bully to guard his or her tongue. After the first few weeks, two of the older students, Tadeusz and Agnete, elected themselves her deputies and held the others in order whenever she was out of the room.

She had divided the room up into two unequal sections: the smaller was for the infants, the larger for the older children. Not all the older ones came on both days – many of the poorer families depended on every member bringing in earnings – but she scattered her regular students around the room so that they could help those who could not come so often. Every child in her school spent at least three or four days working to

160

supplement the family income – that, after all, was the reason. they could not attend the 'steamer' classes in the public schools – and some of the older ones had only the one day, the school day, free. Even the smallest child worked, boxing matches, rolling cigars, wiring up silk flowers for fashionable ladies' corsages, or watching over the baby while the mother scrubbed floors or hunched over the sewing machine, fitting in as much piecework as she could get.

Some of the families were well-educated; a number of the Poles, Russians and Magyars were intellectuals who had become involved with revolutionary movements and fled their homeland just before the secret police knocked on the door. Some, like Agnete's family, were peasant farmers exhausted by subsistence farming, who had come to America to find a softer, more welcoming land to farm, one which did not demand so much in sweat and blood; others without land had read of government land grants and looked forward eagerly to theirs.

Whatever the reason for leaving their homeland, they had all come to America with hope in their hearts that this would be the new land of plenty, the land of milk and honey, but for many the struggle to keep their families housed and fed was every bit as heart-breaking in the New World as it ever had been in the Old. All of them, whatever their origin or religion, were determined that, however hard it was for them, things would be better for their children – and many of them saw education as the key to that better life.

Each day she began with a long session of basic English reading and writing which everyone, large or small, joined in. At each table there was at least one child with a reasonable knowledge of English, and she made sure that the nationalities were well mixed too. Some of the older ones had had a reasonable education in their homeland and in the afternoons she would set them more difficult tasks in arithmetic and history, limited only by their grasp of English. Tadeusz was a particular challenge to her: well read as she was, she barely managed to keep ahead of him. Once his English improved, he would be able to hold his own in any college.

All the students, perhaps aware of the limitations that kept their parents in poverty in a land of plenty, were eager to

161

learn. She taught them basic arithmetic, she showed them how to read and write, and in a few weeks she had most of them up to a reasonable level. She hoped the doctor would be satisfied.

But the school took up only two days out of the week. At first she spent her free time walking about the estate, or driving round it with Max Ellsky, when he was free, or in the library, sorting, rearranging and dusting the collection of books. She spent some time packing up Mrs Carter's ornaments, ready to send on to New York, but when it was done, she found herself with time lying heavily on her hands. Sometimes, if she could be certain that Olsen was working in the gardens, she would wander out to the stables with apples and sugar lumps for the horses.

The most sought after task in the Orphanage, one which the children would have fought for if Matron had let them, was the trip to the local dairy to collect or return the churns on the little wooden trolley. It was not just for the treat that Mrs Evans always gave the messenger – a glass of thick buttermilk or a hunk of tasty cheese – that Melisande would have fought along with the others, but for the joy of sitting on the warm pavement and feeding the cart horses sugar lumps or pieces of apple through the bars of their basement stable. She would stroke their velvety noses through the grating, their steamy breath hot on her hand; if Mr Evans or his strapping son were at home, they would let her help groom and feed them and even occasionally ride one of them round the little yard. In her imagination she rode over hill and dale, with the fresh country wind in her face, a knight off to the Crusades, or young Lochinvar's bride, flung over the saddlebow, galloping through the Border Country, her hair streaming behind her with the horse's mane. Dobbin and Ned had served for a while to fill the terrible empty gap in her life that Lizzie had left; she had had no qualms about stealing specky apples from the Orphanage kitchen for them – even though she knew it meant more black marks against her in the Recording Angel's Book.

One morning, as she left the stables at Springs House, she heard the sound of melodious singing coming from one of the outhouses. She followed the sound, opening a door to be met by billows of steam through which at last she made out a stout red gleaming face.

'Bridie O'Hara,' explained Mrs Chobley later. 'What she's got to sing about I never could tell,' she said with a disapproving sniff. 'Barely thirty and she looks seventy. Married to a drunk and works her fingers to the bone to keep him in whiskey and six little 'uns fed. You can tell her there's a cup of tea for her here when she has time to stop.'

Bridie O'Hara had come out as a young bride, to join her husband's family who had come out earlier in one of the great waves of Irish emigration that followed the disastrous failure of the potato crop in Ireland. 'Full of hope we was, Jackie an' me, an' prayin' for a fresh start,' she said, in a brogue as strong as if she had stepped off the boat only yesterday. 'But the streets paved wit' gold we never did find, nor work for Jackie. Brought up on the land he was, like his father and his grandfather before him. Oh, that man knew land, so he did. When the crops failed again and we lost the land, he lost everyt'in'.' She sighed reminiscently. 'Mistake we made was in stoppin' over in New York. If we coulda come straight up here, where there's land and fields and beasts, the Good Lord only knows what that man could have done. But in the big city he was like a lost soul. Only work he could get in New York was wit' a cousin, may the Lord forgive him his sins. I never was too sure what Seamus was doin'. Politickin', Jackie said. Whatever 'twas, 'twas mostly done in the bars and that was the undoin' of my Jackie.'

'So it all falls on you.'

'Oh, I'm not afeared of hard work,' she said with a grin that took years off her. 'And this place is a treat to work in, so it is. Spoils me fer the rest of the week, does this,' she said, looking admiringly around the outhouse, with its water pump, gleaming wood-burning stove and heated iron-stand. 'There's the guid man settin' up a laundry fit fer a quain and then there's meself the other foive days workin' in gloomy holes not fit fer pigs, haulin' me own water meself, scrubbin' me knuckles raw wit' not even a washboard besides. Is it any wonder I gets up from me bed wit' a spring in me heels every Wednesday?'

Melisande was allowed to help Bridie with the sorting and folding of the clean linen, that being deemed by Mrs Chobley to be suitable work for a young lady. It was not very demanding work but, as she said: 'At least it makes me feel I'm doing something to earn my keep!'

'Don't talk such nonsense, girl!' said Cook sharply. 'You're a young lady, and don't you forget it! You do more than most young ladies already, with the schoolteaching.'

'Then I think young ladies must be confoundedly bored!' said Melisande roundly. Perhaps you had to be brought up to a life of leisure, she thought, and determined that, by hook or by crook, she would find herself something to occupy her time.

'I shall have to mend this,' said Bridie one day, looking critically at the fraying edge of one of the linen sheets. 'The guid man's set up one of those wondrous new sewin' machines in the house for me, but truth to tell, I'm that nervous of it, I'd rather take this home and hem it by hand.'

'A sewing machine? Here?'

'In the butler's pantry. But neither Mrs Chobley nor me can get the hang of it at all.'

At the sight of Mr Singer's splendid machine, its ornate black and gold metal work gleaming in the shaft of sunlight, Mel's eyes lit up. She had only ever seen one in a shop window, but she had often day-dreamed about possessing such a machine in the long and tedious hours spent mending in the Orphanage or seaming in Madame Chantal's basement and it did not take her long to familiarise herself with its workings. She took over the sorting and mending of all the household linen and found time too to brighten up the navy wool skirt by stitching some Russian braid along the hem; one day she cut round the faded parts of an old brocade curtain that Bridie pronounced beyond repair, to produce a pieced skirt that had more fashion in it than either of Mrs Chobley's staid purchases. She wore it on the Sunday when she took tea in the drawing room and could hardly keep her face straight when she saw that the two chairs on either side of the escritoire were upholstered in the identical fabric!

Max Ellsky often drove her round the estate, introducing her to McNair, the gruff farm foreman, and a number of the tenant farmers. One fine sunny day he drove her out to Carfax Farm.

164

The farmhouse was like one she had once seen on the way to Epping Forest, a long low building, half clapboard, half tile-hung, with farm buildings on either side, forming three sides of a square round a grassy yard. A stocky black man was standing in the farmyard, throwing grain to the chickens pecking around his feet. As they drew into the yard, he tossed the last of the grain on the ground and went to the horses' heads.

"Day to yo', Mr Ellsky,' he said in a deep voice, patting the horses on the nose.

'Good day, Samuel,' said Max, climbing down. 'Family all well?'

'Sure are, thank yo' kindly.' His voice had a leisurely Southern drawl to it. He reached up a calloused hand to Melisande to help her down. 'Will yo' step into the house, sah, you an' the young lady. Was you wantin' t'see the books?'

'No, no!' said Max hurriedly. 'Purely a social visit. I'd like you and your wife to meet Miss Stevens.' He turned away to fend off the attentions of an enthusiastic black and white dog that came bounding out of one of the barns to fawn over him.

'The new schoolteacher?' He looked her over with a shrewd eye. 'Surely am pleased to meet you, Miss Stevens ma'am!' He shook her hand vigorously. 'Step 'long into the parlour. Missus Jefferson'll be 'long any minute now. She's just over in the bachelor's barn.'

Melisande blinked rapidly. 'The –'

'– bachelor's barn,' he repeated, as though he imagined she were hard of hearing. 'Redding it out for the boys. They all goan be back soon. Lordy, I cain't hardly wait to see 'em all!' He rubbed his hands together enthusiastically.

He ushered her into the house, through an airy hall to a spacious room where sunlight streamed in through long windows to shine on floorboards waxed to a golden honey brown. Bowls and vases of flowers stood on every surface, and the air was heavy with scent.

'What a beautiful room!' she exclaimed. 'And so many flowers. I don't think I've ever seen so many flowers before.'

'Thass Missus Jefferson for you,' said Samuel with a high-pitched laugh that didn't match his burly frame. 'She's surely a great one for the flowers. Why, she's already got 'em dryin' down the chimbly end, ready for the pot pourri bowls.' She followed his hand and saw the bunches of brightly coloured herbs and grasses and seed heads hanging from the beams above the inglenook.

A light footstep fell on the boards in the hall and she turned to see a slender woman dressed in a fashionable olive dress step into the room. She was very pretty, with glowing hazel eyes set in a creamy complexion, and luxuriant light brown hair piled up of the top of her head, which gave her the illusion of height.

'Here's Miss Stevens come to see us, dear,' said Samuel, stepping forward. 'The new schoolteacher, you know.'

Mrs Jefferson held out a dainty little hand. 'A belated welcome to Eden Springs, my dear Miss Stevens,' she said in a lilting voice. 'I hope you have settled down well in the school.'

'Thank you, yes.' She looked at Max who had just come in, hoping for some enlightenment.

'I have an unfair advantage,' said Mrs Jefferson with a smile. 'I am one of the trustees, you see. So I know all about you! Do sit down, Miss Stevens.' She waved her to a chair. 'I hear you have made quite an impact on Edensville.'

'I – thank you. I – do all I can.'

'My husband has offered you refreshment, I hope?' said Mrs Jefferson.

'Mr Jefferson? I –'

Too late Melisande saw that Mrs Jefferson was smiling at Samuel, and remembered that he had called Mrs Jefferson 'dear'. She hoped she had not let her surprise show in her face.

'I'll have Tessie bring some coffee,' he said, disappearing down the hall.

The rest of the visit passed in something of a haze for Melisande. A red-cheeked Irishwoman brought in a tray with coffee pot and delicious biscuits. She sipped at her coffee and listened while Samuel Jefferson talked to Max about crops and 'beeves' and market prices, but she was too aghast at the blunder she had almost made to hold much part in the social exchanges.

'You are not the only one to fall into error,' chuckled Kingsley, when he heard from Max what had happened.

166

'Most people take Mrs Jefferson for white and Samuel for black – until they see them together. But they both have the same heritage.'

'It doesn't seem possible.'

'She was a Jefferson before she married. They are distant cousins, both descended from Thomas Jefferson.' He mistook her frown. 'One of the Founding Fathers who made the Declaration of Independence,' he explained.

'I know who he was,' she said impatiently. 'But weren't they all –'

'White? Yes. But then independence – and freedom and liberty and brotherhood – *were* only for the whites. Many of the Founding Fathers were slave-owners. Jefferson himself had a number of children by his daughter's black maid. Some married up – like Mrs Jefferson's family; they are small farmers over by Owenstown. Others, like Samuel's family, remained in slavery and only came north on the Underground Railroad.'

'The – ?'

'Underground Railroad. It wasn't a railroad at all, but a system of safe houses that helped runaway slaves to get to the free states of the North. Samuel's mother was a runaway slave.' He looked at her quizzically. 'You know about slavery?'

'A little.'

'From Mrs Beecher Stowe's book, no doubt.'

'*Uncle Tom's Cabin*? No. I've heard of it, but –'

'I didn't think there was an educated English speaker left who hadn't read it!' he exclaimed.

'Sarah thought it unsuitable,' she explained lamely.

Her life soon fell into a steady rhythm. Two days a week she travelled into Edensville to teach the children, who had settled in rapidly and were making excellent progress. At Springs House she lent a hand when she was allowed to, hovering between the house and the servants' quarters, taking her meals not in the kitchen with the maids and the hired women, nor in the main house with the doctor, but with Mrs Chobley in her room. When callers came, as they often did, she kept well out of the way.

167

On Sundays, however, she was summoned to take tea with Doctor Kingsley and Max Ellsky. One day she arrived in the drawing room to find them absorbed in a heated discussion about a revolutionary new plan the doctor had for Springs House.

'I am sure Cook would appreciate this,' he said, flourishing a sales brochure. 'Lighting in all the rooms without the need to trim lamps and in summer a modern stove without the need to stoke up the oven.'

'I don't see how you can cook without a fire,' she objected.

'Look at this.' The doctor thrust the brochure into her hand and bent over her to point at each page. 'Electricity run by water power. Of which we have plenty up stream at Eden Falls. The electricity is carried into the rooms and connected to lights; it can also run an electric stove. We might even be able to provide heating in all the rooms. Imagine! Warm rooms in winter even before the fires are laid. And no more draughty corridors!'

'If it's that simple, why has no one done it before?' she asked, as Hetty carried the tea tray into the room and set it down before her.

'The heating? They have,' he said smugly, as she poured the hot water onto the leaves. 'The Duke of Wellington heated his house at Stratfield Saye by that method many years ago. Although he used a furnace. That heated the water and it was carried through the house in a series of interconnecting pipes.'

'The present Duke?' said Ellsky.

'No.'

'You surely cannot mean the Duke who beat Napoleon,' said Melisande with a smile.

'The very one. Installed a central heating furnace in his house in 1833. As far as I now, it's still working. We'll go further and light the house at the same time.'

'I thought you must prefer oil lamps,' she said. 'Otherwise you could have installed gas lighting.'

'Mrs Carter would not have gas,' said the farm steward. 'No piped water because the servants could do it just as well, and no gas because it would have dirtied the ceilings and the paper hangings.'

'But electricity is very clean,' said the doctor enthusiastically. 'A number of American cities are now lit by it. And it is now more than seventeen years since the first play was lit by electricity. One of Mr Gilbert and Mr Sullivan's musical comedies, though I forget which one.'

'But how do you bring in this –'

'Electric current,' said Ellsky.

'Easily. Max and I were just working out the practicalities.' Ellsky raised his eyes to Heaven with an expression of resignation. 'The falls will drive the generator, though we must be sure to dig a subsidiary channel for the big spring thaw. They failed to do that at Godalming – they lit the whole town there as far back as 1871, run by a pump powered by the River Wey, but it foundered when the river flooded. We must learn from the experience of others.' He thrust an advertising pamphlet into her hand. 'Look at that!' he said excitedly, leaning his arm on the back of her chair. 'Just think of all the things we could run from that power! Lighting, machinery in the kitchen, an electric stove for the summer months, hot water throughout the house, in the laundry too – even power driven mangles and presses!'

Melisande looked up from her perusal of the booklet with a mischievous smile. 'Better see if you can persuade an – an incandescent to light first, or the generator to work, before you become too enthusiastic!' she commented dryly.

'What a little sceptic you are.' But there was no stopping him now, and her lack of faith seemed only to act as a challenge to him.

'But the time, Adam, the time,' protested Ellsky. 'Surely you already have too many irons in the fire! What with the estate and the school and the clinic . . . I know Miss Minton –'

Doctor Kingsley's eyebrows snapped together angrily and Ellsky's face reddened. She looked at them in puzzlement: there was a communication going on here of which she understood nothing.

'However, I'm sure you'll find the time,' said Ellsky after a moment's uncomfortable silence. 'You always do. And of course Jefferson will be back soon to help you.'

She looked up with raised eyebrows, hoping that someone would enlighten her, but both men had fallen silent. With a sigh she picked up the teapot and poured the tea.

Kingsley looked up from the papers on his desk. Through the half open dispensary door he watched her slim figure, hurrying back and forth as she rearranged bottles and phials on the tall shelves, singing softly under her breath. She had confined her hair in severe braids today – in an effort to make herself look a little more mature, he imagined – but little curls and strands kept drifting out and he found it hard to keep his eyes from her.

He shook his head to dispel the wayward thoughts that kept slipping past his guard, and forced himself to concentrate on the print before him.

So much for his intentions of keeping their lives separate! he thought with a sigh. He was not quite sure how the situation had come to pass, but almost before he knew it, he had found her working alongside him, helping him sort out some of the chaos which Doctor Carter had left behind him. She was very efficient with the paperwork, but she had also proved very useful in the dispensary at Springs House, helping him to label some of the unidentified substances which had been left scattered around in Doctor Carter's time, and might have gone to waste, all but for the want of a little time and effort. With luck he would be able to equip Harbourside Dispensary almost entirely from this one.

And when high summer and harvest time came, he would be able to spend a great deal more of his time with Max on the estate, leaving his secretarial work to her. He'd get someone in to look after his patients, of course, he already had that in hand, but it would be a relief to know that she was keeping everything else up to date, writing up the patient's notes in her neat hand, transforming his scrawled jottings into sensible, ordered sentences and saving him from being overwhelmed by a mountain of correspondence when the harvest was over.

If the residents of Springs House thought they had heard the last of electricity, they soon realised their mistake. Within a week, the doctor had persuaded nearly all the leading members of Eden Springs society to join with him in the project, the Mayor even going so far as to suggest including some street lighting. Before long, Eden Springs was invaded by an army of workmen.

170

They made Springs House their first call. They laid in cables to carry the current throughout the house; they set up a large boiler in the outhouse and laid what seemed to be miles of piping to carry hot and cold water to the upper landing, the dressing rooms attached to the main bedrooms and the kitchen and scullery. Alongside each dressing room they installed a large bath with shining brass taps and mahogany shelves and frames and a much decorated porcelain flushing water closet. On each floor, even the servants' floor, one of the smaller rooms was converted to a bathroom; another flushing water closet, elaborately engraved with gilded lilies, was set in the cupboard under the stairs.

Melisande had never seen anything like it in her life. Sarah had often spoken wistfully of having them installed, but the money had gone before she could do it. Used to earth closets, Melisande was rather nervous of using the new closets, terrified that they might start flushing prematurely!

To Dr Kingsley's infinite regret, it proved impossible to heat the water by electricity. 'Seems that they haven't quite got the workings sorted out,' he explained after a long conversation with the engineer. 'We could have had gas heaters, but they can be dangerous. There have been a number of accidents with boilers collapsing if too many people draw off water at the same time.' Reluctantly he had to settle for a furnace, fuelled by the abundant wood from the estate.

The day the workmen connected up the boiler, Melisande ventured out to the outhouse to see for herself, causing Cook to prophesy a nasty fate for her 'if that there new-fangled contraption explodes'.

The foreman took great delight in explaining to her the intricacies of the system. 'Course, the heating's easy,' he explained. 'A furnace is nothing new. But the lighting was much more difficult.' His face lit up. 'It's the turbines up at the falls that caused us the most problem. A fascinating challenge. Fascinating.'

The maids were intrigued by the new electric lighting and the new bathrooms, but not Mrs Chobley. 'Come Hell or high water, I'll take my bath in the tub in front of the fire like a Christian!' she insisted. But the hot and cold running water piped into the kitchen and scullery from the furnace in the outhouse she admitted was an improvement.

Melisande looked up from the table where, bent over the slate board, she was helping Natasha with her sums. 'What is it, Tadeusz?' she asked.

'There's a lady at the door,' he said, the gleam in his eye telling her that it was a young and pretty lady. Tadeusz was growing up fast.

'Don't leave her out on the street. Ask her in.'

'She would not come in, not to disturb you while you teach.'

As he spoke the distant chimes of the clock on City Hall struck the hour.

She rose and shook out her crushed skirts. 'I'll go and see her,' she said. 'Will you see that everything is tidied away? Natasha, will you stay a moment while we finish off these sums? Agnete, perhaps you could wait and see her safe home?'

The older children began to look to their duties; one cleaned the chalkboard, another collected in the copybooks, a third went round closing the windows, a fourth supervised the smaller children as they began, reluctantly, to tidy everything away and collect their hats or shawls, those who had them.

Melisande, blinking as she emerged into the bright sunlight, at first saw no one; then she sensed a movement to her left. Under the broken canopy stood a petite young lady, dressed in a rather severe dark blue robe, the only touch of frivolity a delightful bonnet lined in cerise which framed an enchanting face with the bluest of eyes in a pale porcelain complexion. She looked like a figurine that had stood on the mantelpiece in the drawing room, before the doctor had had Mrs Carter's ornaments packed up to send on to New York.

The resemblance to the Meissen shepherdess was swiftly shattered. 'Harriet Minton,' said the young woman in vibrant tones, thrusting her hand forward to take Melisande's. 'You must be Miss Stevens.'

'Y-yes.' Melisande took the proffered hand and found her fingers gripped and shaken enthusiastically. 'Won't you come

172

in? I don't know what Tadeusz meant by leaving you standing out here.'

'Good Heavens! Didn't want to come in and disturb you. Vital work you're doing here. Vital. Didn't realise you were so young, though.'

'You won't be disturbing me,' said Melisande, rather taken aback. 'The children are leaving now.'

'Lead on!' said Miss Minton.

She consented to take a seat, flapping impatiently at her skirts. Her dress was very simple, with none of the fashionable frills and ruffles, but to an eye trained in Madame Chantal's cutting room, the material was clearly of the best quality.

It took only a few moments to finish explaining the sums to Natasha and then Agnete clapped the child's hat on her head, collected Mariika from the porch and set off for Harbourside.

'A long and tiring day,' commented Miss Minton as Melisande closed the door behind the children. 'May I make you a cup of tea? I am sure you would appreciate a cup of tea. Where is the kettle?'

'I – I am sorry, I can offer you no refreshment,' she stammered, seeing her words as a criticism. 'There are no facilities.'

'Good Heavens! Oh, I am not concerned for myself,' said Miss Minton, flapping her hand dismissively. 'But you look in need of a cup of tea. The trustees should have seen to that. I had thought Doctor Kingsley – but of course, one can hardly expect a man to think of such matters.'

'You are one of the trustees?' she asked, as Miss Minton paused for breath.

'Among other things. Oh, don't look so alarmed,' she said with a delightful tinkling laugh that was at odds with her customary forthright manner of speech. 'I am not here on a tour of inspection – although from what I hear, you have no need to fear, even if I were! I hear nothing but praise from the mothers of Harbourside for the work you are doing here.'

'Th-thank you, ma'am.'

'Don't ma'am me!' said Miss Minton, in what was perilously close to a snap. 'Can't abide it!'

'Very well. Miss Minton. Then how may I help you?'

Miss Minton drew a small book from the capacious bag on her arm. 'I understand you speak a number of languages?'

'Yes.'

'Then I would like you to translate this into all the languages you know.'

Melisande craned her neck to read the title: *The Fruits of Philosophy* by C. Knowlton.

'Not the whole book,' smiled Miss Minton, opening the book. 'Only these pages.' She drew out a few leaves that appeared to have been detached from the spine – a crime in the eyes of one to whom books were precious. 'And I am sure I need not impress on you the need for secrecy. If word were to get out, and the authorities interfere, then the whole scheme could founder.'

'Miss Minton, I must confess I am very far from understanding –'

'Look at the pages. Then I am sure you will understand.'

On the first page was a diagram: an inverted triangle like a funnel with tubes leading in and out of it roughly on the three corners. Various points had been numbered and at the bottom of the page was a key.

'We shall reproduce the drawings, though I doubt they will mean much to these poor ignorant women,' said Miss Minton. 'What we really need are translations of the names. Until we know what words they use – the vernacular, naturally – we cannot explain the function.'

'The – vernacular?' ventured Melisande cautiously.

'The scientific names would be no use,' said Miss Minton, tapping impatiently with a slim finger at the list of words – Latin words? – on the numbered key. 'They would mean little to the women of Harbourside.'

Melisande scanned the list in some bewilderment. 'I'm sorry to tell you, Miss Minton, that they mean nothing at all to me,' she said at last, and as she spoke, she heard the sound of the buggy drawing up outside in the yard. 'Doctor Kingsley!' she exclaimed. 'And I'm not ready!'

Miss Minton, who had been staring at her in baffled silence, started to her feet. 'Take your time, Miss Stevens,' she said briskly. 'I would appreciate a word with him.' And she swept up her papers and hurried out into the yard, leaving Melisande to tidy away, fetch her coat and hat and lock the door behind her.

The drive home was accomplished in almost total silence. As they turned on to the road to Eden Springs, Melisande ventured a cautious comment on the weather, but when she received only a growl in return, she settled back in her seat with a mutinous sniff and decided to keep her silence.

She thought she would be left to get down from the buggy as best she could, but the doctor looped his reins and came round to help her down. He held on to her hand a moment longer than necessary and she found herself experiencing once again that strange, slightly shaky sensation in her stomach as he gazed down into her eyes. Then he broke the spell.

'I am sorry you should feel unable to help us in our work at the clinic,' he said abruptly. 'Had I realised you had such scruples, I would not have permitted Miss Minton to approach you. I –'

'What clinic?' she asked in some confusion.

'Did Miss Minton not explain to you?'

Melisande shrugged. 'Miss Minton asked me to translate – I did not understand then and I do not understand now!'

He seemed to be struggling to control his temper. 'Will you come to my study this evening, Miss Stevens?' he asked, grinding the words out between his teeth. 'There are some matters I feel we need to discuss.'

All through dinner that evening in Mrs Chobley's room, she racked her brains to think what she had done that might have annoyed or vexed him, but she could think of nothing.

In rising trepidation she went to her room to tidy her hair and fetch the school register, before presenting herself outside the study door.

This time she did knock, as this was her employer's private domain rather than a public room.

The door opened almost before she had withdrawn her hand.

'Come in, Miss Stevens,' said Doctor Kingsley coldly, crossing the room to draw out a chair for her. She was surprised to find Mrs Chobley already seated in front of the desk. The doctor seated himself in his leather chair, fingers steepled beneath his chin and a grave expression on his face.

Melisande bit her lip. She wished she knew what she had done wrong.

'I have brought the register,' she said at last, when she could bear the silence no longer.

Kingsley waved it aside. 'This is nothing to do with the school,' he said impatiently. 'I have brought you here to try to persuade you to change your mind.'

'But I –'

'If you would do me the honour of hearing me out, Miss Stevens, I would be grateful,' he said, and his voice was as bleak as his expression. 'If, in the end, your moral or religious principles preclude you from being associated with contraception, I will try to understand.' His face became suffused with an angry flush. 'Although how anybody –'

'Everyone's entitled to their own view, Doctor,' said Mrs Chobley with a warning look. 'And you promised me –'

He let his breath out on a long sigh. 'I know. No pressure.'

'Contra what?' queried Melisande.

'It's not what I hold with, mind, to be talking of such things to young unmarried women,' said Mrs Chobley firmly. 'Considerin' anyways I'm hardly the one to talk, being as how my Albert and me was never blessed with little 'uns. 'Course, Miss Minton's a law unto herself, as they say, but –'

'Thank you, Mrs Chobley,' said the doctor, interrupting what was obviously a well-worn argument. He turned to Melisande. 'Pray tell me, Miss Stevens,' he ground out the words between his teeth, 'precisely what are your objections to birth control?'

Melisande looked at him blankly. 'Birth control? Is that about having babies?' Sarah would have had a fit, she thought. Talking about babies in front of – no, *with* a *man*!

'It's about *not* having babies, you silly wench!' snapped Mrs Chobley.

'But if I don't even know how you –' She stopped, appalled, at what she had almost said – and in front of Doctor Kingsley too! A wave of hot colour washed up from her shoes and bathed her whole body in a comprehensive blush. She dropped her head and looked steadfastly at her hands.

'You mean – you didn't refuse to translate the diagram on principle?' said the doctor carefully after a moment.

She shook her head. 'Was *that* what . . . ?' Her voice trailed away. 'I didn't know what . . . I – didn't understand.'

She looked down at her shoes, her face scarlet; she could never be more embarrassed, she decided, not as long as she lived.

She looked up cautiously at a sound from the other side of the desk, but when she realised that Kingsley was chuckling, indignation swiftly replaced embarrassment.

'I know I should not,' he said with an apologetic look, 'but – that was the last thing I thought of! My dear Miss Stevens, you are a teacher, an educated woman!'

'I know what I have been taught,' she said in a small voice. 'That is all. And Sarah decided what I should be taught.'

'Dear God!' His face became grim once more. 'It is no laughing matter, you are right. Such ignorance is unfortunately not rare. And when just a little knowledge could save the lives of so many. . . '. He drew Miss Minton's book out of his desk drawer and pushed it across the table. 'Let me explain,' he began.

'You will do no such thing!' exclaimed Mrs Chobley, surging indignantly to her feet. She stood her ground until the doctor had been ejected unceremoniously from his own study and only then did she sit down again, take a deep breath and begin to explain.

'There's a lot to be said for being brought up in the country,' said Mrs Chobley, shaking her head. 'Book knowledge is all very well, but nature's a better teacher than any books. Now, girl, do you know where babies come from? No shrinking now. Out with it boldly.'

Melisande raised nervous eyes to the door to the dispensary. 'Don't worry about him,' snorted Mrs Chobley. 'He's going out.' And sure enough the door to the outside closed with a click. 'There now. This is just woman to woman. Come on, gel, they can't have been that mealy-mouthed in an East End Orphanage.'

'Aggie told me –' she coloured as she spoke ' – she said babies came from out the belly button.'

'The belly button?'

'Yes.' She pointed to her belt buckle.

'Did she reckon they got in the same way?'

177

'I never found out. I did ask, but Matron heard us and we got a good whipping and – and –' And the door punishment. But she dared not let her mind dwell on that memory.

'A whipping? Whatever for?'

'For talking dirty,' she whispered. She had been twelve years old, Aggie a bare year older, and the memory still reduced her to jelly. At the Orphanage there had been times when she had done her share of mischief, but on the whole she had been pathetically eager to please those who had taken her in. The thought that she had grieved them – for of course Matron had told Sarah about her fall from grace – still made. her feel almost as wretched as the awful punishment that had followed.

'Good job she didn't get round to telling you,' said Cook grimly. 'Out of the belly button indeed! Small wonder so many poor girls get into trouble! Now look at this, girl, and make sure you listen carefully . . .'

Mrs Chobley was country born and bred, and explained everything in great detail, without mincing words. It wasn't the first time she'd had to do it either; none of the servants in her charge was allowed to remain in ignorance, for Mrs Chobley had no patience with the modern mealy-mouthed approach to life. Nor had she any desire to find herself with a pregnant maid on her hands, just because the girl's mother had failed to do her duty. By the time Cook had finished, Melisande was round-eyed with amazement. It wasn't just the practicalities of the matter that seemed to her so astounding, but the fact that men and women apparently indulged in such strange activities even when they didn't want children.

'You'll understand when you grow up,' said Mrs Chobley comfortingly.

'I am nineteen!' Melisande reminded her.

'Hard to remember sometimes,' she observed. 'Them at that Orphanage seems to have kept you in short skirts in your head as well as everywhere else.'

'Why didn't they tell me?' she said in a small voice.

Mrs Chobley shrugged. 'There's many as think it's best to keep girls innocent. Most girls only gets told these things when they marries. And only then if they're lucky, which makes for some awful wedding nights, *as* you can imagine.

178

And then the girls away from home – in service and so on – that's often too late for them. And their poor babies.' She looked at Melisande with a frown. 'Though how they managed to keep the men away from a pretty girl like you, I can't imagine. Do you mean to say you've never had aught to do with a man?'

The ready tears filled her eyes. 'I never meant to . . .' she began with a sniff.

'Never meant to what, dear?'

'Sarah said I was a whore. That I led him on. But I never did! And I only went to tell Mr Vilaghy about his wife. And he –' She bit off a sob. 'Perhaps Sarah was right.'

'I shouldn't think so for a moment. And believe me, I've seen all sorts coming through while I've been in service. Come on, gel,' said Mrs Chobley encouragingly. 'Best tell me what happened.'

Behind the half open dispensary door, Doctor Kingsley ground his teeth in fury as she poured out the tale of her sufferings at the hands first of John Thomsett and then Vilaghy; he clenched his fists as she told of her fear that she might have a baby after Vilaghy's assault, but careful questioning from Mrs Chobley soon established the truth and he let his breath out in a long silent sigh of relief. He found himself willing Cook to find the right words to put the girl's mind at rest, but he need not have worried: Mrs Chobley had dealt with generations of girls as ignorant as Melisande.

'All seems a bit strange now, I'm sure,' she said at last, 'but when you find yourself a feller, you'll see it all different.'

Kingsley's face twisted with an unpleasant grimace and he shifted uncomfortably from one foot to the other. He was finding it increasingly difficult to keep up the detachment which usually served him so well with his female patients.

'But what about – what the doctor was talking about?'

'Birth control?' Mrs Chobley sighed. 'That's for another day, child. You take this book and go away and think about what we've talked about. Any questions, you just let me know.'

To Melisande's relief, Kingsley had visits that took him out of the house for the whole of the next day. She did not feel capable of meeting him and looking him in the eye until she had come to terms with all the new information Mrs Chobley had given her.

Strange how everyone expected her to be so worldly wise because she had been brought up in the slums; if they had met Matron and Sarah, they would have understood that the one did not follow from the other. And she was beginning to realise that she was probably even more ignorant than the rest of the orphans. They at least had gone out into the wide world at fourteen to have the corners knocked off them by knowing contemporaries, while she, thanks to Sarah's proprietorial interest, had stayed for far too long in the artificial, over-protected world of the Orphanage. Looking back, she saw how what had at first been a safe haven had all too easily become a cage. Living in the greatest metropolis in the world, she had scarcely stirred more than a street away from the Orphanage in six years. Even the trips to Evans's dairy and to Smithfield and the other markets had ceased once Sarah had taken her in hand.

Ironic that she, at the admissions desk, had dealt every day with the orphans, the products of that aspect of life of which, till yesterday, she had understood so little. Of course Matron had told her about the wicked women in the dockside taverns, girls who had gone to the bad 'from listening to disgusting talk'. Maybe dusky Aggie, whose own mother had come from the docks, might have told her about them too, but then Aggie had died, like so many others, in the scarlet fever; somehow, after the epidemic, Melisande had never returned to her old bed in the dormitory, but to the supervisor's truckle bed outside Matron's door.

For some weeks she had found herself thinking with less and less enthusiasm about her upbringing and now she forced herself to face what she had so long denied: that what the Orphanage had made of her life they had made for their convenience, not hers. They had trained her – but for what? To be another Matron, or another Sarah! When she thought how Sarah and Matron between them had kept her tied to their apron strings, educated and yet at the same time totally ignorant of real life, she was shaken by the rage she felt towards them. She no longer regretted Matron's dictate that

180

she was not to write, apart from one letter to confirm her safe arrival, for fear that she would pine for London and not settle in her new life. Oh, she would settle, she told herself savagely! If only to show them!

She had been forced to re-examine her life and it had thrown her into complete turmoil. She moved restlessly about the house; for once she felt no inclination to walk out in the gardens, despite the bright warmth of the summer day. She found herself mid-morning in the library, but today even books had no appeal for her. As she crossed to the window she caught sight of the door to the drawing room and knew at once what she needed to soothe her restless spirit.

She pushed the door open as carefully and as fearfully as if it were the door to Bluebeard's chamber and crossed to the alcove where the piano stood, in its all-embracing velvet swathes. Pushed up against the stool was a sort of chest, its lid left open by a careless housemaid. She reached over to shut the lid and her eye was caught by the name on the spine of a leather bound folio lying on the top. Hesitantly, her nerves on edge lest someone come in and find her prying where she had no right, she drew it out. *Complete Art of the Fugue*, she read. J.S. Bach. Her heart thudding, she laid it aside and drew out the next collection. Chopin. With gathering excitement she found all the pieces she had worked on at Sarah's and a few more by composers she had only heard of.

She listened fearfully, but no one came up the stairs to reprimand her for her boldness. She ran her fingers longingly over the polished satin sheen of the wood, then, with a defiant· gesture, opened the lid and sat herself down on the little stool.

She picked out a few notes and the sound reverberated around the room, sparking off something in her soul. Her fingers flew over the keys and she soon lost herself in the music, putting out of her mind the worries which tormented her soul. She had not lost the fluency of expression and accuracy of technique which she had developed over the years under, though at the same time, in spite of, Sarah Thomsett's strict tuition.

She played for hours, lost in the music, her confused spirit transported beyond her earthly concerns, unaware of anything or anyone else, until she heard the rattle of wheels on the gravel drive. By the time the buggy drew into the stableyard, she had closed up the piano, tidied the music back into the chest, and scuttled back through the library and into her own room, where she stayed until dinner.

She looked forward with mixed feelings to her next day in the school. She had been forced to take a fresh look at her life and had not liked everything she had seen; although the familiar tasks of the school day would be balm to her soul, there was the journey to be got through first. For once she found herself hoping that Max would drive her in, or even Olsen. But it was Doctor Kingsley.

Melisande had feared the journey might prove a strain, but Doctor Kingsley did not broach the subject of the translations again. Instead she asked him about the reports of war she had read in some of the morning's newspapers.

'I don't understand it,' she said. 'When the *Maine* sank, the papers were full of praise for the Spanish warships that went to the rescue of the survivors. Havana couldn't do enough for them, they said. But now the *Tribune* says that it was the Spanish who sank the *Maine* in the first place! It doesn't make sense.'

'Nothing to do with war makes sense,' he growled. 'And this is just the war-mongers making the sinking of the *Maine* a pretext for war.'

'Do you think the Spanish really sank it?'

'I doubt it,' he said. 'It was probably an accidental explosion – all warships these days are floating volcanoes, with their gunpowder stores and their torpedoes and charges, not to mention the plain old-fashioned danger of boilers exploding. But it's the nature of such an explosion to destroy the evidence. I don't imagine anyone will ever know for certain. That won't stop the hawks, though. They want war and are determined to get it one way or the other, so it's a damned convenient accident for them.'

'But why would anyone want war?'

'Some politicians want land and territories,' he said with a frown, 'an American Empire to rival the Europeans. But that's only part of it. Unfortunately too many of our public figures make their money from war. Gun building, armour-plating, ship-building, supplying the Army and the Navy . . . It's been some time since we last fought a war and the coffers need replenishing.'

Apart from the odd disparaging comment about Crocker and Tammany Hall and corruption in New York City, she'd never heard him say much about politics before.

'I am dining in Owenstown this evening,' he said as he handed her down. 'Max will drive you home if you walk round to Mr Topping's office.'

'I hope you will enjoy your evening,' she said politely. Turning away as he drove off, she saw the children waiting outside in the street and her spirits lifted. The lessons she had prepared went well and the children played together without any of the name-calling that had so often led to fights. Of course that could have been due to Mrs Hedstrom, one of the mothers, who had come by that morning, as mothers occasionally did, and decided to linger a while. A hefty woman with the washerwoman's strong muscular arms, she was not one to argue with.

Mrs Hedstrom was still there, sweeping out the infants' end of the room, when the cart pulled up outside with the two cauldrons of stew that were sent up from the factory kitchen every day wedged in straw-filled boxes, and it seemed only polite to ask her to take a bowl with them. There was always some left over, and today there were a number of children missing, including Agnete. They had just sat the children down when the sunlight that streamed in through the main door was suddenly blocked out.

Melisande looked up to see a burly black-robed figure standing in the doorway.

'Miss Stevens?' He was over the threshold and in before she was half out of her seat. 'I'm Father Kerrigan, the parish priest. You'll have heard of me?'

She hadn't. She held out her hand but he ignored it, his attention drawn to the children, and she hastily dropped it to her side again.

'You're surely never eating without saying a grace?' he demanded, scandalised. 'Will I say one for you? Children, lay down your spoons and –'

'That's a very kind thought, Father,' she said, putting down another white lie to the list kept by the Recording Angel, 'but it wouldn't do at all.'

No one had ever defied him before and his jaw dropped in shock. Before he could take the initiative again, she grasped him firmly by the elbow, for all he was almost twice her size, and steered him away from the tables, towards the door to the yard. 'We have no graces here,' she said sunnily, 'for if we did, what would we use? Some of the children are Catholic, some Protestant, some Jewish . . . Then there are the Orthodox and the Baptists . . . And if I favoured one above the other . . . well, you see my problem. A school of this nature has to steer a careful path. You must talk to Doctor Kingsley about it. Of course, I know that the children in *your* flock do not lack spiritual guidance.'

The children were still sitting with spoons hovering, unsure whether to continue or not. She nodded at Mrs Hedstrom. 'Carry on, children,' she said, her heart in her mouth. She didn't look back to see whether they were doing her bidding but headed confidently for the door to the school yard, chattering on like an uncontrolled parrot, desperate not to give the priest an opening to bring up the subject of the grace once more. 'Do come out into the sunshine, Father Kerrigan,' she said, a plan forming in her mind. 'I would appreciate your advice on a problem. I'm sure you've heard the difficulties we work under in these buildings? No privy – or at least, not one we can use. And with children so young – well, you can imagine the difficulties. Quite a health hazard. Not like your school, of course. I hear the congregation was very generous with the new building.'

She took the priest round the warehouse, asking his advice on some of the problems they were encountering and praising the work of the Catholic schools run by the priests and nuns. 'I daresay some of our children may move on to your schools should their parents decide to stay. Perhaps you could let me have a sight of your syllabuses, so we can prepare them properly?'

Although he had little to do with the running of Saint Patrick's school, Father Kerrigan was only too happy to accept her praises on their behalf; he lingered on for some time, only moving when the children began to rampage around the playground with scant regard for his dignity. But as the children came out, so too did Mr Murphy. The wizened little Irishman erupted out of the back of his sheds to bellow abuse at the children, as he did every day in the midday break, and Miss Stevens fell silent at last, waiting with bated breath for the priest's reaction.

'Sean Murphy, do I hear you blaspheme?' boomed Father Kerrigan, emerging from the shadow of the wall that divided the old goods yard from the back of Murphy's broken down sheds.

'Father! Oh, Father, I wasn't seein' you standin' there!' Murphy's leathery face went pale. 'Twas only those brats of Hell I was warnin' off. This corner here's my land and always was! It's in me deeds and – But I meant no disrespect, Father. You know I would never –'

'I was just explaining to Father Kerrigan how you always used to allow the warehousemen to go across the corner of your yard to get to the privy,' said Melisande, looking soulfully at Murphy.

He was trapped and he knew it. To repeat his prohibitions in front of the priest would show him up in a very poor light. Reluctantly, he said: 'Well, I suppose there'd be no harm in them – only, see, they're not to come into my sheds. Thievin' little. . . .' He caught the priest's eye and clamped his jaw shut on the expletives that crowded up behind his rotting teeth.

'Suffer the little children, Sean,' said Father Kerrigan portentously. 'Suffer the little children.'

Melisande went through the afternoon on a cloud of well-being, trying hard not to giggle as she recalled the look on Sean Murphy's face. It was good for once to be a manipulator rather than the manipulated! And there'd be no more slop buckets for her to empty!

She was just finishing closing up the schoolroom when she saw little Mariika standing on the step, her lower lip quivering ominously. The six year old was usually taken home by Agnete, but she had not come today. Melisande swore softly under her breath. If only she hadn't been so wrapped up gloating over her little victory, she could have arranged for Mrs Hedstrom to take Mariika home instead.

185

'Is your mama coming for you?' she asked the girl.

Mariika shook her head. 'Agnete take me,' she whispered, her pale blue eyes filling with tears. 'But Agnete not here.'

The schoolteacher looked up and down the street, but there was no sign of Mariika's mother. She looked at the clock on the distant church tower and saw that it lacked only five minutes to the time when she was due to meet Max at the shipping office.

She was tempted to send Mariika to find her own way, for she liked to walk to the shipping offices by a roundabout route that took her through the main shopping street, where she could linger, looking wide-eyed at the window displays, but when a huge brewer's dray drawn by a team of heavy horses thundered past, sending a cloud of malodorous dust across the street to settle on the porch, she swiftly changed her mind.

With a sigh she turned back into the schoolroom and wrote a hasty note to pin on the door. 'Come. Mariika,' she said, holding out her hand. 'I'll take you home. Only you'll have to show me the way.'

She had never been into the heart of Harbourside before and the stench of the uncleaned streets in the heat of the summer day hit her like a hammer blow. The tenement buildings leaned drunkenly out over the streets; built seventy years before as offices and warehouse buildings when Harbourside was the commercial centre of Edensville, they had long ago been subdivided into pairs of rooms into which ten or fourteen people now crowded.

The occupants of the main street that ran, arrow straight, through the heart of Harbourside, were mostly Irish, with a sprinkling of German, French, Jewish and Italian – or as Harbourside would put it, Paddy, with an overlay of Dutch, Sabé, Sheeny and Dago. The smaller communities of Magyars, Ruthenians and Scandinavians were mostly tucked away down the side streets. Here there was little traffic, for there was no longer any commerce in Harbourside, and the ragged children played out in the road, drawing patterns in the dust, tossing five stones and knuckle bones or playing hopscotch.

Mariika tugged on her hand and drew her down a back alley that ran between the backs of buildings so tall that the sun was blocked out and they hurried on through cold shadows. Emerging into the brightness once more, they turned left, deeper into the slums of Harbourside; they crossed Bubbly Creek, once a sparkling brook, now the open sewer that drained from the slums into the lake, by a rickety bridge which swayed sickeningly beneath their feet, and then they were there.

It was dark and gloomy inside the building and there was a strong smell of boiled cabbage and damp and mould. Mariika, a smile on her face once more, hurried her up the stairs, not letting her pause for breath until they stopped outside a door on the fourth floor from behind which came a deafening clatter of machines.

The door gave under the child's hand and they walked into a room where six women sat sewing. The fair-haired woman nearest the door looked up in surprise as they entered and said something incomprehensible to the little girl, who promptly burst into tears.

'Mariika, child, what is it?' said Melisande, going down on her knees in front of the weeping child.

'Her mother,' said the woman, in guttural tones. 'She not here. No workin' here today. You take her home, pliss? We no allowed leave machines.'

Melisande wiped Mariika's eyes and resigned herself with a sigh to even more delay; they set off once again through the noisome streets.

At last they came to the house where Mariika's family lived; to reach their rooms they climbed several flights of stairs and went through another tenement, empty apart from an elderly man with a fez who was coughing his heart out into a blood-stained cloth.

They pushed aside the curtain that served as front door and there they found Mariika's mother, lying in a pool of blood in the middle of the floor.

Someone was speaking to Melisande and she came back from a long way off; she felt as though the walls were spinning round her and a hand gripping her throat was stopping her from swallowing.

Mariika was holding so tightly to her hand that it felt as if the bones were cracking; but she knew that was all that held

187

her to reality and stopped her fainting. Moving as if in a nightmare, every second an hour and every minute an eternity, she disengaged her hand from the child's and crossed to kneel at Mrs Vaasanen's side. She lowered her head and listened; the woman was still breathing.

'Run, Mariika, fetch help!' she said, controlling her voice with difficulty. The words, echoing back at her from the damp walls, sounded like a stranger's. 'Send someone to the Dis-- pensary, Anyone! Anyone who's at home!'

As the child dashed headlong out of the door, yelling for help at the top of her voice, Melisande turned back in panic to the body on the floor, desperately trying to think what she should do. The Orphanage had always sent its Infirmary cases to the workhouse; she had never had to deal with anything like this, and knew herself woefully ignorant.

The woman's face was deathly pale. Perhaps if she propped her head up? Melisande reached out to grab the rag mat, trying to ignore the pounding and the dizziness in her own head as she moved. She rolled the mat into a wedge and propped the woman's head on it, then turned her attention reluctantly to the pool of blood, trying to fight her way through the layers of skirts and petticoats, patting frantically at the blood-stained legs to find the wound.

'Let me come to her,' said a soft voice, and she looked up to see Agnete at her side. Firmly the girl pushed her aside, caught at Mrs Vaasanen's skirts and ripped them from waist to hem. Then her face too went pale and she rocked back on her heels, appalled at what she saw.

Her voice sharpened. 'Fetch the sheets off the bed. Quickly!' she commanded. Melisande did as she was bid and looked on as Agnete ripped the sheets and folded them between the woman's legs, staunching the bright blood that streamed out. With a hiss of annoyance, Agnete drew the rag mat from beneath Mrs Vaasanen's head and tucked it beneath the woman's hips.

'Help me turn her round,' she instructed quietly.

Under Agnete's supervision, they pulled the body round; Melisande gritted her teeth as the woman's head beat a tattoo on the rough floor boards but once they had her feet propped up on the bed, a little – a very little – colour came back into her face.

Melisande reached out tentatively and stroked the woman's face with a trembling hand, as if to reassure her that, despite the rough treatment, they meant her no harm. Mrs Vaasanen's eyes flickered and opened. 'Mariika?' she asked, in a thread of a whisper.

'She's safe,' Melisande assured her.

'With Tadeusz's mother,' said Agnete, looking up briefly. 'And Tadeusz has gone for the doctor.'

Mrs Vaasanen moaned softly. 'No doctor!' she panted. 'No . . . money.'

'Don't fret about that now,' said Melisande, patting her hand. In the shadow of Agnete's calm competence she felt rather ineffectual. 'It's all right, we will –'

'Doctors at the Infirmary don't want money,' said Agnete crisply. She looked across at the teacher. 'Talk to her,' she commanded. 'Don't let her drift away.'

Melisande was not offended at this reversal of roles, only relieved that one of them seemed to know what she was about.

'Hold on, Mrs Vaasanen,' she said encouragingly. 'You'll be fine. Once the doctor gets here.'

Mrs Vaasanen jerked convulsively, clutching at Melisande's hand and squeezing it until the bones cracked. Then she drew her knees up sharply and screamed, a long animal shriek. Melisande slipped her free arm around the woman, cradling her in her arms, quite convinced that this was the end. She glanced at Agnete and then wished she hadn't as she saw what the girl held in her hands. With difficulty she swallowed the bile that rose in her throat and resisted the urge to vomit. She turned back as she felt a hand on her arm and looked straight into Mrs Vaasanen's exhausted eyes.

'I not mean to be wicked. I –'

'No.'

'It was only – no more babies. I – could not . . .'

'You went to Mother Wilson's?' said Agnete sharply.

'Did – it before . . .' she panted. 'No trouble . . . that time . . .'

'Mother Wilson?' asked Melisande in a whisper.

'Old witch lady,' said Agnete. 'To get rid of the baby. Sometimes it works, but –'

189

Before she could explain any more, there was a crash of feet on the stairs and Tadeusz shot into the room, followed closely by Harriet Minton and a young black man in a frock coat.

Melisande stood by the fire, gazing at the damp patches on the wall, making faces and shapes out of them while she waited for the pot to boil. She felt totally out of place. Soon after his arrival the doctor had been called away to see to a young boy injured by machinery in the tannery, leaving a competent Miss Minton – a trained nurse, no less! – to see to Mrs Vaasanen. Agnete, seeing that Miss Minton had everything under control, had announced that she had to hurry home to keep an eye on Mariika, Tadeusz had been sent out for some tea and Melisande had taken the opportunity to get out from under everyone's feet.

She poured the boiling water on the leaves and risked a glance across the room.

With a sigh of relief she saw that Miss Minton had finished her bloody work and was bustling about round the table, her back to the bed where the pale still figure lay, her blond giant of a husband towering over her, her small hand lost in his huge paw.

She cleared her throat and carried two cups across to the couple, then poured two more and carried them to the table. There was no milk, but no one seemed bothered.

'Thank goodness you came!' said Melisande in a low voice. 'I felt so helpless. So incompetent.'

'Exactly the way I would feel faced with a class of children,' said Miss Minton crisply, sipping the scalding tea with relish. 'You did the best you could. And you had the good sense to step aside for Agnete. Bright girl, that one.'

Melisande picked up her own cup, but her hand was shaking so much that the hot liquid slopped over the scrubbed table.

'Shock,' said Miss Minton. 'Come, come, now!' she scolded, as Melisande sniffed, trying to hold back the tears that threatened to spill over. 'No point feeling sorry for yourself.'

'I'm not,' she sniffed. 'It's just – poor Mrs Vaasanen.'

'I think she'll come through,' said Miss Minton. 'She's more of a fighter than many I've seen.'

'You mean, other women . . . ?'

'Happens all the time.'

'If only I could have done something!'

Miss Minton looked at her shrewdly. 'You can,' she said. 'Oh, there's a deal you could do. If you are really sure you want to help . . .'

The summer sky had darkened from azure to navy by the time Doctor Jefferson came back. He had stitched young Guiseppe's injuries and then, as promised, he had brought the trap round to drive her home. 'It's on my way,' he said briskly when she demurred. 'I'm staying at Carfax tonight.'

'Jefferson! Of course. I never connected you. . . .' She bit off the rest of what she had been about to say. 'Ought you not to say with Mrs Vaasanen?' she asked anxiously.

'There's nothing I can do that Miss Minton cannot,' he said crisply. 'She is in safe hands with Miss Minton. And many of the immigrants do not like their women to be treated by men, black or white, particularly in such intimate cases.'

'Will she live?' she asked, as he handed her up into the trap.

He shrugged. 'Some do, some don't. Depends how strong a fighter she is. It's all such a waste,' he sighed, picking the horses up with a touch of the reins. 'You see them slipping into Creek Alley one day, you know they'll turn up at the Infirmary the next, crying 'miscarriage'. That's if they're lucky. If not, then it's a painful death from septicaemia or peritonitis.'

'Do you work with Doctor Kingsley at the Infirmary?' she asked with interest.

'Only in the vacations,' he said.

'What?'

He looked down at her, laughing at her puzzled expression. 'I'm still at college,' he explained.

'But – if you haven't qualified . . .'

'In this country anyone can put on a tailcoat and call himself doctor, if he wishes. And claim to cure anything from tumours to consumption! Unless you're black like me, or a woman. They you have to get to college and pass every paper

191

qualification you can before anyone will let you have a look in!'

'Is it hard to get into college?' she asked.

'Not as hard as it was even ten years ago. Though for negroes and women, it's still not easy.' He chuckled. 'But it's amazing how many invincible objections on the score of propriety and prejudice will melt away before the charmed touch of a few thousand dollars!'

'You are fortunate that your parents could afford to send you,' she said, rather stiffly.

'They couldn't,' he said curtly. 'But I had a benefactor. And I'm not afraid of hard work.'

Adam Kingsley had hoped for a quiet afternoon. The sun was shining brightly, the air was heavy with the scent of flowers, and he thought it was about time he had another talk with Miss Stevens.

His heart sank as he heard the carriage draw up on the gravel drive. Sunday callers he could have done without.

He watched with a jaundiced eye as Madame Jouvet, an elderly French widow who was one of the trustees, stepped down from the carriage, but brightened up considerably when she was followed by Mrs Randall, a woman in her late forties, dressed in the height of fashion.

He hurried to the door to greet them.

'Madame Jouvet.' He bowed over her hand. 'And Beatrice!' he exclaimed. 'I thought you were still with John and Bella!'

'I have been home a bare few days,' she said with an attractive smile. 'I am not receiving or paying calls yet, but I felt I must come to see you.'

'I am honoured,' he said gravely.

'You are nothing of the sort, you provoking man!' she said, looking at him sideways as she drew off her gloves. 'And if you had come to church this morning I might have been spared a double journey. Now, what is this I hear of a lady who has moved into Springs House?'

He scowled angrily. 'I see the gossips have been at work again,' he said through gritted teeth.

'The mail still runs between Edensville and Albany,' she smiled, shaking out her skirts. 'Now, Adam, who is she – and what the Devil are you thinking of to move her in here?'

He ran his fingers distractedly through his hair, uncomfortably aware of Madame Jouvet at his side and Hetty hovering in the hallway.

Mrs Randall barely suppressed a smile at his harassed expression. 'Shall we take a turn in the garden?' she suggested. 'You know, of course, that Madame Jouvet is an authority on roses? I have told her about the beautiful gardens at Springs House and she is longing to see them.'

He held the door open and ushered the two ladies out into the sunshine.

'I know little of roses, I'm afraid,' he admitted. 'But I understand Mrs Carter imported some very rare specimens.'

He offered an arm to each lady, but Madame Jouvet darted away down a gravel path, cooing excitedly over a heavily budded apricot tea rose she had spotted.

'Now, pay attention, Adam!' said Mrs Randall, with a smile that robbed her words of any offence. 'This lady who has moved into Springs House . . .'

He cleared his throat. 'But – Madame Jouvet . . .'

'Is tactfully remaining out of earshot. So tell me all.'

'She's the new schoolteacher.'

'Good Heavens!'

'The Harbourside school is fortunate to have her,' he enthused. 'Very good with the children. She speaks a number of languages and –'

'She is an experienced teacher, then? Middle-aged? Elderly? I might have know Eithne Patterson would get everything wrong.'

'Ah – no. Not elderly. Miss Stevens is – er – not elderly.'

'How old is she, Adam?'

'Ah – nineteen years old.'

'And living here?' She raised her eyebrows in shock. 'Adam, it really is not quite the thing.'

'What else was I to do, Beatrice?' he said impatiently. 'She desperately needed the post and the trustees had made no provision for housing.' A glance down the gravelled walk showed Madame Jouvet admiring a particularly splendid lilac

193

rambler trained over a pergola. 'Do you remember that girl I asked you to look for back in the winter?' he asked abruptly.

'The runaway servant girl from the London Orphanage?'

'Just so. She and Miss Stevens are one and the same. And that is for your ears only, Beatrice. If the other trustees were to find that out . . . Well, you know what their reaction would be.'

'Indeed.' She fell silent for a moment while she digested all that he had told her. 'Well, well,' she said after a moment. 'And how does she cope with the work? Nineteen is very young.'

'It's early days yet,' he said frankly, 'but I believe her to be coping well. The teacher at the Orphanage seems to have spotted her potential very early and trained her for just such a position. She had taught the younger orphans.'

'But no formal qualifications, so Eithne Patterson tells me?'

'No. But a bright and enquiring mind, as you may shortly see for yourself.'

'I suppose you hope I'll agree to meet her and give the seal of approval to this unsuitable state of affairs!'

'I might have known that nothing would slip past you,' he said with an answering gleam in his eye. 'But you would like her, Beatrice, I am sure.'

'Possibly. That's hardly the issue, though, is it?'

'She's very bright and –'

'And has an enquiring mind. Very well. But you need not sell her to me, Adam!' she said severely. 'I need no convincing that she is the right applicant for the post. And of course one understands why a girl with such talents did not find the idea of being a scullerymaid very appealing. It's everything else that I find so unsatisfactory.'

'Beatrice, she has lived all her life in an institution. She is not as capable of looking after herself as she likes to think. You were not here. I could scarcely ask Madame Jouvet for a decision.'

'Not without throwing her into a panic!'

'Quite so. Would you have had me send her to Mrs Patterson's to beg for a bed?'

'That's all very well, Adam. But you must see she cannot stay here. It is most improper.'

194

'Mrs Chobley has the care of her,' he said coolly. 'For her to remove from here now might cause more gossip than it saves. Besides,' he chuckled, 'I should be loth to let her go: her novel views on life provide me with endless entertainment!'

Mrs Randall was rather shocked by such a selfish view and told him so, but curiosity overcame all other considerations and she reluctantly agreed that Miss Stevens should be sent for.

Melisande had assumed that the customary Sunday invitation would not stand, as there were visitors, and was about to set out to her usual spot by the brook with a Russian novel she had borrowed on her last visit to Natasha at the Tshenchenyovs, when there was a knock on the door and Jessie burst in, her face red and her eyes wide.

'Oh, Miss!' she gasped, panting as if she had just run all the way up from the basement. 'Mrs Randall and Madame Jouvet have arrived and the doctor says as how you're to go down to meet them!'

Melisande looked at her as if she'd run mad. 'Are you sure you have the message right, Jessie?' she asked in lively astonishment. She could not imagine Adam Kingsley wanting her present when his society acquaintances came to call.

'Oh, yes, Miss!' Not *Mel* but *Miss*. It must be true. 'He said you was to come straight away, no arguments, and Cook said to wear something smart and be sure your hair is neat. Which it is,' she added conscientiously.

Melisande stood outside the drawing room, as smartly dressed as she could be, her hair neatly braided. So great was the sensation of being summoned, as she had been so many times, to Matron's office, to answer for some youthful misdemeanour, that she almost knocked on the door.

She checked herself just in time, bit her lip nervously, pushed open the doors and entered.

'So this is Miss Stevens, about whom we have heard so much!' exclaimed Madame Jouvet, and Melisande nearly turned tail and fled again. But she managed to compose herself while Kingsley performed the introductions and then Hetty almost immediately brought in the tea tray.

The ritual of taking tea gave her something to concentrate on for those first few awkward moments; while one part of her

195

poured water, adjusted the kettle on the spirit stove and offered cakes and bread and butter, another part, aware of Doctor Kingsley's tension, knew a fierce determination not to let him down. She managed to play the gracious hostess and poured the tea with a steady hand, though she almost disgraced herself when Mrs Randall revealed that both she and Madame Jouvet were trustees of the Harbourside School!

'We have heard good reports of your progress from all sides, Miss Stevens,' Mrs Randall assured her, relieving her swiftly of the cup and saucer before it slopped all over her. 'Do tell me more about these mothers who are helping. An excellent scheme and one we should have considered. Do they learn English as fast as their children?'

They talked about the school for a few more moments, then the talk turned to Society gossip, mostly about people unknown to her, and Kingsley watched her sit back with an almost audible sigh behind the tea tray. All in all she had borne her part in the social niceties very well, but he knew it was with something approaching relief that she rose to bid them farewell.

'A most pleasant young lady, Adam,' said Mrs Randall as her host handed Madame Jouvet into the carriage. 'Intelligent, but I hope not above a good gossip about fashion?'

'She is not normally quite so quiet,' he replied.

'The natural hesitation of a younger lady playing hostess to those senior to her. And, of course, judging by the clothes she is wearing, she has not the experience of fashion to venture an opinion.'

'I left all that to Mrs Chobley,' he said off-handedly.

'That, Adam, is obvious!' she said, in tones perilously close to a snap. She permitted herself to be handed into the carriage alongside her friend, and settled her fashionably full skirts around her. 'I shall call next Sunday morning to take Miss Stevens to church,' she said decisively. 'We should like to get to know her a little better, should we not, Ermine?'

Madame Jouvet smiled thinly. 'You must arrange one of your picnic parties, my dear Beatrice,' she pronounced. 'And soon, I think, before the harvest is upon us.'

Melisande did not have much time to muse on her first foray into Edensville Society. On the next schoolday she was fetching the chalk from the cupboard and chatting in low tones to Mrs Walchinski about Mrs Vaasanen while the children settled round the tables when she became aware of scufflings and suppressed giggles behind her.

She turned round, vexed at this unusual behaviour, and was brought up short by the sight of a tall, stooped man with a long black beard and a heavy black and white shawl, not unlike a blanket, around his shoulders, standing just inside the door.

'Good day to you, sir,' she said, laying aside the chalk. Some of the children scuffled to their feet and Tadeusz said quietly: 'It's Rabbi Benjamin, Miss Stevens.'

'Good heavens. I – I mean –' She pulled herself together. 'Welcome to the Harbourside School, Rabbi Benjamin,' she said.

Was that how you addressed a Rabbi? she wondered, in a moment of panic. Benjamin might be his first name, in which case it was a little over familiar of her to use it! How *did* you address a Rabbi? Without thinking, she held out her hand, then wished she hadn't. After all, Father Kerrigan had ignored it. Perhaps ministers did not shake hands, she thought dubiously. She had never come into contact with any but the Minister at St Mark's, and that only rarely. And he had ignored her, as he ignored all the orphans, as a matter of course.

'Miss Stevens.' He took her hand with a considered grace and held it a moment. 'I am delighted to meet you,' he said, his dark eyes lighting up with genuine pleasure. 'We have heard a great deal about you.'

'Really?' She saw out of the corner of her eye Tadeusz shuffling his feet uncomfortably, and smiled. 'Will you take a seat – er – Rabbi?' she said weakly. 'I must just set the children some work. Tadeusz, would you help the little ones?'

'Come, Tadeusz,' said the Rabbi. 'Together we put out the slates. Then you will supervise while I talk to Miss Stevens about education.'

She might have imagined it, but she thought Tadeusz scowled.

She found Rabbi Benjamin an amusing visitor, with very definite ideas on children and their education. Unlike Father

Kerrigan he did not expect them to start with a grace or a prayer. 'Religious observance is hardly possible with such a cross-section,' he said with a sigh. 'Of course, right and wrong are universal. But it would be unreasonable to expect you to. oversee the children's prayers. No, that is for us.'

He went on to chat with her of the difficulties of teaching so wide a range of abilities and languages.

'I can do no more than give them a basic grounding while they learn English,' she admitted frankly. 'Most of them will not stay here long enough to go further. And those that do will enrol in the public schools once their English is sufficiently improved.'

He shook his head. 'Too many of these poor people need their children to go out to work,' he said mournfully. 'For some this will be their only chance. But every day they are here is a bonus for them. For they will make their home in America, most of them; maybe not here, though, where their kinfolk are. Maybe even somewhere where there is no one to speak Yiddish or Italian with. And without English, they will be lost, like the lamb without the shepherd.'

He was particularly interested in the work done by the older children and Melisande showed him the books she was reading with Agnete and Tadeusz and Sophia.

'Agnete is not here today,' she told the Rabbi, 'But I can show you Tadeusz's work.'

The Rabbi made a funny little sound between his teeth. 'I know Tadeusz's work well,' he said, ruffling the boy's hair, much to his annoyance. 'I tutored him a while before the school opened. Oh, I know well what great talents this young man has.'

There was no doubt about it: Tadeusz scowled.

'We should discuss what you are going to do with your talents,' began the Rabbi. 'Perhaps Miss Stevens –'

Tadeusz shot his chair back, his face suffused with angry colour. 'It's no one's business but mine!' he said harshly. 'And if you think you can talk my parents round . . . !' His voice broke and he rushed out of the room.

'I'm very sorry,' said Melisande, startled. 'It's not like Tadeusz at all. I'm sure he will apologise.'

He patted her arm. 'Another time we talk about Tadeusz,' he said comfortably. 'For now, I keep you too long from your class.'

When the Rabbi at last left, Melisande looked for the boy, but he was nowhere to be found. She had no time to do anything about that, for hot on the heels of the Rabbi came the funereal figure of the Lutheran minister, Mr Larssen, followed by Father Kyril, the Orthodox priest, who kept his distance from her as if he felt she would contaminate him, bellowing at her from the other side of the room, and Mr Hamilton, the young Scots Calvinist minister who in contrast was eager to press on her the details of the strict curriculum followed by the children at the school run by his mother. He was more difficult to get rid of than the others and watched her with a strange glow in his eyes as she went about her work with the children. She was glad when he went; he made her feel even more uncomfortable than Father Kyril.

Mrs Randall's proposed picnic turned into a bathing party, to which were invited the residents of Springs House, Madame Jouvet, her niece and her niece's fiancé, who were on a visit from Quebec.

The weather was kind to them, the day dawning clear and warm. Mrs Randall had insisted that Max Ellsky, a particular favourite of hers, join their party: 'For you know full well that once the harvest starts, there'll be no rest for either of you!' The three of them set out in the open carriage, driven by Olsen in a smart dark driving costume, to Mrs Randall's house, which stood foursquare to the elements on a bluff above the lake, a few miles from the main Edensville road.

Mrs Randall greeted them enthusiastically and once the introductions had been made, led the party down a winding path that ran through gardens planted in the English style, to a wide, curving natural beach where a small summerhouse had been built, set back into the shelter of the cliff and affording magnificent views across the lake towards the Canadian shore.

Melisande, following behind Madame Jouvet and her niece, looked enviously at the delicate crepon dress with rustling silk petticoats in which Genevieve made her dainty way down the path, and the matching parasol held carefully above her head by her fiancé, a weak-chinned young man much given to fulsome compliments. She did not envy Genevieve the fiancé, rather wondered how she could bear such nonsense.

Pierre Vaux was fastidiously dressed in white flannels and a loud striped blazer and straw hat. The two men from Springs House were equally casually dressed in white flannel trousers and shirts, but Max's more subdued striped blazer and Adam Kingsley's navy flannel jacket served only to make Pierre's outfit seem extremely affected. The contrast in niceness of taste was even more pointed when, as the sun rose higher in the sky, Mrs Randall gave her permission for the gentlemen to remove their jackets. Pierre was wearing a full-sleeved shirt with a deep-pointed Shakespeare collar; together with his carefully oiled waving hair this was obviously intended to give him a poetic appearance, but it failed sadly, due to an unfortunate tendency to corpulence.

The picnic baskets had been brought down earlier to the summerhouse, and the tables and chairs set out on the verandah. 'Why do not you all take a turn along the shore while Ermine and I lay out the picnic?' suggested Mrs Randall.

'I shall not go,' declared Genevieve. 'The sun is *so* bad for one's skin and I do so abhor a freckle.' She sat on a swing seat in the shade of the summerhouse and prepared to be bored.

'But I am sure that Miss Stevens would love to see the view,' said Pierre, leaping between the two women and holding out his arms to them.

'You will come, won't you, Miss Stevens?' said Max, stepping around Vaux to offer Melisande his arm.

'Miss Stevens will not at all wish to go,' snapped Genevieve. 'The sun is far too hot and all those pebbles turn one's ankles so.'

Melisande had no desire to see her day mapped out by the languid beauty, but nor did she wish to find herself in the middle of an argument. While Pierre and Max stepped round one another, trying to persuade the two ladies to come, Adam Kingsley put up Mrs Randall's parasol and, linking his free arm in Melisande's, walked off with her on his arm.

'Actions speak louder than words,' he said with a smile, squeezing her arm.

She could scarcely suppress the shiver that ran through her at his touch; for a moment she could think of nothing to say, then, recalling Sarah's strictures about immoral behaviour, withdrew her arm under the pretext of going down to the water's edge.

'I cannot imagine why Miss Jouvet would not come!' she said, her voice once more under control. Turning her flushed face to the cool breeze she danced her way down to the water's edge, where little waves rattled musically over the pebbles, lapping over them and then swishing softly back again. She flung her head back and breathed in lungfuls of the fresh cool air. 'This is wonderful!'

'Ah, but beaches are not *à la mode* this year,' he said gravely, catching up with her and taking her arm again before she could withdraw it. 'Not at all.'

'I don't see that fashion can have anything to say about how one enjoys oneself!' she exclaimed in lively astonishment.

'My dear Miss Stevens, how can you say such a thing! I am appalled. One simply must be a slave to fashion. It rules us all. You must know that tennis parties have quite replaced beach picnics this year. *Everyone* is having them. And of course one plays baccarat not whist. Whist is quite *passé*. Balls, not dinners. And at house parties, one must get up concerts this year, not amateur theatricals . . .'

'You are laughing at me,' she said uncertainly.

'Not at you, Miss Stevens,' he said, looking at her with a warm light in his grey eyes. 'With you, I hope.'

They stopped frequently to look at interesting pebbles washed smooth by the endless action of the water, and pieces of driftwood twisted into fantastic shapes. Just before they turned back, Max and Pierre caught up with them, and Melisande was hard put to it not to laugh out loud at some of Pierre Vaux's sillier sallies; she thought it wrong that he should make her such extravagant compliments when he was engaged to Genevieve, but he knew more of the world than she; perhaps that was how Society worked. It seemed to her very odd. Since he clearly held himself to be a man of the world, she did not want to hurt his feelings, so she tried to

201

steer the conversation into a more sensible vein. In this she was ably assisted by Max Ellsky. Adam Kingsley took little part in the general social chatter, contenting himself with watching her reactions to the other two. He linked his arm with hers once more when they turned back, and showed no signs of being willing to relinquish her to Max or Pierre.

When they returned to the summerhouse, they found the table on the verandah set with a crisp damask cloth and covered with a mouthwatering selection of dishes, cold meats and salads of all kinds, flanked by crisp fragrant bread baked by Mrs Randall's cook. Doctor Kingsley poured sparkling wine into crystal glasses and they set to with an appetite engendered by the walk in the fresh air.

'Really, Pierre!' scolded Miss Jouvet as her fiancé helped her to a selection of food. 'What are you thinking of? I cannot possibly eat so much!'

'It's the fashion to eat sparingly this year,' said Adam *sotto voce*, as he handed Melisande a glass of wine.

She almost burst out laughing and had to bite her lip as she turned back to make polite conversation to Miss Jouvet.

Even now she found it difficult not to stare wide-eyed at the spread of food that was produced for each meal; it scarcely seemed proper to eat so much and so well, and of such a variety, when the inhabitants of Harbourside or the inmates of the Orphanage could have lived for a month on it, but she enjoyed a healthy appetite and found it hard to resist the delicacies that were offered to her. She took a cautious sip of the wine – Mrs Chobley had never offered her anything but fruit cordial – but the bubbles tickled her nose and made her feel as though she wanted to sneeze, so she set it down again. Kingsley, seeing her reaction, reached out without comment and replaced the glass with one of Madame Jouvet's chilled lemonade while everyone else's attention was on a story Max was telling.

A selection of savouries and cakes succeeded the salads. Mrs Randall pressed them all to fill their plates, but Miss Jouvet was adamant in her refusal.

'I myself,' she stated in a voice which brooked no argument, 'am banting, as is my dear friend Miss Mabberly. You are sure to have met her,' she said to Melisande.

'I – I don't think so. I –'

But Miss Jouvet had lost interest in Melisande. 'I am sure that the sun has moved around!' she complained pettishly. 'There is not room to put up my parasol. One of the gentlemen must change seats with me.'

Pierre was slow to take the hint, but Max jumped to his feet, nothing loth to exchange a seat between Mrs Randall and Pierre for one next to Melisande. While Madame Jouvet began a long and tedious tale of a friend of hers who could not abide the sun, her niece was already half way across the verandah, pausing only to take a generous portion of almond cake from the delicate rose-sprigged plate as she passed by the table.

Melisande looked up and caught Adam's eye as he came out of the summerhouse with a fresh bottle of wine from the cooler; he was struggling to keep a straight face, his eyes brimful of laughter. She thought it best to look away quickly; his laughter was infectious.

Max paused to hand Miss Jouvet across to his chair, but by the time he crossed the room, Adam had already taken the empty chair next to Melisande. Max had to content himself with talking to his hostess.

'What does she mean, she's banting?' Melisande asked Kingsley, under cover of the conversation.

'You would never guess it,' said Adam frankly, 'but it's a way of eating.'

'Eating extra, as Mrs Chobley made me do?' she said, perplexed.

He shook his head, chuckling. 'No. Far from it. It's a fashionable system of dieting. It was invented by William Banting, a London coffin-maker so obese he could not tie his own shoe-laces. His good work has now, alas, been distorted into a fad whereby overfed ladies delude themselves they can keep or regain their unhealthy handspan waists by pretending to eat less. They don't, of course,' he said scathingly. 'But it occupies their minds.'

Melisande watched round-eyed as Pierre helped his fiancée to the rich desserts set out in crystal bowls. She did not think she would ever understand Society.

After luncheon the servants came down the path to clear away and the two older ladies exercised the privilege of age

203

and retired to the summerhouse to doze in the shade. Conversation was desultory among the others, since the harvest and the Harbourside school were dismissed by Miss Jouvet as 'too, too provincial', the extension of the war in Cuba to the Philippines as 'too, too horrid', and neither Max nor Melisande was able to join in a discussion on fashion.

To Melisande's dismay, Max and Adam, bored, decided to go down to the water's edge to see how warm the water was; she felt bereft without them.

'And so you have only recently come to America, Miss Stevens?' observed Miss Jouvet, fanning herself languidly. 'My aunt tells me that you have done wonders at the school. Did you teach in England?' She sat up abruptly, a look of interest on her face. 'You must tell us about the fashions in England,' she commanded. 'One longs to hear the latest. Not of course, quite up to Paris. Still, the old world, you know . . .'

Fortunately Miss Jouvet never stopped speaking long enough to hear the answer, but Melisande was beginning to feel quite hunted.

'Tell me, Miss Stevens, shall your parents be joining you?' she went on.' 'They are relations of Doctor Kingsley's, one imagines. Tell me –'

To Melisande's relief, Mrs Randall emerged on to the verandah.

'Now then, you young people, who is ready for a swim?' she demanded briskly. 'I should imagine the water is warm enough by now. And it is quite a time since we ate, is it not, Adam?'

'Quite long enough,' he confirmed, coming back up the beach to the verandah with Max.

'I don't think I shall bathe today,' said Miss Jouvet languidly. 'I daresay one of the gentlemen will keep me company.' She turned her limpid gaze on Doctor Kingsley, but he affected not to have heard and carried on talking to Max.

'We shall change in here,' said Mrs Randall, who had no intention of letting Genevieve spoil her little party. ' The gentlemen can change behind the rocks.'

Max had already set off towards the little outcrop of rocks half way along the beach, and Adam set off after him.

'Pierre will stay and bear me company,' said Pierre's affianced bride, robbed of any other prey.

'Dearest Genevieve,' fluted Pierre, 'you hardly need me while you have your aunt to keep you company. By Jove! It has been a long time since I tried bathing and I do not intend to pass up the opportunity on such a splendid day!'

'If you will come in with me, dear child, we will dress,' said Mrs Randall, drawing Melisande into the summerhouse before Genevieve could detain her.

'But I don't have –'

'– a costume? Of course you do not. I have one of my daughter's costumes for you. Have you ever tried sea bathing?'

'No. Never.' She shivered a little. The prospect of the cool water was inviting and yet at the same time terrifying.

'I may be prejudiced,' said Mrs Randall, 'but I think you will find the experience delightful.' She led Melisande into the inner room of the summerhouse where two screens had been set up. Beside them two strange outfits hung on hooks on the wall. Mrs Randall directed Melisande to change behind the nearest screen. 'Tell me when you are ready,' she said with a smile. 'I shall have to be your maid. And you in turn will have to help me with the buttons on my costume.'

Melisande had never seen such an eccentric form of clothing. The costume, which consisted of bodice and trousers made in one in a sort of serge material, reached to the knees, with a multitude of buttons to do up at the back and a belted tunic with red and white ribbons and a sailor collar to go over the whole to disguise the way in which the undergarment clung to the figure.

'How can anyone wear such a bizarre costume?' she asked in amazement. 'I don't wish to be rude, but –'

'Oh, this is nothing,' said Mrs Randall with a laugh, her voice muffled in the layers of her dress. 'If we were bathing in England, then we would have to wear something far more voluminous, and cover up our ankles too. When I was in Brighton soon after I married my late husband – that's where his cousin George first introduced us to Adam's family, of course – we used to have to wear virtually full dress to bathe, petticoats and all! *And* we had to take a bathing machine to

205

carry us out away from the shore, so that there was no risk of the gentlemen seeing us. Even so, some of the young rakes used to walk along the sea front with spy glasses in the hope of spotting some poor female floundering in the water. Thank goodness over here we have so much more freedom.'

'But – can you actually swim?' asked Melisande as she fastened the tiny buttons down the back of Mrs Randall's costume, which resembled hers, though with more frills and flounces on the over-tunic to provide a more complete disguise of the undergarment. 'I don't see how it is possible to stay afloat. I'm sure I shall sink to the bottom!'

'The water will hold you up to a degree. You have only to propel yourself through the water by kicking out with your arms and legs. I think it a very important skill to have, living as we do, so close to the water.'

'Does everyone here swim?'

'By no means. And many in society would think it slightly shocking to have a mixed bathing party as we have today. I taught my children to swim when they were quite young, for children are so adventurous, you know. Usually it is only the young who swim, but I find the exercise so invigorating that I should be loth to give it up. I swim often in the summer – and shall do so until I feel too old for it!'

They emerged from the summerhouse, Melisande very conscious of her legs, bare below the knees, and the lack of enveloping folds of cloth. On the verandah Madame Jouvet had dozed off and her niece was sulking, pretending to read a copy of *Harper's* and taking no notice of the swimming party.

They picked their way across the pebbles to the water's edge. Mr Vaux was splashing in the shallows and when he stood up to greet them, Melisande could hardly restrain a chuckle, for the close-fitting combination garment, almost identical to her own but that it lacked the disguising over-tunic, was not designed to flatter a slight paunch and narrow drooping shoulders.

The water against her ankles was deliciously cool after the heat of the day and the stickiness of stockings and high buttoned boots, and she was not at all reluctant to be led slowly into the deeper water where she watched with fascination as her hostess lay on top of the water and swam around her young friend with effortless strokes.

'Just float on the water,' she said, catching Melisande's hands and towing her along. But when the water caught her face, she spluttered and panicked and grabbed Mrs Randall for support. The two of them ended up floundering in the depths, trying to find their feet again, for Mrs Randall was somewhat shorter than her pupil.

They found their feet and rose from the waves. 'Perhaps I'll go back to the shore,' said Melisande, coughing and spluttering.

'I will see you safely back,' said a voice behind her. She whirled to see Adam Kingsley, a sharp contrast to Pierre Vaux, the wool costume showing his strong muscular body and broad shoulders to perfection. 'Leave her with me, Beatrice,' he said, an amused smile playing about his lips. 'I'll see her safe back. Max has swum out to the island,' he said as she hesitated. 'He's longing to have a race back.'

They watched Beatrice Randall launch herself towards the island with an energetic surge; as the waves from her departure threatened to swamp Melisande, Adam stepped coolly behind her and she gasped as he caught her round the waist.

'Close your mouth,' he said, aware of her consternation; how could he not be when he was experiencing the same sensations himself? He was beginning to think that those who denounced mixed bathing as immoral had a point. He had never thought so before, but then he'd never swum in company with anyone who had such a dramatic effect on him. He took a deep breath to steady the rush of emotions that threatened to swamp him, lifted her easily, clear off the sand, and towed her for some distance through the water.

'But you told Mrs Randall you'd take me back!' she wailed, panic creeping into her voice as she realised he had taken her even further out from the shore.

'No,' he said calmly, holding her firmly around the waist, for although he could reach the bottom, she was not quite as tall as he. 'I told her I would see you safely back. I thought you might welcome a challenge, but if you'd rather give up, I'll take you back to be bored in the shallows,' he said, a note of scorn in his voice. 'You can flounder about there quite happily with Pierre Vaux. I must admit, though, I thought you had more backbone.'

She scowled at him, but behind the scowl he could see pride and fear warring for supremacy. It wouldn't be like her to admit defeat.

'It's just – I *am* scared,' she said, a note of panic creeping into her voice. 'I can't pretend I'm not. The minute you let me go, I'll go under, I know I will.'

'Not if you do as I show you.' He drew her gently forward and held her, one hand under her chin and the other beneath her waist, until she was lying on the water.

He took a deep breath, for the feel of her against his hands, with nothing but a thin layer of wool between them, was having an effect on him that he found hard to ignore. His customary detachment, trained into him over the years, had deserted him.

'The water will hold you up,' he said hoarsely. 'Now – kick your legs.'

It took some time, for he guessed that she too was distracted by the situation, but at last she did as he bade her, moving gently through the water, encouraged by his support.

Twice she clutched at him in panic until he threatened to take her back to the shallows if she did it again. That enraged her, as he knew it would, but it also made her even more determined. She gritted her teeth and launched herself once more; by the time Max and Mrs Randall came back from the island, she was kicking her way quite strongly through the water and had lost a great deal of her fear.

Adam was relieved when Max came back with a flat piece of wood for her to use as a float; he was finding it difficult to keep his hands under control. When Beatrice offered to show his pupil how to hold her breath and exhale under the water, he stepped aside gratefully.

Melisande was a fast learner and once Beatrice Randall was confident that the girl was making good progress and could be left, she challenged Adam to a race out to the island, which he speedily accepted. They were swimming neck and neck when he became aware of someone else swimming behind them. He turned and looked over his shoulder, aware as he did so that Beatrice was surging ahead, and saw Melisande kicking valiantly along in their wake, quite carried away by the ease with which she travelled with the float. He swore under his breath, for Max was nowhere in sight and he knew he would have to turn back to see her to shallower water.

She did not need the angry gesture to turn her back; she knew from the look on his face that he was furious.

'What the devil do you think you're doing out here!' he demanded. 'Get back into the shallows! Now!'

'I – I'm sorry,' she panted, when at last they reached a place where she could touch the sandy bottom. 'I hadn't realised how far out I had gone.'

'What good is sorry if you get yourself drowned – and most likely someone else too, trying to save you!' he said angrily, unmoved by the penitence in her troubled green eyes. 'The tides beyond the island are very strong and even on the shore side the current is deceptive. The water here is fresh from the Niagara falls and if you once get swept out, there's no hope for you.' He saw her lip tremble but forced himself to carry on. 'So if any bright young spark tries to persuade you to go out of your depth, don't listen to him! Is that clear?'

'But I don't know any!'

'But you might in future. So for once in your life, please take advice!'

'What the devil else have I done all my life?' she snapped back. For a moment they stared at each other in silent fury, then she turned back to the shore and, float held out in front of her, kicked her way back to the shallows where, for a penance, she bore with Pierre Vaux's silly remarks until the others returned.

Kingsley swam out to the island and back, exercising his anger away. He need not have snapped at her quite so much, he told himself. A quiet rebuke would have sufficed. She was, after all, no more than a child in some matters, despite her adult years. A word of apology might be called for, he decided. He arrived back in the shallows just as Melisande was leaving the water. In spite of the over-tunic, the wet serge costume clung heavily to her slim figure as she made her way to the wrap which had been left out for her by the water's edge. It was not gentlemanly to stare, but he could not drag his eyes away from the ripe curves thrown into stark relief by the wet and clinging material. He opened his mouth to speak but only a strangled croak came out. The apology, he decided, would have to wait.

When they had changed and rested a little, they played beach tennis and French bowls and collected more shells for Madame Jouvet, who decorated picture and photograph frames with them. Max had brought his camera and a tripod; he took a number of photographs and thoroughly enjoyed himself showing the two young ladies how to operate it, though Adam felt he was spending longer than was strictly necessary under the hood with Miss Stevens.

'Is there a problem with Miss Stevens's eyes?' asked Adam pointedly, as a burst of laughter emerged from under the black cloth.

'None that I know of,' replied Max, emerging somewhat red-faced, leaving Melisande to take the picture.

'Ah. I thought perhaps she was having some difficulty focusing.'

It was a childish remark, he knew. He flushed at Max's puzzled expression and turned away to find Beatrice Randall looking at him speculatively.

As the sun went down and the air grew a little cooler, they made their way slowly up the path back to the house for tea.

'Yet another skill learnt, Miss Stevens,' said Doctor Kingsley mockingly as he gave her his hand up the last few steps. 'The camera,' he explained, as she looked at him, puzzled.

'Oh, it's not the first time I've taken a photograph,' she said, smiling sunnily up at him.

'No?'

'I took my first photograph when I was twelve,' she said. 'A man came to the Orphanage to take photographs for a book. It was called *London Refuges: Secular and Religious*. Price two shillings and sixpence. Page forty-five: the Wapping Home for Waifs and Strays, affiliated to St Mark's Church, photograph of the ragged orphans. When he had finished he let me take one too. He promised to send me a plate, but I never received it.' She shrugged. 'Maybe he sent it to the Vicar. At any rate, I never saw it.'

Tea was served by the parlourmaid in the conservatory, an elegant glass structure filled with exotic plants with heavily scented blooms. They sat in wicker and rattan chairs and she was astonished to find that she had a great appetite for the tea and sandwiches and dainty cakes. Miss Jouvet and Mr Vaux were permitted to leave the company and take a turn together on the piazza, a paved walk between the house and the formal gardens. Miss Jouvet informed her fiancé, in tones more suited to promising a child a treat, that he might give her his arm, if he wished.

The rest of the party moved into the drawing room and the talk turned to the new water system which the City Fathers had reluctantly agreed to lay down after the recent epidemic, and which Kingsley hoped to have extended to Harbourside. Melisande listened attentively; she had not before realised the extent to which the doctor was involved with the poorer part of the city. She watched through half closed eyes the blue sky turn from azure to navy and the bright stars come out, to hang suspended like the crystal drops on Mrs Randall's chandelier.

Mrs Randall was explaining to them her plans to raise money for the Red Cross Auxiliary, which was dealing with the wounded returning from Cuba and the Philippines on sometimes quite unsatisfactory hospital ships.

'You know I'll do all I can to help you,' said Adam, 'but I don't imagine there is much to be done in Harbourside.'

'No. They have enough to do keeping body and soul together,' she said. 'I hope I will not tread on your toes, but I know that some of the women are collecting bedding and cast-offs for Key West. The refugees arriving there from Cuba are in terrible shape, so I hear.'

Melisande sighed softly and slipped down further in the deep cushions of the sofa.

The next thing she heard was Mrs Randall's concerned voice. 'We've worn the poor child out,' she said. 'Better take her home.'

The men chuckled softly at something she could not hear and she sat up with a jerk, her cheeks hot with embarrassment. Her first society outing and she had fallen asleep!

'I'll carry her to the carriage,' said Max.

'No need,' came the lighter voice of the doctor. 'Tell Olsen to bring the carriage round. I'll fetch her out.'

The thought of Adam's arms around her made her blush even more – she did not think she could cope with a repetition of those strange sensations. 'I can walk,' she said, stifling a

211

yawn with some difficulty. She rose and gathered her wits sufficiently to thank her hostess prettily for her hospitality, but once the carriage door was closed on her and the horses picked up their paces, she found herself drifting off to sleep once again.

On the other side of the carriage, Adam Kingsley watched her with a frown in his eyes. It was fortunate that Max was with them, he decided. Otherwise it would be the easiest thing in the world to slip across to sit beside her, to slide his arm round her, draw her head down on to his shoulder and –

She woke as the carriage pulled up outside Springs House and managed to stagger through the door and up the stairs. She could barely keep her eyes open long enough to undress and brush her hair out; she was asleep almost before her head touched the pillow.

Harriet Minton spread the pages out across the table, her eyes running excitedly from the English original to the translations, checking the keys to see that no labels on the diagrams had been left out.

'These are excellent,' she said. 'Exactly what we wanted.' She looked up at her visitor, her blue eyes alive with interest. 'I must say I am surprised. From what Doctor Kingsley said, I did not think you would be able to do it for us.'

Melisande blushed. Did everyone know of her woeful ignorance?

Miss Minton hastened to ease the embarrassment she saw she had caused.

'He explained that you learnt your Russian and French as a small child.'

'And from newspapers. In the Orphanage.'

'Neither likely to produce the kind of wording we were seeking!'

'I hope I have it all correct,' said Melisande, looking in some embarrassment out of the window of the Harbourside Dispensary at the grey and overcast sky. 'I – I had to ask Mrs Wodzinski, and she asked her friends . . .'

'I hope she was careful who she asked.' Miss Minton looked up anxiously. 'We don't want the priests down on us. Let them get one whiff of birth control and –'

'That was what she said. She is not a believer herself, so she was careful only to ask others in the same position. And, of course, they all knew about Mrs Vaasanen.'

'I was just on my way to see her,' said Miss Minton, crossing to take her cloak from behind the door. 'Won't you come with me? I'm sure she would like to see you.' As her visitor hesitated, she added: 'Doctor Kingsley told me he would be delayed. We can leave a note.'

'In that case, yes. I'll walk along with you.'

It was a grey, blustery day with the threat of rain. The two young ladies hurried along the sidewalk past the loungers, hands firmly on hats and holding down skirts which threatened at any moment to fly up as the wind whipped evilly around their ankles.

They had just turned into Harbourside when the sound of running feet behind them made them stop and look over their shoulder.

'It's only Tadeusz,' she said. 'One of my pupils.' Someone opened the door of Muller's Bar and a wave of noise washed over them and receded, leaving behind the smell of beer and sausages to make Melisande's mouth water and her stomach rumble.

'Oh, Miss Stevens,' began Tadeusz woefully, when he had recovered his breath. 'I've been looking everywhere for you! They said you were at the Dispensary, but I went there and you'd gone!'

'Now you've found me, you had better calm down and tell me what is the matter,' she said.

'You must come to Agnete's home. You mustn't let them do it!'

'Do what?'

Tadeusz began to gabble something incomprehensible.

'English, Tadeusz!' she scolded.

He pulled himself together and told her, his words tumbling over each other in their haste.

'She is crying and crying, Miss Stevens,' he said, his English falling apart again in his agitation. 'It is not fair, what is happening to her! Please. You must help! They sell her to some old man . . .'

213

'Tadeusz, no! I am sure you have that wrong!' protested Melisande. She had never heard that they were a feckless family.

'I do not lie!' Tadeusz drew himself up proudly.

Melisande sighed. 'Miss Minton, you must excuse me. I think I must find out what is happening.'

'Mrs Vaasanen can wait,' said Harriet Minton, the light of battle in her eyes. 'I shall most certainly come with you. If what this young man says is true, you may need support.'

Tadeusz led them down a maze of alleys and up several flights of worn stone steps. 'The fourth door,' he shouted, struggling to be heard over the noise of the machines whirring in the adjacent rooms. He hammered loudly on the door. Eventually they heard a shuffling step and the door was opened by a tall man, elderly but still emanating strength. He looked at them under his brows and shouted something incomprehensible. After a moment Agnete's mother appeared, her flaxen hair scragged back from her thin face.

Her eyes went from the two women to Tadeusz.

'What you want?' she demanded angrily. 'I told you, you stay 'way from Agnete!'

'I have brought Miss Stevens, the schoolteacher, and her friend Miss Minton,' he said with a winning smile. 'She wished to come and see Agnete.' Thus implying that he was only there to show her the way. Melisande hadn't the heart to gainsay him.

An old woman coming out of the door opposite stopped, openly curious. It wasn't often that such well-dressed visitors came to the tenement.

'You better come in,' said Agnete's mother reluctantly, opening the door a little wider. To no one's surprise, Tadeusz slipped in on his teacher's heels.

Agnete was kneading bread on the deal table in the centre of the room and she looked up in surprise, her red-rimmed eyes a sorry contrast to her pale flour-smudged face. The old man who had opened the door sat in the chair by the window, his eyes, beneath their bushy brows, fixed on the girl.

'I have your book safe, Miss Stevens,' she said, wiping her hands on a rag. 'I would have brought it round . . .'

Melisande shook her head. 'I have not come for the book, Agnete. Keep it till you have read it.' She crossed to the girl's side. 'We have missed you at school,' she said softly.

Agnete's eyes filled with tears.

'I cannot any longer come to the school, Miss Stevens,' she said, dashing the tears away with the back of her hand. The old man heaved himself out of the chair and disappeared into the next room.

Melisande turned to the mother in surprise. 'You are leaving Harbourside?'

'She goes away to work,' said her mother harshly. 'She is soon sixteen, long past time she should bring more money into the house.'

'Oh.' There was nothing she could say about that. Few families in Harbourside could afford to keep their children at school that long.

'I must look for job for her. She is good nurse, good housekeeper. Already I have two offers for her.'

'Old men!' shouted Tadeusz, unable to keep silence any longer.

'Of course old men!' Agnete spat out. She turned to her mother, her face ugly. 'I am very experienced in looking after old men, aren't I?'

Miss Minton drew in her breath with a hiss, but Melisande looked puzzled. There was a tension in the air that she could not understand.

The mother began to shake. 'Child, you must go,' she said in a hoarse whisper. 'Better you go away to work. Nursing you do well. Old peoples pays well for nursing.'

'You don't have to go! You could come and stay with my family!' said Tadeusz doggedly.

Agnete looked at him, her pale eyes wide and sad. 'Tadeusz,' she said softly, 'there isn't room there for the family you've already got!'

'Your family to take in a Gentile?' sneered Agnete's mother. 'Mad,' she said, tapping her head to show her estimation of Tadeusz's ideas.

'Nursing! Of course, now I've placed you!' exclaimed Miss Minton, before Tadeusz could speak again. She looked at Agnete more closely. 'You're the girl who saved Mrs Vaasanen, aren't you?'

'I only helped Miss Stevens.'

'Nonsense,' said Melisande firmly. 'Credit where it's due . . .'

'Quite so,' agreed Miss Minton. 'Hard to recognise you with your eyes all puffed up.' She looked across at her mother, standing in the middle of the room with her shoulders bowed, as if she were carrying the weight of the world on them. 'You have a talented daughter,' she said briskly. 'It seems a pity to interrupt her education.'

Agnete's mother looked fearfully over her shoulder. 'She can not stay here,' she repeated dully.

'What if I were to find her a place at the Infirmary?' asked Miss Minton. 'There she could have a proper training.'

The mother shrugged. 'Is not possible. I tell you she can not stay here,' she repeated, her face fixed in hard lines.

'We could find her somewhere to lodge – if that was what Agnete wanted.'

Agnete nodded, her eyes brightening.

'They will train you well at the Infirmary, but the pay is small to begin with and the work is hard,' warned Miss Minton.

'But at the end I will be a proper nurse?'

'Yes.'

'Then, please, I would like to go.'

They all looked expectantly at her mother.

After a silence that seemed to go on for ever, Agnete crossed to her mother's side. 'I would send you what I can, to help you,' she murmured.

'No, child. Keep it. You will need it – you will have to make your way without help from here.' The mask slipped for a moment and they saw her face soften. She gave her daughter a brief hug, then turned away. 'Fetch your things, Agnete,' she said, brisk once more. 'If you to go, you go now, before your father come back. The two of them together I cannot face.'

'We'll wait outside,' said Miss Minton firmly. She looked as if she could not wait to get out of the building.

They left Tadeusz hovering in the doorway, waiting to carry Agnete's bag.

'Give them some privacy for their farewells, Tadeusz,' said Miss Stevens.

216

Outside on the pavement Miss Minton leaned against the wall, careless of the dirt and soot on her elegant gown, and breathed in the gusty, redolent air as if it were liquid. 'My dear! I am happy to be out of there!'

Melisande drew in a sharp breath. 'Did I – No, it cannot have been. They didn't mean –'

'Did you understand what you thought you understood?' said Miss Minton crisply. 'The old man and the girl? Yes, you understood correctly.'

Melisande paled visibly. 'Here, you're not going to go all missish and faint on me, are you?' said Miss Minton in some alarm.

'No.' She forced herself to breathe slowly, to fight back the wave of nausea.

'It happens, I'm afraid. With families crammed in on top of each other as they are . . . Perhaps for her we were in time. Better not to ask, I think.' She looked sideways at her companion. 'You must have come across it before,' she said. 'Brought up as you were . . .'

Her heart sank. Someone – Doctor Kingsley? – must have told her. She wondered how many other people knew. 'In the Orphanage, you mean?' She shook her head.

Harriet looked at her curiously. 'For someone brought up in a London slum, you seem to have very little experience of life.'

'What no one understands is that, to all intents and purposes, from the age of ten I was brought up by two elderly spinsters whose sole purpose was to shelter me from any experience of life! But – I'm learning,' she said sombrely. Out of the corner of her eye she saw Agnete trudge out of the door. 'Little by little, I'm learning.'

On the edge of Harbourside they split up. Tadeusz took Agnete's hand in his. 'Oh, Agnete!' he said. 'I wish –'

Agnete put a finger to his lips. 'Don't say it,' she said softly. Then she smiled at him. 'I will see you again. When I know where I am to go.'

'You'll let me know?'

'Of course. And – thank you.' She leaned forward and kissed him tenderly on the cheek. Stunned, he stood rooted to the spot and she slipped her hands out of his and hurried down the lane after Miss Minton.

Miss Stevens looked at him, an indulgent smile on her face at the dreamy expression on his face. 'What do you wish, Tadeusz?' she asked.

He sighed heavily. 'I wish I was old enough to look after her. And I wish – that my – that everyone's problems could be so easily sorted out.'

A window opened across the street and a voice called out: 'Tadeusz!'

'My mother,' he said with a distinct lack of enthusiasm.

The woman leaned over the window sill, rich brown curls bobbing merrily around her pale face, and launched into a rapid fire question and answer with her son.

'Aw, heck!' muttered Tadeusz, who had wasted no time picking up the vernacular from the men down at the shipping office where he swept out after school. 'She wants to meet you.'

'Willingly,' said Melisande. 'But you don't seem very happy about it.'

He shrugged. 'You'd better come up then,' he said with bad grace, leading the way up another flight of malodorous steps. On the third floor he flung open a door.

She did not think she had ever seen so many people in one room. Exactly how many it was impossible to say, for there was a constant to-ing and fro-ing and a tremendous din, each person shouting to be heard above the rest. It amazed her that anyone could think in such a racket, let alone work.

Three girls in their teens sat at a tiny table in the corner wiring silk leaves, petals and flower centres together and tossing the finished product into a box at their side, chattering as they worked; on a low bed along one wall several youths sat cross-legged, plaiting long strips of leather for belts or bags, breaking off every now and again to throw mock punches at each other, or to tease the girls, or to jump up and rivet buckles on to the finished items with a noisy rivetting press at one end of the kitchen table. Everywhere she looked there were small children: under the table, bouncing down the back of the bed behind the leather weavers, reaching up to dip a finger into the pots at the side of the tiled stove in the corner, in front of which, serene and untroubled by the noise stood Tadeusz's mother, holding a child on her hip with one hand

218

while she stirred a huge pot with the other. In the midst of it all, next to the rivetting machine, sat a slim, wiry man in his thirties, darkly handsome with an exuberant beard. His brow propped on his hand, he was reading a leather-bound book, apparently oblivious to the chaos and confusion all around him.

'Welcome to the lunatic asylum,' muttered Tadeusz under his breath.

The clock in the hall struck the hour and Melisande looked up in surprise. She had finished her work some time ago, but stayed on to write a letter to Miss Greville. Foolish, really, to have written so much, as she hoped to see her in the next few days. She checked that she had left everything ready for Doctor Jefferson in the morning, locked the door to the dispensary and turned the lights off. She headed for the back stairs, which she always took care to use when the doctor was entertaining, but as she crossed the hall, someone emerged from the closet. She tried to draw back into the shadows, but too late.

'Well, well!' exclaimed Jeremiah Patterson. 'The new schoolmistress, if I am not mistaken?'

She inclined her head, acknowledging him but not encouraging further conversation. 'Excuse me, sir,' she said politely. 'If I may pass?'

'Why such haste, my dear?' he murmured, and she smelt the strong brandy fumes on his breath as he leaned towards her. 'I have been looking forward to meeting you. As son of one of the trustees, I think we should get to know one another a little better, don't you?'

What could she say? What could she do? She could hardly make a scene in the middle of a dinner party. She heard once more Sarah's words echo round her head. *But it's not my fault, Sarah!* she protested silently. *I did nothing!*

She struggled to get a grip on herself, fight down the panic that threatened to overwhelm her. 'I – I should be pleased to welcome you and your mother at the school, Mr Patterson,' she began breathlessly.

He slid his arm around her waist and drew her closer, too close.

219

'If you please, Mr Patterson!' She struggled to evade his hand, but he backed her into a corner on the bend of the corridor. As his hand slid up from her waist, she brought her heel down on his foot and swore at him.

As he recoiled she saw her chance to escape, but his hand shot out, quick as a flash, to close round her wrist like a vice.

'So!' he hissed. 'The insolent seamstress! Of course. Those eyes. I should have seen . . . And living under the same roof as the good doctor.' He leered down at her. 'Not a fool, is he?'

'What do you mean?'

'Wouldn't the good people of Edensville be scandalised to find they have had a seamstress foisted on them! How will they feel when they find that they are paying Kingsley's mistress to teach the slum brats?'

'What are you saying?'

'My dear mother would be fascinated to hear how the trustees were deceived,' he said caressingly. 'Unless you could make it worth my while not to?'

The door at the end of the corridor opened and David Jefferson came in, calling for Mrs Chobley. Patterson, startled, looked over his shoulder and she took advantage of the brief slackening of his grip to wrench herself free. She fled back into the study, where she bolted the door and leaned against it, her breathing ragged.

Kingsley never sat long over his port when the Pattersons came to dine; little though he relished Sophia's simpering, he found Jeremiah even less congenial. The arrival of Hetty with a note was a welcome diversion.

'My apologies, ma'am,' he said with a bow to Mrs Patterson, resplendent this evening in purple satin. 'I must beg you to excuse me for a few minutes.' His lips twitched at the grimace that passed across Max's face. 'Max will entertain you,' he said with a ghost of a smile. 'Hetty, please fetch the tea tray up directly.'

He paused a moment outside the door and looked thoughtfully at the note once more. Then he went swiftly down the stairs to the lower hall and into his study, where Melisande was pacing up and down the carpet, nervously clasping and unclasping her hands.

'You sent for me, Miss Stevens?'

220

'I – I did not mean it to sound that way. But I had to see you, yes.'

A sardonic smile curled his lips as he closed the door and leaned against it. 'A summons it certainly was. But I am still no wiser, and my guests await me.'

She made to turn from him, but forced herself to face him. 'It's Mr Patterson,' she said. 'He's threatening to tell his mother that I . . . that we. . . .' Her speech became incoherent and she turned away, hands pressed to her hot cheeks.

'But you don't know Patterson!' he exclaimed.

'I tell you he recognised me!'

'You've met him before?'

'Yes,' she said baldly.

He raised his eyebrow, waiting for further explanation. 'I went with Madame Chantal to fit Sophia for a dress, and I was sent to the housekeeper's room for a length of silk.'

'And?'

'It wasn't my fault,' she protested.

'My dear Miss Stevens, why should I think it your fault.'

'Maybe it was!' she said, eyes big in her white face. 'Maybe Sarah was right all along.'

In two strides he was at her side. Hands on her shoulders he turned her round and forced her to face him. 'What the Devil are you talking about?'

The feel of his hands on her made the churning in her stomach even worse, but she would never have blurted it out if she hadn't been panicked. 'She said I would come to a bad end. She said I – I was wicked. That I'd seduced her brother and I'd do the same to every man I met.' She could still see Sarah's face, ugly with fury, spitting out that awful accusation. 'She said everyone could see I was a wicked hussy and –'

'Hold on a minute!' said Kingsley.

'But I –'

'Stop right there. What the Devil do you mean, saying you seduced her brother?'

'He was drunk and he –'

'I don't think you seduced anyone. In fact, I don't think you know what you're talking about.'

'I'm not stupid!'

221

'Did you – did you do the things Mrs Chobley talked about?'

'*What*?' She looked at him, appalled. 'Of *course* not,' she exclaimed indignantly.

Damnation! he thought. I shouldn't have said that. After all, she has no idea I was listening in.

'Let me guess,' he said, lips twitching. 'He kissed you and mauled you about a bit.' He asked her a few searching questions and, from her shame-faced answers, it was clear Mrs Chobley had been correct in her assumptions.

'But Sarah said –'

'Never mind what Sarah said,' he muttered grimly. She was clearly one of those genteel spinsters who gave the breed a bad name. He imagined the woman had seen her charge growing up – and growing away from her mentor – and had tried to frighten the girl back again. Or perhaps she had simply been unable to cope with the thought of a once-loved brother so far gone in drink he could contemplate attacking a defenceless girl. 'Never mind her,' he repeated. 'I'm more concerned about Patterson. How did he recognise you? I thought you always wore that dreadful veil when you worked for Madame Chantal?'

'I did. But that time, at his house, he managed to lift it up.'

And those big green eyes would be so very memorable, he thought.

'Though I think what gave me away was when I swore at him. I did the other time as well, you see.'

'Damnation! If only you could learn to keep your tongue between your teeth! This could complicate matters with the Pattersons.'

'That's all very well for you to say,' she flashed, stung by his apparent criticism, 'but no one pens you in a corner and tries to maul you about!'

'I know. I'm not cross with you, don't think it. But it is a cursed difficult situation you have placed me in. If you must swear, why must you use the gutter language you learnt at the Orphanage?'

'I didn't! I swore in French. That's why he recognised –'

'Your mother taught you to swear in French?' he said, taken aback.

'No. I learnt it from my father. After my mother died he –'

'Girl! My hat and cane!' It was Patterson's voice and his heavy footstep on the stairs. 'Tell Doctor Kingsley I must take my leave!'

Adam pushed Melisande unceremoniously into the dispensary and went out into the hall.

'Leaving so soon, Jeremiah?' he enquired politely, taking the hat and cane from Hetty and dismissing her.

'Quite so. Business appointment,' said Patterson with a lecherous wink. 'I shall send the carriage for the ladies at eleven.'

'Step into my study a moment before you go, Patterson, would you? I have something to say to you that would be better said in private.'

Patterson strolled into the office. 'Do be brief, my dear Kingsley,' he said, affecting to suppress a yawn. 'My business appointment, you understand.'

'Another poor girl to be terrorised, is it?' Adam raised his hand to stem the flow of denial from the other man. 'No, I'm not really interested. But I am interested in threats made under my roof.' His voice dropped. 'Let me clarify the situation for you, Patterson. There are two points you should understand: firstly, if Miss Stevens were forced to leave Springs House through any action of yours, the trustees would then have to house her at their own expense. Knowing her care of money, I doubt that would please your mother greatly. Secondly, Miss Stevens has no family here to protect her reputation. She is well chaperoned in this house by my housekeeper and if I hear one whisper against her good name or my professional reputation, I shall knock your teeth down your damned throat, then sue your family for every penny they have.'

'You wouldn't do that!' blustered Patterson. 'We all know you're going to marry Sophia.'

'Am I? I do not believe I have yet made a proposal.' He picked up Patterson's hat and cane and handed them to him. 'Your urgent appointment awaits you,' he said, holding the door open. Patterson debated the desirability of arguing the matter, but one look at Kingsley's icy face and he decided that presence of mind required absence of body.

223

As the front door slammed behind him, Melisande peeped around the door. 'Has he gone?' He nodded. '*That* will show him!' she exclaimed. 'Oh, you were marvellous!' She looked up at him, green eyes big in her face. 'Would you really have knocked his teeth down his throat?'

'I had forgotten your presence,' he said, pushing his hair back from his face with an impatient gesture. 'I should not have said such a thing in front of a lady.'

'Oh, fudge!' she said airily. 'I don't have to be a lady with you: you know exactly what I am.' She paused, head on one side, regarding him gravely. 'But would you really have fought him?'

'It would have been an unequal fight,' he said with a boyish grin. 'I was captain of boxing at Harrow.'

He fell silent for a moment, remembering the fights he had been forced into to silence the bullies who would throw his past in his face. He had been so unhappy at first, but things had grown better with time.

He came back to the present with a jolt, catching sight of himself in the mirror above the mantel. He was smiling down at Miss Stevens with a most foolish smile on his face. He shook his head sharply.

'I must return to my guests,' he said abruptly.

But he found himself going slowly, reluctantly, up the stairs to the drawing room. Sophia Patterson's ponderous attempts at flirtation set his teeth on edge even more than usual and it was with a sigh of relief that he finally saw them to their carriage.

He returned to his study and poured a generous measure of whisky into a crystal glass. He took it across to his desk and opened up the latest journal. He tried to concentrate on it, but the words ran into one another and all he could see was the reflection of himself in the mirror, gazing foolishly down at Melisande. And her smiling up at him.

When he remembered the poor frozen waif Max had brought home with him, he felt a fierce longing to go to her and tell her that never again need she fear hunger and cold, for he, Adam Kingsley, would look after her for the rest of his life.

Folly!

And yet in spite of himself he felt an aching wave of protectiveness towards her. His only desire was to ensure that she spent the rest of her life laughing: there had been enough misery in her life.

But as the night wore on and the level in the decanter fell, he drank himself beyond such dreams and back to reality. Practicalities began to emerge from the mists of alcohol that wreathed their fumes about his brain. His family would hardly enthuse about an alliance with a nameless waif, he told himself, and he could not risk cutting himself off from his father's bounty; until the estate became profitable, his father's contributions to the dispensary and the school were vital. And just because his desire for her was strong, did not mean he could make her happy: he had proof of that in his own immediate family. But he was honest enough to know that that was not the real reason. What could he offer her? Only the exchange of one clouded past for another.

Besides, there was Max. He would be better for her, Adam was quite sure. They liked each other; the rest would come, given time. Max would be better for her in so many respects: he was closer to her in age, could offer her a stable background, and had a more even temperament.

'Have to encourage that,' he said sombrely to his reflection, but in spite of all he could and did say to himself, that earlier reflection obtruded on his vision. With a growl he pushed the decanter away, loosened his necktie and laid his head on the desk.

Melisande opened the door, letter in hand, and the bright shaft of sunlight fell across the desk. Kingsley sat up with a grunt, shielding his eyes against the dazzle.

'Would you post my letter on the way to the meeting?' she began. One look at his face and she cast the letter aside and hurried over to the desk. 'Doctor Kingsley! What's the matter? Shall I call Doctor Jefferson?'

'No. No need.' He tried, and failed, to rise to his feet. Necktie awry, he looked blearily up at her, groaning at the effort.

She caught a blast of his breath. Wrinkling her nose she picked up the decanter and looked at it in disgust.

'Well! You certainly won't be going to any meeting today,' she said with asperity.

'Send Olsen in to me,' he muttered.

'Olsen is in Edensville,' she said with admirable restraint. 'You sent him there.'

'Oh. Yes. I remember.'

'You do surprise me.' She crossed to the windows and flung back the curtains.

He winced at the sunlight that flooded in and pressed his hands to his eyes in anguish. With an effort he rose unsteadily from behind the desk and staggered across to the sofa where he collapsed, head swimming. 'Send Max. Or David.'

'They are both out. But I could fetch Hetty,' she offered. 'Or would you prefer Mrs Chobley?'

He shot her a look from under lowered brows. 'If you want to play ministering angel, you can fetch me a whiskey,' he mumbled. 'Large one.'

'I shall fetch you some coffee,' she said. 'Black.'

She left the room, closing the door behind her with a crack that made his head reel.

A few minutes later she came back into the room with a tray bearing a jug of coffee, a cup and saucer, a bowl of sugar and two glasses of water. That was what Matron had sent her to fetch whenever Doctor Morel was 'unwell'.

First she made him drink the water. When it came to the second glass, he told her she was a shrew.

'I'll go away then,' she said with a half smile on her lips. 'And send Mrs Chobley in . . .'

After two cups of sweet black coffee, he began to feel – and look – more human. With her assistance he managed to stagger across the hall and up the stairs, and the next he knew he was lying on his bed with a wet cloth on his forehead and the drapes drawn against the sunlight. He was about to drift into a blissful sleep when he was struck by a sudden thought.

Painfully slowly he forced one eyelid open. She was standing at the bedside looking down at him. How easy it would be just to reach out and catch her wrist. Even all that whiskey had not depressed his desire for her. But that way lay disaster. He gritted his teeth and clenched his fists by his side.

'You'd better go,' he said dully.

226

'When I am sure you will be all right,' she said, blissfully unaware of his turmoil. 'You probably ought not to sleep on your back. If you are unwell, you might –'

'Go!' he roared. He winced and fell back against his pillows, ears cringing at the sound of his own voice. He dropped to a husky whisper: 'And if Patterson saw you now? In my room? What then?'

She coloured as she followed the drift of his words, pressed her hands to her hot cheeks and fled.

It was late afternoon when Adam joined her and Max in the orchard where the tea table had been set up. He looked pale, but managed to smile politely and accept a cup from her, though he rejected the offer of cake with every sign of loathing. When Max was called away to speak to Olsen over by the picket fence, Adam took the opportunity to apologise, albeit rather stiffly, for his behaviour.

'I am quite accustomed to seeing men in liquor,' said Melisande crushingly. 'Sarah's brother was almost always drunk.' She refilled his cup. 'But I thought as a doctor you would have had more sense.'

'What had the fair Sophia said to put you in such a melancholy mood?' teased Max, who, to Adam's vexation, had returned in time to overhear the last remark.

Adam scowled and put his cup and saucer back on the table with a force that chipped the fine china. He was in no mood for Max's heavy humour today. But even more, he was appalled to realise that he had put himself on the same level as the drunkard who had driven Melisande away to America in the first place. Pleading pressure of work, he took his leave as swiftly as he could.

She watched in brooding silence as he walked across the orchard and disappeared into the house. 'Is he really going to marry Sophia Patterson?' she asked Max after a moment.

He shrugged. 'Everyone seems to think so. He's never thought fit to disillusion them.'

'If she came to Springs House, there would be no place here for me any more,' she said in a small voice.

'You could always marry me,' he said awkwardly.

227

She stopped pouring, the teapot in mid air. 'You? But I – I hardly know you. Besides, you do not want a nameless orphan for your wife.'

'It's – you should give some thought to it,' he said, his already ruddy face turning a deeper hue. He reached out and patted her hand awkwardly. 'I am sure we could be comfortable together.'

All in all, a most eventful day. The next morning Melisande drove into town with Doctor Kingsley in total silence. She alighted at the post office, where she posted Miss Greville's letter herself, and made her way to the school so deep in thought that she never even spared a glance for the new displays in the shop windows. She was not so distracted, however, that she did not notice that Tadeusz was in a terrible mood.

'That's the third time you've snapped at one of the little ones,' she reproved him as Nella wiped Monika's tears and took her out into the yard with the rest.

Tadeusz scowled. 'I'm sorry,' he said curtly.

'It's not like you, Tadeusz. What is it?'

'Nothing,' he muttered. He gave a cry of frustration and drew his foot back and kicked the desk savagely, making her jump. 'Nothing! Everything!' He looked up at her and she could see that he was fighting to hold back the tears.

'Tell me, Tadeusz.'

He looked at her uncertainly. 'You won't tell my parents?'

She shook her head.

'I'm – I have to leave home.'

'Leave home?'

'Run away,' he muttered.

'But why? Your parents love you. They send you to school as often as they can. They even give you the extra lessons with the Rabbi.'

'Because education is the key,' he said, in cruel imitation of his father's heavily accented speech. 'Yes, I know. But the Rabbi has persuaded my father that I should go away to study.'

'Don't look so desperate!' she laughed. 'It would be no bad thing, I should have thought. I can't teach you much more. And how you manage to work with all that noise . . . !'

228

'The cousins? Oh, you get used to it.' He said it without much conviction.

'Of course we'd miss you, Tadeusz, but an opportunity to go to college –'

'You don't understand!' he cried despairingly. 'It's not college, it's the Hebrew Seminary! He wants me to be a rabbi!'

'But –'

'How can my father be so blind? So busy trying to outscore the Rabbi in those endless arguments that he hasn't noticed Rabbi Benjamin's twisted my mother round his little finger! Of course she's always been a believer, not like my father. . . .' He sank his head in his hands. 'It's no use, I tell you. I shall have to run away.'

'No, Tadeusz!' She caught his thin wrists, drew him across the room and sat him down in the chair by her makeshift desk. 'I can't make head nor tail of this,' she said, standing in front of him, arms akimbo, 'but I am quite sure you should not act in haste.'

'I tell you, he's left me no choice!'

'What about Agnete?' she said. 'What of all your hopes for the future?'

'What hopes? What hopes of a life with Agnete if they send me to be a rabbi?' He looked up at her, desolation in his eyes. 'Hard enough to marry out of the faith anyway. Even my father, an unbeliever, still married in.' Suddenly new light shone in his eyes. 'I shall run away with Agnete, that's what! We will go west, find work. Then when we're old enough, we apply for our own land grant!'

'Tadeusz!' Her angry voice brought him to a stop. 'If you do any such thing, it would be the most selfish action I have ever heard of!'

'Why? She loves me and –'

'And she might, in a fit of misguided loyalty, throw everything up and go west with you. Abandoning her training, abandoning all hope of ever becoming a nurse. Is that fair to her? And what of Miss Minton? Does she deserve that after all she has done for Agnete?'

He looked up at her and his shoulders slumped. 'No,' he said with a groan.

'Promise me, Tadeusz, that you won't do anything imme-diately. Leave it a few days and I'll think what we should do.'

'There's nothing you can do,' he said miserably.

'Let me speak to your parents. No.' She held up her hand to stem his anxious words. 'I won't mention your plans. I just want to see what theirs are.'

'But his English is so appalling, you'll never understand him!'

'Between us we'll manage something, I'm sure.' Like all educated Poles, Tadeusz's father spoke excellent Russian. She would speak to the Rabbi too, but she saw no need to mention that to Tadeusz.

She saw the Rabbi sooner than she had expected. She had just turned the corner past the new Reform Synagogue when she saw him striding down Madison, his housekeeper, Widow Salomon, puffing valiantly behind him like a black galleon in full sail.

She wasn't sure whether he would greet her, in front of one of his flock, on the open street, but she need not have worried.

'Miss Stevens!' he said, gripping her hand with every sign of enthusiasm. 'I wanted to come to see you about our Tadeusz. What do you think of these plans for our fine boy, eh? Hebrew College! No one in his family has ever made college before. His father, of course, was worthy, but –' Before she could answer he waved his hand at the elderly black-clad woman who had just caught up with him. 'Mrs Salomon, you haven't met Miss Stevens, have you? Runs the classes down on Harbourside.'

Melisande held out her hand with a 'pleased to meet you', but all she received was a curt nod before the housekeeper turned her attention back to the Rabbi. 'I don't get to Horowitz's soon, you can sing for your salt fish!' she scolded. 'And you – you stand round on this windy corner too long, you catch a chill again!'

'Oy-yy!' said the Rabbi on a long breath as she sailed off around the corner, shawl flapping in the light breeze. 'There's the woman should have had all those children to look after. Nothing an old man fears more than a mother hen with no chicks!'

She couldn't help smiling. The Rabbi was no more than forty, and hale and hearty. She was sure he enjoyed being mothered, but just felt obliged to protest a little now and again.

'I have sent a long letter to the Board of Admissions at the Seminary,' he said. 'They are concerned that he has not attended religious classes, of course, but under the circumstances, they are prepared to overlook that if his academic achievements are such that . . .'

'I would be quite happy to write to them, if you wished it. But Rabbi, I –' She took a deep breath and launched into it. 'Do you really think a Seminary is the place for Tadeusz? I don't think he has the qualities for a priest – I mean, for a rabbi.'

'Miss Stevens!' He clapped his hands theatrically to his cheeks. 'You do not think I send Tadeusz to train as – No, no!' He chuckled deep in his throat. 'A rabbi? Not our Tadeusz!'

'He thinks that's why you want him to go.'

Rabbi Benjamin raised his eyes imploringly to Heaven. 'That boy!' he exclaimed.

'If that's not your intention – then why the Seminary?'

'They produce Hebrew scholars as well as rabbis, you know.'

'But Tadeusz –'

'Not the most likely candidate, perhaps,' he said wryly. 'Maybe in time he comes to see . . . Like his father. An unbeliever, that one, but a noted Jewish scholar. Oh, he can out-argue me on some points of the Talmud and the Hebrew law . . .'

'I'm afraid he has not passed that on to Tadeusz.' She took a deep breath. 'To be brutally honest, Rabbi, I cannot think of a worse place to send Tadeusz than this College. I am not even sure he would stay there.'

'Better than trying to study in the tenement with all those cousins! I know his parents are an example to us all, taking in the orphans, but I cannot even think straight when I am there.'

'And that's why you lose the arguments?' she suggested wickedly.

231

A twinkle came into his eye. 'So I should argue with him only on home ground,' he agreed. 'But you see the point I make? Surely the Seminary must be better than home.'

'Thanks to your teaching and his father's, Tadeusz could go far in the world. Lawyer, doctor, politician . . . I don't know and I don't think he does yet. But I believe he needs a wider world than –' she had almost said 'than the Jewish community' – 'than Harbourside. It shouldn't be a choice between staying in that mad-house or training for a totally unsuitable future.'

He sighed ostentatiously. 'Very well, Miss Stevens. So we put on once more our thinking caps, heh?'

She had taken to meeting Kingsley at the Dispensary after school. Suddenly gazing into shop windows seemed a very futile activity. Far better to do something useful, if it was only to make tea for the staff who, on a busy day, often worked right through without a break.

Today there were only a few patients still waiting to see the nurse: Guiseppe, the boy injured in the tannery, come to have his dressing changed, a baby with the croup and a couple of women, one of them Mrs Vaasanen.

'I'm glad she came,' said Harriet Minton, snatching a moment to sip at the hot tea. 'Catch her before the problems start again.'

'Miss Minton –'

'Do call me Harriet.'

'Very well. Harriet –'

'Mmm?'

She could feel herself blushing, but forced herself to go on. 'In that book, it said that – that satisfactory methods of – of – limiting births were the same that had been used to protect men against disease for many years.'

'Yes.'

'So why – if people have known about these methods 'for many years' . . .'

'Why Mrs Vaasanen and the others like her?' She looked at her visitor over the rim of her teacup. 'The trouble is, the men don't have the babies so they haven't the same urgency about contraception as their wives. It gets caught up with other

232

worries: about their manliness, about being a good provider for their family. And they haven't the same drive to disobey the priests as a woman dragged down and worn out by a succession of children she doesn't want and can't feed. A woman can't count on a man to take care. Much better to show women how to limit births.'

'Can they? I mean, I know it said in the book . . . but I confess, I didn't really understand.'

'We've gone back to the Ancient Greeks. They knew a thing or two. If you soak a sponge in certain liquids, lemon juice or vinegar, it will form a barrier to the man's seed and in most cases prevent conception.' It never ceased to surprise Melisande that Harriet spoke about such matters without any embarrassment, in the same kind of tones she would use to ask if you took one lump or two in your tea. 'It's been used for centuries, though not right across society. Unfortunately so · many women now consider it indecent to speak about sex that even if they have the knowledge, they no longer pass that on to their daughters. So we must do it instead.'

'But if it is that easy, why cannot everyone be told about it?'

'Because there are some people in power who consider such matters obscene. Heard of the Comstock laws?'

'No.'

'Prohibit publication of so-called obscene texts. Like the one you translated for us. It's just a medical handbook, only four pages dealing with contraception, but the doctor who wrote it and the printer who printed it went to jail.'

'Are you in danger too – you and Doctor Kingsley?'

'Oh, yes. Comstock and his team are almost as much a threat as the priests. If they knew what we were trying to do here they would close us down. Adam in particular could be in serious trouble.' She didn't seem too perturbed.

'But the women who come to the clinic –'

'We don't give anyone contraceptive advice,' said Miss Minton with a coy smile. 'Endless pregnancies cause more than just poverty. So we prescribe application of a sponge dipped in solution to cure – ah – irritation of the internal passages. While such a cure for such a problem is being undertaken, it is unlikely they will conceive. It's juggling with words, of course. A means to an end. But few women are likely to discuss such intimate matters with their men, least of all with the priests. And what the men and the priests don't know can't hurt them.'

Washing up the cups, Melisande thought about what Harriet Minton had said; it occurred to her that she too could get into trouble for her part in the translation, but it didn't worry her. She felt a great sense of pride that she too was helping the Mrs Vaasanens of Harbourside!

'Have you heard how Agnete is?' she asked Miss Minton when the clinic had finished.

'Making excellent progress at the Infirmary,' said Harriet. 'And Adam found her a very nice family to stay with. They can use the money.'

'But she had no money for lodgings. How –'

'Adam is paying, of course. Nothing grand. Just a small house, so nothing too overwhelming for her. And they make no objection to Tadeusz visiting. Such a pleasant boy, is he not?'

'Poor Tadeusz has problems of his own at the moment, I fear.' She needed little bidding to tell her about Tadeusz and the Rabbi, though she left out Tadeusz's wilder plans.

'It is very difficult when someone like the Rabbi gets a fixed idea in his mind,' agreed Miss Minton. 'But to send a non-believer to a religious establishment would be folly. Seems to me he's a case for the Bachelor's Barn.'

'The *what*?'

'The Bachelor's Barn.' Miss Minton looked up with a smile from the card she was writing notes on. 'Adam has not told you of it?'

She shook her head.

'It's out at Carfax Farm. Right handy for the college in Owenstown. Been going a couple of years now.'

'I've been to Carfax. But I didn't realise –'

'It was Samuel Jefferson's idea. He and his wife wanted to show their gratitude to Adam for fighting to get their son into medical college.'

'David? Yes, he told me something of the problems he had encountered. I didn't realise it was Adam . . .'

'. . . who had helped him? Yes. And so in return the Jeffersons took in others whose parents could not afford to send them to college. Only boys, so far – hence the Bachelor's Barn. Some of them are studying at Owenstown College, one of them is at Medical School with David and only home in the vacations. I imagine Agnete will be the first of many young ladies for whom he will set up something similar.'

No, thought Melisande with a churning of pride: I was the first.

'We must arrange for Tadeusz to go out to Carfax to help with the harvest,' said Miss Minton, chewing the end of her pen while she stared into the middle distance. 'All the bachelors will be there then – they all help with the harvest. Oh, except David and Anton.' She blushed unexpectedly, looking suddenly much younger, more vulnerable. 'They'll take over Adam's work, good experience for them. We can see how Tadeusz fits in. And if it works . . . we can present the Rabbi with a *fait accompli*.'

It was David Jefferson who came to drive Melisande back to Eden Springs that evening. She spent much of the journey questioning him about his studies, and Doctor Kingsley and the Bachelors' Barn. The minute she got back to Springs House she marched into Kingsley's study.

He looked up from the letter he was writing. It was not like her to disturb him when he was working and he immediately assumed there must be a problem. 'Miss Stevens?' He ran his fingers through his hair. 'Is there something I can do for you?'

'Doctor Kingsley,' she said determinedly. 'I have come to say I'm sorry.'

His forehead creased in puzzlement. 'Sorry for what?'

'I –' How could she begin?

'You've broken the second best vase,' he joked.

'No. It's more than that.'

'The best vase!' he exclaimed. 'Not the Spode!'

He was laughing at her, but she tried to keep her face straight, determined to say what she had come to say.

'I'm sorry I said you were like Mrs Patterson,' she blurted out. 'You are not like her at all. You do so many things: the school and the clinic and helping those students and –'

'I detect the fell hand of Miss Minton,' he said grimly, pushing the papers aside with a muttered oath. 'Damn Miss

235

Minton!' he muttered as he strode past her and out of the door.

Melisande had been a little concerned that the easy relationship she had with Max Ellsky might have been damaged by his unexpected proposal, but she need not have worried. Max could think of nothing else but the harvest. At school, too, all the talk was of the coming weeks when school would close and the older children – and some of the mothers too – would hire themselves out to the farmers as extra field-workers.

'Och, it'll be a fine chance for the bairns to get away from the dust and the stink,' said Mary Maconochie. 'I mind fine the wonderful times we had when we went out o' Glasgee the summer, to help bring in the harvest.'

Although it was industry and shipping and factories that sustained Edensville year round, the land still exerted a strong pull on its inhabitants, and everyone had a comment to make on the harvest. Even Miss Greville, calling by the school one lunch-time, spent much of the time – when she had finished exclaiming over Melisande's good fortune in finding herself such a post – prognosticating an excellent harvest. 'The Tschenchenyov's bailiff said – the last time I went to see young Natasha, just before they left for their country estates – that they expected a bumper crop all round!'

Mrs Chobley was the only one to sound a cautionary note. 'There'll be a deal of work before then,' she said bluntly, rolling up her sleeves with a will. 'Ah, and not just in the fields either. There'll be all the food to prepare for the Harvest dance for all the farm workers and the servants – quite a shindy it is too. And if the master decides to have a Harvest Ball here like we did last year, then there's the whole house to be shone from top to bottom . . . All the nobs come to the Harvest Ball: all the old families, the councillors and the judges. Leastways they did last year, when Doctor Carter was still alive.'

Kingsley was satisfied with the arrangements he had made for the Dispensary: Hubner and Jefferson, though still officially students, were as good as many of the doctors who had hung out their shingle in Edensville in the last few years, and with

236

Miss Minton they would be able to keep everything running smoothly. And they could call him in in an emergency. That left only the school; he decided the time had come to make his report to the trustees before the harvest was upon them.

He had always driven Melisande to the corner and left her there. Originally this had been so that she could make her own mark, but it meant that he had never set foot inside the old warehouse.

He entered quietly by the side door, ducking his head as he passed under the low beam. To his left sat a small semi-circle of boys and girls, ranging from about five to eight, listening raptly to a story being read to them by Miss Stevens. He stood quietly in the shadows, thinking himself unseen, until he felt the strange sensation of eyes watching *him*. Seated on an upturned packing case, watching him suspiciously, was a thin young woman dressed in a skimpy black blouse and ill-fitting skirt.

He raised a finger to his lips to silence her questions, and sat down on an adjacent box, careless of his fine wool trousers. The movement caught the teacher's eye but after a slight start she carried on as though there had been no interruption. After a few moments she brought the tale to an end and set the children to copying on their slates the new words she had picked out of the story and written on the board.

'Doctor Kingsley!' Here, on her own ground, she exuded a quiet confidence. He took the proffered hand and bowed over it. 'Something is wrong?' she asked with a look of concern.

'No, no.' He hastened to reassure her. 'I have to make a report to the trustees and thought I would take the opportunity to come myself and see how things are progressing.'

The thin woman was bobbing a nervous curtsey and trying to back out of the room.

'I would like you to meet Mrs Giovanni, Doctor Kingsley,' said the teacher.

He gave her a brief bow and begged her to be seated again.

'Is there somewhere we can talk privately?' he asked, turning back to Melisande.

'I don't know about privately,' she said with a twinkle in her . eye, preceding him to the corner where she had set up a board on two rickety trestles to serve as a desk. She sat down with a

237

swish of skirts on one battered chair and motioned him to take the other.

'I don't recall anyone telling me about Mrs Giovanni,' he observed, stretching his long legs out before him.

She flushed. 'I did not think you would mind,' she said defensively. 'They take it in turns, two a day, and they help me with the children. Mrs Lenkova is out in the yard,' she said as he looked around the room. 'She's very good with the older ones. Without supervision they sometimes start fighting. And Mrs Giovanni helps me with the little ones, takes them to the privy, helps them with their dinner.'

'And how much are the trustees expected to pay them?' he asked, his eyebrows drawn together in a frown.

'Oh, they don't want payment. They have a free meal each and some of the milk you persuaded Mr Randolph to send in to us. And they've all learnt to write their names and read a little,' she finished triumphantly.

'It sounds a fair arrangement,' he admitted. 'But how did you manage to persuade them?'

'Wasn't that difficult. They all work at the canning factory when they can, but only a certain number are set on each day. The rest came to see what was going on and they sort of stayed.'

He spent most of the day at the school, observing with great interest the children's progress. He even found himself helping one of the youngest with her sums when Melisande was busy, but for the most part he tried to keep in the background. He was outside in the yard, examining the state of the building, when two of the older boys fell into a quarrel which looked like developing into a fist fight, but before either he or the formidable Mrs Lenkova could intervene, Melisande had stepped between the two youths and with a few caustic words in Russian, sent them back to their games with a joke and a smile.

She breathed a sigh of relief as the boys went back to their friends with grins of their faces. She desperately wanted everything to go smoothly today, for she felt very much on trial in front of the doctor. She had planned a hygiene lesson for that afternoon, one of several she had worked on. Her first instinct was to abandon it, for fear of getting something wrong

238

and making a fool of herself in front of Adam Kingsley, and only her pride stopped her. She had told Mrs Giovanni she would be talking to them about typhoid and cholera, twin scourges of the slums, and if she did not, then Mrs Giovanni at least would know why. It had taken her so long to win their confidence and she would not risk throwing it away now.

Quaking in her shoes, she turned to the board, nervously marshalling the facts that she had gleaned from the books in the library, hoping her voice would not shake. She took a deep breath, chalked up the various stages and linked them up to show the chain of infection which leads up to an epidemic; she talked about ways in which the children and their families could avoid infection and minimise pollution of the water supplies. She asked questions of the older children, initiating a lively discussion of ways and means, encouraging Sasha when he spoke scornfully of the standard of the water supplies that came to Harbourside. She steered them skilfully to the correct conclusions without seeming to do so, and the two mothers nodded sagely in agreement.

At last the day came to an end. The children tidied up, took their slates and departed in little groups down the hot and dusty road, back to the tenement slums, festering in the shimmering heat. When the last child was gone, Melisande slumped against a packing case, exhausted.

'Are you always this worn out?' he asked anxiously. When he saw her at the Dispensary, she was always bright and cheerful, full of the funny things that had happened that day.

She opened her eyes and looked up at him. 'Not usually,' she said frankly. 'But then I don't usually do anything so foolish as talk about epidemics with a doctor listening with such a critical eye.'

Their eyes met and they both burst out laughing at her confusion.

'Are you ready to go?' he asked, when at last they stopped laughting.

'A moment to tidy up,' she said pushing her hair out of her eyes. She straightened up the room, tidied her desk, then crossed to the little storeroom to fetch her coat. As she opened the door, he heard a sharp intake of breath and saw her shoulders stiffen.

In two strides he was at her side. 'What is it?' he said. He put his hands on her shoulders, feeling her tremble. Gently he put her aside and saw the floor of the little room black and moving, alive with huge cockroaches.

'So silly,' she said with a shaky laugh. 'I can bear the mice and rats, but these I cannot abide. Jim sees off the mice and the rats,' she said, locking the door behind them and checking the yard, 'but he won't touch the 'roaches.'

'Who is Jim?' he demanded, handing her up into the gig. 'Another cleaner you've employed?'

She shook her head with a gurgle of laughter. 'Jim is a cat. I bought him from Sasha. His cat had kittens. I didn't use the school funds,' she said anxiously, seeing the frown on his face. 'I paid for him myself.'

'You should have told me,' he said harshly. 'It is for the trustees to keep the building clean. You should not have to use your money.'

She shrugged. 'I have little else to spend it on.'

'That's not the point! But I shall see it does not happen again. And you will apply to me if you need anything else for the school. Understood?'

She nodded. 'And – your report?' she asked anxiously.

'My report will be favourable.' She wriggled happily in her seat. 'There's just one point.' She looked up at him, a little nervously, head on one side, like a bird waiting for crumbs. 'The children take their slates home. Isn't that asking for trouble?'

'There might be accidents, I suppose. But they are my teachers, you see. Max suggested it. They teach what they have learned to their older brothers and sisters, who are already working.'

'An excellent idea,' he allowed. 'But if you have things to discuss, discuss them with me, not Max. I am chairman of the trustees after all.' As he said it, he knew he was being churlish. Max might not be a trustee, but he was one of the most enthusiastic supporters of the Harbourside school.

'What I mean is – I should like to be kept in touch with what is going on,' he said. 'So if you discuss your ideas with me first . . .'

He knew in his heart that it was foolish to resent the time she spent with Max; but when he saw them walking round the estate, their heads together, deep in discussion, he had to stop himself setting his work aside and hurrying out to join them.

He would have to learn not to be dog in the manger. Since he had reached a conscious decision to spend only as much of his free time with her as was unavoidable, he could scarce complain if she chose to spend her free time with Max.

The Harvest Ball was one of the traditions Doctor Kingsley did not intend to change. The invitations were duly sent out, on gilt-edged cards, beautifully written by Melisande. 'I really haven't time for this,' said Adam as he headed off for the fields. 'Besides, your handwriting is so much better than mine!'

She dutifully wrote out the cards in her best copperplate, but her heart knew no joy, for she was up against a problem which had confronted every member of her profession for over a hundred years: was the teacher, in Society terms, considered to be above or below the salt? Springs House seemed to have solved the dilemma by ignoring it, for while the small tenant farmers were invited to the barn dance, and the Jeffersons to the Harvest Ball, she was on neither list.

There was no school to take her mind off such matters; with a heavy heart she helped prepare Springs House for the ball, supervising as the ballroom was opened and aired, the gallery prepared for the musicians who were to travel up from Albany; the chandeliers were unswathed from their Holland covers and washed until they sparkled and extra footmen were hired for the week, to Mrs Chobley's relief and Nancy's delight.

For a whole week the weather was hot and sultry, with no hint of rain. They woke every day to a brilliant blue sky, scattered with a few fluffy white clouds, and a fiercer sun than any she had know in England. Everyone seemed to be holding their breath, waiting for the decision that the harvest was ready to bring in.

The day came when the horse-drawn charabancs clattered up the hill from Edensville with their burden of temporary agricultural workers of all ages. Max, having seen the harvest started, drove over to Carfax to check on progress there.

Melisande, who had been trapped indoors for days, oversee-
ing the work, decided to go along for the ride. It would be an
excellent opportunity to see how Tadeusz was settling in.

It was a delight to be out in the fresh air after being shut up
indoors. The drive to Carfax in the gig was invigorating and
while Max talked about the crops he planned to introduce the
following year, she turned her face to the warm sun and
breathed in great lungfuls of the sparkling air.

She stepped into the kitchen at Carfax to find a hive of
activity: Mrs Jefferson had her own harvest to see to. Teresa
and her sister and their wizened mother were busily cutting
and stoning fruit while Blanche Jefferson oversaw the boiling
and setting and potting of great vats of plums and peaches.

'I never thought . . .' said Melisande, colouring uncomfortably; once again she had shown herself to be appallingly
ignorant in anything beyond book learning. 'I should not have
come.'

'Busiest time of the year for a farmer's wife,' said Samuel
Jefferson cheerfully as he and the hired man carried earthenware jars of beer and cider and hampers of bread and pies out
to the wagon, ready to drive out to the harvest fields. 'All the
workers to be fed and all the preserving – why, Missie, round
here there ain't hardly time to spit!' he finished with a high-
pitched laugh.

'Don't tease the girl, Sam!' said Mrs Jefferson, turning
away from the stove. 'I guess you've come to see how young
Tadeusz has settled in,' she said, turning to Melisande with a
smile.

'You're far too busy. I should have realised. . . .'

'I guess I can snatch a few moments,' she said, dipping fruit-
stained hands in the sink and drying them on a huckaback
towel. 'Tadeusz isn't here, of course. The boys are out in the
fields. Been out since sun-up, most of them.'

In the yard they met Anton Hubner, a big bear of a man
with a dark moustache and a ready smile; he offered to show
her round the old barn and Mrs Jefferson barely suppressed a
sigh of relief before hurrying back to the kitchen.

'So you're the teacher Tad told us so much about!' said
Hubner with an admiring gaze. 'Reckon he has a lot to thank
you for.'

'It was Miss Minton who suggested sending him here. . . .' she began.

'Ah, yes. Miss Minton.' He stroked his chin and a smile turned up the corners of his wide mouth.

'. . . and Doctor Kingsley who organised it.'

The shingle-hung barn, which formed a right angle to the main house, had been carefully converted to provide half a dozen rooms, each simply furnished with a small chest, a wash stand and a desk for study.

'We thought Tad was probably another of Adam's waifs and strays,' said Hubner, leading the way up the stairs, 'though Tad said he had never met him.'

'I suppose he is in a way,' she said with a smile. 'Are there, many like him here?' she asked curiously.

'They come and go. All waifs and strays.'

'Somehow I cannot see you as a waif,' she said. 'You look far too –'

'Solid?' He gave a deep chuckle that seemed to come up from his large shiny boots. 'Perhaps not a waif. But certainly a stray. My parents died soon after we arrived in America. I had only just started at medical school. David told Adam of my difficulties and he arranged with the Jeffersons to give me a home so that I could continue my studies.' He shook his head as if to dispel unhappy memories. 'This is Tad's room,' he said, flinging open a door on to a sun-filled chamber. 'Of course, the chest was a little empty at first; he had not much more than he stood up in. But Mrs Jefferson had some of David's old pants and a jacket. You would not recognise him now!'

'Is he happy, do you think?'

'Oh, sure,' replied Hubner easily. 'It was a bit strange for him at first, and I guess he missed his family the first few days. Said he'd never heard so much silence!' he laughed. 'But now he's got to know us, he seems a bit brighter. He is a little younger than the rest of us, but he gets on very well with us all.'

'Is he keeping up with his studies?' she asked, looking at the neat stack of books that the Rabbi had sent out with him.

'Just now he is a mite busy with the harvest. But he reads whenever he can. Adam has persuaded the authorities to let him start studies at Owenstown, even though he is so young. Me, I think he will cope. Though the last word stands with his parents, of course.'

Hubner, standing in for Doctor Kingsley during the harvest, was heading for Owenstown Infirmary. Melisande was reluctant to disturb Mrs Jefferson again and as Max, discussing weighty matters with Samuel, appeared to be set for the day at Carfax, she persuaded Anton to give her a ride back down the valley.

Where the track led off back to Springs House he stopped the gig and handed her down.

'Are you sure it is not too far?' he demanded anxiously.

She brushed aside his concern. Bidding him farewell with a cheery wave she set off over the shoulder of the hill into the next valley. Breasting the hill she could just see beyond the green and gold patchwork of the fields the rooftops of Eden Springs, nestling cosily in its hollow; from here too she could see that she had rather underestimated the distance to Springs House. She would have to do the journey in two stretches, she , decided, and stop off at the barn where she could see the men working in the fields, perhaps even beg a lift back with the cart that brought the food and drink out to them.

She set off down the hill with a spring in her step: it was a beautiful day and she had been indoors for far too long. She could certainly do with some exercise.

The birds were singing overhead in an intense blue sky as she strode out across green meadows starred with the myriad colours of wild flowers, their hearts open to the warmth of the sun, and skirted fields with golden ears of wheat and corn heavy on slender stalks. Strange to think that on the other side of the world, under a still hotter sun, Americans were fighting Spaniards in a group of islands that most, until very recently, had never even heard of. She had worried for a few days that Tadeusz, in his discontent, might offer to fight for his new country, but he had been so insulted by the statement in the newspapers that recent immigrants were not being encouraged to volunteer due to their unhealthy and often defective physique, that that danger had soon passed.

Once she was down in the valley she could no longer see the barn, and with the sun high in the sky she began to feel very tired and thirsty, From the hill it had all seemed so much closer.

As she topped a small rise, she saw at last, down to her left, the men busy at work in the fields of grain and Adam, standing on top of a wain with a pitch fork, piling up the sheaves as they were passed up to him. He was wearing a floppy straw hat, a pair of old-fashioned breeches, and his shirt sleeves were rolled halfway up his arms. The muscles stood out on his tanned forearms and he looked very different from the suave figure he usually cut.

By the time she was half way down the hill, the cart carrying beer and bread and cheese was drawn up in front of the barn and the men had laid aside their scythes and pitchforks and were resting in the shade.

Adam was in the lee of a small copse talking to the mechanic when he saw her.

'What the Devil . . .' he began as he strode across to her. 'Have you walked all this way in the noonday sun without a parasol?' he demanded furiously.

'Only from Carfax,' she said blithely, wondering why he was making such a fuss about nothing. 'Anyway, I don't have a parasol.'

'From Carfax? You little fool! The sun is much stronger than you think!'

'I hadn't realised quite how hot it would be,' she admitted, . passing a weary hand across her forehead.

'Since you're here, you'd better come into the shade and have something to eat and drink,' he said curtly, gripping her wrist in a painfully tight grasp and drawing her to the shady side of the barn, where he sat her down with more force than politeness.

In the shade of the wood-lapped barn the men who, like him, had been working since sun-up, laid aside their straw hats and ate their bread and cheese and drank beer while they took a well-earned rest.

'I hadn't realised how thirsty you could get, just walking,' she said with a sigh, as one of the men passed her an earthenware beer jar. To her intense annoyance, Adam reached out lazily and took the jar from her.

'But I'm thirsty,' she complained.

'Water,' he said firmly. 'Beer'll make your head swim.'

But it was swimming very nicely without any help from the beer. She shook her head impatiently, forcing herself to concentrate.

Adam spread his kerchief on her lap and passed her a hunk of bread and a slab of cheese. 'Thank you,' she said huskily. She picked up the bread, but it was not as easy as it should have been to find her mouth. She had thought she was hungry, but her face felt stiff and she found it difficult to get her jaws around the food.

On the other side of the field the mechanic from Edensville started up the mechanical reaper and she found herself hypnotised by the motion of the red spiky arms, turning like windmill sails. Adam said something to her and she tried to tear her eyes away from the reaper and focus on his face, but her neck was stiff and her muscles would not do her bidding.

He spoke again, more sharply, and she forced her upper body round, but his features blurred into one another.

'Excuse me,' she gulped. 'I – I – don't feel very well.'

'Come on. I'll get you back to the house.' He slipped a hand around her waist and drew her up on to unsteady feet. She struggled to lock her knees, but to her vexation she found herself sagging against him.

'We'll put you on the cart,' he said. 'Here. Put your arm around my neck.'

'I – can – not.' She struggled to enunciate her words clearly. 'It would be best if –'

She shook her head, then wished she had not done so. 'I – I think I am going to be sick,' she said in a strangled voice.

Before she knew what had happened, he had whisked her behind the barn, out of view of the men. The whole world was a blur and then pain seemed to travel up from her boots and she was violently ill. He supported her until the spasms had ceased to rack her body, then wiped her face with his kerchief.

'We'll rig up a canopy over the cart,' he muttered, 'to keep the sun off you.' Bending down he lifted her as if she were a featherweight. To his intense annoyance, as he rounded the corner of the barn with her in his arms, he saw the back of the cart disappearing down the track to Springs House.

With a muttered curse he carried her into the barn, spread his jacket over the hay in a shady corner and laid her down on it.

'So silly,' she muttered.

'Shh!' He smoothed back her hair from her pale face with a cool hand. 'Rest now. I'll take you back when we've finished this field.'

She slept, her dreams a confusion of people from past and present. She was playing the piano in Sarah's house and the rattle of the reaper and the creak of the cart wheels blended into a favourite Chopin study. John Thomsett was watching her, but she turned and it was no longer John Thomsett: it was Adam Kingsley.

The music faded away until all that was left was the sound of the waves and she was in her cabin on the *York*, searching desperately for a chair to jam under the door handle. 'Got to keep Vilaghy out,' she kept telling herself, and her voice chanted the words in time to the waves, but somehow she knew that if she opened the door she would find, not Vilaghy, but Adam.

She felt a hand on her forehead and opened her eyes to see him looking down at her, concern in his face. 'I'll take the chair away in a minute,' she said, but her tongue seemed to be several sizes too big for her mouth and the words came out in a jumble.

He wiped her face with a kerchief dipped in water. 'Sleep,' he said softly.

When at last she awoke it took her a little time to collect her thoughts and remember where she was.

'Better?' asked a voice. She sat up and turned around slowly to see Adam in the barn entrance, silhouetted against the setting sun.

She put her hand to her head. 'A little. I don't feel sick any more, but my eyes ache and my head too.'

'Can you walk back, do you think?' he asked. 'I can send for the cart.'

'No. I think I'd rather walk.' She rose unsteadily to her feet, but the worst of the giddiness had passed and her legs felt once more as though they belonged to her.

'Good. Take my arm, you can lean on me,' he said, slipping an arm round her waist.

She felt herself shiver at his touch. 'It's much cooler than it was,' he said. 'You don't want to catch a chill. My jacket –'

'No. I'm warm enough,' she said hurriedly. She didn't want to wear his jacket, warm with the smell of hay and the smell of him. She shook her head and tried to chase away the foolish thoughts that were crowding in on her, unbidden.

Outside the barn the reaper was still, the men and the horses gone. 'We'll begin again at sun-up tomorrow,' he said. 'We should have all the harvest home by Saturday. If Samuel's doing as well over at Carfax, we'll have a bumper one this year.'

They walked along under the sapphire blue sky as summer day slipped imperceptibly into summer night and as he listened to the calls of the night birds and the chirrup of the crickets, he felt at one with nature and at peace with the world.

They stopped at the little wooden bridge below the falls to watch the moon rise. She leant on the rail, but still he left his hand round her waist.

She drew in her breath sharply. 'It's as if we're the only ones awake in the whole world!' she said in an awed voice.

Below them the light of the harvest moon flooded the landscape, picking up details that were usually lost in the haze of sunshine. The air was so clear that they could see to their right as far as the bluff above Edensville, a faint smudge of smoke hovering above it to mark the position of the city. To their left they could see across vast dark fields of waving corn and pale meadows to the sparkling blue-black waters of the lake.

They stood a while in silence, leaning on the rail, awed by the beauty of the scene before them. 'I always loved harvest-time in England,' he murmured into her hair. 'Never thought I'd be bringing in my own!'

'I never saw a harvest,' she said in a sad soft voice, leaning against him as tiredness began to overwhelm her. 'Only ever read about it. England to me was dirt and dust and sour fogs. All the country I ever knew was Epping Forest – one day a year.'

'Oh, Melisande!' he said on a long sigh, and knew a sudden fierce longing to tell her that she need never again know such unhappiness.

She turned sharply, puzzled at the strangeness in his voice, and the pain shot fiercely through her head again, making her wince.

'We'd better get you back home,' he said, tightening his arm around her waist and biting back the words that threatened to burst through his customary restraint. Along the uneven path she leaned naturally into him, her head just reaching his shoulder, and he found his breathing quickening at the nearness of her and the perfume that rose from her hair.

By the time they reached the house she was almost asleep, walking stiffly like a clockwork tin soldier, her head thumping in time to her steps. She winced at the light from the hall lamps, closing her eyes tightly against the dazzle.

By the subdued light of the green-shaded lamp in his study he looked into her eyes.

'Sunstroke,' he said grimly, and poured her a draught of evil-tasting medicine. She forced herself to swallow it, but she choked on the last mouthful, tears springing to her eyes.

'Poor lass,' he whispered softly. He picked her up easily in his arms and carried her up to her room. She was almost asleep as he drew back the coverlet and laid her tenderly on the bed.

He perched on the edge beside her, remembering that moment on the bridge over the little stream. Was he glad or sorry that she had broken the spell before he could blurt out everything that was in his mind? He could not decide.

She stirred a little, murmuring something unintelligible in her sleep. With a heartfelt sigh he gazed down at her, brushing her hair out of her eyes with a shaking hand.

It was as if he were looking down at himself from a great distance, watching his hand cupping her cheek, watching himself lowering his head towards her where she lay, pale and vulnerable, on the crisp sheets.

What the Devil did he think he was doing? He couldn't believe he was acting this way! Appalled at himself, he jerked away from her as if she had the plague. He turned away from the bed, shaking. He should stay to remove her shoes and belt, but he could not trust himself. He turned back to draw the cover over her; in spite of his earlier resolution, he bent his head and dropped a gentle kiss on her cheek, then, hands rigidly at his sides, he left the room, closing the door quietly behind him.

She slept deeply until just before the dawn when the scenes she had relived in the barn came to fill her dreams, causing her to toss restlessly from side to side and mutter under her breath.

Someone was shaking her. She opened her eyes expecting to see Adam Kingsley's face, expecting to find herself being cradled in those strong but gentle arms. Instead she found herself neatly tucked in her own bed, with Mrs Chobley's anxious face hovering above her.

'Thought you'd never wake up, gel,' said Cook with a sigh of relief. 'Gave up with you altogether last night, though it went against the grain to leave you to sleep in your clothes. I took off your shoes and loosened your lacings. Good job you don't wear stays!'

She turned over on to her side, chin propped on one hand as the events of the previous night came flooding back to her. Had Adam really carried her up here or had she only dreamt it, as she had dreamt that he had kissed her? She shivered as she remembered the delightful feelings that had run through her at his touch – or had she dreamt that too?

'Doctor said as how you're to drink that,' said Cook, setting a glass of milky liquid on the bedside table. 'Mind you do, now, or that headache'll come back again, sure as eggs is eggs. Better get a move on, gel,' she said a little sharply, as Melisande lay, half awake, half dreaming still. 'Mrs Randall is calling for you at ten to take you into Edensville.'

'Whatever for?' she asked, sitting up quickly.

Mrs Chobley shrugged. 'Not my place to ask.' She fished in her pocket and drew out a letter. 'You're to give that to her when she arrives.' She set it beside the glass of medicine. 'Now, up you get. I've drawn a bath for you.'

'You shouldn't be waiting on me, Mrs Chobley!' she protested. 'It isn't proper.'

But Mrs Chobley had already departed.

Emerging from the bath, she dressed herself as quickly as she could. It was going to be another hot day, but to her vexation her lightest skirt was so crumpled from being slept in that she could not possibly wear it again. She pulled on the cotton blouse with the Puritan collar and a print skirt which she had made herself on the Singer's machine from a length of upholstery fabric she had found in the linen room. Not very fashionable, but certainly serviceable. She was half way down the stairs before she remembered the draught and had to run back up to her room to drink it. She set the glass down with a grimace, snatched up the letter and headed for the stairs again as she heard the knocker being plied vigorously. She reached the hall as Nancy opened the massive front door to admit Mrs Randall.

When the greeting were completed, Nancy took Mrs Randall's fashionable light wrap and led her into the morning room, leaving Melisande to bring up the rear.

'Sunstroke, eh?' tutted Mrs Randall as she cast her eye over the note. 'And how do you feel today?'

'Much better, I thank you. I –'

'Have you eaten this morning? I imagine dining was the last thing on your mind yesterday.'

'I – I fear I rose rather late. And I don't wish to hold you up.'

'Nonsense, child!' said Mrs Randall briskly. 'I won't hear of you leaving without breakfast. To spend the day trudging round the shops in this heat on an empty stomach would not be at all wise.' She turned to Nancy with a smile. 'Would you please bring some bread and butter and coffee for two to the dining room?'

Nancy took her indignation to Cook. 'She's only a servant!' she said angrily. 'What gives her the right to eat in the dining room?'

'She's breakfasting with Mrs Randall, sourpuss!' snapped Mrs Chobley. 'You'd hardly expect *her* to eat in the kitchen!'

'Well, I'm not waiting on her!'

'Then Jessie had better do it. Time we started training her upstairs,' said Mrs Chobley malevolently. 'When Hetty marries her young man, we'll be needing a new parlourmaid.'

They set out in the carriage after breakfast; Melisande, seated next to Mrs Randall, looked down in delight at the

251

folds of the smart Indian silk shawl that covered her shoulders, transforming the plain outfit she wore, and twirled the pretty cream sunshade, edged with broderie anglaise, that protected her head from the sun.

'I've been of a mind to look them out for some time,' said Mrs Randall. 'My daughters no longer live at home and the style is too youthful for me.' Melisande accepted them gratefully, revelling in their stylish elegance.

'Why are we to go to Edensville today?' she asked at last.

'I can no longer bear to see you in that same stuff dress and homemade shirtwaist,' said Mrs Randall frankly. 'It is past time that we purchased a more suitable wardrobe for you. Modiste first, then milliner's, then bootmaker's,' she said, marking them off on her fingers.

'But I have not enough money for all that!' exclaimed Melisande.

'My dear Melisande – or may I call you Mel? So much easier! – Doctor Kingsley has given me the money for all the months you have worked for him as unpaid secretary. He said if he gave it to you, you would probably spend it on the school, which was not what he intended at all, so he has given me *carte blanche*. You surely do not desire to go about looking like that much longer?'

Melisande looked at her drab clothes and Mrs Randall's elegant gown and wisely decided not to argue.

By the end of the morning, no one could any longer have described her as drab. She was dressed in a cream pleated high-necked chiffon blouse with modest gigot sleeves and a frill down the front; over flounced muslin petticoats she wore a gored skirt in a moss green silk that perfectly matched her eyes. Somewhere in the pile of boxes was a matching gilet for cooler days. The second modiste they visited had a stock of English tailor-mades, two of which they took away with them, one in a warm golden tweed and the other a walking costume in a mid navy blue with an umbrella skirt, darted close to the hips and flowing down to the ankles.

She sat speechless in the little salon when Mrs Randall reeled off an order for two more walking outfits, three day dresses, another skirt and two more blouses and three evening dresses.

'Dear ma'am,' she protested while the modiste was out of the room, 'I can have no need of so many clothes! Pray do not purchase any more!'

'Dear child,' said Mrs Randall, patting her arm, 'I can only repeat: I have had my instructions, and by heavens, I intend to carry them out! And as I intend to enjoy it,' she added with a mischievous grin which made her look of an age with her companion, 'you might as well do so too.'

So Melisande gave up the struggle and threw herself into the task wholeheartedly. She stood in silence while the two women discussed the rival merits of gauze de soie, crepe de maretz and Lyons heavy silk, but her time at Madame Chantal's had given her an eye for style and colour and she rejected the more extreme gigot sleeves, double skirts and pleated bishop sleeves out of hand.

'But the bishop sleeves, miss! They are the very latest look,' insisted the modiste. 'Straight from Paris, ma'am!' she said, turning to Mrs Randall for support.

'Anything too broad or over-elaborate only looks well on a taller woman,' said Melisande decisively, rejecting out of hand the fussy flounces and double revers. 'I would prefer simpler lines, more fluid and sweeping, if you please.'

The modiste was rather taken aback by this show of obstinacy from one she had mentally pigeonholed as a quiet little country cousin.

For that, Mrs Randall was sure, the hair style was to blame and when they had finished at the modiste's she swept her off to Monsieur Pesquale to have her waist-length honey-blonde braids trimmed and dressed in a soft chignon high on her head.

Melisande looked at herself wide-eyed in the mirror. The hair piled up and fluffed around her face made her look at once more sophisticated and yet more fined down, emphasising her tip-tilted eyes and making her cheekbones more prominent.

'Ma'mselle, she 'ave the vir' good bones,' said Monsieur Pesquale obsequiously. Mel found it hard not to burst out laughing. How could anyone enthuse about 'good bones' when they were the result of years of undernourishment?

From Pesquale's they moved on to Madame Brisarde's, where they bought more hats than she could ever envisage wearing, and then, to her relief, they paused for breath and lunch at the Albany.

She was appalled to see the pile of bandboxes awaiting them in the foyer – for they had added gloves, lace-trimmed handkerchiefs, an evening shawl and a mantlet, silk stockings, boots and shoes to their purchases – but she would have had to be made of wood not to feel a certain frisson as she entered the dining room, carrying a crystal-handled fringed pagoda parasol in moss green to match her skirt, with a neat little jockey hat with tassels perched on top of the chignon – and all heads turned.

They were shown, at Mrs Randall's request, to a private alcove, as they were dining unescorted; the young waiter held out a chair for Melisande and stood admiringly by until recalled to a sense of his duties by the maitre d'hotel.

Mrs Randall drew out her lorgnette and made a show of consulting the menu before ordering 'my usual light luncheon, Hawkswood. You know the kind of thing I like.'

'There is only the ball gown left,' she said, consulting her list while the first course was served. 'We shall go to Lasky's for that. She always dressed my daughters.'

'But I can have no earthly use for a ball gown!'

'And what, pray, do you intend to wear for the Harvest Ball?' demanded Mrs Randall with some asperity.

'But – but I am not invited.'

'Invited?' Her plucked brows rose until they almost disappeared into her curls. 'You live there, you foolish child! I would never have consented to be Adam's hostess unless I was sure you would be there to support me. He tells me you have done sterling work preparing the house.'

'I – I thought I might be invited to the Tenants' Ball.'

'Quite unsuitable!' said Mrs Randall firmly. 'We will *open* the Tenants' Ball, of course, with Adam and Max, but we will come back to the house directly to receive our dinner guests. I wonder Adam or Max did not explain all this to you. I suppose they have been busy with the harvest and they assumed –'

'They assume too much!' snapped Melisande, angry spots of colour on her cheekbones. 'One moment I'm a housemaid who's not subservient enough, the next I am supposed to

254

know I am to be hostess at a ball to which I have not even been invited!'

Mrs Randall heard only the first part of her speech. 'Never – *never* – refer to that time again!' she commanded, looking nervously over her shoulder. She shuddered expressively. 'Society may be more liberal here than in England, but there are still some matters which should not be spread broadcast.'

Melisande looked mutinous, but as the waiter was hovering with another covered dish, she had perforce to drop the subject and turn her attention to the delicacies before her.

The meal was simple but excellent. Unlike the diners on the adjacent table they did not work their way through the entire menu.

At the end of the luncheon, Mrs Randall signed the reckoning and led the way out to the carriage, Melisande following her obediently.

'Put up your parasol,' instructed the older woman. 'For if we have any more of this nonsense, going bare-headed in the hot sun, you will be in bed instead of at the ball, and that would never do, would it?'

No, that would never do, she agreed. Like Cinderella, she would go to the ball. And if it all turned to ashes the next day, she would at least have had her moment of glory.

Then, quite suddenly, reality set in, bringing panic in its wake. She had never been to a ball before, so how was she to know how to behave? There would be many, not least the Pattersons, eagerly waiting to see what mistakes she made.

She turned and looked at Mrs Randall. 'I can't do it,' she said wretchedly. 'Not possibly.'

'Fiddlesticks,' said Beatrice Randall coolly, marching ahead of her into Madam Lasky's. She turned to the girl, frozen on the sidewalk. 'Come along, Mel. Madame is a busy lady and so am I.'

'But there's no point. I –'

'Save your breath, my dear. I don't have time to listen today. I shall call on you tomorrow and you can tell me then all the reasons why not.'

Madame Lasky herself hurried to attend on them and of course it was impossible to continue the discussion in front of her. With a sigh, Mel gave herself up to the assistant to be measured. Fortunately Madame had just such a ball gown as Mrs Randall considered suitable and she promised to have it altered to fit by the next morning.

Mrs Randall stopped only long enough to write a note to the doctor before calling for her carriage and driving back to her own home. 'I cannot stay for tea, I fear, for I have a house guest of my own and must spend some time with him,' she said with a rather smug smile.

'I'm sorry to have kept you from –'

'No need, my dear. I have thoroughly enjoyed myself. Since my daughters married, I have missed our little shopping trips. But I would like to have been here when Ad –' She made a show of clearing her throat: '– when they see you.'

Melisande was restless after her friend's departure. She went to the library to find a book, but could not settle to read it. Every time she moved and the silk rustled, every time she caught sight of her new dress, she remembered the pile of bandboxes on the bed.

She had not brought herself to unpack them yet. She could not rid herself of the conviction that Mrs Randall had made an error, and that the whole wardrobe would have to be returned. And yet she had seemed so certain. She had said too that Melisande was to go to the ball! She shivered. The prospect of the ball enticed and yet repelled her. A mixture of excitement, anticipation and fear overwhelmed her every time she thought about it.

She put the book back on the shelf and returned to her room. She looked at the bandboxes, then with a muttered curse perched the jockey hat firmly on her head and picked up her parasol. As she passed the kitchen door she thought she heard Jessie's voice, but she was set on her path and would not be diverted. Putting up the parasol to shade her face, she set off through the orchard and across the fields to where the men were working.

The spiky red arms of the mechanical reaper came into view first, windmilling busily up and down the field while the men bustled behind, trying to keep up with the voracious monster, binding and stacking as fast as they could. She saw some of the boys from Harbourside, one sitting alongside the driver atop the reaper, the others spread out among the binders or stacking on the wains.

'I see you've split the boys up, Mr McNair,' she said as the grizzled foreman crossed to the cart.

'Wauns, missie,' said McNair, pushing his cap back and mopping his brow. 'We hae a sayin' in the auld country, an' I consider it fits where'er ye find lads – be they Sassenach or Scots, Polacks or Eyetalians – that ane lad is ane lad, twa lads is but half a lad, and three lads t'gither is nae lads at all.'

She chuckled at that, but her face fell when she heard that the doctor had left the fields that morning. 'Rode out to the Hunton's estate,' said MacNair. 'One of the labourer's wives having a difficult birthing.'

When Adam returned that evening he was in high spirits. 'Nothing to compare with bringing new life into the world,' he declared, striding into the study and tossing his leather bag on to the sofa. 'Though I'm sorry I missed the sight of you in your new hat and parasol. Tadeusz gave me a lyrical description.' He looked her up and down and a warm look came into his eyes. 'Beatrice has a good eye for colour,' he said admiringly. 'You look –'

There was a heavy footfall outside the door and he bit off the words, turning away abruptly.

'Ah, Max,' he said coolly as the steward came in. 'Will you join us in a toast to the latest resident of Edensville?' He picked up the decanter. 'Mrs Arkley insists she will name the poor child Adam. If we don't get some new doctors and midwives round here, there will be a whole generation called nothing but Adam and Maud!'

'Maud? Oh, I *am* disappointed,' chuckled Melisande. 'Surely in Edensville the midwife should be called Eve!'

'Then we would only need the serpent!' chuckled Max.

Adam poured her a glass of dry sherry to toast the new baby, but at the first sip she wrinkled her nose and choked on it.

'This we have overlooked!' said Max to Adam in some consternation. 'I don't suppose they drank wine in the Orphanage.'

'And you said Miss Thomsett would not allow strong drink in the house . . .' Which had come first, he wondered: the sister's ban or the brother's heavy drinking? 'That could be difficult. As our hostess –'

'Since no one has even invited me to the ball, the problem is hardly likely to arise!' she snapped.

'Surely Max asked you?' demanded Adam.

Max coloured in embarrassment. 'I thought it was for you to ask her!' he said defensively.

Adam saw the hurt in her eyes and he could have kicked himself – yes, and Max too. He crossed to her side and took her hand. 'Max thought I should and I thought he would,' he said in a tight voice quite unlike his usual decisive tones. 'I'm sorry.'

He saw how she tried valiantly to smile and blink away the tears pricking her eyes. In spite of all she had suffered she had not cried since the first day he saw her – when she thought she had gone blind; perhaps some would not understand why she wanted to cry now, over what was no more than a social misunderstanding, but he understood.

'I am sorry.' He pressed her hand warmly. 'Miss Stevens,' he said with an elaborate bow, 'would you do us the honour of joining us at the Harvest Ball?'

'Wot? Little Milly from Wappin'?' she said in an out-rageous Cockney accent, smiling up at him through the unshed tears. Then: 'Sirs,' she said softly, sweeping an elabo-rate curtsey, 'I should be most happy to accept your kind invitation.'

'Yes, but has she anything to wear?' demanded Max. Adam had noticed before Max's tendency to speak to him about her as if she were not there.

'Fortunately Mrs Randall had more forethought than either of you,' she said before Adam could answer him. 'She purchased a ball gown for me which should arrive tomorrow.' She drew out the note from Mrs Randall and handed it to Adam. 'She left this for you, Doctor Kingsley.'

He read it, colouring in his turn at the polite reproaches in it. The last thing he wanted to do was to offend Beatrice Randall, and not only because her support was vital if he intended to introduce Melisande Stevens into Society. And after her initial criticism of Adam for taking the new teacher to live at Springs House, she had insisted that Melisande should be properly introduced. 'If we do not do so, it looks as though we have something to hide.'

'She hauls me over the coals for not making our intentions clear,' he said gruffly, handing it to Max. 'You should have said something. Asked . . .'

'What was I to ask? I never thought you would invite me to the ball.' Her smile faded. 'I am still not sure it is wise. Have you really considered this, sir? I know Mrs Randall does not like me to speak of my background, but it cannot be ignored. How shall I know what to do? I've never been in polite Society before.'

'You received Mrs Randall and her friend without turning a hair,' he reminded her, crossing to the bell.

'That was different. And it was not a formal ball.'

'It's not as if this is England. Or even New York.' He shrugged. 'This will be just a rural ball; you have only to make people feel at their ease and the hired servants will do the rest. Fortunately you are a quick learner.'

'But I cannot dance!' she protested. 'And as for the dinner . . .!'

'It will be only a little more elaborate than the dinner that is normally served at Springs House,' he said.

'But I –'

'A moment, Miss Stevens.' He cut off her protests as Hetty came to answer the bell. Turning his back on Melisande, he gave the parlourmaid her instructions in a low voice.

She turned to Max. 'Mr Ellsky!' she begged. 'Cannot you make him see sense?'

'I think you make a problem where there is none,' said the steward with a smile. 'Unless – you perhaps do not wish to come to the ball?'

'Yes, of course I do. But I –'

'It is as the doctor says: the Harvest dinner will be only a little more elaborate than any other dinner.'

'Such as the one you will be joining us for in –' Adam drew his watch from his waistcoat pocket ' – in forty-five minutes. Mrs Randall speaks of a lilac dress?'

'Yes.'

'It sounds appropriate. If you would care to change? Then I can sit down to dine with my ward instead of with the schoolteacher. Max, you'll join us?'

Then it was true, she thought. The wardrobe was for her: no one was going to take it away this time. She went upstairs with her head in a whirl, to find Jessie drawing a bath. 'You get in that, Miss, and I'll be back in a trice to help you dress,' said the young maid.

'This is foolish!' protested Melisande. 'I don't need to be waited on. I can dress myself.'

'Seen all them 'ooks down the back?' said Jessie, a sparkle in her eye. 'That dress weren't made for no one to dress single-'anded.'

Adam Kingsley was pacing up and down the drawing room, wondering what he had got himself into – or rather, what Beatrice Randall had got him into. He had overruled all the girl's objections, but one could not pretend they did not exist. When you came down to it, she was a child from a ragged school. Could you count on the education and the fine clothes to disguise her origins?

There was a gentle footfall in the hall outside and he heard Max draw in his breath sharply. He turned to see Melisande standing in the doorway, dressed in a pale lilac dress with a high-waisted sash, of the style made popular by Sarah Bernhardt. She looked exquisite.

His worries and concerns fell away from him as if they had never been. While Max stood rooted to the spot, Adam crossed to offer her his arm and took her into dinner.

Until now he had thought it best for Melisande to dine with Mrs Chobley so he was inevitably a little nervous to see whether she would be overwhelmed by the formal table with its sparkling cut glass and bewildering array of silverware set on crisp damask, not to mention the succession of courses, side dishes and removes, but any fears he might have had that her table manners would reflect her upbringing were soon stilled. She could bear comparison with the best. Thanks to Sarah Thomsett's training, she had no difficulty selecting which cutlery or glassware to use, although she did not seem too enthusiastic about the excellent wines that were always served at the doctor's table.

'You need not finish the wine in every glass,' he said, suppressing a grin at the expression on her face. 'A sip will suffice and the servants will clear whatever is left at the end of each course. Probably better if you don't drink too much: you'll be under the tab –' He cleared his throat. 'You'll be in no fit state for the dancing.'

When the dessert was cleared, he instructed her to withdraw, according to custom, that the gentlemen might enjoy their port in peace.

'Don't the ladies drink port?'

'Under no circumstances! They take their idle chatter to the drawing room.'

'Idle chatter?' she exclaimed indignantly. 'If that is what you think, then I –'

'Not yours,' he chuckled. 'Thank God, you have not yet learned to be as empty-headed as most Society women.' He crossed to hold the door open for her. 'I hope you never will,' he murmured softly.

He had little inclination to linger over his port that evening, however, and he and Max soon joined her in the drawing room. She sat demurely on one of the heavy crimson-upholstered sofas, framed against the heavy red drapes; as they came in, she laid aside the journal she had been leafing through and looked expectantly up at them.

Max crossed the room to open the tall French windows but Adam sat down opposite her, amused. 'You look like a kitten waiting to be stroked,' he said as she looked up at him, green eyes wide.

Over by the windows Max cleared his throat loudly.

The spell that had held them, gazes locked, was broken. She looked away and sought for something to say. 'Now you must tell me what I must do, what I must say,' she said at last, turning to include Max. 'You said you would teach me how to go on.'

'You will have to excuse me,' said Max abruptly. 'I have to ride out to see McNair.'

'Of course. The harvest . . .'

'Stay for tea,' suggested Adam. 'Miss Stevens, if you will ring for Hetty?'

'I can't stay,' said Max curtly. 'McNair will be waiting for me.' He took Melisande's hand, bowed formally, and departed, leaving her to wonder what she had done to offend him.

261

'As hostess, you must ensure that all your guests are comfortable,' continued Adam smoothly as the door closed behind his steward, 'but Max and I will be there to help you. And Mrs Randall. We shall have to practise dancing, but that's best left to the morning when Mrs Randall is here.' He could not admit, even to himself, that her presence alone with him in the drawing room was already sufficiently disturbing; to hold her in close proximity, without the sobering presence of a third person, was more than he felt able to cope with.

'Perhaps you would play for us – for me – until the tea tray is brought in?' he suggested.

She rose to cross the room to the instrument; watching her covertly he saw that the change in her was more than superficial. Her entire way of walking, the sway of her body in the clinging robe, was different – much more graceful, much more sensuous. He tried to consider the matter objectively: since he had solved the matter of the ill-fitting boots she had walked much better, though she had still had a tendency to stride out that contrasted strongly with the delicate steps of fashionable ladies. But now there was a grace and sway to her movements that had not been there before; he imagined that must be due to the dress.

It wasn't entirely the dress, but Melisande, revelling in the strange sensation of the silk underwear against her skin after so long wearing rough cotton or scratchy wool, was unaware of its effect on her – and unaware of his scrutiny.

She seated herself at the pianoforte and was halfway through the Chopin waltz she found on the music stand before she was struck by a sudden thought. She broke off abruptly.

'How did you know I could play?' she demanded accusingly.

'Never seen anyone look more like a pianist,' he said with a ghost of a smile.

'I had rather look like a lady,' she sighed, turning away from the instrument. 'Your guests are sure to see I am an impostor. I don't wish to let you down, but I am bound to do something wrong.'

He shook his head. 'Stop fretting,' he begged. 'After all, you behaved like a lady even when you were supposed to be a housemaid! And what is a lady, when all is said and done?

Someone who knows how to take her part in the little ceremonies and rituals with which we surround our lives, that's all.'

'But I *don't* know. I knew little of society in England: I know even less of American Society.'

What could he tell her? Once Society had been the same on this side of the Atlantic as on the other – a matter of birth. The old Dutch and English founding families had dictated what was or was not acceptable, and for most of them that had included a certain sense of duty, of care towards others less fortunate: *noblesse oblige*. Feudal, but it had had its good · aspects. But now, the leaders of society were those with money.

'I've read about New York Society in Mrs Carter's journals,' she offered. 'The Astors and the Whitneys and the Vanderbilts . . .'

'Not the old families,' he said. 'Self-made men – or the descendants of self-made men. Most of them with more money than they know what to do with. Of course, Edensville society is not the same as New York Society. But it presents the same problems – and the same possibilities.'

'Are they what Sarah used to call the *nouveaux riches*?' she asked.

'A fair description. And they judge as they wish to be judged themselves – by money more than by merit.' Which had its advantages, particularly in his situation. 'Unfortunately their money hasn't necessarily brought them style or manners.'

'Then why do you bother with them?' she asked curiously.

'I want their money,' he said frankly, then gave a shout of laughter at her shocked expression. 'Oh, not for the money itself,' he reassured her. 'It's what I can do with their money - or persuade them to do. You look puzzled.'

'I am. I have seen the bills for the ball.' There had been more money spent on champagne and food and ice than she had ever imagined existed. 'Why not just use *that* money?'

'That money is an investment for the future which will repay itself tenfold. I'm sure the sums involved seem huge to you, but I assure you, they are nowhere near what would be spent on a function in New York or London. An elaborate ball there could cost between ten and fifteen thousand dollars. Even a dinner party would be as much as five thousand.' He laughed at the look of horror on her face. 'But we dine simply here, and use our own produce. Never fear. I have no intention of facing bankruptcy.'

'How can you be sure everyone will come? Mrs Chobley says it's out of season.'

'All the more reason for them to come. The leaders of society will come because it's Springs House, and they have always come to the Harvest Ball. And the *nouveaux riches*, as you call them, will come because, though they have wealth and they have mansions, they do not yet have social acceptability. And they have sons and daughters to marry off. I shall persuade them – without too much trouble – to hold soirées and charity balls in their new mansions, to which I can invite the so-called 'leaders' of society. The money from the charity balls will give me the chance to benefit the school, the dispensary, set up scholarships for promising children –'

'Like Tadeusz and Agnete!' she said, her green eyes widening.

'The next generation won't be the *nouveaux riches* any more; they will themselves be the leaders of Society, with huge inherited fortunes at their disposal. And by then, hopefully, they will be in the habit of supporting my charities.

'But I have neither birth nor money,' Melisande said sadly.

'I warrant you will not find that a bar,' he said stiffly. The thought of all the suitable young men Beatrice had invited did not fill him with enthusiasm. He forced a smile to his face. 'You have looks, you have talents and you have two Society sponsors: me and Beatrice.'

The next morning, Mrs Randall, arriving for an early breakfast tête-à-tête with Melisande, disposed of her objections in much the same manner. 'Take his word for it, my dear child. He knows how shallow Society can be.'

'But he does not need to be accepted,' she pointed out. 'Even though he is English, he is already part of Society.'

'Oh, the English are very much *à la mode*,' said Beatrice Randall. 'Especially with the mamas of American heiresses. They would like nothing better than to marry off their daughters to a title. Even though –' She stopped abruptly and busied herself with fussing over the muffins, which Hetty had set in a chafing dish on the huge sideboard before he left.

'He told me he was educated at Harrow, so his family must have had either money or position or both!' said Melisande, a frown creasing her forehead. 'Do you know, I do not think he has ever mentioned his family. And I have seen no photographs or portraits. Are his parents still in England?'

'He doesn't need a long line of family portraits to introduce him into Society,' said Beatrice Randall a little snappily. 'People welcome him – apart from Mrs Patterson – for who he is.'

'But Mrs Patterson welcomes him,' said Melisande, puzzled.

'Yes. Of course she does,' replied Mrs Randall hastily. 'Now we cannot sit here chattering all day. We have work to do.' And Melisande had a feeling that she had been very firmly headed off.

To her disappointment, Doctor Kingsley was not able to fulfil his promise to teach her to dance, claiming that his presence was required in the fields to supervise the last few days of the harvest.

'Drat the man!' exclaimed Mrs Randall. 'But perhaps it will be better if he doesn't see you until the ball. He will have an even bigger surprise then.'

'I doubt he will even notice me among so many sophisticated people.'

'My dear Mel, what nonsense you do talk! Now, go and dress. I brought one of Amy's old ball gowns for you. We cannot risk marking your own gown before the ball. And be sure to wear the train. You must learn to manage a train before we can begin the dance instruction. How fortunate that George is coming. Otherwise I should have to partner you and accompany you, and that could have been a trifle difficult.'

'George?' she asked.

The doorbell sounded loudly, cutting through the still summer air, and she could have sworn Mrs Randall blushed. 'I imagine this is he now,' she said, making a show of rearranging the ornaments on the whatnot. 'Hurry along, Jessie is waiting to dress you.'

Amy's ball gown was magnificent, and Melisande gave a little shiver as the folds of amber silk caressed her skin. It had a softly draped train, but like the ivory silk gown she was to wear to the ball, it was so cut away in front and at the back, the little lace sleeves so low down on the arms, that it was trimmed with ribbons to fasten on the shoulder to hold it up.

'But, ma'am, I fear it does not really fit me,' she said, hesitating to sound ungrateful. She looked down doubtfully at her bosom. 'I – I seem to be a bit too big for it.'

'No, no,' laughed Mrs Randall. 'All young ladies must wear their gowns décolleté, I assure you. Ankles must never be seen, that goes without saying, but no young lady would consider a gown which does not show off her shoulders and bosom. And your skin is very good: you need not hesitate to wear such a dress.'

She made her walk up and down the drawing room until she had mastered the art of moving gracefully in the elegant robe. 'Very good. Now flick the train to one side as you turn. Catch the loop in your hand to dance. No, not like that. The merest dip of the knees, child!'

At last, satisfied with her progress, she crossed to the door to the library. 'Very well, George,' she called. 'I believe we are ready for you now.'

Colonel Randall was a stocky, red-faced Englishman, a cousin of Beatrice's late husband. 'Delighted to help, young lady,' he boomed, twirling his snowy whiskers. 'Looking forward to the ball. Get to know Beatrice's neighbours.'

'Do you live in New York?' asked Melisande politely.

'Don't live anywhere, m'dear. Been travelling the world looking for somewhere to settle ever since m'commission expired. Couldn't stomach India. Too full of other old colonels and their pauky wives, drinking 'emselves ter death! Thought I'd see how Beatrice was getting along, out here in America!'

'I'm trying to persuade George to become involved with the Harbourside schemes,' Mrs Randall explained. 'Miss Stevens is the young lady who teaches in the immigrants' school, George.'

'Does she, b'Gad! Don't know but what I might take more of an interest there then,' he said, rolling a glowing eye in

Melisande's direction. 'Mind you, if Adam thinks the scheme worthwhile, that's good enough for me.' He turned back to Melisande. 'Known Adam's family for years,' he said with a beam. 'Why, I remember when –'

'Come along, George,' interrupted Mrs Randall. 'To the matter in hand.'

'At your service, Beatrice.'

'Now, it happens that Miss Stevens has not previously had the opportunity to attend a ball, but we do not wish the old tabbies to know that. Could you help me teach her?'

'I could think of nothing that would give me greater pleasure,' he said, bowing to both ladies with a flourish and affording Mel a glimpse of the dashing young subaltern he must once have been.

Mrs Randall sat down at the keyboard and Melisande and Colonel Randall danced the waltz, the polka, the boulanger, the country dances, the Lancers. They danced dashingly, they danced sedately; by the end of the afternoon, with the Colonel's expert tuition and her own natural sense of rhythm, Melisande was confident she could bear her part in any dance which might be danced at the ball.

Beatrice Randall was showing her how to dispose her fan, train, reticule and *carnet de bal* to leave her hands free, when they heard Adam's voice in the hall.

'Quickly, Mel!' hissed her tutor. 'Upstairs now and change! I don't want anyone to see you until the ball.'

Startled, she did as she was bid, whipping her train up as she rushed upstairs in her little satin slippers.

When she reappeared in the drawing room shortly before dinner she had changed into a more demure, but nevertheless fashionable and sophisticated dress in a soft peachy shade, trimmed with blonde lace and braid, delivered from the modiste that morning. As she came in the two men were engaged in a vigorous discussion of a suitable hairstyle for a debutante to wear. 'For you must agree, Colonel,' said Adam, standing with his back to the empty fireplace and a glass in his hand, 'that she has rather too much curl in her hair.'

Melisande was not sure that she relished being discussed in the abstract, as if she were not there, though perhaps she should regard their interest as flattering.

267

'I am insisting, Mel, that you have your hair done by my dresser,' said Beatrice Randall. 'In the present rage, you know, after the Princess of Wales.'

'With a crimped fringe?' She wrinkled her nose. 'I think my hair is quite curly enough, without any more . . . If you please, ma'am, I have a suggestion.'

She whisked herself back out of the door and ran to the library. She scrabbled through a pile of periodicals stacked on a small inlaid table till she found what she was looking for.

Back in the drawing room she placed it timidly in Mrs Randall's hands.

'Goodness, child!' she exclaimed, looking at the fashion plate in question. 'What a hideous gown!'

'Yes, but what about the hair? Will it do?'

Mrs Randall placed a hand over the offending gown and looked critically at the hairstyle in which the hair was drawn up smoothly into a coronet, set on the crown of the head with a rope of pearls around it. As unlike the fashionable frizz as could be.

'It's certainly something quite different. But flowers instead of the pearls, I think, and little wisps around the face to soften it. No, Adam, you may *not* see it. You must wait with the others to see the transformation.' She closed the periodical, looking scathingly at the front cover.

'Typical of the kind of rubbish Almeria Carter filled her mind with,' she sniffed. 'And now, let us go into dinner. Melisande, Colonel Randall will take you in.'

She sat at the foot of the table with the Colonel on her right and Mrs Randall on her left, chatting to each in turn, performing with natural ease her duties. But when, in response to a sign from Mrs Randall, she rather self-consciously rose to lead the way to the drawing room, the older woman very firmly took her arm at the door and told her to bid the gentlemen good night.

'You will need all the sleep you can manage,' she said. 'I doubt you'll see your bed tomorrow night.'

She took her leave of the gentlemen with a polite curtsey. At the foot of the staircase she turned impulsively to her friend.

'Dear Mrs Randall, you have been so kind and helpful. I hope I will not let you down.'

'Stop fretting, child. You will do very well. I would not be at all surprised, Mel, if you were to be the Belle of the Ball!'

Melisande shook her head. 'I expect Adam and Max will partner me, and the Colonel, just to be kind,' she said. 'But no one else will want to dance with a nobody.'

But even if she did not dance at all, at least she had a beautiful gown to wear.

Shrugging herself into her new lace-trimmed nightdress, made of the finest Hindoo muslin, she shook her head to clear away such thoughts: the Harvest Ball was an unexpected treat, one that would almost certainly never come her way again, and she was determined to enjoy it to the full. And if at midnight the golden coach turned back into a pumpkin and her clothes to rags – well then, no one could ever take away her memories of the time Milly from the Wapping Home for Waifs and Strays played Society hostess.

Society Lady

She was woken next morning by the sound of the heavy curtains being drawn open by the hired maid, and lay a moment with her eyes closed, basking in the warmth of the diffused sunlight filtering through the fine muslin drapes on to her cheek.

'If you please, miss, Mrs Randall has arrived and they're waiting breakfast for you,' said the girl, setting down a tray on the bedside table. 'Your maid is drawing a bath for you.'

She was out of bed and bathed and dressed in no time. As she rushed into the dining room she apologised for her tardiness.

'Dear Mel, *never* run,' said Beatrice reprovingly. 'A lady always walks and a lady is *never* late.'

Adam Kingsley looked over his shoulder from the side table where he was helping himself from the chafing dishes – for the servants never waited at breakfast and only appeared to replace dishes or replenish hot water – and smiled at the look of puzzlement on Mel's face. 'You were not late, we were here too early,' he explained, his grave expression belied by the dancing imp of humour in his eyes.

She suppressed the answering laugh with difficulty, but Mrs Randall was after all the arbiter of accepted behaviour, her guide through the labyrinth of this strange land called Society, and she would have to accept whatever she told her. Storing it away with the rest of the information she was accumulating, she hurried round the table to take her seat.

As she drew the chair out from the table Mrs Randall turned a frosty look on her host.

'My dear sir, how can you expect anyone to treat Mel as a lady if you do not?'

Adam coloured and set his dish aside, coming round the table to hold her chair out for her before returning to his own.

'But you need not,' she stammered. 'You know I am not and – and –'

'Yes he does need. And yes you *are*,' said Beatrice severely. 'So let us hear no more about it.'

They began to breakfast. Melisande, embarrassed to think that she was forcing the doctor to act in a most hypocritical way, felt at first unable to contribute to the light chatter, until she was brought to attention by Mrs Randall. 'It is your duty, my dear, to join in the conversation, to stimulate it, in fact, if it begins to flag. If all else fails, talk about the harvest, or the school, if appropriate, but whatever you do, do not allow the conversation to die.'

Just then Hetty showed the Colonel in and when greetings had been exchanged he consented to take a cup of coffee, having breakfasted some hours before. While Hetty bustled about with fresh coffee, Melisande began to construct conversations in her head.

'But, ma'am,' she said as the maid left, 'what am I to say if anyone asks me where I come from? Who my family is – was?'

'If anyone is so ill-bred as to ask you direct – that would be completely out of the question in London or New York, but here I fear we cannot entirely rule it out! – you need say only that you lived most of your life in England and that your family did not go about much in society. Do you think that will suffice?' she asked Adam.

'That will do very well. And as so many of them are themselves new families . . .' He saw Mel's worried frown and his hand went out to her across the table. 'You need not be ashamed of your background, Melisande. But I see no need to shout it to the world either.'

He looked as if he were about to say more, but compressed his lips and fell silent. As he dropped his eyes abruptly back to his plate, Mel looked up and caught a grave exchange of glances between the Colonel and Mrs Randall.

Later that day they went for a drive in the carriage; Beatrice looked on with barely suppressed amusement as Adam and

271

Max indulged in a little polite skirmishing as to who should sit next to Melisande, attired in one of her smart walking costumes and with the neat tasselled hat tipped audaciously over one eye. They drove sedately out to the valley road and then walked a little way, skirting the stubble fields, to where the last stand of wheat stood ready to be cut. The farmworkers, a mixture of Poles, English, Scots, Ukrainians and Italians, had all brought over their traditions and one of the strongest was the bad luck associated with the cutting of the last stand.

The farmworkers were in their best clothes, some of them with little ribbon decorations at the lapel or in the buttonholes or pinned to straw hats, drawn up in a circle around the last stand of golden wheat, scythes in their hands. Leaving the Colonel to hover solicitously around the ladies, Adam and Max crossed the field to join the men.

There was a lot of shouting in many languages, and a flask was circulated among the men. Then they formed a circle, Adam raised his hat and called out: 'One to get ready!' And as the men drew back their arms the sun winked on the oiled and sharpened scythes. 'Two to get steady!' And they braced themselves. 'Three to – GO!' he bellowed, and the scythes whistled through the air and clattered against each other as they sliced through the golden stalks. The four gang leaders each took a handful of the wheat, stripped the ears and scattered the grain to the four corners of the field, an oblation and an apology for confusing the harvest gods. The remaining ears were then gathered up to be decorated with red ribbons and carried home in triumph. After a brief appearance in church next day the sheaf would be divided up, the stalks woven into traditional shapes and hung up over hearths until the next harvest.

She did not see Adam again for the rest of the day, for while he changed and rode off after a light luncheon to see how his namesake was faring, Mrs Randall insisted that Mel went to her room to rest. She went reluctantly, protesting that she was not in the least tired – and anyway, she was far too excited to sleep. But when she slipped between the cool linen sheets her eyes closed in spite of her determination.

She had a light meal on a tray in her room, where she was joined by Mrs Randall: 'For it will be a long time before either of us can sit down,' she said, nibbling daintily at an almond cake while she racked her brains to see whether there was anything vital she had forgotten to instruct her protégée in.

Then the maid came to tell them that the hairdresser had arrived and it seemed to Mel that that was the last moment of peace they were ever likely to have. She had fretted earlier in the day while the maid washed her hair, irritated to have to sit while someone else did something she felt quite capable of doing herself, but now she was content to sit in a turquoise dressing robe while the clever agile fingers of Monsieur Pesquale trimmed and twisted her hair into an elegant style that she knew she could never have attained herself. She looked in the mirror when he had finished the transformation and hardly recognised herself. Soft curls wisped around her ears while the rest of the hair was swept up into a coronet of plaited and entwined locks. It made her look, she thought, oddly hollow-cheeked and a little distant.

'It will look less severe when we have pinned in the flowers,' promised Mrs Randall. 'But not yet.'

She watched, fascinated, as Miss Timms, the dresser, arrayed Mrs Randall in an elegant robe of deep sapphire with rows of beading around the corsage. 'It should be black, of course, but I never could abide black and Jack, my late husband, made me promise never to wear it.' She hooked a splendid pair of sapphire and diamond ear drops in her lobes and Miss Timms set a matching tiara on her crimped hair.

'You look magnificent, ma'am!' exclaimed Mel.

'Good!' Her eyes crinkled in a smile. 'That was what I aimed for.' She turned, skirts swishing, to check her back view in the cheval mirror. 'But you positively must cease calling me ma'am. It makes me feel so old!'

'But what will I call you?'

'Could you bear to call me Aunt Beatrice? I quite feel like an aunt at the moment, preparing you for your debut!' she laughed.

'I should be honoured . . . Aunt Beatrice.'

'Good.' She patted her hand. 'My daughters will be among the dinner guests: nice girls, though I say so myself. If you need any help, turn to them; they will be only too pleased, I know. And their husbands – Good gracious, child! What have I said to make you cry?'

273

'Nothing. Oh, no, it is nothing you've said. Just . . . everyone is being so kind to me!' she said with a watery sniff.

'Why not? Do you have a monopoly on being kind to others?' demanded Mrs Randall briskly. 'Now, here's Timms to help you dress. Wipe those tears away. We cannot have you greeting our guests red-eyed, can we! That's it, underskirt first,' she said, as Timms set it out on the bed.

The girl stroked her hand over the confection of silk and lace, itself so much richer than any robe she had ever had. She started to say something, then broke off as she saw the expression of wrath on the older woman's face.

'What are those?' demanded Beatrice Randall, a look of loathing on her face.

'Corsets,' said Timms woodenly.

'I can see they are corsets,' replied Mrs Randall in something ' perilously approaching a snap. 'And if by now you don't know what I think about corsets –'

'They came with the dress, ma'am,' said the dresser.

'That doesn't mean we have to use them.'

'But the line of the dress . . .'

'She hasn't worn corsets before, thank Heavens, and she will not start wearing them now.'

'As you wish, ma'am.' The dresser turned away with a disapproving sniff.

'Sarah said she would buy corsets for me when I was seventeen,' offered Melisande.

'And did she?'

'No. She – I suppose she forgot.' But in her heart she knew that it was just another way in which her teacher had tried to ignore the fact that her pupil was growing up.

'Then let us be thankful for small mercies,' said Mrs Randall briskly. 'We bring up our children to be fit and active, then, just as the body matures, we clap it into a cage! Just when it needs exercise we put it in a strait-jacket so it can hardly move!' It was a subject on which she felt strongly. 'And then we are surprised when the muscles of the body give up! Of course, it's a self-fulfilling prophecy: by the time we are middle-aged, the body can no longer cope without the strait-jacket. Not to mention the dangers of fainting and the compression of the inner organs . . .'

Timms was not willing to give up without a fight. 'But fashion, ma'am,' she bleated.

'If nature had meant us to be rigid, Timms, the good Lord would have given us a shell. Exercise and a good diet are all that is needed to keep a healthy body. Remember that, Melisande.'

'Yes, ma'am . . . I mean, Aunt Beatrice.'

'A fit mind and a healthy body are more important than an eighteen-inch waist.'

'But, ma'am,' said Timms, in a last ditch attempt, 'all the other young ladies will be tight-laced. And surely, if the doctor paid for the dress he will expect the young lady to follow the fashion?'

'No, he will not!' said Mrs Randall decisively. 'As a medical man he should be against it. And anyway,' she concluded, 'he ought not to know about such things.'

Defeated, Timms picked up the overdress and cast it over Melisande's head, taking care not to disturb her coiffure. Mel shivered at the feel of the silky folds on her skin. The dress, of ivory satin embroidered with scattered rosebuds, was hooked up, the sash of moss green velvet which matched her eyes was tied in a soft bow below the bust in the new Directoire fashion, the satin and lace train arranged to hang in soft folds from the shoulders. It would be removed before they want to the barn, of course, for fear of dirtying it on the earth floor.

'Perfect,' approved Mrs Randall, unwrapping the tissue-wrapped rose pink satin slippers. 'Not too overdone. Simple.'

'Some jewellery?' suggested Timms.

'Hmm.' Mrs Randall stepped back to look at her. 'Diamonds would be unsuitable for a debutante, of course.'

'Just as well I have none,' said Melisande with a chuckle.

As if on cue a knock fell on the door and Timms opened it to find a footman bearing packages.

'Flowers from our beaux!' jested Beatrice, handing Melisande one of the two long boxes. Mel's heart jumped as she recognised Adam's firm handwriting, then fell again as she saw that she had Beatrice's box. She switched them round with a smile and saw Max's solid inscription on her box, which opened to reveal a spray of tiny rosebuds.

275

'Your first bouquet, miss,' said Timms, smiling rather foolishly as she pinned the spray to Mel's dress. 'Will you open the other boxes, miss?'

She looked at Beatrice for approval. 'Open them, my dear,' she smiled, as Miss Timms pinned the hothouse orchids to her corsage. 'They are for you.'

Melisande opened them with trembling fingers; never before had she had so many gifts. There was a fan from the Colonel, of delicate carved ivory sticks with mother-of-pearl handle, a dainty evening bag from Max, a pair of pearl drop earrings from Aunt Beatrice, and a single pearl on a green velvet ribbon signed flourishingly 'Adam'.

Overwhelmed, she could hardly get a word out, hugging Beatrice enthusiastically while the dresser threaded the earrings on to gold wire screws – for Beatrice flatly refused to pierce her ears there and then.

Coming back into the room after fetching her evening bag Beatrice saw, out of the corner of her eye, Mel slipping one of the cards into her reticule. She thought she had a good idea which one it was, but said nothing.

Timms twined the rosebuds into Mel's coronet of hair, sprayed her with a light perfume and declared her at last ready to be seen.

On the landing at the head of the ornamental staircase which led down in a graceful curve to the saloon, which in turn opened on to the ballroom, Beatrice paused.

'Wait till I get to the bottom before you start, Mel,' she instructed. 'In case you tread on my train,' she added, inventing a reason where she could not confess the true one.

Melisande watched in some trepidation as Beatrice set off down the stairs, her train swishing behind her. She could see Adam and Max waiting for them in the hall below, formally attired in swallow-tail coats and trousers, white bow ties and black buckle-fastened pumps. Adam wore a red silk cummerbund and his unruly black hair was for once brushed flat and off his forehead. She thought how very handsome he looked.

Beatrice was half way down the stairs when Melisande had a sudden overwhelming vision of all the people who would be coming to dine and the others coming to the ball and she was quite sure that she could never do it. Panic washed over her:

her heart began to pound furiously and her legs would not do her bidding.

Beatrice stopped at the turn and looked back with a question in her eyes.

'I – I can't,' she whispered.

Beatrice's eyes crinkled in a smile and she held out her hand to the girl.

'Come along, Mel,' she said softly, 'or we'll make everyone late.'

And then the prospect of letting Beatrice and Adam down was suddenly far more alarming than the thought of all those guests and before she realised what she was about, she had picked up her train and set off down the stairs after her friend.

The two men looked up and smiled as Beatrice sailed regally down the stairs, then their eyes went past her to the vision gliding down behind her. Max drew in his breath sharply and Adam ran a finger behind his stiff shirt collar to loosen his bow tie, which suddenly seemed too tight.

Beatrice, suppressing a smile of satisfaction, turned to watch with them. Mel was very pale, as befitted a debutante, but Beatrice was delighted to see that her new style had not flattened the vital personality which had carried her from the Orphanage to the ball room.

Adam stepped forward, hand outstretched, to meet her at the foot of the stairs, but he got himself tangled up with Max somehow and by the time they had side stepped round each other, it was Max who handed Melisande across the saloon while Adam fell in behind with Mrs Randall.

'Thank you both for my beautiful presents,' she said, just before they stepped out to the carriage.

'My gift is not nearly as beautiful as the girl carrying it,' said Max with an unexpected burst of gallantry which made her blush.

Adam merely bowed formally. 'It is a pleasure to be able to express my gratitude for your assistance in the preparations,' he said coolly.

Outside the Great Barn, midway between Carfax and Springs House, were hitched a great number of gigs, carts and saddle horses. As the group from Edensville arrived, McNair and the leader of the harvest gang, dressed somewhat bizarrely in a flower-bedecked hat, came out into the warm early evening sunshine to meet them and invite them in.

Inside, the barn had been divided, one part set out with long trestle tables groaning beneath the weight of hams, pies, roasts and huge harvest loaves set between barrels and flagons of cider and ale, the other with a wooden floor erected over the earth for dancing.

The band struck up a lively jig as they entered, and the men and women formed an aisle down which they passed.

McNair rose to his feet to make a short speech of welcome and as she sank onto the chair that was being held out for her by a blushing beardless youth, Mel caught sight of David's mother and smiled at her.

She was sorry the Jeffersons had declined the invitation to the ball, but Blanche Jefferson had been adamant.

'David will come to the ball, of course,' she said, 'but Samuel and I will be much happier at the Barn Dance.' Dressed in a pretty print dress, arm in arm with a beaming Samuel, she gave no sign that there was anywhere else she would rather be.

Adam rose to answer McNair's speech of welcome. 'Friends,' he began, his deep voice carrying across the barn, 'I hope you have as much satisfaction as I have in this splendid harvest. We have been blessed this year with superb conditions, for the crops and for the fruit. Prices are high, and there will be a share of the profits for all.' His next words were almost lost in the cheers and hand-clapping that followed: at a guess some of the men had already broached the barrels. 'Thank you all for your hard work,' he concluded. 'Now – on with the celebrations!'

Jem Radley, the man in the flower-bedecked hat, stepped up on to the platform.

'Friends, I won't keep you long from the dance,' he said. 'But I'll thank Doctor Kingsley right heartily for his kind words. You'd go far to find a better man to work for, aye, and Mr Ellsky too, this side the ocean or the other!' The men cheered and clapped his words. He took a glass from the table at his side and raised it with a flourish. 'So we'll drink to the harvest and the land and the springs and the beauty of all our ladies!'

'The Harvest! The Springs! Beautiful ladies!' came the ragged echoes, and the men raised their glasses high and drained them. Then, to Mel's surprise, Jem Radley bowed to her and, taking her hand, drew her from her seat and across the barn as the band struck up a strange, rather haunting tune.

She looked at Adam in startled enquiry as she passed him, but he only smiled and continued talking to McNair, arranging for the remnants of the Harvest Supper to be taken to the poor families living on the edge of Eden Springs.

Jem Radley stopped in front of a striking woman in the crowd, tall and stately with a dark, almost swarthy beauty and, bowing, held out his free hand to her. One on each hand he moved down the length of the barn and Mel struggled to pick up the elaborate figure he was dancing.

'Don't try to work it out, m'dear,' called the dark woman across him. 'Just go with the music.' And so she did, and the three of them moved rhythmically around the room, others falling in behind them as they passed.

At the end of the dance Melisande felt alive, tingling with suppressed energy. When Adam announced that it was time to leave the barn she felt oddly reluctant, but her time there was, after all, just a dress-rehearsal for the main event of the Ball.

'She has not drunk any of that cider or ale, has she?' asked Adam anxiously, noting the flush of colour in Mel's cheeks. She looked like one of those glossy-leaved hothouse plants that suddenly runs riot, producing exotic, heady-perfumed blooms in uncontrolled abundance.

'She has no need of cider – or champagne,' laughed Beatrice. 'She's drunk on the occasion!' She looked fondly across the barn at her protégée. 'I am pleased to see how very much at her ease she is – and that makes the others feel at ease too. I anticipate no problems.'

As they left the barn, Mel became separated from the others for a moment by the press of people who came to see the carriage off. The dark woman came up to her with a smile and stood at her side.

'Don't take it ill I should talk to you so,' she said, 'but there's good fortune for you here, missie, same as there's been for me.' She took Mel's hand and looked down at it with a little crooked smile. 'You're not like all the other young girls who comes to

279

Margaret to hear their fortunes told. There's more to your life than just finding yourself a man. Shows in your face, as well as in your hand. Even so, you'll be wed within the year.' She saw the look of surprise on Mel's face and laughed. 'It won't be to the first, nor yet the second or third as asks you. Do but have faith, dearie.'

Melisande smiled and thanked her politely, but something of her doubt must have shown for the other woman said grimly: 'Aye, you're another disbeliever. I sees it in your face. But if I told you your folk loved music – what then?'

Again the lift of the curtain and the sound of a woman singing, the flicker of candlelight in a hushed, crowded room.

'But you've known poverty and misery too,' added Margaret.

She bit her lip. Was her secret out? Was she to be exposed as an impostor even before the ball began? How could this woman know?

'Sure, and no one told me,' said Margaret. 'I have the sight.'

'The sight?'

'Second sight, missie. So your secret's safe with me, never fear. Go now and have the best evening of your young life. The gods watch over you.'

Back at Springs House, Beatrice whisked her off to the dressing room where Timms was waiting to tidy her hair and arrange the lace train. Beatrice began to get flustered, thinking of a thousand and one things she had omitted to tell her charge.

'Of course all the young men will want to take their partners out on to the piazza. Such a warm evening and –'

'The piazza?'

'Outside the ballroom. It is not unacceptable, but it is for you to make sure they toe the line. An arm around the waist is one thing, but do not be letting them take liberties.'

'But I –'

'Drat! There are the first dinner guests arriving. We shall have to hurry or we shall not be there to greet them. Have you not finished there yet, Timms?'

'Finished, ma'am,' said the dresser, adjusting a straying rosebud in Mel's coiffure.

'Then come along, child. And remember everything I've told you.'

'But, Aunt Beatrice, I –'

They reached the top of the stairs just as the first carriage debouched its passengers into the hall where a stately butler directed them to the dressing room to leave their wraps, and then preceded them up the stairs and announced them in sonorous tones.

'It's only the Patterson women,' said Mrs Randall to Adam with a frown. 'Don't know that I would have hurried so if I had realised.'

While Mrs Randall exchanged vapid pleasantries with Mrs Patterson, Melisande found a moment to peek at her *carnet de bal* nestling between the bowls of lilies on a small table. To her surprise, a number of names were already written in: Max was down to open the ball with her, then the Colonel had inscribed his name against the second, Adam against the third. Someone else, whose name she could not quite make out, had written 'engaged' against the supper waltz. She prayed it was not Mr Patterson. Three of the dances after supper had also been marked.

'Seven dances!' she whispered to Beatrice, in a brief lull between greeting the dinner guests. 'I don't care if I sit the rest out,' she breathed, eyes bright with excitement, 'for I am to dance seven dances, and nearly all with my friends!' Beatrice smiled quietly to herself as she turned to greet the next guests, an ironmaster from Edensville and his mousy wife. She thought it unlikely Melisande would sit out a single dance: already out of the corner of her eye she could see the ironmaster's son marking his name on the *carnet de bal*. She was particularly pleased she had made Max and Adam sit up and take notice; they had been taking her protégée far too much for granted.

Introduced to Melisande, the dinner guests looked curiously at her as they bowed over her hand or exchanged curtsies before passing on to greet Adam and Max, but as no explanation was forthcoming, speculation continued unchecked. Some of the Edensville residents already knew of her work at the school, but where she had come from no one seemed to know.

281

Melisande was delighted to see the Colonel and hurried forward to thank him for his gift.

'M'dear girl, the fan was m'wife's and she'd have been as delighted as I am to see it adorning so beautiful a wrist.' He bent to kiss her hand and then her cheek before turning to greet Beatrice in a far from avuncular manner.

Mrs Randall's daughters turned out to be as charming as their mother, whom they greatly resembled, though Amy was a little fairer and Bella much darker. Their husbands were complete opposites: Tom Bennett was a big bear of a man, tall and very quiet, while John Wintour was a smaller, wiry man with an excess of energy which seemed to trip out of him in all directions. Amy and Bella were pleasant and friendly and Melisande found herself chatting to them without reserve, which added fuel to the rumour flying around the dinner guests that she was in some way related to them, possibly through their father who had, after all, been a relative of the Colonel's.

The dinner was splendid. She had never seen so much food on a table at any one time. Course followed course as footmen glided silently in and out bearing new delights, removing empty plates, filling glasses, while the twenty elegantly dressed men and women chattered gaily to one another about the political news, the latest gossip, the newest fashion or the success of the harvest. Down the table she could see Harriet Minton chatting easily to the ironmaster who in spite of his great wealth and position in Edensville Society looked even less at ease than she felt with the vast array of crystal and silver on the table.

She was talking to the Reverend Elias James about her school and hoping he would not ask her why she did not attend his church, when Beatrice Randall caught her eye. She brought their talk to a conclusion and she and Beatrice rose to their feet together.

'Ladies,' said Beatrice, 'let us withdraw.'

The gentlemen surged to their feet as the ladies departed in Beatrice's wake.

'Well done!' whispered Adam and Max in unison, as Mel, bringing up the rear, passed through the double doors to the saloon. They smiled, a little shame-faced, at each other, then returned to their brandy and cigars.

By ten o'clock the drive was full of carriages, some with liveried coachmen, jostling to set down the rest of the ball guests. The saloon and the ballroom were rapidly filling with a brilliant and richly-dressed throng; conversation and laughter rose confusedly on the heated air and the musicians filled the night with lively and entrancing melodies.

'Glad to see such a crowd of young people here,' said the Colonel, surveying the ballroom with satisfaction. 'Be able to start the dancing early, instead of all that tiresome promenading they go in for in New York.'

As the musicians struck up for the first dance, Melisande took Max's arm and followed Beatrice and Adam on to the floor where they were to take a few turns before the guests joined them.

'You have done an excellent job, Beatrice,' said Adam, watching Melisande out of the corner of his eye. 'She moves with such grace and assurance.'

'Oh, I don't take the credit for it all,' replied Beatrice with a sidelong glance up at her partner. 'She has a pretty elegance all of her own.'

'Nevertheless, I am amazed at the transformation you have wrought,' he insisted. 'Though a new hairstyle and a fashionable gown can make such a difference too.'

'The beauty and the sparkle have been there all along,' she said shrewdly. 'But now she knows what it is to be cherished, she is unfolding her wings like a butterfly.'

It was an apt description, for Mel flitted from one partner to the other through the evening, exciting admiration and speculation wherever she went. She might have aroused less tender feelings in mothers of plainer daughters as the young men thronged about her, were it not that she put on no airs and danced as enthusiastically with the older men as with the younger, and when her card was full and she had to disappoint a suitor for a dance, always made a point of introducing the disappointed applicant to one of the unpartnered girls sitting out, so that even the most critical mama was forced to concede that she seemed a charming girl.

She had never imagined an evening could hold so many varied pleasures. Max was rather overcome by her frank enjoyment of it all. He was not a good dancer and never felt comfortable with such large gatherings. An evening with friends or a quiet dinner party with people he knew well was much more in his line. To find himself opening the ball with a beautiful girl who was the focus of all eyes, was for him a double ordeal; for a few moments he felt quite unable to speak. Her ready sympathy was aroused by his nervousness and she began to talk to him, not the kind of conversation which required answers, but idle comments which soon set him at his ease once more.

Truth to tell she was not entirely at her ease herself: being held in the arms of a young man with a warm glow in his eye was not at all the same as dancing with Colonel Randall!

As she spun away and then back into his encircling arms and her bosom brushed against his jacket she felt the colour rise into her face. How strange it was that a society so nervous of the body that it swathed its swimmers in tents, banned all mention of legs, even in some houses going so far as to swathe the legs of tables and pianos in thick cloth, should encourage the members of the higher echelons of society to flaunt their almost naked bosoms. Some of the ladies had even lower décolletés than she had; indeed, one or two of the plumper ones looked as though they were in imminent danger of bursting out of the tops of their dresses. Those older matrons who still wore bustles looked to Melisande's eyes quite ridiculous, forced as they were by their tight-lacing into a sort of tortured S-shape. One extremely large middle-aged woman was dancing with a man much shorter than she, and they made a particularly incongruous partnership as he seemed to be permanently backing away from her overhanging bosom.

'I dread to think what will happen if she stops suddenly!' Melisande whispered to Max as the two couples passed. But he only looked embarrassed and hurriedly introduced another topic of conversation.

Her next dance was with the Colonel, and they moved and talked together with an ease that supported in the minds of many the gossip that Miss Stevens was in some way related to the Randalls.

When the dance finished there was a break in the dancing and the Colonel went off to secure refreshment for her. She looked around her and her heart sank in her slippers as she saw Jeremiah Patterson approaching, a smile on his thin lips. 'It is so devilish hot in here, is it not, Miss Stevens?' he said. 'Will you take a turn in the garden with me?'

'Thank you, Mr Patterson, but no,' she said firmly. Just then David Jefferson and Anton Hubner came up to join her. 'But I would dearly love a glass of lemonade.'

She knew he would not be able to deny her request if he was not to lose face and appear incredibly boorish in front of the other men.

'Your servant, Miss Stevens,' he said with the smallest of bows. And of course, by the time he arrived at her side with the glass, she was already sipping the drink the Colonel had fetched her.

'No matter, Miss Stevens,' he said coldly. 'I shall look forward to our dance after supper.'

She would never have allowed him to write his name against any but a country dance. 'But I–'

He took her *carnet de bal* and pointed to a squiggle against the boulanger. 'Mr Ray has kindly granted me his dance,' he said. 'Until then, Miss Stevens.'

She rose to protest, but Adam was at her side.

'Patterson,' he said, acknowledging him with the slightest of nods. 'Miss Stevens.' He bowed to her formally. 'My dance, I think.'

She pulled herself together with an effort. 'Indeed, Doctor Kingsley.' She placed her hand on Adam's proffered arm, nodded coolly to Patterson and stepped onto the dance floor.

She was not prepared for the shock that seemed to go through every fibre and nerve of her body as Adam's arm went round her waist to guide her through the throng of dancers. He said something to her, but it was some time before she could collect her senses together sufficiently to answer him.

'I asked if you were enjoying your first ball,' he repeated gently. 'I hope that Patterson has not overset you?'

'No, it wasn't –' She stopped herself just in time. Better that he should think her upset by Patterson than that he should realise what an effect he himself had had on her. 'I am having a wonderful time,' she said, albeit a little shakily. 'Better than I ever imagined. I can still hardly believe I am here and not down in the kit—'

'Ssshh!' He put a finger on her lips in a curiously intimate gesture. 'Someone might hear.'

She tried to speak, but the words would not come; the feel of his hand against her face had lit a flame inside her and she knew a mad longing to kiss the finger on her lips, to nestle closer into her partner's embrace.

Again she was struck by the old fear: perhaps Sarah had been right; perhaps she was a wicked harlot . . . but no. Had not both Mrs Chobley and Adam himself said that such feelings were perfectly natural? But Mrs Chobley had also said that you had to keep such feelings under control. And she was right for, ball gown or no ball gown, Melisande and Adam were a world apart. Between the Harrow educated man and good family and the teacher from Wapping there was a chasm that could never be bridged.

They did a few graceful circuits of the ballroom and Adam, a more natural dancer than Max, tried a few more intricate steps and was delighted to see her following his lead. She was doing what Margaret had suggested: letting herself go with the music; it worked to perfection with such a graceful partner as Adam. When at last they left the floor after a dance that seemed to have lasted twice as long as the others, several young men hurried to her side, some clamouring to take her out on to the piazza, others offering to fetch her a glass of champagne. Cutting them out with practised ease, Adam led her to a little alcove behind a pillar where he had arranged to have two glasses of champagne cup ready. He raised his glass, smiling at her over the rim.

'To a successful debut, Miss Stevens.'

She smiled back at him. 'To the man who made it possible,' she replied.

At that moment, the band struck up again and the stout woman promptly steered the little man back on to the floor.

'I wonder what will happen if she stops before he does?' said Adam with a conspiratorial smile.

She giggled, choking on the champagne cup, the bubbles tickling her nose until her eyes watered. He watched in some amusement until the choking subsided, when he handed her his handkerchief. 'I did not think it quite that funny,' he commented.

286

'I know! But I said just the same thing to Max while we were dancing,' she said, mopping her eyes. 'He was covered in embarrassment and promptly changed the subject!'

'He shares Society's notion that men may be risqué, but ladies may not be anything other than proper.'

'It seems so very unfair!'

'Undoubtedly. But it is the way of the world. Many things are permissible for a man, even encouraged, while if a lady did the same thing, she would be ostracized.'

'Then I had better guard my tongue.'

'With others, yes, or they will look on you askance and hint at unladylike behaviour.'

'But to you –'

'To me you may be as frank as you wish.'

'It's not that easy to be a lady,' she said with a sigh, handing him back his handkerchief.

'But it will be worth the effort. Look at all the young men clamouring round you tonight,' he said, his voice artificially cheerful. 'You will be inundated with proposals before the week is over.'

He wondered why he found that such a bleak prospect.

Just then Warden Hurstpoint, a wealthy young man who had inherited his father's shipping line and fortune far too young, came up to claim the next dance. Adam was down to take out Sophia Patterson, and he knew he should be looking for her, but he stood a moment, watching Melisande on Warden's arm. He wondered if she had realised how much he had wanted to take her in his arms and kiss her, in the middle of the dance floor, in front of all the assembled worthies.

But that way lay madness.

With a sigh he turned and made his way across the floor to find Miss Patterson.

Miss Stevens at first had some difficulty communicating with her new partner, who seemed to have invented his own kind of speech which involved cutting parts off his words. ''Joying 'self?' he asked. And when she had hit on the appropriate response: 'Jawly good.' At one point he said to her with a roguish twinkle in his eye: 'Down fer c'ntry dance af' supp'. Should said Germ'n 'stead.' By which she took him to mean that he would rather have waltzed with her – and the

German waltz certainly gave the partner more opportunities to 'take liberties' than any other – than partnered her in the country dances. Not that he was not enjoying himself. 'Offly jawly dance this, hey?' he commented as they parted company.

In the last dance before the supper waltz, an earnest young man, the son of the Rector of Eden Springs, trod heavily on the hem of her train as they plunged gamely around the floor in a leaden attempt at the polka. She had to retire to the room set aside for the ladies, where the maid helped her to pin it up again. There were already a number of ladies on the other side of the room and she suspected, from the way they fell silent as she entered, that she had formed their topic of conversation. As the maid bent to pin the torn hem, the conversation picked up again.

'I'm absolutely determined,' said one young lady, 'that Papa will not put us off again. Mama says we shall have a Season in England, whatever the cost.'

'Oh! If only my mama would insist,' said a dainty little blonde girl, almost stamping her foot. 'My cousin Amelia went last Season and she was almost offered for by a viscount!'

'And you're so much prettier than Amelia,' said a younger girl. 'You could be sure of a duke at the very least! Miss Stevens, you are so fortunate!'

'Fortunate?' said Melisande blankly.

'Dear Doctor Kingsley being English, you can be certain of the Season. You will be presented, of course?' Melisande looked at her in confusion. 'At court. To the Queen at St James's. When do you sail?'

'Sail?'

They were all looking at her expectantly and she didn't have the first idea what they were talking about. She was just beginning to panic when Harriet Minton appeared at her side and linked an arm in hers.

'Ladies, our beaux will be waiting,' she said with a simper that Melisande felt did not quite sit well on the Miss Minton she knew; then, with a swish of silken skirts, she swept them both back out into the hall.

'If only Consuelo Vanderbilt knew what she had started!' sighed Harriet, rolling her eyes to Heaven. 'Now every

American mama has ambitions for her daughter to marry into the English aristocracy!'

'Is that what all that was about?'

'What else?' said Miss Minton crisply. 'I hope being the Duchess of Marlborough makes up to Miss Vanderbilt for the enmity of every rich papa from here to Washington!'

When they returned to the saloon they found Max waiting by one of the doors that had been flung open on to the piazza. He seemed somewhat taken aback by Miss Minton's presence. 'Ah, Miss Minton! I –' He bowed a little awkwardly in her direction.

'Mr Ellsky.' Her acknowledgement was, for her, so lacking in warmth as to be positively glacial, but as she passed on through to the ballroom, Melisande could see the colour creeping up the back of her neck.

'Would you care for a turn in the garden, Miss Stevens?' said Max, breaking into her thoughts. She wondered if he was the mysterious man who had written 'engaged' against the supper waltz on her card.

'A breath of fresh air would be most welcome,' she agreed, taking his arm. 'Oh! How lovely and cool it is out here!' she exclaimed as they strolled along the paved area and towards the scented gardens where flambeaux lit up the lawns and gravelled walks.

As they turned down one of the walks they heard the subdued sounds of couples murmuring to each other, and the occasional giggle or scuffle and 'Oh, Jack Elmett, what *do* you think you're doing?'

'Look at the stars!' she exclaimed. 'They are so clear here. In London you can scarcely see them for the river fogs and the street lamps.' She ventured a nervous glance at him; she feared from his serious expression he had not brought her out here to look at the stars.

He stopped in the middle of the gravelled walk and took her hand tightly in his.

'What is it, Mr Ellsky?' she asked, trying to ignore the sinking sensation in the pit of her stomach.

'You know what I want to say to you, surely?' he said, his voice thicker and more guttural than usual. 'Mel – I mean, Miss Stevens. I – you know what a deep regard I have for you and I think you like me too, don't you?'

289

'Of course. But I –'

He took her hands in his and gripped them tightly. 'Will you marry me?' he asked.

'M-Max!' With an effort she steadied her voice. 'You have been so very kind to me and – and I'm very fond of you . . . but I cannot marry you. I'm sorry.'

'It is because I am a Catholic?'

'I – I didn't know. And it would not worry me. If I loved you.'

'But you do not.'

'As a good friend, yes. But not as a husband.'

He looked for a moment very dashed down, but then he smiled rather crookedly at her and put his arm consolingly round her shoulders. 'That will have to do, I guess,' he said, a little forlornly.

'Max, you will always, I hope, be my good friend, but I wouldn't make you a good wife.' She smiled up at him. 'You need someone who would like to cook for you, bring up your children, be a home body.'

'Mel – Miss Stevens – you are wrong. Once I thought that, but –'

'And I'm not that. Come what may, I am determined to prove myself a teacher. I want that qualification, if it takes me till I'm an old, old woman.' She smiled up at him, a little mistily, then stood on tiptoe to kiss him on the cheek. He held her for a brief moment close to him, then released her so abruptly she almost fell over.

'I do hope I am not interrupting,' said a harsh voice from behind them.

Melisande stepped away from Max, her cheeks flushed. 'D-Doctor Kingsley.'

'If you are free, Miss Stevens, I believe this is our dance.'

He held out his arm, leaving her no option but to lay her hand on it, and led her through the gardens to the piazza and back into the ballroom without another word being spoken.

As he slid his arm around her waist to guide her through the throng of dancers she felt once more her breath stop in her body and the blood rushing through her veins and making her dizzy. She hoped he could not feel the trembling.

'It – it was not what you thought, Doctor Kingsley,' she said when she had her breathing once more under some control.

'No?' He raised his eyebrows. 'And what makes you think you can read my thoughts, Miss Stevens?'

'I –' She could not meet his angry look; abashed, she cast her eyes down as they began to move around the dance floor.

He relented. 'Come, look up, Miss Stevens, or people will wonder what I am saying to upset you. What was not what I thought?'

'When I kissed Max.'

'You kissed him, did you?' he said, his voice harsh and sarcastic. 'I would have thought it the other way around. He asked you to marry him, I suppose?'

'Yes,' she said baldly.

'You accepted?'

'No. Of course not. I –' She groped for the words for what she wanted to say, but with his arms around her and the blood pounding in her temples she was not capable of coherent thought.

He had steered her, unnoticed, off the dance floor and out onto the piazza.

'Then since I stand *in loco parentis*, it behoves me to tell you that young ladies do not kiss men they do not intend to marry.'

'It was just a friendly kiss,' she said forlornly. 'He has been so kind to me.'

The far end of the piazza was deserted, the music here only a distant sound. 'And I?' he demanded, spinning to a halt. 'Have I not been kind to you?'

His grip on her waist tightened as he drew her closer still to him, tilting her head back, forcing her to look up at him. 'Do I not deserve a friendly kiss?' he said, his grey eyes glittering with a strange light. She looked at him, her own eyes wide and uncertain, and stood on tiptoe to kiss him on the cheek. But then his hand was behind her head and his lips were on hers in a long passionate kiss that seemed to her to last for ever. His mouth moved hungrily on hers, bruising her soft lips, and she clung to him tightly, wanting the moment, the sensation, to go on for ever.

Suddenly, without warning, he jerked his head aside and almost pushed her from him. She staggered and almost fell, for her knees would hardly bear her. Shocked, she caught at the low wall for support and turned to him in confusion.

He was leaning over the balustrade that separated the piazza from the sunken garden, head bowed, his knuckles gripping the elegant ironwork until they showed white in the moonlight.

'I apologise,' he said in gruff tones quite unlike his own. 'I should not have done that.'

'Why not?' she asked in a small voice.

'Because I stand to you in the place of a guardian.' Behind them the music had stopped and in the still soft night it was as if they were the only ones in the world, a world that had shrunk to nothing but the corner of this elegant piazza.

After a moment which seemed like an age to her, he straightened his shoulders and held his arm stiffly out to her. 'The guests will be waiting for us to lead them in to supper,' he said coolly, as if nothing had happened.

She took his arm hesitantly, for even so slight a contact threatened to overset what little composure was left to her.

'But I –' Over to their left, beyond the balustrade, someone giggled.

'You see, Miss Stevens,' he said lightly, 'balls are for flirtations.' He looked down at her in the cool light of the moon hanging low in the sky. 'Don't look so serious,' he commanded more harshly. 'Put on a good face for our guests.'

Melisande bit her lip and did as she was bid.

She regained her composure slowly as she sat in the supper room, nibbling at a few choice delicacies brought her by Adam and sipping at a glass of champagne cup. She could hardly bring herself to meet his eye: she was not surprised that he took the opportunity to slip away when Amy's husband, Tom Bennett, brought the Rector of Edensville's new College across to meet her. They were very interested in her work with the immigrant children and she found, to her surprise, that she was able, despite the pain in her heart, to bear her part in the conversation like a sensible woman.

That was easier by far than the conversation she could half hear behind her. Well, it was less a conversation than an inquisition, really, as Mrs Patterson cross-examined Harriet Minton about David Jefferson.

'I vow and declare to you, Miss Minton, I could not think what was happening when I saw him on the ballroom floor! I thought it was one of the hired servants taken leave of his senses!'

'Goodness!' exclaimed Miss Minton disingenuously. 'I was not aware that David Jefferson could speak French.'

'French? What has French to do with this, Miss Minton, pray?'

'You said you mistook him for one of the servants. I understood French servants were being hired.'

'French and coloured, Miss Minton!' If anyone could be said to thunder in a whisper, then Mrs Patterson certainly thundered. 'Capering about on the floor like a Nigger Minstrel! I –'

'But I found him such a graceful dancer. Did not Sophia? She is such an excellent dancer herself, we must rely on her judgement.'

'I am happy to say Sophia has never had – will never have – the opportunity to put that to the test,' said Mrs Patterson in arctic tones. 'I do not in the least approve of the current fashion for over-educating the Negroes.'

'But surely, Mrs Patterson,' Max's far from dulcet tones weighed in on the side of Miss Minton, 'I understand your son has a supervisor at the factory who is –'

'Oh, a supervisor, Mr Ellsky, yes. By all means make your Negro a scientist, but at all costs not a classical scholar. There must be no attempt to put him on a level with a white man. A scientist Negro, such as our factory supervisor, is much on the same level as an improved cotton gin: that is, a promising addition to the resources of the country. Yes. I can accept that. I hope Doctor Kingsley's man is to be educated as a scientific Negro?'

'He is a doctor, ma'am,' said Miss Minton with some glee.

'A doctor?' said Mrs Patterson faintly. 'You mean, he treats –' her voice dropped to a whisper '– white people?'

'Indeed.'

Mrs Patterson shuddered. Then she rallied. 'What your parents are thinking of, Miss Minton, permitting you to dance with him, I do not know.'

'Unfortunately they could not be here this evening,' said Miss Minton, unperturbed. 'It was my father's night with the prostitutes.' She walked away with a swish of her skirts.

293

'Don't be alarmed,' said Tom Bennett with a grin, seeing Mel's eyes widen. 'She only said that to annoy.'

'I don't understand.'

'Miss Minton's parents run a refuge for fallen women.'

The music struck up again before she could assemble her confused thoughts and, absent-mindedly ignoring the prior claims of the gentleman who had put his name down for that dance, Tom led Miss Stevens on to the floor, continuing their conversation about the Harbourside school, which seemed to interest him greatly.

Her heart skipped a beat as Jeremiah Patterson came up to claim her hand for the next dance.

'But I – no, I –' He was taking her arm. She could not bear it – but how could she extricate herself without causing a disturbance?

'Jack Ray is a friend indeed, would you not agree, Miss Stevens?' said Patterson, a sickly smile on his face. 'To give up a dance with the belle of the ball . . .'

She looked around for a friendly face, but Tom was dancing with his wife, Adam with Harriet Minton, Max with Mrs Randall and John Wintour with Sophia Patterson. No help to be found there.

Patterson drew her into his arms, holding her rather closer than was polite. They had barely completed half a circuit when his hand squeezed hers painfully hard. 'You are indeed a *succès de fou* tonight, Miss Stevens,' he said, and though his lips were smiling, his eyes, black and glittering, were not. 'And what would the good people of Eden Springs say if they knew their hostess was a skivvy, a little bastard shipped out here from the London slums?'

She struggled to keep her composure, though her stomach had knotted and her legs once more felt as though they would give way beneath her any moment.

'Why not tell them and find out?' she managed to say with an assumption of hauteur. 'Then you can see whether their horror – if they believe such nonsense – is sufficient to compensate for the punishment you will undoubtedly receive at Doctor Kingsley's hands!'

His arm tightened round her waist until her face was barely inches from his. 'And if I told them that he had made this same little bastard his mistress and then foisted her on society? I think he would be run out of Eden Springs!'

'You're mad!' she whispered hoarsely.

He went on as though she had not spoken. 'But if you are *very* nice to me, my dear, I dare say I will manage to keep this little gem to myself.' She made to speak. 'No. Don't say it. Adorable as you are when you are angry, we don't want the guests to think we are quarrelling, do we? And if you are willing to share your favours with me . . .' He swore under his breath as she stopped abruptly and the couple behind bumped into them, then tightened his grip until she almost felt the bones crack and could scarce stop herself crying out in pain. 'That's better,' he crooned as she began to move again. 'I shall send you a message when I am ready. Ah, don't look so bereft, my dear,' he said caressingly. 'I am not a greedy man. I am quite content to share you with him.'

With a final wrench she tore herself from his arms and a ripple of shock went round one end of the ballroom at the look of hatred she cast him before hurrying off the floor.

As everyone else moved smoothly back into the dance again, the couples unsighted at the far end craning their necks to see what was happening at the other, John Wintour steered his partner off the floor.

'The little fool!' said Sophia Patterson in rather shrill tones. 'To make such an exhibition of herself . . .'

'But Miss Sophia!' exclaimed Wintour, thinking on his feet. 'Will you not use your good offices to smooth things over? After all, Doctor Kingsley's ward . . . insulted by your brother . . .'

'What do you mean? Why should I –'

'I should not have spoken,' said Wintour contritely. 'Only when my mother-in-law informed me that you and Adam . . .' He saw with satisfaction that he had her complete attention. 'Forgive me. I realise there has been as yet no formal announcement . . . but if the happy announcement we all hope to hear should be brought to nothing by Mr Patterson's unfortunate behaviour, I could never forgive myself if I had omitted to assist you in such a dilemma.'

Sophia Patterson's eyes widened. 'You think Adam would take offence?'

295

'Well, his ward. . . . And such a public insult. If we were to say your brother had overindulged . . .'

They were across the room in seconds, before Adam or Max at the other end of the ballroom were aware that anything had happened. Sophia took her brother's arm and said something sharp to him before marching him across the room and out on to the piazza.

'A little too much of our host's excellent champagne,' said Wintour in answer to a question from an inquisitive matron at his elbow. 'His sister does not wish any fuss. I am sure Patterson will apologise in the morning, when he has come to his senses.'

He knew it would be round the ballroom in minutes.

In the early hours of the morning, the guests went into the second supper. Mel, watching them fill their plates and charge their glasses, wondered how they could possibly eat or drink any more.

To her relief the Pattersons by then had taken their leave. The third time Eithne Patterson had been quizzed about her son's bizarre behaviour she had decided to depart while the family still had some shreds of dignity left. But her cup of bitterness was not yet full, as both Adam Kingsley and Beatrice Randall had made a point of having a 'quiet word' with her.

She left Springs House with her head reeling, scarcely able to believe that her own son had put at risk all the plans she had for her daughter's advancement; she could hardly bring herself to speak to him. However, the conversations with her host and hostess had not left her entirely without hope; with skill and dedication she might still be able to snatch the brand from the burning!

The ball was drawing inexorably to its close but though Melisande was still there in body, her spirit had fled with Patterson's onslaught and while she mechanically danced with the Colonel, with David Jefferson and with Warden Hurstpoint, who had imbibed so much champagne that he declared instant and undying love for her in the middle of the boulanger, her mind was racing round in desperate circles, trying to think what she had to do.

Her whole body shuddered at the thought of Patterson's hands on her, but what was the alternative? If he denounced her, repeated all those evil things he had said tonight, then Adam would indeed be ruined, for she knew how the censorious world would respond to the sort of accusations he would make. It was at heart a hypocritical age: one could do virtually whatever one wished – provided it was not known.

At the end of the boulanger she sank into a chair, head spinning, eyes closed against the bright lights while Hurstpoint went to fetch her some refreshment. She shook her head wearily. Patterson had her at his mercy: she would be ruined if she gave in to him – and Adam would be ruined if she did not.

She opened her eyes and there was Adam in front of her, holding out his arms, as if she had conjured him up out of thin air.

'Poor child,' he said with a smile. 'You look all in. Bear up, it's the last waltz and then you shall go to bed.'

'Should you not ask Mrs Randall?'

'Beatrice is dancing with the Colonel – who would take it most unkindly if I attempted to forestall him. Come! I know I behaved rather boorishly, but I have apologised. And now I am on my best behaviour.' He smiled at her. 'Trust me?'

She nodded. How could she explain that it was not him, but rather her own emotions which she did not trust. As they circled the dance floor she wondered again how he could possibly not feel the pounding of her heart at the feel of his arms around her. She fixed her eye on the top button of his waistcoat, struggled to control her breathing and wondered desperately what she was going to do. Unless she could think of a plan, she might have to go away again, abandon the house, Adam, the school – everything.

Max! she thought suddenly. She could marry Max! That was the answer.

And yet – would that stop Patterson claiming she had been Adam's mistress? No. She concluded sadly that it would not work. Besides, it would not be fair to Max. To marry him without love was one thing, but to marry him loving another was an action she could not contemplate. And she did love Adam: she had known that without a doubt since the moment he had held her in his arms and kissed her. But there was no hope in that direction either. Tonight his family had been spoken of in the same breath as dukes and viscounts – and what had dukes and viscounts to do with nameless waifs from Wapping? It had not needed his recoil from her to show her that they were worlds apart.

And yet she could not regret it: she would cherish for ever that moment when she had loved and felt herself, however briefly, loved in return.

'I was asking whether you would join us at the Harvest Thanksgiving tomorrow,' said Adam, looking down at her with a frown.

'No. I couldn't possibly . . .' she began, blurting out the first thing that came to her. She stopped, biting her lip. And · yet, did it matter what she said? After all, by the time they went to church, she would be well gone.

'I gather you share some of my cynicism over a just God,' he said, 'but I do hope you will reconsider.'

She smiled mistily up at him. 'I hardly think God can be blamed for man's inhumanity to man,' she said, so softly that he had to bend his head to hear her.

'It means a great deal to the farm workers,' he went on. 'Beatrice, of course, would say that it is socially correct for you to attend. And I daresay many of our Eden Springs ladies will be watching out for you.'

'Matron always held that there were better Christians outside church than in. She maintained that half the ladies at St Mark's only went to show off their new hats!'

He chuckled. He always found her views on life in general and society in particular entertaining, and was delighted to find that this evening had not changed her.

'Come with m – us,' he said with a persuasive smile. 'I should be glad if you would come . . . though Heaven forbid I should press you.'

She knew she should be making plans to leave, but the first thin streaks of rosy dawn were already painting the sky. What was another day? she thought. Another day in Adam's company, another day to store away in her memories, a joyful interlude that would have to last her a lifetime.

The sun was coming up over the horizon when the last guest finally departed.

Beatrice Randall collapsed gracefully on to a chaise longue in the drawing room. 'We can congratulate ourselves on an excellent evening,' she exulted. 'And a successful one. Mel is now well launched on Edensville Society.'

Launched and sunk in one evening, thought Melisande.

'What is it, child?' asked Adam softly. 'Why the tragic look?'

'It's nothing,' she said, a little breathlessly. 'Just – a little tired.'

'Nothing else?'

'No. No,' she repeated. 'It just seems so strange to be going to bed in the morning!'

He looked at her a moment longer, then turned away to offer Tom Bennett a nightcap.

'Take her to bed, Beatrice,' he said over his shoulder. 'It has indeed been a long night.'

She looked around the circle of smiling faces. 'Thank you, all of you,' she said, her voice tight in her throat. 'Thank you for giving me such a wonderful evening. I shall always remember it.' The tears shone in her eyes and threatened to spill down her cheeks.

'You shall have many more,' said Amy.

Adam put the bottle down abruptly and crossed to her side. He brushed the tears from her cheeks with a gentle finger, then at a gruff cough from the Colonel, dropped his hand and crossed to hold the door open for her.

'Go to sleep, my dear,' he said softly as she departed. He stood a moment watching her make her way up the stairs, the train swishing softly behind her.

'I'm glad you could join me, Colonel,' said Adam, ushering the older man to a comfortable chair in the study. 'I had hoped to manage without your assistance, but I may need you as a witness.'

'Dashed if I know what's going on,' grumbled the Colonel. 'M'man tells me that Olsen's gone and a new feller's moving his gear in above the stables!'

'Yes. McNair's nephew.'

'But where – and why? I –'

Before the Colonel could finish his speech there was a rattle at the door. A young man with a freckled face and sandy hair appeared in the doorway with Nancy.

'Thank you, Duncan, that will be all,' said Adam. 'Come in, Nancy. Close the door.'

Nancy flew in, her hair all over the place and her uniform looking as though she'd slept in it.

'You got no right to drag me in here like this!' she hissed. 'I'm a free woman!'

'Quite free, Nancy,' said the doctor, unperturbed. 'I just thought we might exchange a few remarks . . . about Olsen.'

'An' that's another thing! Where is he?' she demanded furiously.

'He's gone, Nancy,' said the doctor.

'For how long?'

'For ever, I should imagine. It's a long way to Alberta.'

'Alberta?' The colour drained out of her face.

'Surely he told you before he left?' asked Kingsley.

'Alberta,' she repeated dully. 'Why in tarnation did he want to go to Alberta?'

'Want is not quite the word he would have chosen,' said the doctor. 'But – if you wish to follow him, it could be arranged.'

She furrowed her brow suspiciously. 'To Alberta? Why should I want to go there?'

'Did I say want?' asked Kingsley.

'You can't force me! I ain't done nothin' wrong,' said Nancy heatedly. 'S'pose it was that uppity maid, all set to get me into trouble? Ever since your grand friends have taken her up . . . but she's just a housemaid like me. An' one of these fine days –'

Adam reached into the desk drawer and drew out a length of soft green baize; he unrolled it under Nancy's horrified gaze and out spilled half a dozen pieces of silverware. She gasped and blanched. 'Just a sample of the items you and your fellow thief have been taking out of this house,' he said, watching her closely.

'It weren't – I don't know nothin' –'

'Save your breath, Nancy,' said the doctor, cutting in sharply on her protests. 'The description of you and Olsen was unmistakable.'

300

He opened his desk drawer, took out two envelopes and dropped them alongside the silver. 'You'll recognise Olsen's hand, I'm sure,' he said steadily.

But it was the other envelope that seemed to hold her attention; she was staring at it like a mouse mesmerised by a snake.

'Two?' she said in a hoarse whisper. Her shoulders drooped. 'So Olsen told you about the fence?'

'Would you care to reconsider that offer of a ticket? A court case would be such a bore, but if you leave me no option . . .'

Twenty minutes later a third envelope had joined the other two.

'Sign it, Nancy,' he said levelly. 'And if you will witness it, Colonel?'

'Ain't no need for that. Said I'd disappear.'

'Nevertheless . . . if you please, Colonel? I'd remind you, Nancy, in the presence of a witness, that this confession will be handed over to the law if you ever show your face in this part of the world again.' He was taking no chances that she might sell the ticket to Alberta to some unsuspecting immigrant and come back to New York State on the proceeds.

He took Nancy's confession and laid it alongside the other two envelopes. 'I do hope Mr Patterson paid you well,' he said softly, reaching out for the bell pull.

'Hey! How did you know?'

'You have a slack tongue, Nancy.'

'He said he wouldn't say anything! It'd be just between him and me.'

'And you believed him?'

'Shoulda known better,' she said bitterly. 'But I ain't said a word to anyone else, honest!'

'Honest is a word which appears to hold little meaning for you, Nancy,' said Adam dryly. 'Ah, Mrs Chobley. Nancy is leaving us. Take her to pack her bag, if you please. Needless to say, you will search it before she leaves. And her room. And stay with her until you see her off the premises.'

'Patterson will not be so easily dealt with,' said the Colonel sombrely as the door closed behind the two women.

'I dealt with him last night,' said Kingsley coolly.

301

'How?'

'If I'm honest, I should say Beatrice and John dealt with him.'

'By playing on his mother's ambitions for you and Sophia?' demanded the Colonel, looking up from his perusal of Nancy's confession.

Adam grunted non-committally.

Randall looked at him from under jutting eyebrows. 'Hardly fair to Sophia, m'boy.'

'I know.' He had the grace to blush. 'But it was all John could think of at the time.'

'So that was why she spent the rest of the evening making spaniel eyes at you . . . Good Lord!'

'What is it?'

'These other two envelopes are empty!'

'Good Lord,' said Adam with a lopsided grin. 'So they are!'

'Never thought you had it in you to be so devious, m'boy!' exclaimed the Colonel. He shot the younger man another piercing look. 'Not devious enough to divert me from what I was saying, though. We were discussing Sophia Patterson.'

'You were,' said Adam with a long-suffering sigh. 'I was trying to change the subject.'

'You're not going to marry her, are you?'

'Good Lord, no.'

'That's what I thought.' Colonel Randall made to say something else, then thought better of it.

The ray of sunlight stole through a chink in the curtains and shone on the halo of golden hair on the pillow. Mel stirred and opened her eyes drowsily. Memories of the evening's gaieties flooded in with the light and for a moment she stretched and smiled, basking in the memory of Adam's arms around her, his lips on hers, reliving the feelings that had swept over her, causing her body to tingle with an intensity she could not remember feeling before. . . . Then the memory of her conversation with Patterson pushed its unwelcome way in and blotted out her joy as surely as a black cloud covers the sun.

She sat bolt upright in bed, tossing her hair behind her, pressing her hands to her eyes in an attempt to blot out the memory, but in vain. She could hear his sneering voice as

302

clearly as if he were in the same room: 'Once it has been said – you will both be destroyed. But if you share your favours . . .'

That day she lived every moment as if it would be her last; every word, every gesture, had an intensity never before experienced, as she folded each conversation, each meeting, away in her memory. This will be the last day I will spend here, she told herself; the last breakfast, the last walk through the orchard, the last time I shall look across the room and see Adam.

Mrs Randall remarked on her rather frantic air to the Colonel. 'Nothing to fret about, my dear,' he said comfortably. 'Excitement and exhaustion combined. Still, I'm pleased she agreed to come to the service with us.'

Exhaustion seemed to be the most likely explanation, so much so that at the end of the Harvest Thanksgiving, Mrs Hutchinson twice addressed a remark to Melisande without receiving an answer, and Mrs Randall had to bring her sharply back to them before she was able to bear her part in the polite exchanges. But then Mrs Matthias admired Mrs Hutchinson's new hat, and Mel, catching Adam's eye, had to turn away quickly, muffling her laughter in her handkerchief.

The Randalls looked bemused, especially when they saw Adam's shoulders shaking with the effort of suppressed laughter. They thought it wise to make their adieux and leave.

But a shared moment would not last a lifetime. Alone in her room at last, Melisande forced herself to face up to the reality of the situation. She tried to think out a sensible plan for her departure, but her head was pounding and she had great difficulty thinking beyond the moment when she would leave Springs House. She would only pack the blouses and skirts, she decided; there was no purpose in taking the elegant dresses she and Beatrice had chosen so short a time before.

And where was she to go? Edensville was out of the question: she must get as far away as possible from Jeremiah Patterson – and from Adam.

She knew a sudden illogical longing for London and Sarah Thomsett, but that was foolish. Sarah had turned her back on her, and her background – and John Thomsett – would always stand in her way.

She wandered forlornly into the library and through to the deserted drawing room. Crossing the room, she ran her hand over the satinwood piano. She had been happy here, happier than she had ever thought possible. She loved her work, both for the sake of the children and for the opportunity to show that she was more than just another nameless orphan.

If only she had not met Jeremiah Patterson. If only Nancy had not hated her so. If only she had not fallen in love with Adam . . .

Her eyes widened and she collapsed on to the piano stool with a gasp. Across the room she caught sight of herself in the mirrored overmantel, face white with shock, mouth agape as she took in the enormity of what she was confronting. And as she remembered how he had looked at her last night, she knew she could not simply walk out of his life again without a word of explanation.

For the third time Adam looked up eagerly from perusal of the journals as the door to the morning room opened; last time it had only been the Colonel; this time it was Tom Bennett. With an angry gesture he tossed aside the journal and announced that he was going to his study to work.

He was in the dispensary when he heard the knock on the door. 'Come in,' he called gruffly, expecting to see the Colonel. After a moment he peered round the door and came face to face with Melisande.

They stood a moment, inches apart, looking deep into each other's eyes. Registering the pain in her green eyes, he felt again the twisting sensation in his chest, as if someone had turned a knife in it.

With a superhuman effort, he resisted the temptation to take her in his arms and kiss away the hurt; he tore his gaze away at last and stepped into the study, closing the dispensary door.

'Please . . . Miss Stevens. Sit down,' he said with an assumption of ease he did not feel.

Struggling to control her ragged breathing, she crossed to sit on the leather Chesterfield, one of the few pieces in the house to reflect his taste and not Almeria Carter's, arranging her skirts around her and trying not to remember that this was where they had put her the night she had come to Springs House.

He sat in the armchair, as far away from her as he could, and contemplated her a moment from under lowering brows.

'Doctor Kingsley –'

He interrupted her. 'You must leave Springs House,' he said abruptly.

His words, echoing so sharply her own thoughts, took her aback completely.

'Why?' she whispered. There was no immediate reply. 'Because you kissed me?'

'No. My unmannerly conduct has nothing to do with it.'

'Then you are bored with having me as a ward.'

He smiled, and the relaxation of his stern expression made him look years younger. 'No.' He chuckled softly. 'I have often been maddened and infuriated – but never bored.' His face hardened again. 'But you must leave, and it would be best if you left today. The necessary arrangements –'

She stood up abruptly. 'You need not trouble yourself,' she said with icy dignity. 'I shall make my own arrangements.'

'You will accept Max?' he demanded.

She looked at him with a puzzled frown. In the agitation of the moment, she had all but forgotten Max's proposal. 'No,' she said at last.

'He is a good man.' He forced himself to say it. 'And he has – a great affection for you.'

'And I for him. But I could not marry him,' she said flatly. 'I do not love him.'

'Love might grow between you,' he suggested. 'Many marriages –'

'Not in this case,' she said decisively. Not while she had to see Adam almost every day. How could he be so blind as to suggest it!

He turned away from her and walked across to the window, unable to bear the raw pain in her face. He cleared his throat of an unaccountable lump.

'I – I regret if my ungentlemanly behaviour last night led you to expect . . .' God, this was terrible! How could he say it?

'I expect nothing,' she said softly. 'But I – I thought perhaps you might care for me a little.'

He said nothing.

305

'I should have known better,' she said bitterly. 'I should have remembered: I'm only a foundling, an orphan from the slums.'

'Stop that!' He crossed the room to her side and gripped her shoulders painfully hard. 'You're a teacher,' he said, almost shaking her. 'A well-respected member of the community.' His mouth twisted as she looked up at him, hurt in her deep green eyes. 'The belle of the ball,' he said softly.

'Then why?'

'Melisande.' He let his hands fall to his side and turned away from her to gaze unseeingly out of the window, blind to the beauty of the neat flowerbeds and the riot of blooms in the shrubbery that all too soon would be reduced to bare twigs by the autumn winds. 'Melisande, I – I can't marry you. It just isn't possible.'

'I never expected you would,' she said, chin up as she tried to collect the rags of her pride around her. 'As I said, I know what I am. And what man from your background wants a nameless orphan?'

'I never said anything about not wanting,' he said tiredly. 'Only that I cannot.'

She stood stiff-backed by the empty fireplace, only her pride stopping her from giving way to her emotions and blurting out the words that crowded her brain.

It was a struggle to speak, for her voice was threatening to drown in the tears that filled her throat. 'I hope you will find a new teacher soon,' she said at last.

He looked up at that. 'New teacher?' he said with a frown. 'Why the Devil should we want a new teacher?'

'I have to leave. Leave Edensville. I came to tell you. Someone is . . . has . . .' She took a deep breath, struggling to steady her voice. 'Someone is . . . going to say . . .'

'You need not put yourself out to protect Jeremiah Patterson's name, I think,' said Adam harshly.

Startled green eyes flew to his. How did he know?

'I just thought that if – when – I go away, then you and Miss Patterson could explain to him that he is mistaken, persuade him not to say such things . . .'

'You may safely leave Patterson to me,' he said, his eyes glinting dangerously. At last he dragged his eyes away from hers, unable to meet that vulnerable gaze, and crossed the room to fiddle aimlessly with the pens on his desk. 'Sit down, Miss Stevens,' he said after a moment.

'No. I'm –'

'Sit down!'

She subsided on to the couch once more.

'And so you would leave us, would you? Go far away from Edensville?'

'I thought it best.'

'And if you are not to marry Max, what had you in mind?' he asked, the muscle working at the side of his mouth.

She shrugged. 'Back into service, I suppose.' Her voice was barely a whisper and the tears she had held back for so long spilled down her cheeks.

'Into *service*?' His rage exploded out of him and he crossed the room to stand in front of her, arms akimbo. 'You little fool! After all you have done to escape it?' He dropped his voice again as she shrank away from his anger. 'And you thought we would let you?' he said softly.

She said nothing, just looked up at him through tear-drenched eyes.

'Dry your tears,' he said thickly, holding out his hand-kerchief to her. When she didn't move, he squatted down beside her, cupping her chin in his strong lean fingers while he wiped away the tearstains. 'Better now?'

She nodded, swallowing a shuddering sob, her eyes still shimmering with tears.

'I should never have brought you here,' he said abruptly.

'I –'

'No. Listen to me. Tom and Amy have offered you a home with them in Edensville. She will take you about in society. And you will still be able to teach at Harbourside.'

'You will not be my guardian?'

'No. This – this will be more suitable.'

'I am fortunate to have so many kind friends,' she said in a flat voice.

'Jessie is packing your trunks. You will be leaving within the hour.'

As if on cue, a knock fell on the door. 'Ah! So you are here,' said the Colonel. He looked at Adam, eyebrows raised. 'Have you – ah – discussed . . .'

Adam nodded.

'They are bringing the carriage round,' he said to Mel. 'When you're ready, m'dear.'

'A moment,' she said, rising to her feet and pulling herself together with a visible effort. 'Doctor Kingsley, what about Mr Patterson?' she said anxiously. 'If you antagonise him . . . there is the school and the clinic to consider . . . and Miss Patterson, of course. I would not wish –'

'No need to concern yourself with that, m'dear,' said the Colonel jovially. 'Adam's dealt with it.'

'It appears Doctor Kingsley has dealt with all the problems,' she said bitterly. 'Me included.'

'I'll wait for you in the hall,' said the Colonel gruffly, going out and closing the door behind him. 'Don't be long.'

'I must not keep the Colonel waiting,' she said with a bright artificial smile. 'Would you tell Mrs Chobley I will write? And say goodbye to Jessie for me. I don't think –' she bit her lip '– I don't think I can manage any more goodbyes today.'

Adam walked across to her side and took her hand in his. 'I hope you and Amy will visit,' he said, forcing a smile. 'Tell us about your gay life in the big city.'

She tried to smile back at him, but the smile went awry. She went to shake his hand, but he almost overset her once more when he raised it to his lips.

'Melisande . . .' he began.

'Yes?'

'It will pass,' he said, in a voice so low she could scarce make out the words. 'It won't always be so painful.'

'How do you know?' she snapped, snatching her hand away. 'How can you tell me how I feel?'

'I didn't –'

'If you'd ever truly cared for anyone, you – I'm sorry. I think I'd better . . .' She turned and fled the room before the tears betrayed her once more.

'I can see you've done what was proper,' said Beatrice as the carriage disappeared down the drive and out on to the Edensville road, 'but I admit I'm at a loss to know why? Is it to launch her into Society? To silence Patterson? Does she go for her sake or yours?'

He shrugged fatalistically. 'She could not have stayed here any longer, even if Patterson and his poisonous tongue had not interfered. Tom's offer came at just the right time.'

'And if it had not?'

'Then I suppose I would have done what I ought to have done in the first place: asked you to look after her.'

'I could have done that six months ago,' she said placidly. 'Why only now?'

'Oh. dammit, Beatrice! Don't you see? I kept her here, pretending to myself and the world that there was no impropriety in it, because I came to enjoy her company so much.' He turned away to pick a blown rose from a bush by the walk, crushing its faded petals in his hand. 'For the first time in my life I had my own real home and she completed it for me. It is only in the last few days that I have come to realise that . . . I can protect her from other men, but I can no longer protect her from myself.'

'Does it not occur to you that she might not want protection from you?'

'No!' he exclaimed harshly. 'Even if I could offer her marriage – and you of all people know that I cannot – would it be fair to take such advantage of her? She has persuaded herself that I am some sort of fairytale prince: King Cophetus and herself the beggar-maid. You know how far that is from the truth.' They had paused on the edge of the orchard and he leaned against a fruit tree, running his fingers slowly over the rough bark. 'Amy will be able to take her about in society – she's met no other men but Max and me. How could I take advantage of such inexperience? There's another consideration too. Don't forget I am entirely dependent on my father for the money for the Harbourside school and the new dispensary.'

'You are so sure he would disapprove?'

'Oh, yes. Make no mistake about it: both he and the Duchess are anxious that I marry a woman of good family and some fortune,' he said bitterly. 'As you are aware, that's why I was sent out here in the first place.'

'Not *sent*, Adam. They –'

'It doesn't matter,' he said impatiently. 'It's all ancient history now. But it's still a case of don't do as I do, do as I say.

And Mel, when all is said and done, is a nameless orphan. God knows what her family was.'

It was late before Adam went to bed that night, and he lay tossing and turning, unable to get comfortable. He blamed it on the turmoil of the ball, too much champagne and the late night brandy he had consumed. And of course the scene with Melisande.

'If you'd ever truly cared . . .' she'd said to him. And when he closed his eyes, it was to dream, not of Melisande, but of his own personal nightmares.

He remembered that day as vividly as if it were yesterday. His mother had pinned her best feathered hat on her head and taken him to the school gate; he had kissed the perfumed cheek so reluctantly offered and then run into the playground to join in a game of tag with the other six year olds. He could recall in crystal clear detail the scene that afternoon in the headmaster's study, the tall man and the elegant lady perched on the leather chairs while portly Professor McCann cleared his throat uncomfortably.

'Brent, my boy,' he said at last. 'Here is your father come to see you.'

'But I haven't got a father!' Had his mother not always told him that his father was dead?

The Professor had slipped tactfully away and the tall man drew the boy to his side and told him, as gently as he could, that he was his father.

There had been no easy way to explain why he was back in his son's life again. At last he'd said: 'Your mother is to marry again and – and it is thought best that you should make your home in future with me.'

'Cannot I live with her?' he'd asked, bemused.

'It is not certain whether her new husband likes children,' said the lady softly. 'But I – we – would very much like you to come and live with us.'

The truth, which came out over the next few years of increasingly unhappy visits, was that Swinton liked his own children well enough, but saw Adam as a stain, a millstone round his mother's neck. When he realised that his mother felt the same the visits ceased, to everyone's relief.

His father and stepmother did their best, but all their love could not compensate for the fact that his own mother had abandoned him. When at the age of eight he took his father's name, he suffered a great deal of ragging from his fellow schoolboys, ragging which culminated in the most monumental fight the small school had ever known. One of his rivals called him a bastard and was punched on the nose. His friends weighed in to the mêlée and before it could be stopped, half the Middle School had received bloody noses and black eyes.

He had made his point so decisively that when he went up to Harrow, there was no more taunting – a wise decision since he had a certain gift in the field of pugilism and went on to box for school and county, until his better self decided such skills were inconsistent with his desire to become a doctor.

As he grew up and won the respect of his fellows, he almost succeeded in forgetting the unhappiness of his early days, supported by the love of his father and stepmother, who loved Adam as if he had been her own son, a love more admirable as she was unable to have children of her own. He had been well on the way to forgetting his miserable start in life when he met Cecilia.

Cecilia was the beautiful sister of a fellow student with whom he went to stay one summer vacation. The Harveys were genteel but not wealthy, and Alfred was one of his closest friends at St Bartholomew's, where they had both trained together. It had been an idyllic summer and Cecilia, the eldest of Alfred's four sisters, had encouraged Adam to believe that she was as deeply in love with him as he with her. He had written to ask his father's approval to propose for · Cecilia's hand in marriage and was only awaiting an auspicious moment to press his suit.

It had been a warm clear day, the kind of day that comes as a beautiful summer slips, almost unnoticed, into the mellowness of autumn, and Adam had come across her in the arbour, cutting the last late rosebuds for a table centre, the sun drawing blue highlights from her raven's wing hair and setting little golden lights sparkling in her violet eyes.

He had proposed, been accepted, with the proviso of parental approval, and permitted to kiss her on the lips. They sat on the rustic bench, her tiny hand resting in his, while he talked excitedly of the future – their future.

311

'Dear Adam.' She smiled her dazzling smile. 'Surely when we are married, you will not persist in this foolish notion of being a doctor?'

'Foolish?' he said, somewhat taken aback. 'My sweet, it is what I have been trained for. Like Alfred.'

'Oh, Alfred.' She dismissed her brother with an airy wave of her hand. 'Alfred has to find a profession. A younger son. He has no prospects, unless our uncle Samuel can be persuaded to name him in his will, but –'

'But Cecilia,' he said in some confusion, 'don't you understand? It's what I've always wanted to do.'

'I must suppose that is why your father indulges you in this,' she said, a frown marring her alabaster forehead. 'But why in such a poor district? Surely you could set up in a more fashionable practice? Harley Street would be quite acceptable. And when you inherit your father's estates –'

'Cecilia, my darling,' he said gently. 'I'll never inherit. I'm not my father's heir.'

'But of course you are. You are your father's only child! Alfred said.'

'But not his heir, Cecilia. There will be something for me, of course, but the estates are all entailed. They will all go to Edward Kingsley.'

She went perfectly white as she realised the implications of his words.

'I am so sorry, Cecilia my dear. I thought you knew.'

'Knew? Knew? Do you think I would ever have encouraged you had I known the dreadful truth!' she screamed, her mouth ugly and twisted in her fury.

He left Alfred's house that night and within the month had turned his back on England. And vowed that no woman would ever again have the power to hurt him.

Melisande tried hard to settle into her new life in Edensville and, if she never quite felt as much at home with the Bennetts as she had at Springs House, they were in no way to blame, for the young couple gave her a warm welcome to their home, a smart white weather-boarded villa on Hamilton, one of Edensville's elegant new boulevards.

She sorely missed Springs House, and all the people there, although she tried hard not to give into her misery, not

312

wanting to hurt Amy's feelings. Starting back at the school again gave her another focus for her attention; it seemed strange without Tadeusz and Agnete, but there were new faces to work with, more lost and frightened children relying on her to help them make sense of the bewildering new land in which they found themselves.

'Quite a challenge for her,' said Amy.

'And God knows she needs one at the moment,' observed Tom with ready sympathy.

The hope of the trustees that the work of the Harbourside school would soon be at an end proved unfounded. Wave after wave of immigrants still poured into Edensville, adding yet more variety to the colourful mix of people who called Harbourside home, and replacing those who had moved on that summer to homestead on the prairies or to try their fortune in the Yukon.

After the harvest break, the school soon fell back into its old routine. Father Kerrigan seemed to have washed his hands of Melisande, but much to her delight, Rabbi Benhamin fell into the habit of coming in once a week, bringing newspapers with him. He would read the news, national and world events, and discuss them with the older ones; while he was there she could concentrate on teaching the little ones their alphabet. The older ones who had only a limited time in the school he showed how to make sense of job vacancies and helped them write an application for a post – though they had to pick their way carefully round the ones that specified 'no Jews or Irish need apply' or 'no Greeks', according to whatever prejudice the prospective employer might hold. The children had already found out that America wasn't all milk and honey; now they had to learn that it wasn't always the Land of Liberty either.

Tom and Amy were both very supportive of her work at the school and she enjoyed many an evening chat with Tom – it seemed strange to think of him as a Professor – about current theories of education; when she proposed extending her work to help in the dispensary, however, Amy put her foot down.

'I promised Mama that I would take you out into Society,' she said firmly, 'and that is precisely what I intend to do.'

'But Miss Minton combines her work in the dispensary with a social life!' Melisande protested.

313

'And you can combine your work at the school with your social life,' said Amy briskly.

Amy's mother, seeing the dark circles under Mel's eyes and hearing from her daughter that the girl still cried herself to sleep almost every night, was brusque and to the point.

'Where is the sense in going back to the dispensary?' she demanded. 'You are not a nurse. You are not needed there.'

'But the immigrant women –'

'If Miss Minton has need of you, be sure she will send for you.' Beatrice took her hand. 'Mel, I understand that you want to be there, to see Adam again.'

'No, I –'

'And if you do, what then? It will only open old wounds.'

'But surely I shall see him anyway? The school . . .'

'There are many other trustees, my dear,' said Beatrice. Her heart went out to the girl, but she had to be cruel to be kind. 'Put him and Springs House out of your considerations,' she advised. 'Concentrate on your work at the school and your Society debut. Goodness knows that would be more than enough for most girls!' She took Mel's hand in hers. 'Tom and Amy have given you a superb opportunity, but only you can decide what you make of it. And if you are forever feeling sorry for yourself, and harking back to the past, what can you hope to achieve in the future?'

'I know.' She smiled at her friend, albeit somewhat shakily. 'I will be better soon, I promise you. I will not disappoint you.'

'Good girl!' approved Beatrice briskly, folding her in a soft embrace. 'Now work hard, keep your tongue under control – and get rid of those shadows under your eyes before I see you again!' She left in a flurry of furs and ribbons, leaving behind her the heavy scent of late roses.

Soon after her mother's visit, Amy began to take Mel round with her to the 'At Homes'.

These visits, exchanged between the hours of four and six in the afternoon, were a strange mixture of the formal and the informal; calling at Mrs Hurstpoint's vast mansion on Adams Street, designed for her by the fashionable architect Richard Morris Hunt, they were shown without ceremony into the parlour, the first of a seemingly endless series of interconnecting rooms. No one was announced or introduced as they had

314

been in Springs House, but a bevy of young ladies, nieces or cousins of the family, seemed always to be on hand to show everyone round, to take the strain off the hostess, who sat on the sofa surrounded by her closest friends, holding out a languid hand to be shaken.

'Has she hurt her leg?' asked Melisande in a whispered aside.

'No,' said Amy, puzzled.

'Then why does she not rise to greet her guests?'

Amy laughed. 'It is perfectly correct! She would only rise if Mama were here.'

'Because she is older?'

'Heavens! Don't let Mama hear you say that! No. It's partly because Mama is a leader of Edensville Society, but also because she's the daughter of an English peer.'

'And the English are in fashion this year.'

'You are learning fast!'

'Goodness!'

'What is it now?'

Melisande gazed wide-eyed around the room. The parlour was redolent with the heavy scent of autumn blooms. Wherever she looked, ferns, smilax and flowers dripped from chandeliers, cornices and mantelpieces; balls of flowers hung from the ceilings, plateaux of flowers were banked against the walls, and in every room, on every surface, there were arrangements of moss and ferns, from which branched sprays of exotic waxy blooms.

'It is like a hot-house!' She looked at Amy who was struggling to suppress a giggle. 'I know,' said Mel with mock resignation. 'It is this year's fashion.'

She saw Warden Hurstpoint making his way through the fashionable throng towards her.

'Oh dear!' she said.

Amy followed her gaze. 'The price *you* pay for being this year's fashion,' she said gravely.

Max often stopped by at the Bennetts when he was in town, and was occasionally roped in by Amy to escort them to some social function or other if Tom had a meeting at College or had to dine with the Dean.

He would have spent all such evenings dancing attendance on Melisande if she had let him, but she made a point of

315

introducing him to as many of the other young ladies as she could. One of them, Michaela Jennings, made a set at him straight away.

She was a pleasant young lady, pretty, though not especially beautiful. Her brother would inherit the considerable Jennings fortune, but Michaela was an heiress in her own right through her mother and would not have to limit herself like so many other young ladies to marrying a man of fortune. She was much admired by the more flirtatious young men – to whom Max was a challenging contrast! – and very adept at keeping them all on a string, but social ease and a wide knowledge of precedence and etiquette, although impressive to one who was just finding her feet, was not the same as intelligence; although Mel had at first encouraged the friendship between Michaela and Max, she became sadly aware as time passed that there was considerably less to her new friend than met the eye.

At the Hurstpoints' ball, Michaela spent much of the evening, in Max's absence, flirting outrageously with a visiting French count, whom Beatrice had tartly stigmatised as yet another European bankrupt in search of an American fortune to restore his chateau.

'It so rarely works,' she said with a sigh to her friend Mrs Matthews. 'The families want the money, but not the rather more independent-minded young women who go with them.'

'But surely Consuelo Vanderbilt –'

'The Duchess of Marlborough? They say that everyone in England loves her – except the Duke.'

Melisande found Michaela out on the piazza, sulking after a sound scolding from her mama. 'I often wish that I were a poor girl,' she sighed dramatically, 'so that people would like me for myself.'

'That would hardly help in the case of the count.'

'Why not?'

'Because if you were a poor girl, you'd be too busy scrubbing floors or sewing all hours in a sweatshop to speak to him at any length about his reasons for loving you,' said Melisande robustly. 'Assuming you ever met him, for really it seems unlikely that the count would visit the slums to seek a potential bride.'

'I never thought of that,' said Michaela, heaving another sigh.

It was fortunate, thought Mel, that Adam was not present, for if she had caught his eye, she could never have kept a straight face.

Without Amy and Michaela to guide her, however, she would have found her way through Society beset by more pitfalls than she could have avoided herself, so she tried to be tolerant of her new friend's foibles.

Entertaining in Edensville was only slightly more casual than in New York. There, if you were not among the 'Four Hundred' – those people claimed by Ward McAllister to be the inner circle of New York Society, limited to the number that could comfortably fit into Mrs William Astor's ballroom – you might as well give up and go back to the prairies, but here, socialising of necessity involved a wider group.

'Which at least means you meet the occasional interesting person,' said Amy, on one of their rare evenings home.

'Not many, but more than in New York,' agreed Tom, peering over the top of his paper. 'That fashionable ass McAllister and his Four Hundred would flee in a body from a painter or a musician. But you can meet some pleasant intelligent people in Edensville,' he said, pushing his wire-rimmed spectacles back on to his nose. 'Most of them men, I fear. The women are proper, well-behaved, censorious – and deadly dull.'

'That is hardly their fault,' protested Amy. 'All that's expected of daughters is to be moderately well-educated –'

'Such a very narrow education, though! Any girl who can play the piano, recite poetry and recognise famous paintings and sculptures when her parents whisk her off on the Grand European Tour of museums and palaces, is spoken of as clever!' he said scornfully.

'She must also be able to supervise a large household, entertain guests, and be passable in summer sports,' pointed out Amy in defence of her own sex.

'And that's more than many of the young men would be capable of,' said Melisande scornfully.

'Ah! An evening spent with Warden Hurstpoint?' hazarded Tom, cocking an inquisitive eyebrow.

317

'As you would know if you had come to the Tranters' ball,' scolded Amy.

'Hurstpoint at least started out a fool,' said Tom caustically. 'It's the others I feel sorry for, the intelligent young men who fail under the challenge of emulating their father or grandfather. I have one in my class who has turned to scholarship in the hope of making his mark in a different field, but his brother is turning into an alcoholic under the · strain of competing with the dead grandfather who made the family fortune.'

'To have so much and throw it away!' exclaimed Melisande. 'I'd send them to the slums, to the orphanages – make them appreciate what they have!'

'That's what Adam does,' said Tom, oblivious to his wife's frown. 'If you cannot compete with the family history – the times after all being quite different – then make your mark as a philanthropist. It seems to work.'

Mel was glad to discover that it seemed to work for Amy too. While she stressed the need to join in whatever fashionable diversion was offered, she rarely missed an opportunity to encourage the ladies to support her charitable causes. Last year it had been the Harbourside school; in the summer it had been the Red Cross Auxiliary, in support of the soldiers fighting in Manila and Cuba; this season it was a new lying-in ward for the hospital – the rich of course could command the services of skilled attendants in their own homes.

Melisande was full of admiration for the skilful way in which Amy introduced the subject, which was made doubly difficult as the ladies themselves never mentioned pregnancy. In the same way that they pretended that tables and pianos had no legs beneath the draped, fringed cloths, so too they found it necessary to adopt euphemisms when mentioning anything to do with the female anatomy. No female, if their conversation were to be believed, existed at all below the waist. Melisande sometimes had a vision of them all floating along on wheels.

An old schoolfriend of Amy's who had been married for some years, suddenly announced that she was 'not at home' and absented herself from the splendid ball given by the Fenns to celebrate the engagement of one of their many daughters. Maria, whispered Michaela Jennings, was in an interesting condition. Melisande, who found everyone interesting, could not imagine how shutting oneself away in the middle of the Season could make one more interesting.

'It's quite simple,' said Amy with a chuckle when Melisande sought enlightenment in the carriage on the way home from the Fenn's. 'Maria is to have a baby.'

'Then why did they not say so?'

'They – I don't know. It's just thought not proper to know these things. And it is certainly not proper to discuss it in mixed company.'

'You don't mind, do you, Tom?' asked Mel anxiously.

'Not at all,' he said sleepily from the corner. 'Though I don't think that's quite the point.'

'It's very odd,' said Melisande. 'I thought I was the only ignorant one.'

'Unfortunately it's the fashion to bring children up in ignorance,' said Amy, heroically ignoring her husband's attempt to catch her eye, 'and the affectation to pretend ignorance oneself. But not us. Mama brought us up to be honest.'

'Like everyone knowing that Mrs Henderson and Mr Fenn are having an affair, but pretending that they don't?' she said.

'Quite so, young lady,' said Amy in dry tones. 'But even less do they talk about something like that!'

'You are growing up fast, Melisande,' said Tom as he handed her out of the carriage. 'I think your erstwhile guardian would be surprised to see how much you've changed in so short a time.'

'I don't think he'd even notice,' she said sadly. 'Besides, he's washed his hands of me.'

She had not seen him since the day after the Harvest Ball. She had steeled herself to meet him again with a semblance of calm and self-possession, but he had not come. It was a constant pain to her to listen to the other guests speculating on the reason for his absence from the balls and breakfasts.

She could have told them. Obviously he had only been waiting for the opportunity to be rid of her, otherwise why had he not come to see how she had settled in? Even Colonel Randall, who had taken a large house on the corner of Fifth

319

and Erie and who was going about a great deal in society with his cousin's widow, had commented on his absence.

Many of the hostesses, who had counted on him for their balls, were quite cross about what they saw as sheer dereliction of duty. 'For one can never have too many gentlemen, my dear,' said Mrs Jennings at Maria Choat's engagement ball. 'So many of them come only to watch or to drink. He is one of our best dancers. Sadly missed, sadly missed.'

'And Max has not come either,' said Michaela, who had been looking forward to a good flirtation with Pierre Pellisson under Max's glowering eye.

'You should remember, Michaela, that his time is not entirely his own,' Melisande reminded her friend. 'He runs a vast estate – he has to work with the seasons like any farmer.'

'Oh, what boring stuff!' said Michaela, wrinkling her dainty little nose. 'I wanted to tell him a German riddle that I learned today from my governess.' Her face fell. 'Not that I have really made the progress in German which I had hoped for. And you know I have quite set aside French and Italian for the moment, in spite of Mama, who thinks that German is too harsh and quite distorts one's lips. But I insisted on German, even though I am well aware that Italian is *le dernier cri*.' Melisande wondered whether she was under the illusion that Max was German. Michaela was prattling on, as she so often did, without waiting for a reply – but then, thought Melisande fair-mindedly, in the Jennings family, how often would a reply be worth waiting for?

'However hard I work at my German, I don't seem to make any progress,' complained Michaela. 'If I could go to Germany, now, it would make the most tremendous difference. Always to hear German spoken, would that not be perfect?'

'Then why do you not go?'

'I shall!' Her eyes lit up at the prospect. 'I shall go next winter and live with a German family. As a governess per- haps.' Melisande raised her eyebrows at that. 'Spend a month or two in Dresden in a German family,' she went on, growing more and more excited. 'Father, mother, daughter my age and – and perhaps a son. Yes. A very interesting son.'

'Twelve or so. That's an interesting age . . .'

'Don't be a goose, Mel,' she said tartly. 'Twenty at least.'

'And the younger children?'

'No.' She frowned. 'No younger children. I detest younger children.'

Melisande bit back the question of why the family would need a governess in the first place.

'I would hear and speak nothing but German. We would have such delightful excursions. I would discuss philosophy and art with the son. And then, in the summer, I would tear myself away, to journey to Florence and study Italian in the same way. *En famille.*'

'And discuss the Renaissance with the son, assuming he is of an age?'

'Yes, of course.' Then her face fell. 'But it cannot be this winter, as Mama believes Bailey – Bailey Crichton, you know – is coming up to the mark. So it would scarcely be sensible to go now. Though you must agree that it would be an excellent plan.'

And Mel, under the pretext of fanning herself, bit her lip hard and agreed that, yes, it would be hard to think of a better.

Melisande herself was not short of admirers, many of them intrigued by her mysterious background, or dazzled, like Hurstpoint, by her radiant looks; the confirmed bachelors, particularly the older men, found her extremely good company, so different as she was to the usual simpering Society miss. At first she found their adulation set her pulses racing, but before long, even their attentions began to pall and cloy and she found it harder than ever to be civil to some of the younger men with their foolish compliments. She would have given anything to look across the room and exchange a smile with a pair of hard grey eyes. The world seemed a hollow place without a like mind to share it.

But depression never lasted long with Melisande and it took no more than a walk through Harbourside to lift her spirits. If the people of Harbourside, slaving away day in and day out to give their children a better start in life, could smile at her and call cheerfully to one another from the tenement windows, what had she, wafted miraculously from a slum orphanage to the lap of luxury in less than a year, to complain about?

321

It might have consoled her to know how difficult Adam was finding it to keep away from Edensville, though not to anybody, even Max, would he have admitted how much he was missing her. Wherever he looked, whatever he did, there would be some reminder of Melisande. During the harvesttime she had been in and out of his study, keeping the notes up to date, making sure that Jefferson and Hübner had left the place in order. Now, every time the door opened, he expected her to walk in and found it hard not to take his disappointment out on whichever person happened to walk in in her place. And of course Mrs Chobley never stopped talking about her or reading snippets from her frequent letters.

It was not much better at the dispensary, especially when the town hall clock struck five.

'Strange not to see Melisande walking in through the door,' remarked Miss Minton one day as the last chime died away, and was quite surprised to have her head snapped off for her trouble.

He avoided the balls, pleading pressure of work after the harvest when Mrs Patterson taxed him with his absence. Not that he could entirely avoid the Pattersons: until Mel was thoroughly established in Society he would have to keep the pressure on Patterson through his sister. Besides, he did not foresee spending the rest of his life as a bachelor; he was not cut out to be a monk, and commonsense and the horrors he had seen as a medical student kept him from seeking solace elsewhere. He could do worse than Sophia Patterson, he told himself sternly; with her inheritance she could keep the school and the hospital going for years. Besides, it would be a favour to her to get her away from her mother's influence. At least, that was how he reasoned it out to himself, but he always found an excuse not to take matters any further.

Melisande often spent the evening with Colonel Randall and Aunt Beatrice at the theatre or dining in the Colonel's handsome new house; she enjoyed their company and it meant that Tom and Amy, who had not been that long married, had some time to themselves. The older couple had constituted themselves to some extent her guardians.

'Godparents, if you like,' said the Colonel gruffly one evening as the two of them sat around the fire together. 'If you were younger, child, I would suggest adopting you,' he said, 'but I recall Beatrice telling me you will be of age soon.'

'In July, as far as I know,' said Melisande. 'And while I suppose I am a little old for adoption, I cannot think of anyone I would rather have as godparents. But I thought you had planned to go back to England soon?'

The Colonel twirled his moustaches rather self-consciously. 'That was before I had really come to know Beatrice,' he said. 'Don't know but what I might –' he cleared his throat '– might well decide to settle down here.'

'For ever?'

'Well, that depends . . .'

'On Aunt Beatrice?' she said shrewdly.

He chuckled, but would not be drawn any further.

He took his position as her unofficial guardian very seriously, questioning her closely about the school and about her admirers. One day he turned up on horseback followed by a flat cart with something large under a tarpaulin.

'Present for you, Mel, m'dear,' he said, and drew off the tarpaulin to reveal a bicycle.

Her mouth fell open and she gave a gasp of surprise.

'It's a Pierce Safety, m'dear,' explained Colonel Randall. 'Ladies' version, of course. Plunger brakes, pneumatic tyres and so on. Thought it might be useful with all that to-ing and fro-ing you do to Harbourside.'

'Useful?' said Melisande in awed tones. 'It will be wonderful!'

It took her only a few days to work out how to ride the bike and before long she was cycling all over the town, not just to the school. She loved the sensation of the wind on her face as she swooped downhill to Harbourside and, truth to tell, cherished the independence it gave her. The Bennetts had just the one small carriage and now, freed from the necessity of waiting on its availability, Mel no longer had to rely on others to fill her days. The first time she mastered the bicycle she travelled out of town to call on Miss Greville, and the next day went to see . Natasha.

Beatrice gave George Randall a tremendous scolding when first she saw Melisande perched on the bicycle; it was hard to

323

tell which she disapproved of the most: the bicycle, which she thought unladylike in the extreme, or the freedom it gave Melisande to come and go pretty much as she pleased.

Natasha, on the other hand, was overjoyed to see her friend again. She was obviously very happy with the Tschenchenyovs and cherished her position. But then Matilda, the Bennetts' maid, was happy too. Perhaps a lot depended on your employer, thought Mel, as she cycled back down Main Street. And yet the doctor had been a good employer and still she had not wanted to be a servant in his household.

But not all employers were as considerate as the Bennetts and the Tschenchenyovs. She remembered how she had commented to Amy, on one of their earlier social calls, what a strange coincidence it was that all three of the first footmen in the houses they had visited that week should be called James and the parlourmaids Mary. With a casualness she found chilling, Amy had pointed out that servants in most large households would not retain their own names at all, but be called James simply because they *were* the first footman.

Mel had been horrified. To take away a person's name seemed to her to set that person at naught.

Amy had shrugged. 'To be a servant in a reasonably prosperous household is the sum total of many a poor girl's ambitions,' she pointed out. 'If she is sensible and honest, she can rise through the servants' hall to a position of trust. She will have no expenses or living costs, so when she leaves to marry – perhaps to a tradesman she has met while in service – her savings will often make all the difference between grinding poverty and a degree of respectability.'

Mel was musing this over, cycling absent-mindedly down Ontario Street back from a visit to Natasha, the day the first snow fell. She had watched the preparations for winter without really believing it was upon them: the boats being pulled up from the lake's edge and upended, logs being stacked almost feverishly on verandahs, sledges being drawn out into stableyards for the runners to be oiled. 'Snow comes the first week in November,' Rabbi Benjamin told her. 'Second at the very latest.'

'Every year?'

'Without fail.'

She drew her bicycle into the side of the road and stood there, catching snowflakes on her outstretched hands and opening her mouth to the cool feel of them on her tongue, and thinking that this year when the sledges came she would be in them, wrapped snugly in furs, well-fed and well-dressed, not cold and starving as she had been in the last snows, terrified of being swallowed up by the drifts, desperate for shelter – any shelter.

With the first heavy fall of snow the bicycle had to be put away, but with the Harbourside school and the society visits, Christmas was upon them almost before Melisande could draw breath.

Christmas Eve was to see the opening of the new lying-in ward at the hospital and by mid December only one more fund-raising event remained: Amy's own contribution to the festivities.

She had organised a musical evening, several of the ladies of her circle having been persuaded to sing one or two of the sentimental ballads so popular this year. Colonel Randall had offered his house for the soirée, since the Bennetts' home had not sufficient space, even when the two main reception rooms were thrown into one. An elderly gentleman of Amy's acquaintance had been dragooned into reading from Charles Dickens' *Christmas Carol* and Madame Pellisson, mother of the indigent count, had promised to play for them on the harp.

'You can accompany the singers,' Amy informed Mel the week before the concert. 'And I rely on you to provide at least two other items.'

'But I've never played in public before – only to you and Tom. And Adam.'

'It's for a good cause,' said Amy briskly. 'And I won't take no for an answer. I had hoped to get Dame Adelina Patti, but she has had to alter her schedule, drat the woman, and she's already left for Chicago.'

Melisande thought she would make a very poor substitute for the operatic diva.

325

Anxiously she smoothed down the lace-panelled sleeves of her heavy silk evening blouse, and straightened the edging around the wrist.

'Stop fiddling Mel,' said Amy. 'You look perfect.'

'But I –'

'Here are the first guests,' said Amy, taking a firm grip on her arm and leading her, with a rustle of silk taffeta under-skirts, to stand with Tom and Colonel Randall at the top of the elegant staircase in his splendid mansion to welcome the guests who had come to support Mrs Bennett's charitable efforts.

'Nervous?' asked the Colonel.

'A little,' admitted Melisande. 'But I will not let Amy down – not after all she has done for me.'

'You'll do, m'dear,' he said with a warm smile, turning away to see to his guests' comfort.

They had been to many such evenings before and, in the absence of any great names, were prepared to be faintly bored, especially the husbands who had been dragged along under protest and were counting the moments until they could slip away to spend the shank of the evening in their clubs, playing a frame of billiards, blowing a cloud and cracking a bottle in convivial company. They knew what kind of fare would be served up: some amateur wailing away at Tostig's *Goodbye* or Arthur Sullivan's *Lost Chord*, and some-one's spoilt daughter plodding through a nocturne or a so-nata, with little accuracy and less feeling.

When they were all seated comfortably in the saloon, there were almost a hundred leading members of Edensville Society present. As the entertainment began, the audience ceased its whispering and settled down to listen.

The first performers came up, or rather down, to their expectations. Mrs Hutchinson had only a moderate voice, which although competent enough for the sentimental ballad with which she began, was not at all equal to the challenge of Tostig's famous song with which she followed it – in any case 'Goodbye' was scarcely a song with which to open a concert! The accompanist, however, was able to disguise the worst mistakes and the applause at the end was sufficient to send Mrs Hutchinson back to her seat with a glow of pleasure.

She was followed by Mr Webster reading selected passages from *A Christmas Carol* between the musical items. He had a good voice and an entertaining style. Beatrice Randall's elderly neighbour informed her that he had been privileged to hear the author himself on one of his triumphant tours of America and that Mr Webster 'wasn't half bad'.

Madame Pellisson closed the first part of the evening with a competent rendering of a popular song, accompanying herself on the harp, and then it was time for refreshments to be handed around. The Colonel had not stinted on these.

'In my experience of musical soirées, the audience is in far greater need of sustenance than the performers!' he'd said gruffly. A number of the gentlemen, having imbibed a great deal of champagne, were quite prepared to doze off, discreetly of course, for the remainder of the evening.

As one of the hostesses, Melisande found her time so taken up with seeing to their guests that she had not time to be nervous about her own performance. She went from one end of the room to the other, supervising the servants, stopping for a brief chit-chat with Michaela, making sure that all the guests were happy. Before she knew it, she and Amy were ushering their guests back to their seats. Turning away from an elderly lady she had assisted to her chair, Melisande bumped straight into Adam Kingsley.

'I'm so sorry, I hadn't seen you. I – I did not know you were here . . . I mean . . .' Her voice trailed away as she realised that she was babbling.

'I trust you do not object to me coming in half way through?' he said coolly. 'I have been with a patient.'

'Of course not,' she said breathlessly. 'I will tell Amy.'

'No need, Miss Stevens,' he said. 'Tom is fetching me a chair.'

'A glass of wine, then?' She signalled to a servant standing nearby.

'Thank you.' Adam took two glasses and handed one to her. 'A pleasing turnout,' he said, but all the time his eyes were on her.

'Yes. Amy says –'

'You look very well,' he said abruptly, seemingly unaware that he had interrupted her. 'Edensville suits you.'

327

She inclined her head graciously and took the smallest sip of the sparkling wine. She thought she could hardly say the same about him. He was looking somewhat drawn and haggard, his face all hard planes and shadows, harsh without the redeeming smile to lighten it.

'And the school?' he asked. 'Is all well with the school?'

She took another sip of the wine to give her courage. 'If you want to know about the school, Doctor Kingsley,' she said coolly, 'you have only to come and see. You are, after all, a trustee. Pray excuse me. I must see to my other guests.'

'Oh dear,' said Amy, watching Mel turn away. 'I hope they have not argued!'

'Don't worry, my dear,' said her mother. 'It would do Adam a world of good if –'

'Adam?' exclaimed Amy. 'I am not in the least concerned about Adam. I just hope he has not upset my star performer!'

'Whatever can you mean?' demanded Beatrice.

'Wait and see!' said Amy with a chuckle.

As the audience settled once more into their seats, Melisande set down her glass and walked up the seemingly endless room to take her seat at the piano, conscious of every eye on her. Why did she always feel as though she had lost several layers of skin when she was with Adam? Now every nerve was on edge: she felt as though she could feel every knot in the carpet beneath her satin slippers, and the rustling of her silken skirts seemed abnormally loud in the expectant hush.

She struggled to get a grip on her emotions; she would not let him throw her. Stepping up on to the little dais, she took a deep breath and steadied her voice.

'I should like to play you Beethoven's Rondo in G Major,' she announced. 'Also known as "The Rage Over a Lost Penny".'

The title was enough to make even the most somnolent member of the audience sit up and take notice, even if Beethoven was considered sadly passé, and when her hands began to fly over the keys as she started on the developments and embellishments, they sat entranced. The applause when she finished was more than polite, it was wildly enthusiastic, and they would not let her leave the keyboard without an encore. She chose another well-known piece by Beethoven,

328

the 'Moonlight' sonata and this time she did not have to worry about catching the audience's attention: she had them in the palm of her hand.

Adam, watching her from the back of the saloon where he sat with Tom Bennett, felt a stab of pain as she began to play, for this was one of the pieces he had chosen and left in the chest for her to find, as if by accident, when she stole into the drawing room, thinking herself alone, and played her heart out.

And she was playing equally well tonight. He supposed he was pleased to see that the recent disruption had not affected her skill at the pianoforte.

'She seems to have settled well in Edensville,' Adam said to Tom when the last haunting notes had died away and the audience had burst into applause once more.

'Very well,' he replied, forcing himself to ignore the note of bitterness in Adam's voice. 'All the young men are fascinated by her, because she is so different from the usual simpering miss.'

'They don't realise just how different!' said Adam, struck by a sudden unexpected vision of the time he had confronted her in the library at Springs House and finding himself unexpectedly aroused by the memory. 'And which of these young men does she favour?' He forced himself to say it with a casualness he did not feel.

'None of them, I fear,' sighed Tom regretfully. 'She told Amy she finds them all rather silly and young. Indeed she seems to have more in common with the older men, like Alderley and Poynington.'

'Those rakes?' said Adam scornfully. 'She will do her reputation no good if she associates with *them*!'

'I told Amy not to push the girl,' Tom went on. 'She may just not be ready to settle down yet.'

Adam opened his mouth to retort, but the next performer was taking her place on the dais and they had, perforce, to drop the subject.

The last item on the programme could not have been termed a success. They had tried in vain to persuade Agatha Feyden to sing earlier in the programme, but that lady, insistent as ever in such matters, had pointed out that her

329

seniority entitled her to the honour of closing the programme. And close it she did. Her rendering of 'Home, Sweet Home' made everybody think longingly of theirs and within half an hour the saloon was empty.

Some of the guests had lingered long enough to praise Amy's talented young friend and a number of them commented rather acidly on Mrs Feyden's unfortunate habit of trying to grab the glory without having the ability.

'We got off lightly,' Amy confided to her mother. 'Agatha *had* intended to finish the programme – in George's honour, you see – with 'Rule Britannia!' You can imagine how that would have gone down with the audience!'

'Offended every one of 'em,' said Tom grimly.

'And offended George too,' said Beatrice, 'when he heard how she could murder it!'

The talk in Edensville, and in the Society journals that week, was all of the talented Miss Stevens, but much to Amy's pleasure and Tom's surprise she did not allow it to go to her head. On the contrary, after a few days of being gushed over, she confessed herself heartily tired of all the nonsense.

'You should have heard Warden Hurstpoint!' Amy said to Tom, with a gurgle of laughter, as they sat at dinner together one evening. 'Told Mel that her playing was as angelic as her face and her behaviour!'

'And what did you say to that?' Tom asked Melisande.

'I told him that his remark should rather have been addressed to Madame Pellisson, since it was generally believed that angels played the harp, not the pianoforte.' She heaved a long-suffering sigh. 'But I think that was beyond him.'

'Then you do not hold the same estimation of young Warden's prospects of winning your hand as he does?' enquired Tom mildly.

'Goodness, no! If I were going to marry anyone, he'd have to have a good deal more brain than poor Warden!' She laid down her fork. 'But I don't think I shall ever marry.'

'That would be a shame,' said Tom.

'Are you thinking you will never be rid of me?' said Melisande. 'You need not, you know.'

'That wasn't at all what I meant,' he said, shaking his head. 'We are only too pleased to have you for as long as you want to stay.' He twirled his wine glass and grinned down the table at his wife. 'And the world is full of married men and women who said 'never'!'

'Tom!' Amy blushed.

'But I'm pleased to hear that rumour was false in this case,' he went on. 'And now that you have set my mind at rest, I can go ahead with an idea I have.'

Amy was as intrigued as Melisande by this incomplete hint and both clamoured to know what he had in mind, but with a grin that his fond wife did not hesitate to tell him was as infuriating as it was ungentlemanly, he refused to be drawn on the matter, excusing himself after the dessert 'to write an important letter'.

Just after the tea tray had been brought in, there was a knock on the door. Amy laid aside the tapestry she had been working on – not because she wanted to sew, but to stop herself asking Tom about the letter, as she was sure he wanted her to do.

'Whoever can be calling at this hour?' she demanded. 'Are you expecting anyone, Melisande?'

'No,' she replied, looking up from the silk handkerchiefs she was embroidering for Christmas gifts.

'It's probably someone for me,' said Tom, in an absent manner guaranteed to infuriate his fond spouse.

'Then I shall retire,' said Melisande, folding her work away, but before she could leave, Matilda came in.

'Mr Smeaton has sent up his card, ma'am,' she said. 'Are you at home?'

'Show him up, Matilda,' said Tom. 'Melisande, I would particularly like you to stay and meet him.'

He crossed the room to greet Mr Smeaton, a round, plump man with a fixed vacuous expression.

'My wife. Our friend Miss Stevens. Amy, Melisande, I'd like you to meet Mr Smeaton, Dean of Admissions at Edensville College.'

Mr Smeaton shook hands rather perfunctorily with Amy then turned to Melisande with enthusiasm.

'So you're the young lady who wants to go to college, are you?'

Tom stepped forward, grinning broadly at their startled expressions.

'Do sit down, Mr Smeaton,' he said.

'Mrs Bennett?' He waited for Amy to take her seat.

'Of course! Of course! What am I thinking of?' She waved him to a chair. 'Matilda, another cup for our guest. Your pardon, Mr Smeaton, but we are, as you can see, both dumbfounded.'

'Thought you would be,' said Mr Smeaton with rather grim satisfaction.

'Our college runs a course for teachers, as you know,' said Tom, 'but this year we have admitted –'

'– as an experiment only,' interjected Smeaton.

'As a very successful experiment,' Tom went on, 'we have admitted those who have already had experience of teaching, but have no formal qualifications.'

'To improve the standards, you see,' said Smeaton with a beam.

'For them the course lasts anything between a few months and a whole year,' added Tom quickly. 'And one of Mr Smeaton's teaching students has had to drop out of the course due to a family crisis,' he explained, 'which leaves a place free . . .'

'Quite so. And –'

'And if we can persuade the board that Mel's teaching experience is sufficiently extensive, she could be taken on for the teaching diploma –'

'– which can be completed by the summer –'

'*And*, what's more, the Dean of Music will let her join his students!'

'Provided, of course, that she passes the entrance examination.'

'Which she will – with flying colours!'

The two men came to a halt and smiled beatifically at each other before turning to look expectantly at their audience.

'Oh, Tom! Mr Smeaton! That's wonderful!' exclaimed Amy.

Melisande's face had lit up with an excited smile as the two men spoke, and when they finished, she jumped up, clasping her hands together. Then, in an instant, the excitement was wiped off her face to be replaced by a look of pure misery.

'Tom – Mr Smeaton – it is so very kind of you,' she said with a catch in her voice. 'But I – I couldn't do it.'

Tom's face fell.

'Melisande!' said Amy sharply. 'What nonsense is this?'

'I can't,' she said wretchedly. 'How can I let the children down?'

'The children?' Mr Smeaton's cherubic face was a picture of warring emotions as he struggled to make sense of what she was saying.

'The children at the school. Harbourside.'

'Ah. *Those* children,' he said, nodding his head. 'Of course you may have to shorten your days a little, but I do not imagine there will be a problem with that.'

'Shorten my days? I – I don't understand.'

'I assure you, neither the trustees nor the children will have cause for complaint. Since they are sponsoring you, we would hardly deprive them of your services, Miss Stevens.'

'Sponsoring me?' faltered Mel.

'The Scholarships have already been awarded for this year. And without sponsors we could hardly have accepted you.'

Christmas passed in a whirl of fancy dress balls and parties, to which they went wrapped in fur rugs in bell-hung sledges; Amy could only persuade Mel to come by promising that she should have the days undisturbed to study for the examinations she had to sit in the New Year. When she did go, she threw herself into the festivities with wholehearted enthusiasm and energy, but she looked in vain for Adam Kingsley: he had gone to New York to stay with friends, leaving his patients to the tender mercies of David Jefferson. Anton Hübner had gone too, declaring his intention to seek his fortune out west in Oklahoma.

'So vexing,' said Beatrice to her daughter as they watched Melisande talking animatedly to Harriet Minton at the reception to celebrate the opening of the lying-in ward on Christmas Eve. 'I thought for certain Anton would make a match for Harriet.'

'You do not think that Harriet and Adam –?'

'They would not suit,' said Beatrice Randall decisively.

'That's never deterred anyone before,' observed Tom.

'True,' said his mother-in-law. 'But – Harriet Minton and Adam? No. They would make each other very unhappy.'

333

'I swear you are in the direct line from Old Father Noah!' teased Tom. 'This obsession with pairing everyone off!'

Beatrice smiled quietly to herself.

'I know,' said Tom, reaching for his wife's hand and squeezing it. 'Some of us need a little more help than others. But if Harriet and Adam are not to make each other unhappy, then clearly we shall have to find someone else for her.'

'Tom, really!'

'At least she is not wearing her heart on her sleeve.'

'Any more than Melisande is.'

'Hard to tell which of them is putting on the bravest face,' said Tom wryly.

As Tom had prophesied, Melisande passed her entrance examinations with flying colours and was accepted into the college. Mr Smeaton's vacuous expression had proved deceptive, as she discovered when he produced for her a comprehensive timetable fitted around her commitments at Harbourside.

'And so you are to go to college!' said Beatrice proudly when she heard the results. 'Not that I ever doubted they would take you.'

'Thanks to Tom – and you. I am sure you persuaded the trustees.'

Beatrice waved her thanks aside. 'If the trustees want an efficient school, they must be prepared to train the teacher. Besides,' she added shrewdly, watching Mel's reaction in the mirror where she was adjusting a dashing new hat, 'I cannot take the credit, for it was Adam's idea.'

She swept out to her carriage, smiling to herself at the warm glow in the girl's eyes.

Melisande's first day at college was the longest she could remember. She had declined Tom's offer to take her in, feeling that she had to stand on her own two feet, but when she alighted from the sledge that carried the students up from the town, her heart sank into her high-laced boots.

Edensville College was an impressive building set on a hill overlooking the town. Built in the 1880s as an exact copy of a vast baronial castle somewhere in the highlands of Scotland, complete with turrets and castellations, it had weathered in the course of a dozen fierce winters until it looked as though it had been there for ever.

She stood a moment irresolute while the other students, calling cheerily to one another, disappeared in twos and threes around corners, up staircases, through doors, until at last she was left alone, standing forlornly between the banks of snow that had been cleared from the path.

'Miss Stevens?' She turned to see a young man standing beneath the portico, a smile in his brilliant dark eyes. 'Professor Bennett has asked me to be your guide for today,' he said in a warm friendly voice with a trace of an accent to give it added charm. 'I am Gilles de Villeneuve. I'm in my final year. We attend the same music classes today, although I must study English while you major in French. A pity we cannot exchange: we would do so much better in our native tongue, would we not?'

The world seemed a friendlier place with Gilles at her side. He introduced her to his friends, ensured she found out everything she needed to know.

At lunchtime Sally Harding, whose brother James had decided in the first class that he wished to further his acquaintance with the new student, took Melisande under her wing, showing her to the ladies' common room where a warm fire crackled welcomingly.

'I'll introduce you to the others when they come in,' she said, making them both a warm drink. She hesitated. 'They may seem a little stand-offish at first, but it's only envy.'

'Envy?' said Melisande, startled.

'For spending so much time with Gilles. My dear, everyone here has a crush on Gilles! He's just so adorable!'

'Adorable? I suppose so,' said Melisande with a shrug. But what was adorable without strength and dedication? she thought, remembering a pair of hard grey eyes in a strong face.

Over the course of the next few weeks, as they realised that Melisande had no designs on Gilles, most of the young ladies set their reservations aside and made friends with the new girl. She found it amusing that they should all be languishing after the same young man, for charming though he was, she felt there was little depth to Gilles. But she would always be grateful to him: he had been a very pleasant introduction to what could have been a nerve-wracking experience.

The interview with the Board of Examiners to discuss the results of her entrance examination was another hurdle to be overcome, but their views, she found, reflected her own. In her French studies, her language skills were satisfactory, although her reading had, of necessity, been restricted. In music too, her practical skills bore comparison with and in most cases surpassed those of the other students, but of musical theory she was abysmally ignorant. If she was to be permitted to sit her final examinations with the rest of her class at the end of the academic year, then she had very little time in which to improve her weak subjects.

Without delay she set to work with Tom to plan out a course of study which would concentrate on her weak areas without affecting the time she spent preparing her work for the Harbourside children. Once the frantic pace of the first week had subsided, Mel found herself more at home with her new life than she had ever thought possible. At first it had been a little unnerving, for she had never had to compete with other young people of equal ability. She who from the age of twelve had taught others was now herself a pupil. It helped that she was not the only one in that position, for many of the students for the teaching diploma had, like her, taught for some years, and had come, some of the older ones much against their will, to train for a diploma many of them thought superfluous, as it would only enable them to do the same job they had been doing all their adult lives. But Melisande remembered the schools inspector and the disappointment she had gone through when the orphans moved to St Mark's; if Eden County wanted a teacher with a diploma, then Eden County should have one!

Not many of the teaching students came to the music classes. Most of them had no greater ambition than to be able to thump out a tune while the children marched round the hall, or accompany carols and harvest hymns. The students in the music department were nearly all the sons and daughters of wealthy families, who had been playing their instruments since they were small children, studying under the best French and Italian instructors that their parents' money could buy. She was at first envious of them for their greater knowledge, but as the weeks went by and the piano teacher Mr Farson managed to rub off some of the rough edges, she realised that she could, with practice, be every bit as good as them.

'Better, in fact,' said Mr Farson, with his booming laugh. 'Most of them have become poor imitations of their tutors, but you, Miss Stevens, have had no one to imitate, and so you have developed a delightfully original style.'

Of course there were weaknesses, but she attacked them fiercely. As the weeks went on, she found that, as Mr Farson had promised, musical theory fitted in so logically with what she had learnt from her practical work that she no longer saw it as a problem and in the evenings, after she had practised on the Bennetts' instrument, she often went to her room to read or to familiarise herself with new pieces, which provided her with an excellent excuse not to impose herself as a third on the young couple.

Each day the wind grew a little more bitter and she was glad of the fur-trimmed cape Colonel Randall gave her to wear over the deep blue covert coat. Each day as she climbed the hill to the college, the mantle of snow lay deeper and crisper and colder than the previous day over the hedges, walls and rooftops of Eden Springs, until the day when every feature of the landscape had been obliterated into nothingness.

Days at Harbourside took on a different aspect in the harshness of winter. The children, ill-clad and ill-shod, struggled through the snow to reach the school, but the chill of the dank tenements and snow-filled alleys seemed to have penetrated their brains as well as their bones, and in spite of the bellied black stove Adam had had installed in the corner, they seemed to take all day to warm up. Progress was slow until she and Max hit on the idea of providing a cup of hot broth as soon as the children arrived at the school. She made a point of asking Rabbi Benjamin's opinion when he came in to work with the older ones, and the next day there was a large pot waiting for her on the doorstep when she arrived, alongside a box of battered tin mugs.

It was a good chicken broth, still savoury even after it had been heated up on the banked down stove and watered down with water from the kettle. As each child entered, stamping the snow from their shoes, Melisande bade them good morning and handed them a mug half full of broth; round-eyed. they took it from her and sat at their desks, hands cupped eagerly round the tin mugs, eyes closed as they breathed in the tempting aroma, sniffing the fumes as though they would thaw them from the lungs out.

Each evening the scrubbed pot was left out on the doorstep; each morning another was in its place. It wasn't always the same pot. Sometimes it held beef broth, often it was chicken, occasionally only a rather thin vegetable soup, but the effect on the cold and hungry children was dramatic.

'I wish your benefactor could see their little faces,' said Melisande the next time the Rabbi came in.

'No need,' he said. 'I'm sure he knows.'

And Mel, suppressing a smile with difficulty, was equally sure of it.

Through the bleak winter she would walk home from Harbourside, along the frozen sidewalks, the snow crisply crunching beneath her feet, past the City Hall shining in its crystalline overcoat of hoar frost and reaching the house, pausing only to tear off her coat and hat and greet Amy, would set herself down at her desk to dash off pages of ideas and practical observations on the day's work. And occasionally as she worked her eyes would stray to the window, with its view of the lake, and she would try not to think of Eden Springs – and Adam. The joys and delights and hopes of the summer days at Springs House faded into the increasingly bitter cold of the city by the lake, and her love for Adam she folded away in her heart like a faded photograph of someone once greatly loved whose constant memory is too painful to bear, to be brought out only in the quiet, sad moments and laid carefully away while she concentrated on her work.

The early March wind plucked little snow devils from the surface of the snow pockets that lingered in the lee of tall buildings or on the patches of waste ground, sucking them up into powdery miniature whirlwinds. The worst of the winter was over and as the piled up banks of snow that lined the road slowly thawed, the winds and severe snowstorms were facing

338

into no more than an alarming memory. As Mel walked across City Hall Square shafts of early sunlight thawed the overnight frost and glinted feebly on the stallholders setting up their tables in the open air market, spotlighting the bright reds and golds of the hothouse fruit against the muted greens of the early spring vegetables.

Among the shoppers on the far side of the square she could see Mrs McPherson, Amy's housekeeper. She wondered with a deep sigh who would be served up at dinner this evening.·

Amy had taken most seriously the 'task, given her by her mother, of introducing her house guest to all the eligible young men of Edensville, and had been working on it ever since Mel first came to live with them. Mel had been polite to them all, and many a young man like Warden Hurstpoint had gone away bowled over by her charm – only to be completely nonplussed on their second meeting by her coolness. Recently Amy had abandoned the sons of hopeful Society mothers and begun to invite Mel's fellow students in the hope of finding one who would catch her friend's fancy.

She had had great hopes of Gilles for a while, especially when he had invited Mel and the Harding twins to his family's farm for the Sugaring-off party.

"I can't tell you exactly when it will be,' he had said, his eyes resting warmly on her, 'for we have to wait on nature for the timing.'

'Sugaring-off?' said Mel with a puzzled frown. 'Whatever is that?'

'One can see this is your first winter in this part of the world,' he said teasingly. Remembering what her first winter had been like, she was not going to disillusion him. 'Not know what a Sugaring-off party is? Why, you haven't lived till you've been to a Sugaring-off party!'

Just as the main snows melted away and the early spring flowers began to emerge in the deep forests, in that stage between winter and spring when it wasn't too cold and it wasn't too warm, the soft 'sugar snow' fell, covering the young daffodils with a thick cool white carpet and signalling the running of the maple sap from the big sugar maple trees.

All through the woods and forests around the lakes, the big trees were tapped with hand-whittled wooden spouts through

339

which the thin sap coursed into strong buckets. And then the Sugaring-off party began.

The maple sap was poured into iron cauldrons slung on stout poles between two trees and throughout the night a crackling hot blaze was stoked up. Friends and neighbours came from miles around to join the party. Anyone who could play the fiddle or call the barn dances was particularly welcome and while some helped stir the boiling sap until it began to thicken, the older folk grilled food over smaller fires and watched the more energetic dance the traditional reels to the sound and the stamp of the caller. It was as different from the formal balls as it could be, and Melisande though it was wonderful.

When the first batch of syrup was poured off, the rest was left to boil and crystallise, when it would be transferred to pans to harden into crumbly dark maple sugar. Gilles, elegant veneer gone as if it had never existed, showed them how to drizzle the syrup on to plates of snow to make taffy: 'for the children', he said, though they ate a goodly quantity of it themselves!

'Oh, I ate so much,' groaned Mel on her return. 'I don't think I'll ever eat another sweet thing as long as I live!'

'So kind of Gilles's family to invite you,' said Amy. 'Such a delightful young man – and of course, you have so many interests in common . . .'

'Yes. He's very sweet,' said Melisande. Then she wrinkled her nose. 'But he's a little like maple taffy: there's a very fine line between sweet and cloying.'

It was a quiet day at Harbourside and while she took the class through the elements of multiplication, Melisande found her mind drifting away on thoughts of sunshine and the warmer seasons to come. Seeing the haze of green on the solitary tree in the sheltered yard, she wondered whether she could persuade the Colonel to allow her to bring out her bicycle again, now that the roads at least were free of snow. She realised how much she had missed the freedom to come and go as she pleased.

Her mind was still on thoughts of bicycle rides and freedom when she waved goodbye to the last of the children and

340

locked up the school. It was so long since she had enjoyed a leisurely journey and she longed to feel the wind in her face once more. She rather thought she would go home the long way round this evening; even though the sun had gone, the cold air was crisp and invigorating and it was an age since she had last looked in the shop windows.

In the shadow of the warehouses the snow was lying longer and down at the end of the street a few of the boys, having shivered their way through the winter, were determined to catch the last of its joys and had stamped themselves out a snow slide which as the temperature fell had acquired a dangerous top polish of ice which glistened evilly in the light of the streetlamps.

'Watch ya step, miss!' shouted one, Brooklyn heavily seasoned with Ruthenian. 'Wouldn't want ya t'go ass over –'

Feodor cuffed him into silence. 'You wan' slide, Miss Stev'n?' he asked, smiling his infectious grin. 'Is good fun!'

She remembered the time when Aggie and Tom had made a terrifying slide down the Cut and dared everyone to go down it or be called coward. She had been frightened almost witless, but she had gone; she could still, even today, recall the thrill and the terror of that long uncontrolled descent.

Peter said something scornful in German about her being rather too old for such things and without further thought she thrust her basket of books into his hands and threw herself on to the slide. Her stomach churned, her head span as the wind whistled past her ears and she felt once more that potent mixture of terror and exhilaration as the ice took direction of her boots and whisked her, willy-nilly, down the slope and round the corner . . . and straight into a man coming out of a door.

'Ouf!' There was a violent exhalation of breath as she struck the man with full force just below the ribcage.

Her feet shot from beneath her and she felt herself start to fall only to be brought up short as a grip of iron fastened itself around her. Her face was pressed with some force into the cape of a vicuna overcoat.

She subsided with relief into the unknown embrace, heart pumping madly, lungs working like bellows to catch her breath, and legs which suddenly seemed to have lost their bones dangling helplessly several inches off the ground. At last her panting slowed and her breathing gradually matched itself to the rhythm of the man holding her; she dragged her face out of the smothering folds of overcoat and looked up into Adam Kingsley's hard grey eyes.

It could only have been the briefest of moments that they stayed, gazes locked, but it seemed to Melisande like an eternity. Then the crowd of boys catapulted round the corner, all shouting over each other in a variety of languages, all eagerly demanding to know if 'Miss Stev'n' was hurt. Adam set her down on her feet again.

As Feodor was shouting loudest, she started with him. She answered him at first in Russian, reassuring him that she was quite unhurt.

He continued to gabble at her until she said firmly: 'English, Feodor!'

'You tell me, Miss Stev'n, and I punch him real hard for hurtin' you!'

She looked at Feodor, all of five foot, every inch of him bristling with righteous indignation as he looked up at Adam towering above him, and had to suppress a desire to laugh. Instead she said soothingly: 'All's well, Feodor. No one's hurt. Except the doctor.' And that only in his dignity, she thought mischievously.

A slim figure in a heavy cape appeared from behind the doctor. 'That's enough, boys!' said Miss Minton firmly. 'Home, now, all of you!'

As the last of the boys disappeared round the corner and back to Harbourside, Kingsley turned back to Melisande.

'Of all the mutton-headed, irresponsible idiots,' he began wrathfully before she could utter a word. 'What the devil do you want to go on a slide for? Are you trying to break your bones? Don't you think there are enough people in the Infirmary without you adding to them? And as for setting an example to the children. . . . You, of all people. Their teacher!'

'For Heaven's sake, Adam,' said Miss Minton briskly. 'What a to-do over nothing!' She smiled up at him. 'Did you never go a-sliding when you were a child?'

'Miss Stevens is not a child!' he said angrily. 'And what's more –'

342

'Oh, I think there is something of the child in all of us,' she said, trying to pacify his anger. She linked one arm in his and the other in Melisande's. 'Come! Let's remove from this horribly draughty corner. You can see Mel safe home after you've taken me back to the Refuge.'

'I daresay that would be best,' said Adam icily, taking the basket of books from the pavement where Peter had left them.

'There will just about be room for us if you squeeze up next to Adam,' said Miss Minton cheerfully as Mel climbed up into the gig and, heart pounding once more, wedged herself and her basket between Adam and Harriet. Until she alighted at the Refuge, where her parents had an apartment, Harriet chatted to Melisande about the school, the clinic and her college course. Her manner was as friendly as ever, but Melisande felt a stab of jealousy every time Harriet said 'Adam and I'.

At the Refuge, the door was opened by the Supervisor, a tall woman with striking looks, her once golden hair now streaked with white. Herself a reformed prostitute, she ran the establishment with the Mintons, Harriet's mother and father, and her own 'husband', a former safe cracksman who had seen the inside of Eden County jail more than once.

Despite her jealousy, it was with genuine regret that Melisande waved goodbye to Harriet, for the journey from the Refuge to Amy's was conducted in icy silence. Melisande, uncomfortable, tried to apologise to the doctor, but he would not be pacified. 'I think the whole incident is best forgotten,' he said curtly.

Outside Amy's, he hitched the reins to the picket fence and insisted on seeing her safely in.

'Adam! An unexpected pleasure,' said Amy, who was crossing the hall. 'Are you hurrying back to Springs House or can you stay to dine with us?'

'I dine with the Pattersons this evening,' he said stiffly. 'I am escorting –'

'If you will excuse me, Amy, Doctor Kingsley,' interrupted Melisande. 'So much work to do before I go out,' she said with a tinkling laugh that bordered on artificiality. 'So kind of you to see me safe home, Doctor.'

Amy looked at her in surprise. 'But –'

'You and Tom will be able to dine *à deux*,' said Mel, picking up her skirts and running lightly up the stairs. 'I too am dining out.' Seated at her writing table she dashed off a note to Clive Trensham, one of her college admirers, and sent Sam round to deliver it.

Folly to have spent so many months thinking about Adam, she berated herself savagely. While he – what with Harriet Minton and Sophia Patterson, no wonder he had no time to come to the school! She had not expected him to take up where they had left off, she told herself, tearing a nail trying to unlace her dress herself, but she certainly had not expected to be shouted at either! Well, she would mope for him no longer.

Adam clicked his tongue at the horse and set off morosely for the Pattersons' mansion on the corner of Madison and Fifth. What little enthusiasm he had had for the evening had evaporated completely and he wanted nothing more than to take himself home and shut himself in the study with a large bottle of whiskey.

He had worked so hard to cure himself of his infatuation with Melisande, burying himself in his work, throwing himself into the plans for the new hospital and the new water system which they had at last persuaded the City Fathers to lay in the spring. The evenings he had spent with Max, making plans for the estate, choosing to grow a wider variety of crops to protect themselves in the case of another market collapse like the one at the end of the 1880s. And he had kept his vow to stay away from the balls and receptions in Edensville, limiting himself to flirting rather ponderously with Miss Patterson and rather more frivolously with Harriet Minton – though that, of course, was only to take her mind off Anton's departure. There was no harm in that, for both Harriet and Sophia had been brought up in Society, and knew how to play the game, to keep the flirtation light and within its limits.

He had even gone to New York with Bella and John for the New Year celebrations, to avoid any risk of a chance meeting with Melisande over the festive season; at the house party he had taken up a flirtation with the bolder of John's cousins, a free-spirited young lady of one and twenty who had cornered him in a cupboard in a rather childish game of hide and seek and kissed him soundly, making it clear to him that she would not object to him taking further liberties. It had been an enjoyable interlude, and he had been prepared to declare himself cured of Miss Melisande Stevens, but today, when she had crashed into his arms, he knew he had only been deluding himself.

'This is very pleasant, to have my wife all to myself for once,' said Tom, raising his glass to Amy.

'Yes, but I wish I knew what had got into Melisande,' she replied with a frown. 'She told me last week that she had declined young Trensham's invitation to the concert because she had far too much work to do. I could hardly believe it when she sent that note round to say she would go.'

'Is that Clive Trensham?'

'Yes. Studies music with Mel. I say nothing against her going to the concert with him –'

'Which is just as well, my dear, as she has already gone!' said Tom, rather amused at his wife's agitation.

'It's all very well for you to laugh, Tom, but we're responsible for her and she said if he asked her to supper after the concert, *she'd go!*'

'My, oh my!' he chuckled. 'That's throwing down the gauntlet with a vengeance!'

'But he's not at all the right man for her,' objected Amy crossly, nibbling absently at a petit four from the silver dish.

'What about James Harding then?'

'No. Even worse. Oh, I know he would do anything for her, but she has no respect for him. He could never hope to call his soul his own again.'

'The same could be said of all husbands, my dear,' said Tom, rising and coming round the table to grin lazily down at her. 'Are we not all victims of our wives' tyranny?'

She pulled a face at him as he slid his arm suggestively around her shoulders. 'Yes, but –'

'Never fear, my love,' he said softly, his finger against her lips. 'I doubt she has any intention of marrying young Trensham – or James Harding.'

'Then she should not go to supper alone with him!'

'If I am not mistaken, that is simply to pay Adam back for his poor taste in escorting Sophia and her appalling mother. Where are they going, by the way?'

'To the concert!' she said.

'Ah.'

'Quite. So what do you think, Tom? Will she –'

'What I think, my love, is that I should very much like to be there when they all meet up!'

It had not been a very satisfactory evening for Adam Kingsley, and by the interval he was already thoroughly bored. It was not that the performances were not worth listening to, but the stultifying effect of Sophia's conversation meant that his mind was numbed before he reached the concert hall, so much so that he had omitted to order refreshments brought to their box and, much to Mrs Patterson's displeasure, they had had to leave the box to seek them. So when a slim, fair-haired, smartly dressed young man stumbled against him in the crush and slopped wine down his jacket, Adam was not minded to be very charitable.

He had just begun to tell the young man what he thought of his manners when he caught sight of Miss Stevens, elegantly attired in the height of fashion in a lace-trimmed evening dress, at a nearby table and bit the blistering words of censure off short.

His face stiff with disapproval, he gave her an infinitesimal bow.

'I say, sir,' said the young man. 'You a friend of Miss Stevens? Do come and join us. And accept my apologies. Waiter!' he called, rather too loudly. 'Another bottle of wine over here!'

'My own party –' began Kingsley.

'I see you are with the Pattersons. Oh, they must join us. By all means! Great friends of my mother's, y'know!' Adam suspected the young man, who was shepherding the Pattersons to his table and effusively bidding them welcome, had already imbibed rather too much wine, but people were beginning to stare and to refuse would bring even more unwelcome attention on them.

Mrs Patterson was shooting him angry glances through her lorgnette, but he could only shrug.

It fell to Melisande to make the introductions, but obviously Mr Trensham was not used to letting anyone else hold the floor.

'Excellent concert, don't you think, sir?' he said heartily to Adam. 'Don't know when I've heard Thomas in such fine voice, though I suspect Madame Kentner had a *touch* too much vibrato in that last aria.' And as he proceeded to give them his far from modest opinion on each performance, even Mrs Patterson found herself reduced to a stunned silence. Adam tried to interject a comment or two, but when Trensham appealed, in far too friendly a manner, for Melisande's support of his views, Adam retreated into a glowering silence.

Melisande was furious with both Clive Trensham and Adam Kingsley, the one for being so over-effusive and obvious in his attempt to make an impression, the other for not supporting her attempts to meld together the ill-assorted party. But Adam's abdication angered her most and she found herself, to her vexation, enthusiastically seconding Trensham's exaggerated opinions. Emboldened by her encouragement, he soared to new heights of daring and, as the interval bell rang and Adam's party had risen to leave, was so bold as to invite Miss Stevens to partake of a light supper at the Clayforth Hotel after the concert.

Adam, following in the wake of the Pattersons, caught the end of his speech and turned back in annoyance. 'Out of the question!' he muttered angrily, keeping his voice low so that the Pattersons would not hear.

'That would be most pleasant, Mr Trensham,' said Melisande, propping her chin on her hand and gazing up at her escort through long, undoubtedly darkened, eyelashes.

Adam's face went white. Without another word he turned on his heel so abruptly that he almost took an old gentleman off his feet.

'Come, ladies,' he said, catching up with Sophia and her mother. 'We must take our seats.'

A wiser man would have realised that the display was being put on purely to make him sit up and take notice, but jealousy

347

can make the wisest behave foolishly. He only just stopped himself from inviting the Pattersons to sup at the Clayforth; only the knowledge that it would be seen as the next step towards the hoped-for engagement saving him from the folly of spying on his ex-ward.

Damn Almeria Carter! he thought for the thousandth time. If it had not been for her cursed unbridled tongue he would have avoided this endless pursuit, for Mrs Patterson, under other circumstances, would hardly have considered a country doctor a worthy match for her cossetted only daughter.

And so Melisande was left undisturbed to dine *tête-à-tête* with the dazzled Mr Trensham, where she drank far too much wine and responded teasingly to his more daring sallies.

'I was quite shocked, as you may imagine,' said Mrs Henderson to Mrs Randall the next day. 'Because I thought her such a quiet, modest girl, you know, and to behave so in a public place . . . But I said to my brother and sister-in-law – the Judge and his wife, you understand, over from Rochester – I said to them, she must be betrothed to him, unknown to us, for I am sure Beatrice would not countenance such behaviour else.'

'Certainly not!' said Mrs Randall, swallowing a desire to consign Mrs Henderson and the Judge and the Judge's wife to a hot place. 'I consider her far too young to be betrothed to anyone.'

'But she must be twenty if she's a day.'

'After a restrictive upbringing, it is inevitable that these young girls should want to break loose now and again,' said Mrs Randall casually. 'I shall have a word with her myself. And I am sure I can rely on you to keep this to yourself, for I would not wish the more censorious in our little society to try to ruin her social career.'

'Especially as she is in your daughter's care.'

'Quite. You understand, I am sure, that I take a personal interest in dear Melisande?'

Mrs Henderson took the carefully disguised warning to heart: she had no desire to antagonise Mrs Randall, one of the leaders of Edensville Society, even though Miss Stevens's shocking behaviour would have made for an excellent good gossip with a number of ladies of her acquaintance. But Mrs Henderson had very little money and three plain daughters to launch into society over the next few years; without Mrs Randall's active assistance, their debut could be most awkward.

Beatrice waited until she could be sure that Melisande was at college before visiting her daughter to discuss the vexed matter of Mr Trensham with her. When Amy told her Tom's opinions on the matter, she nodded her head in agreement.

'Really, Amy, I never cease to be amazed that such a studious man could at the same time be so *au fait* with more worldly matters.'

But with Mel herself, arriving home soon after, flushed and windswept on her bicycle, with Mr Trensham in attendance, she was rather more severe.

'I am well aware, Mel, that you have no intention of marrying Mr Trensham,' she said when he had gone. 'A pleasant enough young man, I allow, though with a deal too high an opinion of himself. A gentle flirtation is quite acceptable and I daresay Trensham and that nice young man Harding will recover from the inevitable rejection eventually.' Melisande had the grace to blush. 'But to put people's backs up as you did the other evening, is to go beyond the bounds. Proper young ladies, even liberated students, only dine alone with family or fiancé. You have neither.'

'I did not think . . .'

'I know. You see, I also heard who was there when Mr Trensham was rash enough to ask you to supper and you were foolish enough to accept.'

Mel turned sharply away to the window, the colour suffusing her face.

'Don't think I don't understand, my dear. If you want to make him jealous, well and good, but if in the course of it you compromise yourself so much that you have to marry Mr Trensham or face social ruin, you have achieved nothing but your own defeat!'

She was pleased to hear from her daughter that her advice had been taken to heart and though Mel still saw a great deal of Clive Trensham, she was careful to see that it was generally in a group or with another couple.

Truth to tell, she was beginning to find both Clive Trensham and Gilles de Villeneuve rather young and immature.

'Then why not mix a little more in Society?' asked Amy in exasperation. 'There are any number of more mature men there who would be delighted to spend time in your company.'

'What about Mr Douglas?' she suggested.

'Mr Douglas?' shrieked Amy. 'Mel! He must be sixty if he's a day!'

'But such a romantic figure!'

The story was that Davie Douglas, a poor Scot, had emigrated to America earlier in the century armed with letters of introduction to van Rensselaer and other men of wealth and influence. But Douglas had not used the letters. Instead he had built up from a small forge to a small factory, from orders for nails and horseshoes to contracts for the iron spikes for track laying on the burgeoning American railroads. Only when he had made his first fortune did he invite the would-be sponsors to dinner and present them with the undelivered letters. 'Just like the Count of Monte Cristo!' exclaimed Mel dreamily.

'Mel, I cannot believe you are serious!'

She would have liked to continue the tease, but found that keeping up the lovelorn expression was too much for her and she burst out laughing at the appalled expression on Amy's face.

'What about Henry Foxendale?' persisted Amy. 'He's looking for a wife. And if you're looking for a more mature man . . .'

'Henry?' she exclaimed. 'Henry can talk of nothing but stocks and shares and horse racing! At least Clive and Gilles and James Harding can share some of the subjects that interest me.' The prospect of marriage to a Society man such as Foxendale, the thought of voluntarily confining herself to his narrow set, was horrifying. 'Marrying someone like Henry would be like putting myself back in the Orphanage, Amy,' she said sombrely. 'Henry doesn't understand the things I care about any more than the other orphans did. To give up all those discussions and good arguments, to give up talking of books, of music, even of politics . . . I'd hate it.'

But as the term wore on there was less and less time for socialising. She had far too much work to get through. Each of the music students had to prepare several concert pieces, solo and ensemble, to be played before the Board of Examiners. By tradition the best of the solo performers would be asked to perform with a visiting orchestra in the annual summer concert in the City Hall. Even before Easter, the students were searching frantically for pieces to suit their abilities, debating whether duets or trios were to be recommended.

Clive Trensham had asked Melisande to play a duet with him and they had arranged to meet up with Mel's friends, Sally and James Harding. Mel had sat up late the night before writing up her notes on the week's teaching and Amy, unaware of her plans, told the maid not to disturb her.

Waking late, Mel threw on her new sailor suit with its braid-trimmed sailor collar, wide skirt and matching beribboned straw hat. She barely had time to snatch a quick cup of coffee and a muffin before dashing out to the stables to pull out her bicycle. She thrust her music hastily into the basket hanging by the handlebars and pedalled rapidly out of the yard, her skirt flapping wildly around her ankles in the strong breeze that blew off the lake.

She met the Hardings on the corner of City Hall Square and, not for the first time, found herself envying Sally her more practical clothes: Mrs Harding had insisted Sally wear the new divided skirts whenever she was cycling. But Mrs Randall had refused Mel's request for the same. 'Liberal I' may be,' she said, 'but I cannot approve of young women wearing breeches.'

'But I wore trousers when we went to Madame Pellisson's!'

'The Turkish evening,' said Beatrice repressively. 'I can't say I approved of that either : grown women in trousers with their hair around their shoulders! But fancy dress is very much the fashion this year . . .'

'Bicycling skirts aren't really breeches,' coaxed Melisande. 'They are more accurately described as divided skirts and –'

'To the staider members of our society, they are breeches,' said Beatrice firmly. 'And you are much more open to criticism than Sally.'

351

'I don't see why.'

'Because – because Sally always rides with her brother.'

It seemed to Mel very odd that Society should allow her – nay, encourage her – to go to a fancy dress ball in Turkish trousers, with her hair loose, and yet disapprove when she wore divided skirts for bicycling.

'Come along, Mel,' called James Harding, breaking into her thoughts. 'We'd almost given you up. If we don't hurry, all the practice rooms will be taken!'

'I say, Mel, that's a new costume, isn't it?' said Sally admiringly. 'It does suit you. Mrs Randall does give you such perfect outfits.'

Mel looked ruefully down at her skirts. 'I'm very lucky,' she agreed. 'But, oh, Sally! There was a cycling skirt to match it, just like yours. I wish she had rather let me have that!'

'Come *on*, you two!' hollered James impatiently.

As they sped down Buchanan to the junction with College Street, enjoying the sensation of speed as the wind whistled past their faces, one of the new motor cars pulled out of a side street to drive up Buchanan towards City Hall, only to find its ascent impeded by a carriage and pair making its way sedately up the street.

With a muttered imprecation the young man checked the speed of the automobile, which spluttered protestingly, then back-fired with an ear-splitting bang.

The horses reared up in terror, catching the coachman unawares, and bolted across the road, straight into the little group of cyclists.

'Doctor! Doctor! Come quick!' screeched Feodor, rushing into the Dispensary.

Harriet Minton dropped her pen and looked up in alarm.

'What is it?' she said as the boy began to babble in high-pitched Russian. She turned to one of the woman who sat, head swathed in a shawl, baby in her arms, waiting to be seen. 'What is he saying?'

The woman looked up from her baby, her eyes wide.

'He say accident,' she whispered. 'He say, teacher lady, she dead.'

'Dead?' Adam had come out of his room to see what the noise was about, just in time to hear this. 'I don't believe it!'

352

'Is true!' said the woman, indignant at being disbelieved.

Adam turned to the boy. 'Your teacher lady?' he demanded, the colour draining from his face. 'Miss Stevens?'

Feodor nodded, his grubby face a picture of misery.

Adam grabbed his arm. 'Where?'

Feodor looked up at him in some alarm and lapsed back into his own tongue.

'For God's sake, boy!'

'He say three of 'em killed dead,' said the woman. 'Buchanan Street, he say. You gotta go with him.'

Adam averted his eyes hurriedly from the tangle of wheels and handlebars that lay on the roadside and with a hollow feeling in the pit of his stomach followed Feodor into the shop.

Inside there was chaos. A young man in a dust-covered suit with a rent in the sleeve was being restrained with some difficulty from punching a young man in leather gloves and a black leather driving helmet, several stout ladies were demanding at the tops of their voices why no one had gone for a policeman, the coachman was telling anyone who would listen that the accident was no fault of his and that if it had not been for his superb driving skills, those danged fool young folk on the danged fool contraptions would all have been stiffs by now, and the shopkeeper was wringing his hands at the prospect of a corpse on the premises and asking frantically why no one had sent for a doctor.

'Stop your wailing!' one of the bystanders chided him. 'Here's Doctor Kingsley. Hi! Get outa the way there and let the doctor through!'

'This is most improper!' said the storekeeper, turning his complaints on Adam. 'This kind of thing will do my store no good at all. Trade is bad enough without people bringing corpses into the store. I ask you, what am I supposed to do? I told them, the hospital is the place for –'

Adam shoved the storekeeper out of the way, and knew a mordant satisfaction as his doctor's bag caught the man behind his pinstriped knee and almost felled him. But the brief moment's satisfaction rapidly dissolved as he caught sight of Melisande. She had been laid on a couch and her hair, shaken from its bands and pins, spread out around her white face like a halo. Her eyes were closed and someone had folded her hands on her chest. The drowned Ophelia, he thought irrelevantly.

It can't be! he thought. She can't be dead! His mind was a maelstrom of images and sounds: Melisande dancing, laughing, teasing, Melisande in his arms on the night of the ball, kissing him. He wanted to throw back his head and scream out loud in defiance that she wasn't dead, she couldn't be dead, and only the years of training stopped him. The roaring in his head subsided and he took a deep breath to bring himself once more under control. Then his eye moved to a young lady, a stranger to him, kneeling at the side of the couch, waving a borrowed bottle of smelling salts under her friend's nose.

He was at her side in two strides. 'Tell me what happened!' he commanded.

'She fainted,' said the young lady tearfully. 'She was all right when we disentangled her from the bicycle. But they would insist on moving her and when her foot touched the floor she swooned.'

Adam almost hurled himself down at her side and lifted Mel's limp wrist. Sweat broke out on his upper lip as he felt a weak but definite pulse.

'Will she be all right?' asked Sally anxiously.

'I believe so.' He lifted her lids and examined her eyes. 'We'll know better when she regains consciousness.'

'Thank goodness!' Sally bit her lip and struggled to hold back the tears.

'You are not going to faint on me too, are you?' he demanded, taking in the ruffled clothing. 'Miss –?'

'Sally Harding. And that's my brother James,' she said in a rather wobbly voice. She took a deep breath. 'I won't faint, I promise you. It's just – we all had such a fright, and it's so hot in here.'

Melisande stirred and muttered something.

'What's she saying?' he asked Feodor who had wriggled through the crowd and taken up position by his teacher's head where he scowled at the shopkeeper, fists clenched, as if daring him to make a move towards her. Now, as she muttered something else, he ducked down to listen and a smile lit up his grubby features. He nudged the doctor in the ribs. 'Eh, she thinks you be her papa!'

There was a rustle of interest and the crowd behind tried to press closer. Adam spoke over his shoulder to James Harding, who was still squaring up to the motorist. 'Stop this pointless wrangling!' he commanded. 'Mr Harding, if you wish to be of assistance to the ladies, I suggest you persuade all these people to give us some air. And you, sir,' he said to the storekeeper, 'would do better to stop complaining and fetch me a bowl of water.'

James coloured up at the rebuke, but he was a fair-minded young man and had to admit the justice of the criticism. He turned away to persuade the crowd to withdraw: the automobile driver drew his case from inside his Norfolk tweed jacket and pressed a card on James, who took it with ill grace; then the driver, still arguing about damages with the coachman, withdrew to survey the damage to his shining new machine, followed in dribs and drabs by the rest of the crowd. After a few conciliatory words from Sally, the storekeeper stalked off to fetch water, injured dignity in every step.

As Adam turned back to the couch, Mel gave a muffled groan and her eyelids fluttered. She spoke again.

'What's she saying, Feodor?' he asked over his shoulder.

'Feodor's gone,' said James Harding, coming to join him. 'I thought you wanted to clear the crowd, so I sent him to look after the gig.'

'Damn!' he muttered. While she thought he was her father, he might have got her to say something interesting; he might have been able to fill in some of the gaps in her past.

Then he remembered how she herself had brought the boys to order when they started speaking Russian in front of him, the day they had collided on the ice slide.

He put his hand on hers. 'English, Melisande!' he said severely.

'Yes, Papa.' She spoke in a little girl's voice. 'It's my ankle, Papa. I've hurt my ankle. I didn't mean to be naughty, Papa. I just borrowed mama's satin slippers. The ones she wears for the recitals. With the heels. And I fell down the stairs . . .'

'Poor Melisande,' said Adam, stroking her forehead gently. 'Let me look at it. I shall try not to hurt.' He caught

355

hold of her boot, noting as he did so the shredded hem of her skirt. He could feel the ankle swelling over the sides. 'And where is Mama now?' he asked casually, taking out his pocket knife.

'In her dressing room. Zéphine is dressing her.' She winced as he cut the laces. 'You have not forgotten, Papa, that the prince comes tonight?'

'I had not forgotten,' he said.

'And I may still come down to see him?'

'I am sure you may. And Melisande –'

'Here is the water you wanted,' said Sally Harding.

Adam bit off a curse.

'Oh, my ankle!' exclaimed Melisande, reverting to her normal tones. Her eyelids fluttered and she tried to sit up.

'Adam?' she asked, focusing her eyes with some difficulty.

'Yes, I'm here,' he said levelly.

She looked at him, green eyes wide with longing. 'Don't go away again, will you?' she said in a thread of a voice.

His heart went out to her and it was all he could do not to take her in his arms there and then. He knew she had said the first thing that came into her dazed mind, without any thought for the proprieties.

'Don't fret, Miss Stevens,' he said in a matter-of-fact voice that belied his emotions. He took her hand and patted it. 'Your friends are here, Miss Harding and her brother. They have been looking after you, and when you are feeling a little stronger we shall take you home.'

She wanted to throw herself in his arms and say : 'Yes. Yes, take me home, Adam, home to Springs House.' Then she opened her eyes wider and saw Sally looking anxiously down at her, and the storekeeper hovering nervously behind James with a bowl of water. 'I'm sorry. Didn't mean to be so foolish,' she said, biting back the tears. 'Only my head hurts so and . . .'

'It is sure to hurt, Miss Stevens,' he said, with an unsteady laugh as he wrung out a cloth in water and placed it over a small cut on her forehead. 'There. Hold on to that. You have had quite a knock on your head. I should not be surprised if you had a black eye tomorrow.' He turned to Sally, who was looking in some confusion from one to the other. 'There is no

356

need for you to stay longer, Miss Harding. You have done all you can here, and I thank you for it, but there is no need to detain you any longer.' He picked up his knife again and went to work on the boot, cutting it away and the dark stocking with it, to expose the bruised and swollen ankle beneath.

'But had we not better see her home?'

'I shall see Miss Stevens safe home,' said Adam in tones that precluded any argument. 'Mr Harding? If I could leave you to deal with the bicycles?'

'Of course, sir.'

'Tell Clive I shall come to college tomorrow,' said Mel weakly, 'and –'

'You will not be going anywhere!' said Adam firmly. 'Not tomorrow nor the day after!'

'But I have to choose my duet!'

'Damn your duet!' he said wrathfully.

'Stop fretting, Mel,' said Sally hastily. 'I'll explain.'

As the Hardings left, Adam turned his attention back to her ankle, but she cried out as he probed it.

'I think I'll get you home before I prod it any further,' he said, sweeping her effortlessly up into his arms and carrying her out to the gig. He made her as comfortable as he could, then took the reins from Feodor, slipping him a coin as he did so.

Amy hurried to open the door as they arrived and Tom, coming out of his study to see what all the fuss was about, helped Adam to carry Melisande in. He was as gentle as he could be, but she bore the examination with some difficulty, the tears trickling from beneath tightly closed lids.

'Finished now,' he said finally, smiling up at her from the end of the couch. 'I'll bandage it up. It's not a break. Could be a chipped bone, but it's more likely a severe sprain.'

'It was a chipped bone last time,' she said watcrily.

'The day the Prince came?'

'Yes. He –' She looked at him curiously. 'How did –'

'How old were you when you fell down the stairs in your mama's slippers?'

'Six or seven. Strange, I had forgotten.' She smiled. 'That was before –'

'Before –?'

She shook her head, eyes blank. 'No. It's gone.'

He found it hard to suppress his feeling of frustration; he was so sure that they had almost broken through the barrier when Sally Harding interrupted them.

'That should be a little more comfortable,' he said, tying the bandage. 'I shall come and see you tomorrow.' He resisted the temptation to kiss her goodbye.

'I'll leave a draught for her to take every four hours,' he said as he followed Amy into the hall. 'Sleep will work its own cure.'

'Don't worry. I'll look after her,' said Amy.

'I think I'll spend the night with George, so you can send for me if you need me.'

Although it was only ten o'clock in the morning when he rode up to the Bennett house on a handsome bay gelding from Colonel Randall's stable, his doctor's bag slung from the saddle, Adam was not by any means the first visitor.

As he entered the hall, his eyes were met by the sight of several huge bouquets of flowers arranged tastefully in bowls and vases.

'Good God!' he exclaimed, looking around him.

'You should see the study,' said Amy. 'There's barely room for the couch! The callers we've had! And every one of them seems to have scoured the nursery gardens and hothouses on the way. I should think Cotton's must be full of nothing but empty vases!'

'I thought she was a friendless orphan!' said Adam savagely.

Amy turned away to hide a smile, making a show of adjusting one of the vases. 'Oh, Adam, you are out of date.' She counted on her fingers. 'There's Warden Hurstpoint, Jim Harding, Clive Trensham, Gilles de Villeneuve, a melancholy composer with an unpronounceable name and a drooping moustache . . . Oh, and Mr Brett called – he was the automobilist, you know. And General Stratton, whose carriage was involved in the accident, sent his man round as well, to enquire after her. And Ross Jennings, of course. Which means that the news will have reached Eden Springs by now.' She saw the look of incomprehension on Adam's face. 'Ross

Jennings is brother to Michaela, the young lady who has been making such a play for Max – as you'd know if you'd bothered to attend any of the balls and soirées this Season.'

Adam looked stunned. 'Of course I know Michaela,' he said impatiently. 'She has visited Springs House on several occasions with her aunt, but I didn't realise she and Max . . .'

'I daresay you had other things on your mind,' said Amy innocently.

'And I certainly didn't know she had a brother.' He looked around him. 'I should have thought to bring flowers,' he said angrily.

'I doubt she'll notice your omission,' said Amy with a smile. 'Among so many.'

'I'd better go and see how she is,' he muttered.

Melisande was sitting up on the makeshift bed in the study, a silk shawl draped modestly round her shoulders.

'Good morning to you, Doctor,' she said, holding out her hand coolly. 'I am sorry to receive you in such a state.'

She was using her most formal and distant manner to him, to balance out, she hoped, the naïve and gauche words she had used to him in the shop when she woke and found herself in his arms.

But he was not deceived. He thought she looked beautiful, with her hair tumbling down her back, a fitting focus for the heart of her flowery bower.

In response to his anxious questions, she told him she was feeling much better and tried to persuade him that she was well enough to get up.

'My head hardly aches any more – nothing like yesterday, I promise you.'

'And you are so eager to show your black eye to the world?' he said with a grin.

'Oh.' She looked at him wide-eyed. 'Have I really?'

'A real shiner,' he said gravely.

'That's why Amy wouldn't let me have a mirror,' she sighed.

'And that's probably why she's not letting visitors in to see you.'

'Visitors?'

'Hordes of 'em, I hear.' There was a harsh edge to his voice. 'You'll have to ask Amy the details.'

359

'But she let you in.'

'I pulled rank.' She looked puzzled. 'As your doctor.'

'I hadn't expected to see you today. I hope you did not travel all the way in from Eden Springs just to see me.'

'I haven't been home,' he said. 'I spent last night at the Colonel's house.'

'Was he . . . was he very cross about the bicycle?'

'Not cross. Just very worried about you.' He turned to rummage in his medical bag. 'He takes his duties as your guardian very seriously,' he said in a tight voice.

He had only heard last night that the Colonel had proposed himself as her guardian and had been quite hurt at the discovery.

'Surely if anyone has acted as her guardian, I have!' he had protested.

'An older man would be more suitable for the position, I feel,' said Colonel Randall. 'And –'

'She might have discussed it with me first!'

'Dammit, Adam, Beatrice said the girl as good as asked you to marry her and you rejected her!' roared the Colonel. 'And without a word of explanation!'

'I had my reasons and –'

'And damn stupid ones they were too!' He took a deep breath to calm himself. 'But that's not the point, is it? The point is that your feelings for her – and don't pretend you don't have any, for neither Beatrice nor I are in our dotage yet - your feelings, I say, hardly suit you to give her impartial advice, do they, hey?'

'Well, I – no, I suppose not.'

'Beatrice recommended me, y'know. And I'm honoured. My late wife and I never could have children and even if Beatrice and I . . . well, we're past the age now.' He looked at Adam from under bushy brows. 'I've a strong affection for Mel, y'know. Plucky little fighter.'

'You scarcely need to tell me that, sir,' growled Adam.

'Daresay that's why I overruled Beatrice and gave her that damn' bicycle. Thought she could do with some spoiling. And fond as I am of you, Adam, friend of your father or no, I'm damned if I'll let you foul up her life!'

'I'd never dream of –'

'You want to throw away your chances, that's for you to choose. But don't play dog-in-the-manger. I know Beatrice has her reservations, but this fellow Trensham seems a nice enough young lad. Think I'll look into his background once Mel's on her feet again. Don't think he'll care much about *her* background: once the legal papers are signed and they know I'm her guardian, that's all they'll see. They'll be round her like flies round a honeypot!'

'They already are,' growled Adam. 'As to her background . . .' He hesitated.

'Yes?'

He told him, as concisely as possible, about what Melisande had said in her confusion the day before.

'Don't put too much weight on that m'self,' said the Colonel, after a moment's contemplation. 'Children tend to embellish their early life, often confuse fairy tales with reality.' He thought Adam snorted. 'One ought not to generalise, of course.'

'I thought of sending the information to England, to my father. Ask him to look into it. There cannot be so many musicians who habitually gave recitals – with or without princes in the audience – and dropped abruptly from view twelve or thirteen years ago.' He looked at the Colonel's frowning face and added sourly: 'With your permission, of course, sir?'

'Don't be impertinent, boy!' said the Colonel with a grin to soften the rebuke. 'Yes. Do that if you wish. But I don't want her to know.'

Adam looked across at him, a question in his alert grey eyes.

'Keep me up-to-date. I'll decide what to tell her.'

'But –'

'I don't want her hopes raised just to be dashed again.'

Adam had spent the evening writing to his father. From time to time he looked up from his work, trying in vain to banish the unwelcome memory of Mel with young Trensham. And now, the sight of her surrounded by flowers from her admirers brought the painful image back again.

He shook his head angrily. He *had* to separate the personal from the professional.

'How is your ankle?' he said now, running his hands over the joint, probing it, testing its flexibility.

'Hardly hurts at all.'

'Liar,' he said softly as she winced.

'It is much better. Really. Can I not get up?' she pleaded.

'In a few more days. And then you will have to use a stick.'

She pulled a face. 'Can I try it tomorrow?'

'No. It is not just the ankle. Remember you had a bang on the head too.'

'Oh, please. I –'

'Missing your admirers?' he said acidly.

'Missing my lectures, Doctor,' she replied stiffly. 'And I still have to choose my duet – for the examinations, you know.'

'With Clive Trensham?'

'Yes. How did –'

'I think you have talked quite enough for today,' he said abruptly. 'I will leave a sleeping draught with Amy.'

'I am bored with sleeping draughts!' she snapped.

He grinned at her. 'I sympathise, believe me. But sleep is the best thing I can prescribe at the moment. It's nature's way of encouraging the body to mend.'

He had promised to report back to the Colonel before going to the dispensary. When he arrived, he found not only Colonel Randall but also Max and Beatrice, waiting anxiously for news.

'Though how the devil the news reached Eden Springs I can't tell!' said the Colonel. 'Of course if you'd had a telephone apparatus installed, like any sensible man –'

'Oh, that will be Max's Pocket Venus!' interrupted Adam with a teasing smile. 'Better by far than any telephone service.'

'Who? What?' chorused the Colonel and Beatrice together.

'If you mean Michaela Jennings –' began Max, blushing all over his face.

'Who else?'

'But you should not call her so, Adam.'

'Why not? I said it to her face and she was flattered. Michaela has called on us once or twice at Springs House,' he

362

said to the others. 'Though I confess I thought at the time that it was to see me.' He grinned at Max. 'Now I know better.'

'Ross Jennings's sister,' Beatrice explained to the Colonel. 'Mr Jennings is one of Mel's admirers.'

'One of many,' said Adam bitterly.

The Colonel frowned at Adam under his bushy brows. 'I still don't see where Michaela Jennings fits into all this,' he muttered.

'Since she was introduced to Max last fall, she seems to have discovered an abiding interest in estate management,' said Beatrice with a grin. 'I have met her occasionally at Eden Springs where she has an aunt. I believe she is staying there at the moment.'

Colonel Randall, however, had lost interest in Michaela Jennings. 'May we see Mel today?' he demanded.

'She's sleeping now. Try this afternoon. Though I warn you, Amy is repelling all boarders, so you'd better take Beatrice with you. She may not let *you* in, Max. She has a splendid black eye!'

Mel was up and about in less time than Adam had forecast, although her ankle was still bruised and she could only hobble about with the aid of a stick. She was not up in time, however, to escape a visit from Mrs Trensham, a little bird-like widow who divided her time between extolling the virtues of her beloved only son and fussing around Melisande until she almost drove her mad. Fortunately she was rescued by a visit from George Randall.

'See, Uncle George?' she said, demonstrating her agility with a stick when Mrs Trensham had at last taken the hint and left. 'I can even manage the stairs now. Even Amy thinks I should go back to college.'

'Well, if you must, you must,' said the Colonel unwillingly. 'But you'll go in my carriage.'

'But your coachman won't want to wait around all day for me!'

'That's what he's paid for. Might as well hang around up there as down here.'

'But what if you need the carriage?'

'Beatrice's coachman can fetch me,' he said gruffly. 'I'm having one of these telephones put in in my house. Persuaded

363

Beatrice to have one too. You should persuade Adam to have one. As a doctor –'

'Oh, I have no influence over Adam, Uncle George,' she said with a brittle laugh. 'You had really much better speak to him yourself.'

She had not returned to college a moment too soon. Clive Trensham had chosen a demanding duet for their examination and they spent several hours each day working together. She worked with him on his violin solo too, but whenever she suggested that he work with her on her piano concerto, which she had been persuaded by her tutor to consider putting forward for examination, he always found an excuse to put it off to another day.

'I don't know what Farson is thinking of, letting you loose on the Tchaikovsky,' he said with a frown. 'I'd have thought he'd have offered it to me, or Harper. Much more in our line.' All the pianists had worked on Tchaikovsky's demanding first piano concerto that spring, as a class exercise, but Mr Farson had decided that only Melisande should be encouraged to offer it for examination. 'Too flamboyant for you by half,' said Clive dismissively.

That had been her own reaction when her tutor suggested it.

'Flamboyant?' said her tutor, his eyebrows shooting up his domed forehead. 'Well, it certainly is that. But it's not a circus act as Trensham or Harper would make it - it's a genuine dialogue between piano and orchestra.' He jumped up and began to stride about the room, waving his hands about in his enthusiasm. 'The piano must sing and swell with sound, but the pianist must not seek merely to dazzle, but allow complete equality to the orchestra. Here,' he returned to the piano and leafed through the score, 'you see, where the woodwind take up the theme, and here, where the lower strings reveal the structural features of the concerto, they must be able to take the stage and not be swamped by the flood of sound produced by the piano. I've been waiting years for a student who could take this on. Oh, I've had some with hands as good as yours, with the reach and the flexibility, but they've always lacked either the sensitivity or the self-control. And they are vital.'

Her self-esteem had been boosted by Farson's confidence, but she was still far from sure that she was ready for solo public performance of such a demanding concerto.

'I've promised Mr Farson I'll continue to work on it,' she said to Clive, 'but it's by no means certain I'll enter it.'

'I should think you'll have all your work cut out with our duet,' said Clive, disregarding the fact that he himself was submitting a violin solo, a piano concerto and the duet with Melisande for the exhibition. 'We'll try the duet one more time, shall we?'

The Harbourside school welcomed her back as effusively as Trensham had. She hadn't been quite sure what she would find when she returned, but fortunately Feodor had had the sense to tell Rabbi Benjamin about the accident; he had borrowed young Mr Hamilton from his mother's school and they sat in with the classes when they could and arranged for a group of mothers to take it in turns to sit with the children when they could not.

'Good to see you back, Miss Stevens,' he said, taking her hands. 'We did our best, but the children have really only been marking time while you've been gone.'

She threw herself back into the school work with enthusiasm, noticing a few new faces, asking after those who had moved on, discussing with Rabbi Benjamin one or two of the older ones she thought might benefit from the Bachelor's Barn.

And then Clive Trensham asked her to fit in an extra practice on the Wednesday.

'I cannot,' she said. 'Not until the evening, anyway. You know it is one of my teaching days.'

'I should think that ragged school is the last thing you need while you're taking your exams,' he said pettishly.

'On the contrary. I find it a great help with my teaching certification. Of course I may have to come in more often next year, if the school becomes attached to the state education office. Especially if the numbers of immigrants continue increasing as they are. But I shan't have to do the two days the week of the final exams. Rabbi Benjamin has promised to step in and –'

'Oh, damn the school!' he said irritably. 'And damn Rabbi Benjamin too!'

'Clive!'

'Why you have to teach those filthy brats, I'll never know!'

'It's how I earn my keep,' she said quietly. 'If it were not for them, I would not be here now.'

It was a side of him she had never seen before and she didn't like it one little bit.

'Ah, Adam! Good. Been wanting' a word with you,' said Colonel Randall, bumping into the younger man one day at Beatrice's house. 'Step into the drawing room for a moment. Brandy?'

'Thank you, Colonel.' He almost passed comment on how very much at home the Colonel seemed, but decided against it.

Randall picked up the decanter and poured them both a large brandy, observing the younger man out of the corner of his eye.

'Remember what I said to you a few weeks ago about dog-in-the-manger?'

Adam nodded. 'Yes. And I hope you remember what my reply was?'

'I do. So you can imagine how surprised I was when Beatrice told me of your invitation to her and Mel to spend Easter at Springs House.'

'Your concern is unnecessary, George,' said Adam levelly. 'This is just the usual story of the best-laid plans going completely wrong.'

Randall cocked an inquisitive eyebrow.

Adam sighed. 'Max had invited Michaela and Ross Jennings to Springs House at Easter - he could hardly invite them to his home, a bachelor living alone. Then Ross Jennings cried off. An invitation to a shooting party at his godfather's. And Mrs Jennings asked me who would be chaperoning her dear daughter. I tell you, George, I was tempted to call the whole thing off there and then.' He sipped morosely at his brandy. 'I wish now that I had done.'

'Not worked out according to plan, eh?'

'An understatement, George, an understatement.' He ran his fingers distractedly through his hair. 'I thought I was being very clever. I invited Harriet Minton. She jumped at the chance to get out of the city. No sooner had she accepted than Mrs Jennings told me she does not consider Harriet old enough for a chaperone!' He ignored George Randall's hearty chuckle. 'By then I was committed. I could hardly withdraw the invitation and tell her I only wanted her for a chaperone, could I? And she does need a change and a rest; there is so much coming and going at the Refuge and her parents always try to get her involved.' He sighed. 'But that still left me the problem of the chaperone. So then I asked Beatrice.'

'And the good turn to Max has turned into a veritable houseparty!'

'Yes. For Mel is to stay with Beatrice while Tom and Amy visit Bella and John. Beatrice will come to chaperone, but Mel will have to come too.'

'And what about you, eh?' asked the Colonel shrewdly.

'I can find plenty to keep me busy,' said Adam curtly. 'I shall keep clear of Mel as much as I can. For both our sakes.' He sat up abruptly, struck by a sudden thought. 'Would you care to join us, George,' he said persuasively. 'Or Max will be left to entertain all three ladies!'

'Ah, if I were to come,' said George, stroking his moustache, 'then who would chaperone the chaperone?'

Beatrice, joining them soon after, added her persuasion to Adam's. George demurred a little longer, if only for form's sake, but Beatrice was determined. 'I shall need you to bear me company when these gay young people become too much for me,' she said decisively. Adam grinned. He was sure the Colonel was only to pleased to receive his orders.

'I doubt Mel will be able to join us until later, however,' said Beatrice smoothly. 'She has a number of engagements in Edensville: a bicycle excursion and a luncheon party and I am sure more besides.' Adam glowered. 'She is so in demand these days, you know, so many beaux she scarce knows which invitations to accept!'

George snapped his brows together in astonishment. Dammit, Beatrice was purposely trying to make the boy jealous! Dangerous territory, that. He had better warn her off!

367

He contrived to get her out of the room, but was so taken aback by his own successful manoeuvring that he spent more time pleading his own cause than taking her to task.

The house seemed strangely empty without Amy and Tom. Mel breakfasted alone, dressed in her cycling outfit, complete now with divided skirts, Beatrice having been overruled in the matter by Adam and George.

Outside the sun was shining and she was greatly looking forward to the day ahead, a rare day free of teaching, reading or practising, for she was to cycle out to Stony Creek, a beauty spot a few miles out of town, with a group of friends. There had been a heated discussion as to who should partner Mel on the tandem – it being considered that she was not yet quite strong enough to cycle solo – and she found herself regretting the promise she had made to Beatrice and George not to hurry back into the saddle, even though her own machine was sitting in the stables, bright and shining, with all the damage repaired.

Clive Trensham presented Jim Harding with a *fait accompli* by turning up on the tandem some minutes before the Hardings. Jim and Sally spent the first few moments bickering as to whose fault it was they had come late, until Sally turned her back in a huff and started to chat to Adèle Chalfont, a fellow student, and her brother Jonathan, who had been trying to fix his interest with Sally for some time now.

Jim would much rather have partnered Mel on the tandem, but his innate good manners overcame his jealousy and he cycled alongside Adèle, making polite conversation, and sportingly leaving Jonathan a clear field to manoeuvre his machine next to Sally's.

The sun was shining when they arrived at the Creek; they spread rugs out on the bank in the shade of a small clump of trees and set out the food they had brought: sandwiches, cakes, fruit and bottles of juice and seltzer.

'What's your contribution, Trensham?' asked Jonathan, setting out the contents of the basket he had tied to the front fork of his machine.

With a triumphant smile Clive set three bottles of wine down on the blanket.

'No food?' asked Sally, with a puzzled look.

'Wine for six. That's a fair contribution.'

'I thought we agreed,' said Jonathan. 'No alcohol.'

'Signed the pledge, have you?' sneered Clive.

'No,' said Jonathan stiffly. 'But my mother would not have allowed Adèle to come if she had known.'

'I don't think my mother would have been too keen either,' said Jim, scowling at Trensham.

'Don't be such a bore, Harding,' said Clive. 'No one would think you and your sister are almost come of age. And as for your mother – well, what she doesn't know can't hurt her.'

Jim decided it wasn't worth arguing over, but the incident cast a cloud over the picnic.

After lunch Clive picked up Mel's parasol and insisted on taking her off to see the site where the local settlers had fought off the British Redcoats. The Hardings and the Chalfonts had grown up with the stories of the 1812 war and when Jonathan suggested they give it a miss, Jim, who was meeting with far more encouragement from quiet Adèle than he had ever had from Mel, was quite content to stay where he was.

'Thank God they didn't come,' said Clive as they walked across the soft green grass to the small stone memorial. 'I've been desperate to speak to you alone, and if I had to listen to Sally's nonsense much longer –'

Mel looked at him in surprise. 'Why, Clive,' she said, her voice a soft rebuke, 'I thought you liked the Hardings!'

'Boring and untalented provincials!' he sneered. 'But I didn't come here to talk about them.' He reached for her hand. 'Mel, I –'

She tried to pull her hand away. 'Is that Canada on the horizon?' she said, turning to look across the calm lake to a smudge on the horizon. 'Or is it just another island?'

'I didn't come here to look at the view either,' he said in some exasperation. He put his hands on her shoulders and turned her back to face him. 'Mel, you know how I feel about you, don't you?'

His fingers were digging into her shoulders; it occurred to her that Clive had drunk most of the wine himself.

'We're good friends, Clive,' she said lightly. 'You –'

'More than friends,' he persisted. 'Mel, you know what ambitions I have for the future. New York, Paris, London

369

. . . with our talent, the world is our oyster.' His hands slid from her shoulders and he cupped her face between them. 'You do have the most gorgeous eyes,' he whispered throatily. He lowered his head to kiss her, but at the last minute she moved her head to one side and the kiss landed just below her ear.

Trensham swore under his breath. Matters were not turning out quite as he had planned.

He tried again. 'Mel, it was fate that brought us together,' he said with a fierce smile, catching her hand. 'We shouldn't turn our back on fate, should we? Our future together –'

'Clive, stop!' she said, with a smile to take the sting out of her words. 'All this talk about fate . . . !'

'Such a brilliant future!' he murmured. 'Oh, Mel! You are the most important thing in my life!'

'Music will always be the most important thing in your life, Clive,' she said, trying to inject a note of practicality.

'In yours too, surely? That's what drew me to you in the first place. We –'

'Music is only one side of me,' she said, drawing away again. 'The other parts you would not like so well, I think.'

'There's nothing about you that –'

'Come on, you two!' called Jonathan, coming around the stand of trees with Sally Harding on his arm. 'We're ready to set off back. Sally knows a farmhouse on the lower road where we can have tea.'

Watching Sam rope her trunk on to the carriage to be sent on to Springs House ahead of her, Melisande found herself almost wishing she was going with it. She had been looking forward to the Hardings' luncheon party, but Clive was sure to be there too and after yesterday she would gladly have avoided him.

The luncheon party at the Oaks was being given to celebrate the twins' coming of age. Although somewhat overcast by the news that James was to leave Edensville immediately he had taken his exams, to join an uncle in California, the party was delightful. The guests were a mixture of family and friends, many of them students from Edensville College. The food was excellent and during the speeches there were, inevitably, jokes and humorous stories about double the joy and double the trouble.

'I don't suppose my life will ever be the same again once Jim goes,' said Sally with a sigh to Mel as they walked around the rose garden. 'Maybe it's for the best, I don't know.'

'It won't be for some time yet. Though it must be very difficult, saying goodbye to someone you've been so close to for so long.'

'All my life,' said Sally. 'We grew up together. And because Mother taught us, we didn't even get split up for schooling. I know him so well, you see. He's . . . like the other part of me.' She stopped, her voice choked with emotion.

'Maybe it will be easier when you have graduated, and you know where your teaching post will be.'

'That will give me something else to think about,' said Sally with a brave smile. 'But I shall miss him.'

'You'll get over it. And there is someone I can think of who would like to give you something else to think about . . .'

'Who?'

'Jonathan, you goose!'

'Ah, yes. I'd forgotten –'

'Poor Jonathan!'

As if on cue, he appeared around the trellis with Clive and before she knew it, Sally had gone off arm in arm with Jonathan and Mel was left with the last person at the party she wanted to be with.

But Trensham had thought matters over and was determined not to rush things this time. He had no doubt whatever that matters would work out in the long run just as he had planned: women were, after all, notorious for playing a man along. And once she had heard his news . . .

Mel was delighted to find that he was able once more to talk like a sensible man, but just as she relaxed, thinking that the worst had passed, they came across a little scented arbour and with scant regard for their hosts, he began to pick the pale golden blooms and press them into her hand.

'For you, Melisande!' he said softly, piling the flowers into her arms despite her protests, and backing her into the corner of the arbour until she subsided on to a little stone seat. He sat next to her, slid one arm round her waist and put his other hand on her knee. 'Listen, my dear. Such good news! I've been longing to tell you all through that extremely boring luncheon.'

'Mr Trensham, please!' She tried to dislodge his hand but it was not easy with an armful of roses.

'You remember the impresario I went to see in Albany a while back? He's offered to set up a tour for us: just small towns to begin with, but he has booked us for a concert in Buffalo and another in Toronto!'

'Us? But I –'

'We can get married next week, that'll keep all the old tabbies happy,' he went on, as if she had not spoken. 'Then all we have to do is find a thousand dollars apiece for travelling expenses. Of course, we get that back if the box office receipts are good. So –'

'I'm very pleased for you, Clive,' she said hastily. 'But you know I can't come.'

'Why not?'

'I don't have a thousand dollars for one thing. For another – oh, Clive, even if I wanted to, I couldn't possibly leave the school until they found another teacher.'

'Hell, that's nonsense and you know it!' he exclaimed hotly. 'You don't owe those slum brats anything.' He saw the shock on her face and forced himself to moderate his words. 'You must marry me, darling,' he said persuasively. 'You don't want to stay there forever and turn into a dry old spinster, do you? Anyway, I need you. You know no one accompanies me as well as you.'

'I was under the impression that players in a duet were equal,' she said dryly.

'Oh, that's just so much hot air!' he exclaimed. 'Though you're certainly the best accompanist I've ever come across.' He tried to unravel her hand from the roses to press a kiss on it, but only succeeded in scratching his hand. 'And the prettiest.'

'Even if I did want to marry you, there would still be the money. I know your mother would happily find a thousand dollars for you, but you forget I have no family.'

'The old man would stump it up if you asked him.'

'Who?'

'The Colonel. Mother told me he is your guardian. Just as well,' he went on frankly. 'Wouldn't have been very sensible in my position to marry a girl without prospects. I shall need every cent I can get to promote my career and I should imagine he'll leave you all his money.'

'Clive, I think you must be mad. I –'

'That doctor too. Kingsley. Bit of flattery and sweet talk and you could have him eating out of your hand. What do you say?'

'What I say, Mr Trensham, is what I said yesterday. I will not marry you.'

'If you won't, you won't,' he said with a shrug. 'But it shouldn't make any difference to the tour. People look on these things so much more sensibly now. And it isn't as if you've any family to upset.'

She rose in icy rage, tumbling the roses unheeded into the dust. 'Go away, Mr Trensham!' she hissed angrily. 'Go away *right now* and don't you ever come near me again!'

He smiled at her. 'Oh, I know you ladies like to string a fellow along. I suppose you want me to get down on my knees and –'

'I wouldn't recommend it!' she said furiously. 'Seeing you on your knees might just tempt me to kick you in the teeth, which you richly deserve! And you can bloody well find another *accompanist* for your exhibition!' she yelled. '*I* shall be playing solos!'

He picked up a few of the flowers and thrust them at her. 'But Melisande, I –'

She threw the flowers back at him, broke into a torrent of impassioned French, turned on her heel and fled.

She ran into Jim in the conservatory and threw herself sobbing into his arms. All consideration, he drew her behind a huge potted palm and gave her his handkerchief to wipe her eyes with.

'I must look terrible,' she said at last.

'Not too bad. Tell you what, I'll dip my handkerchief in the fountain and you can – I say!'

'What is it?'

'There's Trensham stamping into the house with as black a look on his face as any I've seen!' he exclaimed. As enlightenment dawned he turned back to his friend. 'You haven't given him his marching orders, have you?'

She nodded.

'Sal *will* be glad. She was most awfully worried that you might not see through him in time. Selfish devil, always was. Thinks he's God's gift to the world of music and the rest of us are only there for the greater glory of Clive Trensham. Matter of fact, I've always had my doubts about his talent. Technically brilliant, of course, but – I say, did he propose to you?'

'Yes,' she said with a watery sniff.

'Doesn't want a wife, wants a slave.'

She muttered something under her breath in French.

'I say! So that was you in the arbour!' He cleared his throat. 'Jolly good command of French you have,' he said, running his finger round his collar.

'Ah. You heard.'

'Only a little. Went away as soon as I realised – Couldn't understand one word in three anyway!'

'Oh, Jim, take me home, please.'

'Thought the Bennetts had gone away?' said Jim, never noted for his quick perception.

'To Eden Springs.' She saw the expression on his face and added hastily: 'The Randalls are there for the week and I am to join them.'

'Ah! Yes, quite so. But it will look very strange if you leave before everyone else, you know. And you don't want to set people talking.'

No, that was the last thing she wanted.

'Don't worry. If Trensham hasn't had the good grace to go home, I'll keep him away from you.'

And so she stayed, bearing her part in the social exchanges without registering what she was doing, moving through the company unseeing, unhearing. The afternoon dragged on endlessly until at last Jim hitched the horses to his father's gig and set off for the Springs.

Monday morning dawned grey and cloudy. Melisande sat up in bed sipping her tea, brought to her on a tray by one of the new housemaids. She looked around her at the spacious guest chamber in which she had passed the night. The pale blue silk hangings at the window and around the bed were very elegant, to be sure, though Almeria Carter's choice of wall-hangings was a little overwhelming, the overall effect a little too cluttered and frilly for Mel's taste. It did not compare to the simple charm of Amy's guest room

She wondered whether Adam had deliberately put her in the guest wing to emphasise her changed status, and knew a sudden strange longing for her old room, for her old life at Springs House.

Adam virtually ignored her on the first day, and she saw him only at the dinner table; Uncle George was paying ever more determined court to Beatrice and Mel felt quite superfluous. Indeed, she felt so much a stranger at Springs House and Michaela seemed so at home there that she felt a spurt of jealousy whenever she saw her and Adam together.

By the second morning, boredom was already setting in, so Melisande suggested that she and Michaela went for a walk after breakfast. She was not surprised when they ended up at the fifty-acre field where Max was supervising some work.

When the strain of listening to Michaela talking as if she actually understood anything about estate management became too much for Mel, she excused herself and left them to it. But she had gone no more than a few yards when Michaela joined her.

'I thought I had better leave him to his work,' she said, linking her arm in Mel's. 'A rather rough man with a *quite* incomprehensible Scotch accent came up to talk to him and –'

'That would be Mr McNair.'

'Don't you think that Max has the most wonderful accent?' asked Michaela. 'He says my name like no one else can, you know.' Max pronounced it with the soft 'ch' of his native tongue, but at the same time managed to invest it with a degree of feeling quite unconnected with the accent. Mel hardly recognised the staid and sober Max in this boyishly exuberant figure.

They arrived back at the house, and Mel was disappointed to hear that Miss Minton had not yet arrived. The prospect of a long weekend listening to Michaela rehashing Max's conversation verbatim did not appeal.

That afternoon the rain set in with a dreary persistence that led the Colonel to prophesy that it would last the best part of the week. He was delighted to be confined to the house, always on hand to untangle Beatrice's tapestry wool, divert her with a game of chess or a hand of whist, or just a cosy chat. Mel, seeing how contented they were with each other's company, was reluctant to force herself on them, but she needed to dilute Michaela's company somehow. Michaela did not play chess and she was such an inattentive fourth at whist that Melisande could almost hear the Colonel's sigh of relief when she took her friend away, leaving him to play cribbage two-handed with Beatrice.

They sat in the drawing room for a further half hour while Mel tried to read a book, but Michaela was so patently not interested in hers that Mel finally gave up reading and scratched around for a topic – other than Max – on which they could talk.

They tried Edensville, American politics, President McKinley's views on the Spanish-American war, books and local gossip, all with little success, each conversation being brought to a decisive end by Michaela stating what 'Max says' on the subject. Since she regarded his opinions as gospel, there was no room for further discussion on the matter. Mel wondered whether a succession of children in his own image would balance for Max the strain of a wife who echoed his every sentiment and had not otherwise two thoughts to rub together.

Mel was not the only one to greet Miss Minton's presence at dinner that evening with enthusiasm; Max spent most of the evening discussing with her the progress of the new lying-in ward, a subject on which Michaela was totally ignorant. Mel watched the way Max came to life when he was talking to Harriet: a contrast to her own laboured conversation with Michaela.

When the dessert had been set on the table, the talk turned to a young lad from Harbourside who had recently been sent out to Carfax as apprentice to Samuel.

'He was a little restless at first,' Adam was telling Beatrice, 'but he seems at last to be settling in. Great skill with the animals, Sam says.'

'I knew we could depend on Blanche to look after him,' said Beatrice.

'I really can't see why you spend so much time and effort on these people!' exclaimed Michaela. 'Schools and clinics and such-like molly-coddling!' Mel, conversing across the table with the Colonel, saw Max's eyebrows rise and made to intervene, for she knew that Michaela was only repeating her mother's opinions on the matter.

'Hardly molly-coddling!' protested Miss Minton hotly. 'The most basic health care and –'

'A family of them came begging to us – though goodness only knows how they got past the lodge. Cook was all for turning them away, but Mama called the little ones back – they had five children, can you imagine? and all quite small – and gave them each one of the tracts we had prepared for Sunday school. I had spent so much time decorating them with little garlands of flowers. They were so pretty, you can't imagine. Mama said that the children might come to the Sunday school, if they washed them, of course. And do you know what the man said to Mama?'

Max shook his head.

'He swore at her!' Her eyes widened with shock. 'Can you imagine? Mama offered him Christian charity and he *swore* at her!'

Max and Adam looked at her blankly, searching for words appropriate to the occasion and finding none. In the end it was Miss Minton who broke the stunned silence.

'I am sure he meant no harm by it, Miss Jennings,' she said with studied calm. 'Perhaps he had simply hoped for something a little more practical in the way of assistance.'

'But to swear! And in front of ladies!'

'He had not your advantages, Miss Jennings,' said Harriet smoothly. 'I fear that fine sentiments come more readily to the well fed.'

'I daresay I must bow to your superior knowledge on the subject, Miss Minton,' said Michaela coolly, and turned her attention to the Colonel on her right. Only Mel, sitting opposite, saw Max press Harriet Minton's hand in gratitude and caught the smile that Harriet flashed at him in return.

Good heavens! she thought. Sits the wind in that quarter? She wondered whether the rest of the party were as blind to the new development as she had been.

The next day, when the rain showed no sign of abating, Max suggested a game of shuttlecock. 'The Carter girls often played shuttlecock in the ballroom,' he said. 'The racquets must still be somewhere around the house.'

Mrs Chobley was consulted and, as usual, had the answer. 'The net's up in the attics,' she said. 'And the stands. And the racquets and shuttlecocks won't be far away, I'll be bound.'

The three girls followed Max up to the attics and had an enjoyable rummage around by the light of the oil lamps until they found what they were looking for.

'Here's the net!' announced Harriet Minton triumphantly. She drew it out and looked at the large holes in the middle of it. 'But I think the mice have been nesting in it!'

At the mention of mice, Michaela put her hand to her throat and swooned into Max's arms as gracefully and accurately as if she had been playing it nightly, twice on matinees, with Wallack's company at the City Theatre.

'Michaela! For Heaven's sake!' Max, more than usually embarrassed, looked to the others for help. Harriet bent her head over the net and Mel, who found the thought of mice very inoffensive compared to some of the creatures who had inhabited the alleys and tenements around the Orphanage, looked studiedly out of the attic windows on to the village street. Max lowered Michaela gingerly on to a nearby chair.

Finding that her artless girlish shrieks had no more effect on Max than her swoon had done, Michaela soon recovered and, picking up the racquets, announced her intention of waiting downstairs for them. Meanwhile, Harriet had found a ball of string and sat down on an old chaise longue to mend the net. Mel went to help, but finding her place usurped by Max, took the other oil lamp and went wandering round the attic rooms, marvelling at the beautiful furniture standing in rows around the walls, covered in thick layers of dust.

At last the net was mended and the stands found and they all went down to the empty ballroom to set up the game. Max was the only one who even vaguely knew the rules and he had an energetic time moving from one side of the net to the other, trying to demonstrate to the other three how the game should be played.

Michaela, finding that she was not to be allowed to partner Max, soon tired of the game, flinging her racquet down and declaring that badminton was a bore. The others refused to be put off, and soon developed a sort of circular game, two against one, where after every few points one of them crossed the net to partner the one who had been playing alone.

Adam, coming in from the stableyard, was puzzled to hear shouts of laughter coming from the back of the house. He put down his bag and crossed the hall.

Hidden by the half open door, Adam stood a while watching them playing, Mel against Max and Harriet, then, as Mel made an awkward shot, he came impatiently to her side.

'No, no! That should have been a backhand. Look, like this.' He stood behind her, his right hand on her wrist to demonstrate the movement. He had told George that any feelings he had for her were well under control, but as their hands touched and their bodies brushed against each other, his hands trembled and the blood seemed to boil in his veins.

Mel had not seen him coming up behind her; her stomach knotted at the sound of his voice and her feet were rooted to the ground. She found herself quite unable to speak and stood there passively, letting him show her how she should flick the racquet from the wrist.

She was relieved when he moved away from her, but her relief was short-lived as he stripped off his jacket and picked up the fourth racquet. Running around the court, she thought he looked like a coiled spring, ready to pounce in any direction.

After a vigorous half hour of play, her ankle began to ache a little and she decided to sit out.

Adam had a quick look at her ankle and professed himself pleased with the improvement. He showed no desire to rejoin the game and in the absence of Michaela, who had wandered off, Max and Harriet played against each other in a game which seemed to provoke a good deal of laughter and badinage.

'I am glad to see this room being put to some use,' said Adam. 'I find it really irritating to have so many rooms unused. Perhaps you and Beatrice could give me some suggestions – otherwise I might be tempted to sell the house and build myself something smaller.'

379

'It isn't so vast,' she said. 'But some of the rooms are badly furnished which makes them so uncomfortable that no one ever uses them.'

'You are right, of course. It is high time I threw out some of Almeria's furniture and chose my own.'

She was about to tell him of their finds in the attic when Max and Harriet rejoined them and by the time they all left the ballroom, Melisande had decided that to tell a man how he ought to furnish his house could very easily be misconstrued: silence would be the better option, she thought.

She could not cope with another afternoon of Michaela and after luncheon she cravenly left Max and Harriet to entertain her, excusing herself on the grounds that she had to read through some notes and prepare her new piece for the examinations.

She didn't emerge until dinner was announced, but immediately she took her place at the table she sensed a tension in the air, something bubbling under the surface. However, she could not quite decide which end of the table it came from, as everyone seemed to be behaving quite unlike their normal selves: Max was unusually verbose and Harriet positively skittish; the Colonel and Beatrice by contrast unusually quiet. Michaela seemed to be hovering on the verge of a sulk, while Adam was watching everyone with an expression of extreme cynicism. She could only hope that the change of mood was not entirely because Michaela was to leave the next morning. Max seemed to be confining his conversation to Harriet, and Mel, struggling to keep a conversation going at her end of the table, felt obliged to make an effort to draw Michaela into her conversation with Beatrice.

As the parlourmaid closed the door behind her, Colonel Randall cleared his throat and rose to his feet.

'I should like to propose a toast,' he said, squaring his shoulders. The others looked at him in some surprise. 'To the beautiful lady who has agreed to become my wife,' he said softly, smiling down the table at a blushing Beatrice.

As the Jennings's carriage disappeared round the curve in the drive the house party turned to go back into the house, each, Mel was sure, suppressing a sigh of relief.

Later that morning she emerged from the drawing room where she had been playing the piano to find Max waiting for her on the landing.

'If you could spare a few moments, I thought we could –' He flushed uncomfortably.

'Of course, Max.' She led the way back into the drawing room and sat down, looking expectantly up at him. Suddenly he seemed very unsure of himself and uncertain of how to begin. He ran his finger round the front of his collar as if to ease it.

'It's very quiet now that Michaela has gone,' she said at last.

'Ye-es,' he agreed cautiously.

'Such enthusiasm for everything!'

'That's it, that's just the problem. I – she –' He took a deep breath. 'Do you think she thinks that I – that we – You see, Beatrice thinks that the Jennings family expects –' He cleared his throat. 'Not that I wasn't flattered by her attention, of course I was. When she singled me out and –'

'And hung on your every word?'

He nodded miserably.

'Don't take it to heart, Max. She does that to all the men who admire her.' It came, she knew, of having not one original thought of her own.

'I was dazzled, I suppose.'

'Yes. She's very pretty.'

'I wasn't thinking straight. And –'

'And now you worried that you have got in too deep to get out?'

'That's it. And the worst of it is that now I realise the woman I really could love –' He turned to Mel with a look of horror on his face. 'Not that I would imply that –' He looked away again, down at the carpet where he fell to tracing the pattern with the point of his shoe. 'Oh, God! I shouldn't be saying this to you at all.'

She took pity on him. 'I don't think you are under any obligation to Michaela,' she said bluntly. 'Her enthusiasms rarely last; she must have flirted with half a dozen different men since she met you.' She crossed the room to his side. 'And I think Harriet Minton would make you a wonderful wife, Max,' she said with a wicked smile.

He looked up from his contemplation of the carpet. 'How did you know?'

She laughed. 'By using the eyes in my head!'

'You don't think she'll think I'm fickle? First you, then Michaela.'

'No one knows about your proposal to me but you and I, Max,' she replied.

'I really thought it might have worked, but once I grew to know Harriet better. . . . Strange, because I've known her – or of her – for a long time. But there were always others around, and when we did meet, we didn't always agree with each other. To be honest, I always thought her rather hard, rather opinionated. And there was Anton, of course. But when I got to know her properly, I – I just suddenly knew she was the one for me,' he said simply.

'Just as well that I turned you down,' said Melisande with a smile that robbed her words of any harshness, 'for then we would both have been miserable, each loving another.'

'Adam?'

'There is no hope there, I know that,' she said. 'But you and Harriet –'

'You understand, I have no reason to believe that she would look kindly on my suit.'

'Then ask her. She is in the morning room, writing to her parents. It's a beautiful morning, Max.' She pressed his hands. 'Suggest a walk. Propose a picnic lunch. But do something, and do it now.'

He went out of the room with a new spring in his step. And neither he nor Miss Minton appeared for lunch.

Adam was harnessing the horses when Mel appeared at his side dressed in her navy blue covert coat and boots.

'Miss Stevens?' His salutation was formal and there was no welcome in his voice.

'Adam, may I come with you?'

'I don't think that would be wise.'

'Max and Harriet are driving over to Carfax, and Harriet will not believe I don't wish to make a third in the outing. And Beatrice and George seem to have me on their consciences, and they *will* keep trying to entertain me!'

'Yes. There is an overwhelming odour of orange blossom in the air,' he said savagely. He ran his fingers through his hair, causing it to flop untidily over his forehead. 'Get in then,' he said curtly. 'But I have a number of calls to make this afternoon, so don't be expecting me to play the polite host.'

'I shall not get in your way,' she said coolly, ignoring his proffered hand and climbing unaided into the gig.

There had been a dramatic change in the weather, and the hot sun was drawing steam from the wet cobbles in the yard, but out on the roads the water still lay in great puddles in the road and the ruts on the smaller lanes were axle-deep in places. Fortunately Mel had had the forethought to put on her stout boots and they were able to leave the gig at the end of the narrower lanes and trudge down on foot.

There were only a few visits, none of them urgent. She found herself wondering whether he had used them as an excuse to get out of the house, a suspicion confirmed when they visited a mother with a new baby, who was most surprised to see them as the nurse had called only that morning.

The sun was almost setting as they walked down the lane from the Pedersens, streaking the azure sky with layers of scarlet and flame. She leant on the barred gate and watched the ever changing colours.

'Best hurry home,' said Adam as the fiery ball of orange dipped towards a dark stand of trees on the horizon. 'It will be dark soon, and Beatrice will worry.'

'I think sunset is the most perfect part of the day,' she said with a sigh of contentment.

'If you stand here much longer, you'll be able to compare it to moon-rise,' he said sarcastically.

'That's almost as beautiful,' said Melisande dreamily. 'I never really saw it in London, because the river mists and the light of the gas lamps always hazed it.' As she spoke she heard once more the mournful sound of a ship's hooter moaning through the banks of thick fog that rolled up from the river to envelop Wapping – and all of London – in its smothering embrace. 'But here it's so clear! Layers of azure, darkening to deepest marine blue until the stars come out and then the moon, like a great sword slash in the sky.' She turned to him, her heart in her eyes. 'Oh, I wish I could express colours in

383

music!' she exclaimed. 'I wish I could write down that fantastical blending and harmony of colours and play it again and again, an entire symphony of light!'

'Your summer symphony,' he said softly, an answering light in his eyes as he was caught up for a moment in her mood.

'Yes.' They looked at each other for a long moment. She thought he was going to speak, but he just looked at her, his eyes fierce and demanding. She couldn't bear it. She had to turn away. 'But then you'd have to have my winter symphony too,' she said, struggling for a lighter note. '*Very* melancholy, I promise you!'

The moment was broken and she did not know whether she was sorry or no. They trudged on down the lane to the gig.

'I fear I have been a poor host,' said Adam gruffly as he handed her up. 'Had I known that the party would pair off so dramatically, I would have made other arrangements for your entertainment.'

'Such as begging the Jennings to let Michaela extend her visit?' she suggested sarcastically.

He pulled a wry face. 'Perhaps not that.'

'Don't make a mountain out of a molehill,' advised Melisande. 'I am not so stupid I don't know why you avoid me.'

'It isn't that. But I –'

'Don't worry. I shan't embarrass you by going over old ground.' She stared out across the fields and blinked hard. 'And please don't insult me by treating me like a formal guest. As if you needed to entertain me!'

'For that you have my apologies,' he said stiffly.

'I don't want or need your apologies!' she snapped. Then, taking her courage in both hands: 'There is a happy medium between love and hate,' she said with a calmness she did not feel. 'It's called friendship.'

He turned and looked at her, then held his hand out.

'Friends, then,' he said.

She put her slim fingers into his hard grip and forced herself to look at him steadily.

'Friends,' she agreed.

It was almost with relief that she returned to college where she threw herself back into work with a will. She stuck to her resolution not to play the duet with Clive Trensham, despite the bouquets and little gifts with which he plied her on her return. She returned the gifts, sent the flowers round to the lying-in ward at the hospital and concentrated on her studies.

The tempo of college life took on a new urgency for the intending summer graduates and the practice rooms resounded with arpeggios, glissandes and flourishes on every kind of instrument. Freed of her commitment to Clive, and determined to show him that she was quite capable of performing without him, she threw herself with renewed vigour into the Tchaikovsky Concerto, which she now had no choice but to enter as her examination piece. She worked on it every hour she could find and progressed so well that Mr Farson insisted she enter it for the exhibition, encouraging the Dean to cherish hopes that one of the teacher students he had fought so hard to have admitted might even walk off with the annual award.

Not everyone was entering for the exhibition: none of the practical teachers, training, like her, on the short courses, nor others like Sally and Jim Harding, who would be pleased with a good pass in the music practical, but there were enough to cause queues for the practice rooms where they worked with the college orchestra. With her work at the school and the impending papers on teaching, music theory and French, Melisande would have her work cut out to have everything ready in time.

The plans for Beatrice and George's wedding were proceeding apace, although Beatrice had threatened to call the whole thing off when she discovered that they would not be back from the honeymoon trip for Melisande's birthday.

'And Tom and Amy had planned to travel to Albany with Bella and John!' lamented Beatrice.

'Then Melisande must go with them,' said George firmly. 'They can go on to New York – you would like New York, m'dear, I promise you.'

'Don't worry about me,' she said with a smile. 'I shall do very well here. After all the examinations, and the exhibition, and the wedding too, I shall want some peace and quiet. Besides there is the school to think of.'

'But your birthday!' objected Beatrice. 'Tom, talk some sense into her. Her first birthday since we became her guardians . . . and such an important one too! I had planned a ball and –'

'Dear Aunt Beatrice,' said Mel with a smile. 'You and George have given me the best possible birthday present, I promise you. And who is to say what date my birthday is? It's always been an arbitrary date anyway, so we can just as well have a ball when you return.'

She bent to lock the schoolroom door and handed the key over to Rabbi Benjamin.

'I can't thank you enough,' she started to say.

'My dear, you've thanked me enough at least ten times today,' he said with a slow smile. 'Go now and do your last minute reading. Not too much, mind, or you'll be too tired to get it all down on paper!' He pressed her hand. 'We will all be thinking of you tomorrow.'

She waved goodbye to him and set off to walk home through the town centre, where she had promised to pick up one or two items. The last day of teaching had gone very well. She had planned another elementary health lesson – only this time she had asked Agnete to come in and give it. An inspired choice, as Agnete had talked to them about her training in the hospital in Owenstown, showing the children and their mothers how high an immigrant child could set her sights.

'So that's Tadeusz's young lady, is it?' said Rabbi Benjamin, who had come in to collect the key just in time to hear the tail end of her talk. 'A fine young lady, that one.'

'I thought – I mean –'

'That I would disapprove? Of course I do. It's a great pity she's a Gentile. It's a great pity you are a Gentile, but there! We cut our coat according to our cloth, eh?' He chuckled to show there was no ill will meant. 'But I can't delude myself that Tadeusz's family care one way or the other.' He shrugged his shoulders fatalistically. 'His father is an unbeliever whose only use for his religious training is to try to better me in an argument, and Tadeusz has been brought up with just the outer trappings of our faith. Of course, this Agnete, she's a sensible young lady. Maybe she'll convert!' But he said it without too much conviction.

Melisande had just reached the bottom of Quincey Street and was turning up to head for Morton's Haberdashery when Warden Hurstpoint appeared in front of her on the sidewalk.

'Miss Stevens!' He tipped his hat to her. 'Jawly pleasant s'prise!' he said ingenuously. 'May I off' you m'escort home?'

'It's very kind of you, Mr Hurstpoint, but do you think your credit will survive being seen in public at this end of town?'

He looked around at the dank warehouses and the unswept sidewalks and shuddered. 'Y'right, 'course. Not kind 'f place I – but, b'Jove, 'f 's good 'nough f'you, I –' He lost himself in his usual welter of half-formed words.

'What on earth brings you to Harbourside?' she asked, torn as usual with Warden between humour and exasperation, and trying not to let either show.

'B'n tryin' see you. Mrs Bennett s'ggest'd I –' He muttered something incomprehensible from which she could only make out 'or country dance'.

'But I'm not going to the Newby's ball, Mr Hurstpoint,' she said.

'Not goin' t' – but –'

She tried to explain that her social life had of necessity to take second place to her studies until her examinations were over, but she doubted she had made much impact on him as he couldn't envisage anything being more important than one's social life.

Crossing the road from the haberdashery on Warden's arm, she saw Father Kerrigan coming out of Mulligan's hardware store.

'Ah, Miss Stevens!' He planted himself in their path.

'Father Kerrigan.' She inclined her head and smiled. 'I don't believe you know Mr Hurstp—'

'Another of your heretics, is he then?' said Kerrigan pugnaciously. 'Another Yid, is it?' Hurstpoint goggled at him, speechless. 'I hear you've handed the school over entirely to the heretics now? Well, they'll have no more of my flock comin' there, I promise you, and so I'll be tellin' the trustees too!' His face grew purple with choler.

'I say!' Hurstpoint made to set himself between the priest and Miss Stevens. 'Can't speak like that t'a lady, m'good man!'

387

Melisande set Warden effortlessly to one side.

'I haven't handed over the school to anyone, Father Kerrigan,' said Melisande in steely tones. 'Rabbi Benjamin kindly offered to step in while I took my examinations. The trustees took up his offer. If you wish to help out as well, I am sure the trustees will be only too pleased to hear from you.'

'Go in that Godless place? I –'

'Godless by instruction of the Eden County Education Board, Father,' she said sweetly.

'What?'

'From next year the Harbourside Trust School will be recognised and funded by the County. And of course as we take in from such varied backgrounds, they agree with us that it would be – inappropriate – to have religious instruction.'

Kerrigan's jaw dropped and his face grew more florid than ever.

'Come, Mr Hurstpoint,' said Melisande, linking her arm in his and dragging him away. 'I believe we must not block the sidewalk. Good day to you, Father Kerrigan.'

Melisande drew to a halt outside the Colonel's house on the corner of Fifth and Erie, flinging herself out of the saddle almost before the wheels had stopped turning. She dashed up the steps, almost falling over the hem of her smart moss green cycling skirts.

'Isn't it a wonderful day, Maggie,' she cried, as the maid opened the door. Thrusting her woollen cape into the girl's hands, she hurried up the stairs.

Dimly she was aware of Maggie calling up the stairs after her, but the maid's thick accent was hard to understand at the best of times and today Mel was driven by excitement and couldn't have stopped if she'd wanted to.

She flung open the double doors of the drawing room and rushed in.

'Uncle George!' she cried. 'Such news!' He hurried across to her side and caught her hands in his. 'I – I've passed all my written papers – distinction in pedagogics too!'

'Oh, my dear girl!' The Colonel's chest puffed with pride as if she were in truth his own daughter. 'That will confound the doubting Thomases, eh?' He hugged her warmly. 'And now, m'dear, let me introduce you to my good friends from England.'

She turned to see a man and woman, both in their early fifties, both very fashionably dressed. The man was frowning, but the woman was looking at her in some amusement. Sitting over by the window they had been hidden from her by the half open door. She blushed as she realised how gauche and ill-behaved she must seem.

'I'm so sorry,' she murmured. 'I would never have dashed in like that if I'd known . . .'

'My ward, Melisande Stevens,' said George, turning with a smile to his friends, who had risen and crossed the room to his side. He put his arm lightly round Melisande's shoulders. 'M'dear, I'd like you to meet James Kingsley and his wife Amelia.'

Adam's parents. Damnation! The people of all the world she'd planned to avoid!

She shook hands with Mrs Kingsley and they exchanged the usual social niceties, then she turned to shake hands with her husband. 'Good heavens!' she exclaimed, taking in the angular face and the alert grey eyes. 'If I had met you in the street without anything else on my mind, I would have known you straight away for Adam's – Doctor Kingsley's – father,' she said frankly.

'We are held to look very alike,' he said somewhat stiffly, and she wondered whether she had overstepped the mark.

'Your hair flops over just as Adam's does,' said his wife with a smile. 'Except that yours is grey, my love. And now, Miss Stevens,' she went on, drawing her over to sit on the sofa, 'I hope you don't mind us sharing in your good news? George has been telling us all about your studies. Do tell me – what the Devil are pedagogics?'

'It's just a fancy name for the theory of teaching,' said Melisande with a smile.

'If that isn't typical of the Americans!' exclaimed the Colonel. 'Never use one word when you can use five!'

The Colonel's visitors chatted easily to her, drawing her out to talk about Harbourside, and the school and the dispensary.

'But you are not American, are you, Miss Stevens?' asked Adam's father, regarding her gravely.

'No. I – I used to live in London,' she said, lifting her chin and looking him in the eye.

'A long way to come to study.'

She wished Uncle George would come to her rescue, but he was gazing out of the window. Perhaps he did not wish to be embarrassed in front of his guests. 'The – the training is more practical here,' she said, somewhat breathlessly. 'I do not believe I could have followed a similar course in London. And then the Harbourside school trustees sponsored me for the course.'

'Are there then no scholarships in London?'

What could she say? Of course there were scholarships – but what use were they without a roof over your head?

Mrs Kingsley came to her rescue. 'James, do stop cross-examining Miss Stevens,' she said, a smile crinkling the corners of her eyes. 'I daresay it is just that one has to know where to look for such assistance. Perhaps they are not as· widely advertised as they could be.'

'Of course they are not,' said Melisande before she could stop herself. 'Too many scholarship girls would damage the supply of domestic servants.'

'You sound very bitter, Miss Stevens,' said Mrs Kingsley, raising her eyebrows.

Melisande bit her lip painfully. She had come very close to blurting out her past to this sympathetic woman and could not understand why.

'I?' She gave a rather forced laugh. 'Oh, no.' She smiled up at the Colonel and this time there was nothing forced about it. 'So many people here have helped me and been so very kind to me. Uncle George, Aunt Beatrice and her family. And Adam – I – I mean Doctor Kingsley,' she stammered, feeling the flush rising from the base of her throat. 'He persuaded the Harbourside trustees to sponsor me.'

Mrs Kingsley leaned forward, a frown between her delicately arched eyebrows. 'Miss Stevens, I –'

Just then Maggie opened the door. 'Mrs Patterson has called, Colonel. And she wishes most particularly –'

A frown of irritation crossed the Colonel's brow, but before he could tell Maggie to deny them, Mrs Patterson appeared behind the maid and sailed into the room, her son and daughter close on her heels.

390

Colonel Randall bit off the words he had so nearly uttered. 'This is an unexpected pleasure, ma'am,' he said with forced civility.

'We came the moment we heard that the Duke and Duchess had arrived,' gushed Mrs Patterson, sweeping past Melisande to fawn on the Colonel's English guests. 'We would not wish to be backward in any attentions . . . so close as we are to Adam.'

The Duke and Duchess!

So now Melisande knew why Adam had rejected her. The son of a duke would hardly be likely to consider an alliance with a nameless waif. Hot tears pricked her eyes and she had to blink hard to hold them back. At the first opportunity she rose and took a disjointed leave of the company.

'I shall look forward to furthering our acquaintance with you,' said Mrs Kingsley – no, the Duchess – in her soft musical voice.

It seemed most unlikely that Adam had any intention of introducing her to his parents, but she did not say so.

She was proved wrong the very next morning when a gilt-edged invitation arrived at the house. Dr Adam Kingsley requested the pleasure of Mr and Mrs Thomas Bennett and Miss Melisande Stevens at a house party the following weekend.

'Oh, Mel,' said Amy, sinking her forehead on to her hand. 'Tom and I have already accepted invitations for that weekend.'

'It really doesn't matter,' she said with a smile of relief. 'I had rather not go.' Amy looked at her suspiciously. 'I have so much work to do,' she said, rather lamely.

The next day Amy was busy arranging a centrepiece of early summer blooms and ferns in a crystal bowl when the maid announced Doctor Kingsley.

'Adam!' She came forward, a smile on her lips. 'How very pleasant to see you. Will you join me for luncheon? Tom's at college and Mel is teaching in Harbourside,' she added as he hesitated.

'Then I shall be delighted.'

'We were sorry to have to pass up your house party,' she said, half way through luncheon. 'I hope we can meet your family some other time. If it had been anyone else but the Principal –'

He looked up, his fork half way to his mouth. 'Miss Stevens is going to the Principal's?' he asked in lively astonishment. 'Won't she find it a bore?'

'I shall certainly find it a bore. But Mel's not coming to the Principal's.'

'Then why did she turn down my invitation?'

'She feels she has too much work.'

'A feeble excuse. She has finished all her written examinations.' His voice hardened perceptibly. 'I hear – from George – that she did rather well.'

'Yes.'

'And she can practise on our instrument as easily as on yours . . .'

Amy gave an embarrassed shrug.

He ran his hand despairingly through his dark hair. 'All I know is that the Duchess has taken a liking to her and insists that she should come. And once the Duchess has made up her mind, there is no moving her.'

Amy thought he looked about as pleased at the prospect as Melisande, and nearly said so, but her nerve failed.

The weather had turned sultry and that afternoon, when Melisande was half way home from Miss Greville's, had produced a spectacular thunderstorm. She had sheltered for a while under the awning outside Schmidt's grocery store, but in the end there had been nothing for it but to push her bicycle home through the torrential rain.

When she reached the Bennetts' house, the gas lights were glowing, the jets spluttering in the damp air. The Bennetts had already left for their weekend engagement, taking the maid with them, but Mrs McPherson, the housekeeper, opened the door to her, tut-tutting over her as she dripped her way across the hall, where her small trunk stood corded and ready, drew a bath for her and laid out her evening attire on the bed.

The hot bath was warming and comforting after the long wet walk, and she could have lain there all evening, but Mrs McPherson was soon rapping on the door.

Melisande drew on her pale silk stockings and the layers of rustling petticoats that went with her evening gown, but she was too nervous to feel the usual thrill and excitement.

'You look more as though you're going to a wake than an evening party!' exclaimed Mrs McPherson. 'It's a pity Mrs Bennett can't be there with you, but her mama will take care of you, never fear.'

Melisande brushed her hair, swept the luxuriant curls up into a neat cluster on top of her head and looked long and hard at her reflection in the mirror. As she had said to Amy, this was not going to be a very comfortable weekend. She could only hope that there would be a large party and that she could disappear among the crowd and not have to speak to Adam or his parents at all, beyond the minimum courtesies.

Mrs McPherson dexterously flung the robe of ivory satin over her head and attached the russet shawl and ribbons to it, which brought out the golden lights in her hair.

'You'll be wanting some jewellery,' said the housekeeper, looking at her critically.

'The pearls,' she said. Not a hard decision, as they were the only jewels she possessed.

Mrs McPherson looked around her. 'I don't see the pearls,' she said, after a moment. 'In fact, I don't see your jewellery case at all.'

'Oh, no!' exclaimed Mel. 'Mathilda must have packed them! I'll have to get them out!' She needed all the confidence she could get. After the way she had behaved the other day at Uncle George's, Adam's parents must already think her naive and gauche in the extreme; the thought of walking into an evening party without a shred of ornament on her made her knees shake even more than they were already doing.

'You'll not have time to uncord it and take everything out,' said Mrs McPherson, and as if to echo her words, the house resounded to the sound of the door knocker being wielded vigorously.

Mel looked at her pale, unadorned face in the mirror and for some bizarre reason wondered what Michaela would do under these circumstances. Without stopping to consider what she was doing, she pulled two of the russet ribbons off her gown: one she gave to Mrs McPherson to thread through

393

her curls, the other she tied round her throat and fastened with a bow at the front. She remembered how Sarah had once told her how French emigrés who had returned to take up their fortunes under Napoleon had often worn ribbons like this: *à la victime*, they had called it, in a grim reference to the guillotine. Only then the ribbons had been scarlet, not russet. It seemed singularly appropriate; she felt tonight as though she were going to an execution, not a ball. Much as she had grown to enjoy the balls and soirées, she could happily have missed this one.

The coachman knocked on the door again. She picked up her shawl and took one last look at herself. She must not keep the tumbril waiting.

At Springs House, Adam drew out his watch for the umpteenth time that evening and swore softly. The Duchess looked up briefly from the tapestry she was working on.

'They will not come any the sooner for your curses, Adam,' she said gently.

'I am sorry, Amelia,' he said, colouring. 'I had almost forgotten your presence.'

'Give you a game of billiards, m'boy,' suggested his father, laying aside his newspaper.

He shook his head. 'I think I had better ride out towards Edensville,' he decided. 'If you will excuse me, Amelia. I'm afraid they might have had an accident.'

'Nonsense,' she said calmly. 'They must have waited until Miss Stevens returned from college. She would have needed to change and dress for dinner. Then again the journey would take twice as long with the roads so slippery.' She looked up at him with wide cornflower blue eyes. 'The Colonel surely has a competent coachman?'

He sighed. 'You are right, of course, Amelia.'

Under her steady level gaze he was forced to cease his pacing up and down. But while the Duchess picked up her work and plied her needle steadily, her eyes went frequently to him and saw that, while he made a show of reading the journal he held in his hands, his eyes and ears were still on the alert for signs of an impending arrival.

When the carriage wheels crunched over the gravel on the drive, he was on his feet and down in the hall almost before the maid had reached the door.

The Colonel had already handed Beatrice down and manners dictated that he should greet her first while George helped Miss Stevens descend.

He led Beatrice into the hall where she greeted her old friends, but it seemed to him that Melisande was taking an unconscionable time to come in.

Truth to tell, she was having a brief moment of panic, wishing that the journey, which had seemed so tediously slow as the coachman nursed his horses over the treacherous surface and along the forest road where they jibbed at the noise of the trees, blowing wildly about in the strong wind, would go on for ever, wishing that she could huddle here under the warm plaid rug and never have to come out. But that was the coward's way, and she was no coward. Besides, she could not embarrass Beatrice and George in front of their old friends.

She had her words ready on her lips, calm and controlled words, formal words of greeting, no more. But Adam spoke first.

'Mel – Miss Stevens –' he blurted out. 'It's so good to see you here again.'

Her answer was lost in a tangle of confused words and blushes. Adam could have kicked himself for his tactlessness.

Beatrice turned from greeting her old friends. 'Come in out of the rain and let Jessie close the door,' she said calmly.

'Where are all the other guests?' Melisande hissed as Jessie took their cloaks.

'Did Amy not tell you?' said Beatrice. 'This is to be just a quiet family house party. We have so much to catch up on: James and Amelia are old friends of ours.'

But not of mine, thought Melisande despairingly. I'm just the charity girl who isn't good enough for their son.

The Duchess, who had been chuckling at something George had said to her, turned to link arms with Melisande. 'I have heard so much about you, my dear,' she said. 'I am looking forward to hearing more about your work and your studies.'

She chattered on as they followed Adam and Beatrice up the stairs, with the two older men bringing up the rear.

Mel had almost regained her confidence by the time they entered the drawing room. There was some polite jostling as to who should sit nearest the fire that blazed merrily in the hearth.

'My dears, you must be frozen from sitting in the carriage in all that wind,' said the Duchess. 'Miss Stevens, do have my seat.'

'No, really.'

'Nonsense,' said Adam, catching her hands to draw her to the fire and sending delicious little shivers up her arms at his touch. 'Mel, your hands are frozen! Madness to wear a summer wrap. You should have worn the coat I gave you.'

There was an audible intake of breath and then an embarrassed silence. If an unmarried man bought items of clothing for an unmarried young woman, everyone knew what favours he received in return. Melisande felt the colour rising up her neck, but her mouth and her throat were as dry as dust and she couldn't have spoken to save her life.

Beatrice tried to leap into the breach. 'Did Adam tell you, Miss Stevens was his secretary during the harvest? Such a good arrangement.'

The Duchess, unperturbed, drew Mel to the fire, sat her down next to her and began to chafe her cold hands. 'James,' she said to her husband over her shoulder, 'do you and Adam take George down to see the new billiards table. I know George is an expert player.'

Colonel Randall took up the cue promptly. 'Ah, dear lady, what else was there to do in India *but* play billiards?' He shepherded Adam out of the room, closely followed by the Duke, a puzzled frown on his face.

As the door closed behind them, Beatrice rushed into speech again but Melisande interrupted her. 'Don't, Aunt Beatrice. I know you mean well, but . . .' She looked straight at the Duchess. 'Adam did give me that coat, your Grace,' she said, with the disastrous frankness Sarah Thomsett had tried so hard to control. 'And it wasn't in lieu of payment for being his secretary. I – I didn't realise then that it would be open to misunderstanding. But I needed that coat. I really needed it.'

She paused a brief moment and looked at her pale, elegant hands, remembering the blisters, chaps and chilblains that had marked them then. 'When I was appointed to the post at the Harbourside school, I had no suitable clothes. I wasn't sent out as a teacher, you see. I was sent out as a scullerymaid.'

She bowed her head and waited for the storm to break.

'Thank you for being so honest with me,' said the Duchess, apparently not at all shocked to find a former servant in the drawing room. 'How fortunate that you were here when the post came up! Though I don't suppose the children realise how lucky they are to have you as a teacher. Oh, by the way,' she added, 'we prefer to be known as Mr and Mrs Kingsley while we are here. It makes life so much easier for – ah – everyone.' Remembering how the Pattersons had fawned over them, Melisande could quite understand that. 'Now, if you have quite thawed out, let us go and find the gentlemen. I declare I am quite ready for my dinner.'

It could not be said that Mel did justice to her dinner that evening. The Duchess – or Mrs Kingsley, as she must remember to call her – had placed Melisande on Adam's right. When he had taken her hands in his in the drawing room, her heart had banged so violently against her ribs that for a moment she had been unable to speak. And now, whenever he spoke to her, or turned to pass her something, her stomach seemed to turn over. From the time they had shaken hands on friendship, she had tried hard to see him only in that light. She had thought herself in control of her feelings for him, told herself angrily that it was nothing but an infatuation with the first gentleman to take notice of her, but here in his own home, in the place where she had first come to know and love him, her emotions were not so easily ordered. She sipped at the delicate warming soup, picked her way through the fish course, hardly touched the game and refused the remove entirely.

She was quite relieved when the talk turned to friends in England and she was able to sit back and listen, not expected to contribute anything to the conversation. She emptied her glass and did not see the frown on Beatrice's face as it was refilled.

'Ah, yes. That was Ernest Moorfield,' said Adam, and she pricked up her ears at the strain in his voice. 'I suppose he married Cecilia in the end?'

'No, no,' said his father. 'Married the Dawsons' younger daughter. What was her name now?'

'Henrietta,' said George. 'You remember her, Adam?'

'I don't believe I do.'

'Surely? Her cousin brought her to Henley in Fothergill's party the year you graduated.'

'Ah, yes,' said Adam. 'Striking girl. Mass of black hair.'

'That's the one,' said George, nodding his head.

'So she married Ernest.' Adam leaned back in his chair, watching the candlelight glint off the red wine in his glass. 'And Cecilia? Who did she marry?'

'She is still unmarried,' said Amelia Kingsley smoothly. 'Although she has several beaux on a string.'

Melisande stole a furtive look at Adam and at the look of pain on his face, it was all she could do not to reach out and take his hand. She looked back down at her plate. What a fool she had been to let her heart run riot when he loved someone else: a girl, well-born, of course, in England. What could he feel for a girl like herself? Nothing, beyond the sense of responsibility for a former servant. Anything else was only in her imagination. *Noblesse oblige*, as Sarah used to say.

And then she looked up again and their eyes met and she knew it had not been all in her mind. He did have feelings for her and even though there was no hope for them, it was curiously comforting to know that she was not the only one to care.

'You do not eat, my dear,' observed Amelia Kingsley.

'I – I am sorry. My appetite has deserted me today.'

'Don't fret, Amelia,' said Adam with a bark of a laugh. 'Mrs Chobley will tell you that Mel is one of those who could live for days on a lettuce leaf!'

When the ladies retired to the drawing room, leaving the men to sit over their port and brandy – 'But not for too long!' admonished Beatrice – Amelia Kingsley took the earliest opportunity to send Mel off to the other end of the house to look for her embroidery frame.

'Well?' she demanded of her friend as the door shut.

Beatrice looked back at her with eyebrows raised.

'I thought you said Adam was considering marrying the Patterson girl?' she said in lively astonishment.

'Indeed he is,' replied Beatrice calmly.

'But he couldn't take his eyes off Miss Stevens all evening, and if he touches her accidentally she jumps like a scalded cat!'

'If you had asked me last year, I would have said he loved her. But then . . .' She looked up at her friend. 'He doesn't confide in me any more, I'm afraid. But at the time, I know, he thought his father would disapprove. And Miss Patterson is much more eligible and – and suitable.'

'Pasty-faced bore!' said Amelia. 'She said not two words when her mother blasted her way into George's house. I find Miss Stevens much more stimulating company.'

Beatrice smiled. 'We all love her,' she said simply. 'But we cannot deny that her background . . .'

The Duchess snapped her fingers in a dismissive gesture. '*That* for background,' she said inelegantly. 'Once Adam would have said the same.' She paused. 'I find it hard to believe he's changed so much.'

When the men joined them, Mrs Kingsley proposed a game of billiards. 'You can partner me, Melisande – I may call you Melisande, may I?'

'Amelia's a dab hand at the game,' said the Colonel with a smile. 'Even better at snooker.'

'I'm afraid I don't play,' said Melisande. 'Perhaps I can score for you?'

'Don't play? Good Heavens. Hasn't Adam taught you?' Mel shook her head. 'Don't tell me the men keep it all to themselves here too? I thought in America at least they'd have lifted that old taboo.'

'I would be happy to watch, ma'am.'

'Nonsense!' said Amelia briskly. 'Beatrice does not play, so someone has to help me keep our end up!'

With three willing teachers in the Kingsleys and Uncle George, Melisande soon got the hang of the game. No one took it too seriously and amid all the laughter and teasing, she soon lost her awe of Adam's parents. She could think of a few egalitarian Americans who behaved a deal more like dukes and duchesses than this friendly couple.

In the second frame she successfully sank the black on a moderately demanding shot and Adam, standing nearby, started to put his arm around her shoulder to congratulate her, then dropped it in embarrassment and turned away, muttering inarticulately, under the pretext of chalking his cue.

The summer storm had blown itself out during the night and by the next morning the sunbaked earth had sucked up most of the surface water, leaving the ground green and refreshed. James Kingsley, who had risen early, suggested that they all ride over to Naskawa Valley to the race meeting being held there.

'Is it a very strenuous ride?' asked Beatrice. 'I am no great horsewoman.'

'Oh, the ground's quite dry,' Kingsley reassured her. 'Going is not too soft.'

'And I have several very docile mounts for you to choose from,' said Adam with a laugh.

'I hope you are not including me in your requirements for a docile mount!' said Amelia. 'I need a good gallop to make up for the last few housebound days!'

'I have just the right mount for you, Amelia. A real demon, he is. I shouldn't dream of giving you a gentle mount – you would only frighten it!'

He saw the frown on Melisande's face. 'Amelia is one of the best horsewomen in England,' he explained, unaware that the frown was due to her confusion at his calling the Duchess by her Christian name. 'I don't imagine we shall see much of her – just a cloud of dust in the distance!'

'Do you have a riding outfit, Miss Stevens?' Mrs Kingsley was always practical. 'You and I are much of a height, and I am sure I can find something to suit you.'

'So kind,' murmured Melisande. 'But I don't ride.'

'You have never been on horseback?'

'No. Well –' She giggled, thinking of Ned and Dobbin. 'Yes. But not on the kind of horse that Ad– Doctor Kingsley has in his stables.' She had loved riding Mr Evans's carthorses, but there was a world of difference between a sedate trot round the dairy yard on steady old Ned and a cross-country ride on an unknown, but undoubtedly mettlesome mount.

But Beatrice was having none of these reservations. 'If you don't ride, then you most certainly must learn,' she said firmly. 'You learnt to ride the bicycle in one morning: you can learn to ride a horse this morning. Besides, I don't believe there is any other way to reach Naskawa, is there?'

'No,' said Adam curtly. 'Not unless you go all the way into Edensville, out along the lake road and back up the Naskawa Valley. That would take hours.' He looked under his lashes at Melisande, who was looking extremely nervous at the prospect. 'But I doubt Miss Stevens has the stamina to see it through,' he said dismissively. 'Or the nerve.'

She bristled angrily at the slur. 'I see no reason why I should not at least try, Doctor Kingsley!' she snapped, chin in the air and the light of battle in her eyes. She rose from the table abruptly. 'You'll see!' she muttered under her breath, and stormed out of the room.

Amelia watched her go with a frown furrowing her brow. 'That was not very kind, Adam,' she said. 'Miss Stevens is after all your guest. And teasing her for her inability to ride has put her in a most uncomfortable position.'

'Worked admirably, though, didn't it, my boy?' said James Kingsley.

'You mean to say that he did this deliberately?' Amelia demanded of her husband.

'I've never known her to shirk any challenge,' said Adam with a rueful smile. 'And God knows she has not been short of them.'

'It seems the two of you have a great deal in common,' said his father wryly.

The men were waiting in the stable yard when the ladies came down. Mel was dressed in a slim-fitting riding habit in Prussian blue, with a jaunty cap to match. She looked across to where Adam was standing talking to Max, who was hitching up the gig for a trip into Edensville. The tweed riding jacket and close-fitting breeches tucked into high polished top boots flattered Adam's well-proportioned figure and she found herself remembering the feel of his arms around her, the feel of his body against hers on the night of the ball. Just

401

then he turned and looked at her and she blushed and turned away, berating herself for her folly in thinking such thoughts about someone who was unattainable.

'We have a problem, Adam,' called Amelia, following her out. 'No boots for Miss Stevens.'

'There were some old riding boots up in the attic,' said Max before Adam could speak. 'You remember, Mel, in the corner where we found all the racquets.'

Melisande lit the oil lamp at the foot of the attic stairs and led Amelia up into the dusty rooms under the roof, torn between hope that they would find boots to fit and hope that they would not, and she would not be able to go. Part of her was eager to join in, eager to show Adam that she was not the coward he had called her, but at the same time she was scared – scared of the horse, scared of falling, scared of making a fool of herself.

'Goodness!' exclaimed Amelia, looking round her in the pool of light. 'How can one hope to find anything up here?'

'Mrs Chobley says that when Mrs Carter refurnished the house, she put all the original pieces up here,' said Mel, running her finger over an old satinwood games table with mother of pearl inlays glistening through the dust. 'I think they are all much nicer than her furniture, which is what Adam is using now.'

'My dear, I share your taste,' said Amelia, lifting a dust sheet to reveal a splendid tulipwood escritoire. 'There is some beautiful Regency furniture here – Federal style, I believe they call it over here. Much more attractive than those hideous over-stuffed sofas and uncomfortable chairs. I never thought very highly of Almeria Carter's taste when we first came out to visit Adam: I would have thought even less had I known all this was up here. I wonder if Adam knows about it? You must tell him.'

'I think not,' said Mel with a forced laugh. 'He would think – and rightly – that I was interfering in matters that did not concern me.'

She set the lamp down and dived into a corner to cover her embarrassment, emerging triumphantly a moment later with a tangled mass of discarded riding boots.

But it was quite beyond their endeavours to lace up the only pair that fitted Mel, for the mice had not confined themselves to the badminton net and as fast as they knotted the laces, another weak spot would snap. At last they admitted defeat and went downstairs to enlist Adam's assistance.

'You go with the others, Amelia,' said Adam, urging her into the saddle. 'The horses are getting restless.' He looked at the boots with a rueful smile. 'I'll sort these out and we'll follow as soon as we can.'

'We'll be off then,' said the Colonel, swinging into the saddle. He turned back in the archway. 'Be careful with Mel, now,' he ordered. 'Don't forget she's a complete novice!'

Adam gave up the struggle with the laces, drew out a penknife and ripped the remains out. She sat on the mounting block and slipped her feet into the boots while he knelt at her feet to thread in a length of twine from the stables. Feeling her gaze on him, he glanced up and found himself looking into her troubled green eyes. In one of those tricks memory plays, he found himself thinking back to the first time he had seen her, that bitter, freezing night when Max had brought her in and laid her on the sofa like the drowned Ophelia. He had unlaced her boots then, he remembered, and her eyelids had fluttered open and those fathomless green eyes had looked trustingly into his . . .

He swore as he broke his nail on one of the tags. She opened her mouth to speak to him, but he scowled at her so blackly that her voice died in her throat.

'There!' he said abruptly, pushing her feet away. 'They're laced now. You can tie them.'

He brought the docile mare over to the mounting block and held her steady while Mel climbed into the saddle. 'She's called Trusty,' he said harshly.

She leant forward to pat the mare's neck and found herself whispering to her the words she had used to the Evans's horses, when she had fed them pieces of stolen apples through the grating of their basement stable.

Adam led her round the stableyard a couple of times, showing her how to use the reins to control the mare, then he mounted his own horse and they set out to follow the others.

It was the first time she had seen Adam on horseback and even to her untrained eye, it was clear that he was an excellent horseman. Thunderer, the glossy black stallion, was obviously ready for a good gallop, but he held him in to a gentle walk through Eden Springs. He kept a careful watch on his companion, but the times with Ned and Dobbin had not been wasted and by the time they reached the next village, where the track led off over the hills to Naskawa Valley, the mare was trotting easily, her rider settled comfortably into the saddle. They rode side by side in total silence, as apart as they had ever been. Mel confined her conversation to her horse.

Spread out below them as they breasted the hill was the Naskawa Valley, its three finger lakes glittering emerald in the bright sunshine, the bubbling Naskawa river foaming silver-streaked down the valley, disappearing into Naskawa Forest and emerging to throw itself under the old covered bridge, through the village, past the meadows where the race meeting was to be held and on, in more stately fashion, to its junction with the waters of Lake Ontario.

They could see in the distance the bright coloured flags and hear the occasional sound wafted back from the race meeting, but Adam looked in vain for the other members of his party. They were either still riding through the forest, or perhaps already at the race meeting. He muttered under his breath something that sounded suspiciously like a curse.

'There is no need for you to stay with me, Doctor Kingsley,' she said. 'I can manage perfectly well now. And I am sure my pace must be most awfully boring for you.'

'Not at all,' he said in glacial tones.

She was irritated by his attitude. 'You cannot pretend that you are enjoying this!' she snapped in annoyance. 'In fact, the more time we spend in each other's company, the less I understand why you ever asked me back to Springs House!'

'Dammit! You don't think for a moment *I* wanted to ask you, do you? Amelia insisted on it and so I had little choice in the matter! Hell, you should know by now, all I want is to keep as great a distance as possible between us!'

They were both thoroughly furious with each other by now and the argument escalated rapidly, Melisande pulling on the reins to move the mare as far from her escort as possible, and both horses growing more restive as their voices rose.

'I'm sorry that I should have been so ill-bred as to force my company on you!' she shouted angrily. 'Of course, the company of a scullerymaid must be vastly embarrassing for you and your noble family!' She let go of the reins to dash away the tears that, to her anger, were beginning to fall and she didn't notice that the mare was perilously close to the edge of the track.

'Look out!' he cried, and as the horse stumbled on the lip of the hill, she grabbed at the reins and attempted to draw her up, but Trusty, thoroughly alarmed, drew herself up from the stumble and set off down the steep slope towards the river, with Melisande clinging helplessly to the pommel, trying desperately to keep in the saddle.

Panic rising in his breast, Adam turned his own mount and set him at the slope. He saw Melisande sway in the saddle as she struggled to catch at the reins; her hat fell off and rolled down the hill in front of them and her hair streamed around her, whipping across her face and half blinding her. Adam tried to call out to her, but no sound came out of his constricted throat. He gave Thunderer his head: even in a panic, Trusty was no match for his mount. He was gradually gaining ground on the runaway mare, but he knew that without the reins Melisande was completely out of control. It only needed a rabbit hole, or a bird to rise from the scrub and startle the mare even further . . .

Melisande had given up the attempt to grab the reins. She was only keeping her seat by sheer determination and effort of will. If she could only stay on until they reached the bottom of the slope, where the ground levelled out, she told herself, the mare would slow down and perhaps it wouldn't matter so much if she fell. She gritted her teeth: she *had* to stay in the saddle till then. Then her right foot lost the stirrup and she felt herself lurching to one side, slithering as the mare skewed to run parallel with the track. Dimly she could hear the thunder of hooves above the wind that whistled in her ears, but whether those hooves were Trusty's or the stallion's she couldn't tell.

She became horribly aware of the speed with which the trees were coming up at them; her hands were losing their grip and she knew that she could hold on no longer, but just as they reached the bottom of the slope Adam succeeded in drawing level with her. Reaching over, he took Trusty's reins just above the bit and rode knee to knee with her for a few

405

yards, rider and stallion guiding the mare, slowing her down, and then the world turned upside down for Melisande as she lost the struggle to stay in the saddle and fell on to the soft damp grass beneath a broad chestnut tree.

Adam flung himself out of the saddle, leaving the horses to go where they would, and raced to her side. He dropped to his knees, anxiously feeling for a pulse, checking her limbs to see that nothing was broken.

'Mel, are you hurt?' he cried in desperation, stroking her face as she didn't stir. 'Oh, Mel, for God's sake speak to me!'

Her eyelids fluttered open. 'I'm not hurt,' she whispered, rolling over to free herself from the clinging folds of the riding habit. 'Just a bit shaken up.' She flicked her hair out of her eyes. 'Look.' She wriggled her toes. 'Everything in working order.'

'Oh, Mel!' he groaned, pulling her into his arms and burying his face in her unbound hair. 'I never meant to . . .'

Without thinking what she was doing, she returned his fierce embrace, revelling in the feel of his arms around her, the pressure of his body against hers as they fell back on to the soft grass. The horror of the headlong flight down the hillside faded and the bruises were forgotten as he rained kisses on her cheeks, her lips, her eyes, the hands that had so recently patted her body to make sure she was unhurt now holding, stroking, arousing.

At last he raised his head, and, gasping for breath, she looked into his eyes, soft with passion.

'Oh, Adam,' she said shakily, running her hand down his cheek. 'I guess I always knew you couldn't marry me, even before I knew who your parents were. But if – if you love me and – and you want me, then – then the rest doesn't matter.'

Her eyes widened with pain as his hands gripped her wrists as if he would crush her.

'Don't *ever* speak like that again, d'you hear me?' he said through clenched teeth, his voice low and impassioned and more frightening than if he had thundered at her. 'Never again!' His eyes darkened and he turned away from her, stumbling in his haste. With a groan he saw the Colonel galloping back towards them. Ignoring George, he caught his horse, leapt into the saddle and headed away through the forest, leaving her standing lost and alone on the river bank.

The rest of the house party would have had to be blind and deaf to miss the uneasy atmosphere which hung between the two youngest members; at the race meeting and on the ride back they did not exchange a single word.

'It's fortunate that Adam has invited guests to dine this evening,' said Beatrice acidly. 'It will give them an excuse to ignore each other.'

'Damned if they look as if they need an excuse!' exclaimed George. 'I've half a mind to have it out with Adam. Why, he's –'

'Leave them, George,' warned Beatrice. 'I think they have to work it out for themselves.'

As both of them decided to work it out by flirting with their guests rather more than was seemly, everyone was rather shocked – all except Warden Hurstpoint who left Springs House with his head in a whirl, convinced that fortune was about to smile on him at last.

The Pattersons were there, mother and daughter, Jeremiah Patterson having been persuaded to plead a prior engagement. Mrs Patterson had been quite shocked at Society's readiness to accept her son in the role of drunkard and villain after the unfortunate incident at the ball, and was not prepared to give Society a chance to point the finger again.

'I don't care who the Stevens woman is or where she comes from,' she had told him irritably. 'She is accepted by Society: neither you nor I can change that now. She is part of the Springs House set, and if Sophia wants Adam Kingsley, then we shall just have to swallow her as well.'

But watching Adam flirting with every female in the party, Mrs Patterson wondered if the damage had not already been done: it no longer looked at all sure that Sophia stood any chance of becoming mistress of Springs House. She herself was no less obsequious in her attentions to the Duke and Duchess, but her hopes of alliance with the English aristocracy were beginning to fade.

Melisande awoke the next morning with a horrid sinking feeling in her stomach, not entirely due to the unusual amount of wine she had drunk the previous evening. In a weak moment the previous night she had allowed Beatrice to persuade her to go to church with the rest of the houseparty and now she was regretting it with all her heart.

407

She could pinpoint the exact moment when she had lost her faith in a benevolent God. She had been summoned to Matron's room one day and had gone in fear and trepidation, wondering what oversight or misdeed she was guilty of. Matron was sitting behind her desk and – wonder of wonders! – the Reverend Widgery was standing by the window.

In the mixture of gentleness and briskness that was her hallmark, Matron told her that Lizzie had died and been buried the previous week. Milly had stood there, frozen to the spot, her mind spinning round and round, coming back always to the fact that she would never see Lizzie again. 'Did you know she was going to die?' she said, when at last she had found her tongue. They looked at her but didn't answer. 'Well, did you? Did you know?' she demanded angrily. 'Why couldn't you tell me? Then I could have gone to see her . . . one last time . . . before . . . before . . .' She stopped, her voice choked with emotion. 'Why did she have to die?' she cried piteously.

The Reverend Widgery crossed the room and patted her on the head. 'It was God's will, child,' he said as he opened the door. She had looked at him in disbelief. If a thunderbolt had come and struck him down at that moment, she would have rejoiced.

Later, when she looked back, she could see how much easier death was for those who could see it as part of God's great plan: He had decreed it, so it had to happen, therefore it must be to some purpose. Melisande was at the same time scornful and envious: how simple it would be to sit back and say *'God's will'*. Yet what could God's purpose have been in bringing poor Lizzie into the world to suffer and die? What purpose in sending her away to strangers, away from those who loved her, and letting her die anyway, all alone?

She sat up in bed with a heavy sigh. She did not want to go to church. She had no desire to see Adam today and would much rather have locked herself away with the piano and spent the day with Tchaikovsky, but she had given her word and would not go back on it now.

Uncle George added his mite of embarrassment on the way to church by recounting to the Kingsleys the tale of Ivan, Miss Widgery and the glue pot, and everyone, including Adam, laughed at the story.

The Reverend James might not be as much a hypocrite as the Reverend Widgery, but his sermons were as long and dreary and she did not take in above one word in twenty. Her mind was beginning to wander when James Kingsley whispered in her ear: 'Does Adam come and listen to this boring claptrap every week?'

She suppressed a chuckle. 'No, not him,' she whispered, under cover of the shuffling as the congregation rose to its feet. 'But Uncle George feels obliged, because of the wedding, and Aunt Beatrice always attends the church in Edensville. It's socially correct.'

Kingsley shook with suppressed laughter. 'Oh dear,' he murmured. 'I'd better behave. Adam is frowning at me. It won't do for me to be reprimanded by my own son.' He raised his eyebrows. 'He's becoming very staid in his middle years,' he said in a stage whisper that reached his son.

'And what were you and James chuckling about in church?' asked Beatrice with a frown as they walked back to Springs House.

'Ah, that's our secret,' chuckled Mr Kingsley, who had come up with his wife on his arm just in time to hear the question. 'But you mustn't blame Miss Stevens. I'm sure she was as riveted by the minister's fascinating sermon as you and Adam were.' He looked up and caught Melisande's eye. A muscle twitched at the side of his mouth and she was hard put to it not to burst out laughing again. Then Adam came up to join them and her face fell. Hard to remember the days when she dared not catch his eye for fear of laughing at a shared joke: hard to remember they had ever enjoyed each other's company. She bit her lip hard and turned away. If only this cursed weekend were over!

After luncheon she excused herself gracefully, citing the need for constant practice as the day of the exhibition drew closer. The piano had been removed from the drawing room to the library so that she could practise undisturbed. She only rejoined the rest of the party for tea in the drawing room, and soon after, the Edensville party took their leave.

Before they were halfway to Edensville the rain had begun to fall again in heavy sheets. Melisande gazed gloomily out of the window, the grey half-light reflecting her spirits.

Adam was in the estate office, burying himself in the accounts, when there was a furious hammering on the door. Hetty was out with her young man so he crossed the hall to open the door himself.

'Why, Fritz!' he exclaimed when he saw the young Prussian who ran the mail office at the station. 'Step in, step in! This is wild weather to come all the way out from Edensville!'

'Ja, Herr Doktor!' Fritz grinned widely, exposing a large gap where his teeth had once been. 'Dis packet I got from der late train and it say on it 'Most urgent'. My Gabi, she say to me: 'Fritzi,' she say, 'I send to doctor to say urgent, he come, rain or hail, so if dis packet say urgent, you get you on dat horse and get!' So I got.' He touched his hand to his uniform cap and clicked his heels together.

When Fritz had been dispatched to the kitchens for something to warm him before he set off back, Adam turned his attention to the parcel, which turned out in the event to be addressed to his father.

'At last!' said James Kingsley, eagerly opening the parcel. 'Damned nuisance George has left. This is the information I've been waiting for about Miss Stevens!'

Colonel Randall took off his spectacles and folded them up, sighing heavily. 'You're quite confident this detective feller has got it right?' he demanded, setting the last letter down on the litter of papers that covered the table.

'Oh, yes. There's no doubt about it,' said James Kingsley. 'The only question now is what we do about it.'

'You have to tell her!' said Adam angrily.

'Of course we shall tell her,' said his father. 'But when?'

'We don't want to disturb her now, with the exhibition only a week away,' said the Colonel, twisting the ends of his moustache in some agitation. 'It might be better to wait until the exams are over.'

'Quite. After all, it's not as though we've found a lost family for her. The news we do have could well wait a week.'

'And if she wins the exhibition? What then?' demanded Adam savagely. 'Wait until that's over?' He crossed to the table and looked sombrely down at the papers. 'I don't believe you have any right to keep such news from her.'

Melisande had promised Amy and Tom that she would not spend the whole evening at the piano while they were at the theatre. She worked for a while on the difficult section in the second movement, then drifted through the house and came to rest in the living room where she sat on the sofa, idly turning the pages of the *Edensville Gazette*.

There was nothing new in its pages: an article on Cuba, one of the new American territories wrested from Spain at the Paris peace conference, an outbreak of yellow fever in New Orleans, a British expeditionary force to bring the Transvaal Boers back into line, yet more stories of fabulous wealth waiting to be discovered in the Klondike. She laid aside the journal, yawned, and stretched like a cat. She was glad she had not gone to the theatre: a little solitude was good for the soul, she decided.

The doorbell rang and she pulled a face. Perhaps she should have told Matilda she was not at home.

On the thought the maid glided into the room. 'It's the Colonel,' she said. 'Presents his compliments and apologises for disturbing you but –'

'Uncle George?' The frown on her face disappeared. 'Show him in, Matilda, if you please.'

'Mr and Mrs Kingsley are with him. And Doctor Kingsley.'

She rose to greet the unexpected visitors, but they all looked so grave that she took a swift step back.

'What is it, Uncle George?' she asked anxiously. 'Is something the matter?'

He took her hands and pressed them. 'James has some excellent news for you, my dear,' he said in a subdued voice. 'Just as I was growing used to having a daughter . . . James will explain . . .' His voice, thick with emotion, tailed away.

She looked to the others for clarification.

'You had better read these, Miss Stevens,' said James Kingsley, drawing a letter from the package in his hand. 'They arrived from England, from my solicitors. On my instructions they had been looking into how you came to be in the Orphanage.'

Her knees gave way beneath her and she sat down abruptly. 'Do not raise your hopes too high,' he warned. 'I fear we have found no lost family for you.'

411

Her hands were shaking too much to unfold the letter.

'I – I can't. Adam, please.' She thrust the letter blindly at him. 'Please read it for me.'

He unfolded the letter and began to read in a steady voice that belied the turmoil of his emotion. She heard what he read, but her dazed mind could not register it all.

We finally traced Mary Crawford, née Timson: nursemaid to the family during their residence in London. She is now living in Northamptonshire, having retired from service. Mrs Timson vigorously denied leaving the child at the Orphanage.

'It wasn't Mary,' said Melisande angrily. 'She would never have . . . Mary loved me.'

They all looked at her expectantly, but she shook her head dolefully. 'I don't remember,' she said. 'Only that she wouldn't have.'

Adam tore his eyes away from her pale face and focused again on the letter.

Timson had last heard of the child Melisande some time in June or July of '84, the year the father died, said child having been taken into the care of a foreign relation of the child's mother. This would be shortly before the child's arrival at the Orphanage. Timson understood . that the child was to be taken abroad, belief confirmed when her letters to the child were returned unopened. . . . Investigations have produced only one possible candidate for this cousin, Anne-Sophie, Frenchwoman married to the late Lord Carlen. I have as yet been unable to communicate with Lady Carlen, who is now believed to be living in Rome, having remarried.

At the mention of Lady Carlen, Melisande drew in a shuddering breath and sat bolt upright in the chair.

'Did you go to France, Mel?' asked Adam softly.

'No.'

'Do you know why the letters were returned?'

Yes, she knew. For the last curtain had finally lifted. . . .

412

For as long as she could remember there had been music in her life. As a small child she would lie in bed, watching the firelight flickering on the nursery walls while the house echoed to music. Sometimes she would be allowed to stay up and peep round the curtain to watch her father at the piano while her mother poured her heart into her song. Once she had even sat through the whole recital, the evening the Prince of Wales had come to the house.

Such happy days. In the elegant house, its tall windows looking out over the gardens of the Square where Mary sometimes took her to play, there had been no shortage of patrons at the exclusive recitals. It was not only her parents' talent that drew the guests, but the added spice of romance that clung to them. Her father Stefan, tall, dark and bearded, with a brooding Russian look about him which lightened only when his gaze fell on his slim, ethereally beautiful wife. She was as fair as he was dark, with a voice which soared like a nightingale whether she sang in her native French, English or Russian. Individually they were splendid, together they were magical, and their audiences loved them.

They had been so happy. Just Maman and Papa and Melisande, and plump, motherly Mary to sit with her, knitting by the firelight, while they gave their concerts. And then, one day, Maman had told her that soon she would have a little brother or sister to keep her company. After a while Maman had stopped singing; each evening she sat to one side, growing ever plumper, while her husband accompanied guest singers.

A few weeks before the baby was born, the doctor sent round a woman to attend Maman. Mary did not care for Nurse Perry and nor did Melisande, but Papa seemed content. Then in the middle of the night, before the doctor could be summoned, Ysabel's baby boy was born dead. Nurse Perry, the worse for drink, delivered the baby and Ysabel fell into a fever for which, despite Mary's protests, she was bled, for bleeding was then undergoing a fashionable revival as a cure for fever.

Ysabel never seemed to recover from the birth. The doctor continued to attend, but as Stefan was too distraught to perform, they could only meet his high fees by selling off, one

413

by one, every item of value in the house. Society clamoured for a while for Stefan to take up his concerts once more. Then a new Italian soprano arrived in London and became all the rage. Society moved on.

It took Ysabel a year to die. When there was nothing left to sell, when even the piano had gone, they sold the house and moved to a less select part of town. Only Mary stayed to care for the child while Stefan frantically sought for a cure which did not exist, from doctors he could not afford. He even wrote to his wife's estranged family for help. There was no reply.

They moved house three times more that year, each time just one step ahead of the bailiffs. They ended up in a slum on the edge of Seven Dials, in a mean pair of rooms in a house occupied by prostitutes and poor students. One of the students took pity on them and brought his friend, a medical student, to see Ysabel. He told Stefan, as gently as he could, that there was no cure.

'You should start to give your concerts again,' he said gently. 'You must consider your daughter.' He looked at the thin pale child in the lace-edged dress and pantaloons which no longer fitted, sitting too quietly on the rickety chair. 'How much longer can she go on like this?'

Stefan looked blankly at his daughter. He had almost forgotten her; he had certainly forgotten Mary. He was totally obsessed with his wife and the terror of losing her. He spent his last pennies on delicacies to tempt Ysabel to eat, but she was beyond all care. The next week she died.

It was midsummer, cholera season; they buried her quickly in a pauper's grave.

Melisande had not only lost her mother, she had lost her father too, for she had become no more than a shadow in his life. As he had been consumed with his love for Ysabel, now grief for the loss of her consumed him.

'Melisande needs you, Mr Stefan,' Mary said, as she rocked the grief-stricken child to sleep.

He turned to her, eyes red-rimmed in a haggard face.

'Ysabel needs me,' he said hoarsely, and rushed out of the room.

A bargeman found him three days later, face down in the River Thames.

414

'There'll have to be an inquest,' said the constable who came to tell them the tragic news. 'Misadventure or suicide. Now, ma'am,' he said to Mary, taking out his notebook and a stub of pencil, 'I'll need to know the next-of-kin.'

And that was why the tall lady had come.

Mary's heart had gone out to the child, huddled under the covers, white as her ill-fitting nightdress, looking wide-eyed at this aloof stranger who had come to take her away.

'But Lady Carlen's family, when all's said and done,' said Mary, 'and I'm not.' It had gone against the grain for her to speak well of a woman who hadn't come near them all the time her cousin was dying. But for all she has a face that'd freeze the well with a look, she told herself, she has the right.

The cross lady took Melisande from the slums and across London to her hotel in a beautiful shining carriage with four gleaming matched black horses, lecturing her throughout the journey on her good fortune in finding a relative willing to give her a roof over her head, despite the regrettable circumstances of her upbringing.

'I trust my children will be able to show you the right and proper path to follow and that you can forsake the evil ways you have trodden these last years,' she had said, her accent so much like Maman's but her words so different.

Melisande barely heard one word in twenty. The shock of her father's death so close on her mother's had shaken her mind temporarily off balance and she followed the woman like a sleepwalker into the splendid hotel, dazzled by the bright lights and frightened by the hustle and bustle.

She was handed over to a brisk nursemaid, crisp in white starched uniform, who efficiently and unemotionally prepared her for bed and then left her. Alone in the dark, lost and unloved, she cried herself to sleep.

She awoke to find herself being stared at by two grave-faced children, aged about ten and eleven. The boy was dressed in a stiff sailor suit and the girl was a hard-faced reflection of her mother, in an elegant pink dress, ruffled at hem and cuff.

'Who are you?' she demanded aggressively.

'I'm – I'm Melisande,' she whispered, resisting the temptation to slide back down the bed and pull the covers over her head and never, ever come out again.

'What a soppy name!' exclaimed the boy. He turned to his sister. 'Mama said we were not to speak to her.' He looked at the newcomer with contempt. 'Her mama was a wicked woman.'

Melisande bounced up in fury. 'No she was not!' she yelled. 'My maman was beautiful and good and – and . . .' Her face trailed off, choked in tears.

'Her?' said the boy scornfully. 'She used to sing at the Opera after she eloped with your papa, and Mama says only scarlet women and whores show themselves off at the Opera. My mama says –'

But they were never to learn what his mama had to say further on the subject, for Melisande hurled herself from the bed. 'You shan't call maman such names,' she panted, her fists flying at the face and throat of her tormentor. She knew what whores and scarlet women were: they were the women who had lived downstairs in their last lodgings, who painted their faces and wore cheap perfume.

A scene of utter chaos met Lady Carlen's eye when she entered the nursery to ascertain the cause of such a disgraceful uproar. Her son was flat on his back with the wretched brat on top of him, trying with a mad strength to throttle him, while Louisa indulged in a fit of hysterics.

For all the child was so thin and wan, it took the nurse and the footman to separate them and by that time both Melisande and her tormentor were scratched and bleeding.

'What – *what* – is the meaning of this disgraceful scene?' demanded Lady Carlen icily.

'I only told the brat we were not to speak to her because her mother was so wicked,' whined Frederick, wiping a bloody nose on his sleeve, 'and she flew at me. I swear she wished to murder me!'

'You shall not say such things of maman,' panted Melisande. 'She was kind and good and not at all wicked.' The footman unwisely slackened his grip and she turned away to steady herself on the night table, gripping the edge to stop herself shaking.

'Your mother,' said Lady Carlen, 'was a wicked, deceitful woman who ran away to live with a man to whom she was not married! She was a disgrace to our family!'

'No!' screamed Melisande in fury, and seized the candlestick from the night table, hurling it blindly in the direction of that vicious tormenting voice. Only the fact that her eyes were full of tears ruined her aim.

Matters moved swiftly after that. She was dressed once more in the clothes she had come in, her shoes were buttoned swiftly; the nurse took her down the back stairs and she was bundled into a hackney carriage with a large man with a flattened nose and heavily scarred face.

'Remember,' said the hateful voice from the shadows, 'as far from here as you can. And don't come back here unless I send for you.'

She could recall little of the journey: they seemed to be criss-crossing the city until she no longer knew where they were. After what seemed an age the cab drew up in a dark and dingy lane that led down to the river. In the distance she could hear voices shouting and ropes creaking. The burly man dismissed the cab, waited until it had disappeared round the corner, then walked her up the lane and down a maze of back alleys. They stopped in front of a gloomy and smoke-blackened building and he beat a tattoo on the door.

As the heavy door creaked open to admit them, Melisande saw a line of children crossing the yard, dressed in serge tunics and Holland aprons. She would have liked to stop and watch them, but the man urged her on through yet another door to where a thin sallow girl sat at a high old-fashioned desk, laboriously copying out rows of figures.

Her escort doffed his greasy cap and cleared his throat. 'Beggin' yer pardon, missie, this 'ere's an orphling.'

The thin girl perked up at the excuse to abandon her labour; she put down her pencil and rose with alacrity.

'Wait here please,' she said, smoothing down her dull brown skirt. 'I'll fetch Matron.'

She whisked herself out of the far door, through which tempting smells of baking bread were escaping. The man patted the child awkwardly on the shoulder. 'You'll be fine 'ere, missie. They'll look arter yer.'

When the girl returned with Matron, plump and middle-aged in a starched nurse's uniform, the little girl was standing lost and forlorn in the middle of the room, weeping.

'They put an advertisement in several newspapers, I recall,' said Melisande softly, her face white with the strain of recalling it all. 'I'd told them about Mary, you see. I didn't know she had gone to Northampton. She would never have seen it.'

Her voice shook as she remembered Mary, plump and warm and loving. 'This lady is your family, child. You must go with her. She has the right.'

'You'll want to read all these later,' said Adam, holding the papers out to her. 'When you're a little stronger . . .'

'My name,' she said softly. 'Did you – did you find out what my name was?'

'Your name was – *is* – Melisande Ysabel Stefanovna Voronzhey,' said the Colonel with a smile. 'Although I suggest you check the pronunciation with Max! Your father was – let me see –' He leafed through the bundle of papers. 'Ah, yes, here we are . . . Stefan Pyotr Vasileevich Voronzhey. But no family has as yet been traced in Russia.'

'And my mother?'

'Ysabel Hélène de Tours de Lovain. The family left France with Napoleon III in 1870. They disinherited her on her marriage. But your parents managed well enough without their approval. I recall attending a recital once, when I was home on leave. Stefan and Ysabel Voronzhey.' He shook his head sadly. 'Oh, they were the toast of English society until –'

Until.

She could see Papa, with that desolate look on his face, crying: 'Ysabel needs me!' and she began to weep, for him, for her mother, for herself.

Adam caught her hands in his. 'Don't cry, my –' He bit his lip. 'Mel, please don't cry.'

'Give me your place, Adam,' said Amelia Kingsley calmly. 'Fetch some wine for her, if you please. She's had a shock. There's no way to prepare someone for news like that. 'Now, my dear,' she said bracingly. 'What good news, to be sure. Now you will be able to graduate as Miss Voronzhey. How proud your parents would have been!' Mel gave a watery sniff. 'I know how hard it must seem, but really you would not have turned out at all well under Lady Carlen's care. Frederick is a wastrel and a spendthrift and that daughter of hers one of the most unpleasant women I know. You would not have wished to be beholden to them, I promise you!'

'It's just been – rather a shock, you see,' said Mel, smiling mistily through her tears. 'To have acquired a background again after so many years of being nameless! And to remember all the things I had forgotten for so long.' Adam handed her a glass of wine and she blushed as their hands brushed.

'Drink it down,' he said levelly. 'All of it.'

She dragged her eyes from him with an effort and did as she was told. As the wine coursed through her she turned back to Amelia. 'If my mother had not fallen ill . . . if they had continued to give recitals and – What would be their – my – position in Society?'

'As Miss Voronzhey? You would have moved in the highest circles, my dear. The Prince of Wales himself was most fond of their recitals. Even now, if you were to return, I could launch you into London Society tomorrow if you wished.'

Mel turned eagerly to Adam, her heart in her eyes, and recoiled in shock at the black scowl on his face.

'You are . . . not pleased?' Her eyes pleaded with him to share her joy.

His eyes glittered angrily. 'Oh, yes. Delighted for you.' He ground the words out between his teeth. 'Now you can throw our help back at us, abandon Harbourside, take the first boat back to England!' He slammed his glass down on the table and turned on his heel. 'I only hope it does not turn out to be empty glory for you!' he said savagely.

'Adam!' Amelia made to follow him, but the door slammed behind him.

'Leave him, Amelia,' said James as his wife muttered angrily under her breath. 'It has been a strange day. I daresay we all need some time to come to terms with the revelations.'

Mel's sleep that night was the deep sleep of emotional exhaustion with the aid of several drops of laudanum administered by Beatrice. Her dreams were vivid, peopled with figures from the past. Now the floodgates of memory had been opened, scenes from her childhood poured from her subconscious and much that she had forgotten came flooding back. But it was all mixed up. One minute she was in the Orphanage kitchen stealing apples for the horses, then Ned and Dobbin were hitched to the cab which had taken her to Wapping. She ran away from it, but when she looked over her shoulder in terror she saw John Thomsett urging his steeds on to overtake her. Next time she looked it was Vilaghy. She could see the tower of St Mark's ahead of her, but she knew she could not reach it before the coach was upon her. Behind her, hands reached down from the carriage to clutch at her. Ahead of her she could see Adam coming down the road, his hands held out to her. Then he looked at her, disdain in his eyes, turned and walked away.

'I really wish Uncle George had consulted us before he spoke,' said Amy, not for the first time. 'To overwhelm her so, so close to the examinations . . .'

'I don't believe she will let it distract her,' said Tom. 'What with that and all the preparations for your mother's wedding, she's scarcely had time to worry about today.'

The subject, perforce, was dropped as Matilda came into the breakfast room with the post, followed by Melisande.

'A beautiful day,' observed Tom. 'Shall you cycle to the college or walk with me?'

She shrugged indifferently. 'It scarcely seems worth going at all,' she said gloomily, helping herself to a cup of coffee.

'Why?' exclaimed Amy in lively astonishment.

'I should have been satisfied with the teaching diploma. It was foolish to be so ambitious.'

'Mel, they wouldn't have let you enter for the exhibition if they did not think you had a chance of taking it,' said Tom with a ghost of a smile.

'Gilles is bound to take it,' she said, refusing to be cheered up. 'Or Clive, if the judges are – who are the judges, Tom? Do you know?'

'The Principal from Rochester University, the head of music here, Professor Chardin, and Madame Giotto, who as you know will provide the other half of the concert. Though why you want to know, if you're not planning to go . . .'

'Tom, don't tease!' said Amy with a frown.

'I'd go if I were you,' he said, unperturbed. 'I agree you have stiff competition from Gilles. Farson says he's matured beyond all expectation these last few months. But as for Trensham – if he wins the exhibition with his cold, passionless playing, I shall confess myself greatly surprised. Of course, there are a number of entrants from out of town, and we don't know anything about them, but I should say you are certainly in with a good chance.'

'But Tom –'

'And it would be a shame to disappoint all your friends,' he said with a grin, passing her a pile of letters.

They had all written to wish her good luck – or nearly all. There was a note from Max, even one from the Jeffersons out at Carfax, but nothing from Adam.

Tom walked her up to college.

'Relax, Mel,' he said, giving her an encouraging smile. 'Remember, you can only do your best.' He put his arm round her shoulder and gave her a quick hug.

She took her place outside the recital hall in the afternoon, and buried her head in her music, preferring not to be distracted by the others. It was a waste of time, of course, since she had no means of telling which part of the concerto the judges would wish to hear. They had heard all the soloists entered for the exhibition in rehearsal with the college orchestra in the course of the last few weeks and today they would specify those passages they wished to hear again. The soloists went in in a steady stream until there was only herself, Gilles, and two out-of-towners left.

'Miss Voronzhey!' She stood up with a start – so Tom had told them to change her name! – and dropped her music on the floor.

'You may take your seat again, Miss Voronzhey,' said the clerk in a high-pitched voice that grated on the ear. 'The examiners will stop for tea after they have heard Mr de Villeneuve. You, Miss Clark and Miss Carlssen may retire and reassemble in half an hour.'

Gilles gave her a strange look – she would have to explain later. She longed to be on her own, to keep up her concentration, but if a half-hour delay was vexing to her, it must be worse for the other two young women, waiting around in a strange college.

'Should you like to step outside for a moment, to catch a breath of fresh air?' she asked.

421

They accepted with alacrity, following her out into the courtyard where the pale stone walls caught the late afternoon sun. She showed them the way to the ladies' common room, in case they should wish to avail themselves of the cloakrooms, pointed out the door in the ivy-hung wall that led back into the corridor outside the recital hall, and then slipped away to try to compose herself once more.

The rest of the afternoon passed as if in a dream. Summoned into the hall, she shook hands with the judges and Mr Farson without really taking in what either she or they were saying, and seated herself at the piano. She began to set out her music like an automaton but then her attention was caught by a ray of sun that slanted across the room, little dust motes dancing in its beam, and she gazed at it fascinated.

'Miss Voronzhey? Miss Voronzhey?' She dragged her gaze back to the judges. 'Whenever you are ready, Miss Voronzhey,' said Professor Chardin. Mr Farson gave her an encouraging smile.

She poised her hands above the keys and heard again that voice saying: 'Go with the music, my darling.'

She took a deep breath. Maman, Papa, she thought, this is for you. And the music flowed from her, a celebration, a triumph, a dedication. As the last resounding chord died away, a bird outside the window began to sing.

By seven in the evening, the judges had finished their deliberations and the candidates assembled in the Perry Hall to hear the results. Tom had explained to Melisande that the graduation ceremony would only be for those who had completed the full course.

'That hardly seems fair,' she said. 'Most of us will have worked far harder than the full-time students in order to fit everything in.'

He shrugged. 'But equally, most of the teachers will be back at their posts by the time the graduation ceremony comes round. They will get their certificates in the post. But all the music graduates get their results on the day of the examinations, when the exhibition is announced.'

A hush fell over the rows of students as the principal, resplendent in his academic robes, mounted the dais, a sheaf of papers in his hands. Professor Chardin and Madame Giotto sat behind him with a number of the other professors.

Melisande couldn't bring herself to listen, couldn't start to think about what would happen next. She knew she had played well today, perhaps better than she had ever played in her life, but the others would have played well too. She wasn't even sure whether she'd be disappointed if she didn't win: she guessed it would depend in the end on who did take it. Gilles on a good day would be most deserving of the prize. Uncharitably she found herself hoping anyone would win – so long as it was not Clive Trensham. She couldn't look at the others; she found herself examining the ornately carved and painted ceiling as if her life depended on knowing exactly how many garlands and sprigs, how many county emblems there were entwined on it.

'In the few years that the college has been examining students for graduation . . .' she heard him say '. . . so much talent . . . every student has been awarded a diploma.' A sigh of relief ran round the hall and she forced herself to attend to his words.

Professor Chardin read out the list of students in alphabetical order. Five students, among them Clive Trensham, Gilles de Villeneuve and Melisande had graduated *cum laude*.

The applause died down and they waited with bated breath while the Principal came forward once more with a card in his hand. He surveyed the rows of anxious upturned faces. 'And now – the exhibition,' he said with a prim smile. 'An extremely hard task to decide who should have the honour of representing us at the City Hall concert.'

'Why doesn't he just tell us and cut the cackle!' Gilles hissed savagely in Mel's ear. She could only agree with him.

'Impossible to choose between them . . . and so with Madame Giotto's approval we have expanded the programme to include both piano and violin solos.'

Mel grabbed Gilles's hand and squeezed it painfully hard. He had been one of the three violinists, together with Clive Trensham and Jeremy Harper, who had submitted both violin and piano pieces.

'. . . and so we congratulate Mr de Villeneuve and Miss Voronzhey.'

She felt like yelling out loud, she felt like dancing a jig in the middle of the hall. Instead she clutched Gilles's hand even tighter and in a daze went up to the platform with him to receive their awards. The Principal shook hands with them and Madame Giotto clasped them both dramatically to her bolster of a bosom. Gilles, emerging from the suffocating embrace, caught Mel's eye and with a quirky lift of the eyebrow acknowledged the comic picture they made. Mel had to bite her lip to stop herself laughing out loud.

There were more speeches before she and Gilles were whisked off to an anteroom where they were honoured to take refreshments with Madame Giotto and the visiting academics.

Tom had to tear her away from Gilles, who was still babbling excitedly to her as she fetched her wrap.

'You can have her tomorrow, Gilles,' he said firmly. 'Tonight I have a houseful of people desperate to hear her results.'

She walked home with Tom through the twilight.

'You have a busy few weeks ahead of you,' said Tom as they walked home through the twilight. 'The concert and then the wedding . . . I don't know how we'll fit it all in!'

'I can't believe this is all happening to me,' Melisande murmured in amazement. 'Me, Milly from Wapping, playing the piano in City Hall!'

'Not 'Milly from Wapping',' said Tom. 'Miss Voronzhey.'

She turned to him, her face serious. 'But don't you see, Tom? However I started out in life, whatever I achieve, part of me will still always be Milly from Wapping, because that was such a large part of my life.'

The others had given up waiting and dined without them, but no sooner had Tom set his hand on the gate than the door flew open and three anxious faces appeared.

'Mel, m'dear,' boomed the Colonel. 'Been thinkin' about you all day. How was it? Not too nerve-wracking, I hope?'

'George, come out of the doorway and let them in!' Beatrice chided him, 'Mel, dear, you have your diploma?'

'Of course she has her diploma,' said Tom, winking at Mel behind everyone's back while he took her coat. 'We're very hungry, Amy,' he said soulfully. 'The Principal is not over-generous with his refreshments and what little there was Madame Giotto disposed of.'

424

'Matilda is setting supper for you in the dining room.'

'The – ah – the exhibition?' said the Colonel diffidently. 'That damned young whippersnapper Trensham, I suppose?'

'No,' said Tom, holding out a chair for Mel as Matilda set the table with a cold collation.

'Dammit, who then?' roared the Colonel.

'George!' exclaimed Beatrice.

'Never known someone make such a hash of telling his tale!' protested George. 'Anyone would think it was a state secret. Dammit, it's worse than drawing teeth, trying to get information out of the boy. Why, he –'

'Gilles de Villeneuve won the exhibition,' said Tom, a look of wounded innocence on his face.

'That's not so bad. He –'

'And so did your adopted daughter!'

Everyone jumped up from the table again and there was a great deal of hugging and laughter. Colonel Randall was inclined to take the huff with Tom for his teasing, but Amy pointed out that if he planned to marry her mother, it was time he got used to his future son-in-law's strange sense of humour.

'To Melisande!' said Tom, raising his glass.

'And to all your achievements,' added the Colonel.

She blushed. 'It's more than I could ever have hoped for in my wildest dreams,' she said softly. She raised her glass to them. 'To all the friends who made it possible.' And, a little sadly, she added under her breath: 'To the one who isn't here.'

It was a frantic week, with all the arrangements for the wedding and the dress fittings to be arranged around the rehearsals in the City Hall. The exhibitioners had only given the final movements in their examinations, now they had to work up the entire concerto with the newly founded New York Orchestra under Emil Paur.

'Nearly a hundred men – and us!' said Gilles with a gulp. And Emil Paur, a striking figure with a leonine head and a reputation that went before him, made it quite clear that he was not prepared to make any allowances for the fact that they were students.

'Perfection!' he demanded. 'We start at eight o'clock Monday morning – and we work until we get it right!'

It was in great fear and trepidation that Melisande and Gilles arrived at the City Hall Theatre, shortly to be renamed the Dewey Theatre, in honour of the victor of the battle of Manila. To play on stage, on a superb instrument, and with such a large orchestra was not at all the same as playing with one's fellow students. But within the hour, their fear had evaporated. Paur might be demanding, but he would always give credit where credit was due. 'You have clearly been well taught,' he conceded at the end of the first day. 'I see no problems in attaining our goal in time. The Midsummer Concert will be the best Edensville has seen!'

Of course Mel couldn't leave without visiting Mr and Mrs James.

'Well, I'll be hog-tied!' exclaimed Mr James when his wife brought Mel upstairs after the first rehearsal. 'Our own Miss Smith, up there on the stage! Whoever would have thought it!'

Certainly not Melisande. She could scarcely believe she had been up on the stage, sitting at the elegant instrument, discussing with the famous conductor, Emil Paur, how she would like the orchestra to take the slow movement!

'We'll have to have a new robe made for the concert, of course,' said Beatrice, looking up, rather harassed, from the list she was compiling. 'It's short notice, but if Madame Lasky's cannot do it in time, we must try Maison Louise. Really, I don't know how we are to manage, with the wedding the day after the Midsummer Concert! If only Tom had told me. . . . Perhaps we ought to postpone the wedding?'

'Under no circumstances!' said Mel, horrified at the suggestion. 'Uncle George would be devastated!'

'But how shall you manage?'

'Very well. Two exciting days and then I daresay I shall sleep for a week while you are away on your honeymoon trip. And I don't want a new gown, Aunt Beatrice,' she said firmly. 'I had much rather wear the one with the rosebuds – the one I had for the Harvest Ball. With the train removed I believe it will do very well.'

'And a lace fichu inset into the decolletage. . . . Yes.' Beatrice tapped the pen against her cheek. 'New slippers and sash, of course. Gold tissue, perhaps? And the ivory satin will stand out beautifully against the black of the orchestra.' She looked at Mel with a small frown between her brows. 'Are you quite sure? You're not just trying to make life easier for me?'

'That too. But I promise you, I will feel much happier in a dress I know, one that won't restrict me. Mr Paur says it's a mistake amateurs often make.'

'That's settled then,' said Beatrice with a sigh of relief. 'When Madame Lasky comes for the fitting for the bridesmaid's dress, she can take your gown away with her.'

Beatrice was now spending almost every day at Amy's house, as it was more convenient for the dressmaker's and all the friends making bride visits and bringing wedding gifts. Uncle George, inevitably, gravitated there in the course of each day and Amy was busy keeping everyone calm and organised at the same time. The little house was bursting at the seams even before Bella and John arrived from Albany and Mel regarded her time at Harbourside school as a welcome break from the constant comings and goings.

She had just finished locking up the schoolroom the last day before the concert when she decided, on the spur of the moment, to call at the dispensary to visit Harriet Minton. She had been inspecting the seating plan in Mr James's office the previous day and found that though the Kingsleys had two seats next to the Randall's party, there was no booking under Doctor Kingsley's name. There were two seats in the name of Minton and one under Ellsky, which made her wonder whether Adam was perhaps coming with Harriet. She desperately hoped so: it was not just because she loved him that she wanted him to be there, but because he was the one man above all who had made all this possible. Without him, she would still be just Milly the housemaid. It was foolish, but she did not want to go into the concert tomorrow without knowing whether he would be there, and if it meant asking Harriet straight out whether she was coming with Adam, then she would ask her.

The sun was reflecting off the warehouse windows as she turned the corner into Harbourside; dazzled, she did not see the two men until she was almost on top of them.

427

'Father Kerrigan! Why, I didn't see you there,' she said, shading her eyes to try and make out the other man's features.

'Sergeant Fielden, miss,' said Kerrigan's companion, touching his cap in a sketchy salute. 'We was just comin' to see you. Seein' as there was no one at the dispensary.'

'I tell you, it's not the dispensary we need to see,' said Kerrigan, his neck bulging redly over his clerical collar as he grew more agitated.

'So you say, Father, so you say. But I think you'd best be leavin' this to me.' He turned back to Melisande. 'Miss Stevens, I'd like to be askin' you a few questions, if that's all right with you?'

Kerrigan snorted derisively. It was clear it was only with great difficulty that he was keeping his temper.

'Me?' said Mel in some surprise. 'How may I help you? Is it one of the children?'

'I'm thinkin' we shouldn't be discussing this on a street corner,' said Officer Fielden. 'Perhaps if we go back to the school?'

'It's the police station you should be taking her to, not the school. Those mothers of hers get a whiff of this, you could have a riot on your hands,' warned Kerrigan ominously.

'Riot?' said Mel, wrinkling her brow. 'Father Kerrigan, what are you talking about?'

Fielden cast a darkling look at the priest. Mopping his brow he turned back to Melisande. 'I don't like to be askin' a young lady like yourself down to the police station,' he protested.

'I wish I knew what all this was about,' she said, a puzzled frown on her face.

'This is what it's about,' said Fielden, drawing a few sheets of paper out of his pocket. His face reddened as he opened them out to reveal Mel's neat handwriting under an illustration. 'Is this your hand or isn't it?'

'It is.'

'Then I am arresting you, Miss Stevens, for publishing abroad – er –'

'Obscene publications!' said Kerrigan under his breath.

Fielden mopped his brow again. 'Obscene publications,' he said in strangled tones, 'in direct breach of the Comstock laws.'

It was a nightmare.

Melisande sat on the wooden bench and looked up at the grille set high up in the outside wall, watching the sky change from pale azure to marine. It was a clear night, but she could only see one star from where she was sitting. She took a deep breath in – one, two, three, four – held it, then let it slowly out – one, two, three, four. If she could keep doing this, she told herself, then the racing of her heart and the thumping in her head would slow down to a more bearable rhythm.

Down the corridor a drunk was shouting for a lawyer, threatening to sue anyone who didn't *immediately* bring him a key and grant him his rights under the Constitution. He'd been shouting the same phrases over and over again for the last hour. Mel knew his speech off by heart. As he paused briefly to rest his tired voice she heard the sound of someone relieving themselves in a bucket.

She had forgotten to count; she had lost the rhythm. Her hands writhed in her lap, her nails digging into her flesh. Panic began to creep over her, panic such as she had not felt for years, not since the door punishment at the Orphanage.

It had been the door punishment above all else that had made of her the biddable child – Matron's little helper, as Aggie had once rather scornfully called her. Until the day of the last door punishment, she had been as mischievous as the others, as likely to get into trouble as anyone else – more so, sometimes, as her quick mind had often been the one to think up mischief: whether putting double measure of yeast in a loaf batch, so that the bread came out of the oven with the tin baked inside it, or convincing Hannah, the bully of the girls' dormitory, that the basement was haunted, and waiting till she was coming up the whitewashed steps carrying a bucket of coal to Matron's room before waggling a sheet on a broom handle round the stairbend at her.

At first she had accepted her punishment, because she knew she deserved it, but two days on bread and water was not that great a punishment for children raised on the Orphanage diet, and Matron turned next to the door punishment, where a child was locked in the narrow space between the two sets of double doors that separated Matron's room from the rest of the building. The first time shut away in the dark and silence Melisande had been frightened; the second terrified; the third time, when Matron had been called away to an accident on the boys' side and had forgotten her altogether, they had found her at the end of the day barely conscious, her fingertips torn and bloodied where she had tried to fight her way through the solid wood.

But she couldn't allow herself to think about that now. That way lay total panic. Now she had to think what to do, what to say. Someone was coming to take a statement from her soon and she had to get it right. She forced herself to shut out the Orphanage, shut out tomorrow's concert and work out how to get out of this mess without ruining everyone else in the process.

Her first instinct had been to demand that they send for Adam, for Uncle George, for anyone who could get her out of the jail, but caution had stepped in and shown her the folly of first instincts. She remembered what Harriet had said about the dangers of their work. If she involved Adam in any way, he could be sent to prison for years, like the printer. He might never be able to practise again; the dispensary would be closed down and the Mrs Vaasanens of Harbourside would be driven back to the butchers to save their health and their sanity.

No. Adam and Harriet must be kept out of it, she decided. In which case she would have to have her own story ready. She had, after all, already admitted that the translation was in her own hand.

Adam was playing billiards with his father when the letter came for George.

'Boy as helps out in the stableyard back of the police station brought it,' said the maid. 'Said it was urgent.'

Kingsley frowned at the badly folded, rather grubby piece of cheap paper. 'Perhaps I'd better send Jason over with it.'

'No need,' said Adam, laying his cue aside. 'Time I set off back home. I'll drop it in on my way. You've beaten me fair and square.'

'You could stop by anyway and congratulate Mel on her success,' said his father rather sharply as the door closed behind the maid. 'Beatrice told Amelia Mel was quite hurt that –'

'I'd be grateful if Beatrice and Amelia would refrain from discussing me and my affairs!' snapped Adam furiously. There was a moment's uncomfortable silence. 'No, I didn't mean that, Father,' he said stiffly. 'I apologise. But at the moment I can do nothing right as far as Melisande is concerned. The last thing I want to do is upset her at such an important time, so it's best if I just keep away from her.'

He had intended to drop the letter at Amy's house and not stop, but when Matilda opened the door, George was standing in the hall, shrugging himself into his coat.

'A little late for your club?' joked Adam. 'And quite twenty-four hours too early for a stag party, I'd have thought.'

'Enough of your cheek, young man,' said George frostily. 'I have more important matters on my mind than clubs, I promise you. Melisande hasn't returned home from Harbourside.'

'*What?* But she must have finished hours ago!'

'As a matter of fact I was just coming to see your father. Ask him to sit with the ladies while Tom and I go out looking for her.' He looked at him under his brows. 'You haven't seen her?'

'No.' Adam held out the letter. 'But there is this.'

'Oh Lord,' said the Colonel in a hoarse whisper. 'Do you think her nerve has cracked? Did we push her too far?'

'Nonsense,' said Adam briskly. 'She coped with the concert at Christmas, didn't she? Besides, this doesn't look like Amy's usual scented notepaper to me.'

'Of course not.' George perked up again. 'Probably nothing to do with Mel. She –'

Adam felt his stomach sinking. 'George,' he said sombrely. 'Your maid says this was brought by the boy who works in the stableyard at the back of the police station.'

He wished he hadn't spoken as George turned a very unhealthy shade of grey. 'Come into the study,' he said with a calmness he didn't feel. 'Let's not go thinking the worst before we've even read it.' He turned to Matilda. 'Would you please ask Mr Bennet to join us?'

Dear Guardian,

431

There has been a slight misunderstanding over some assistance I was able to render to one of the Harbourside women and I am at present being held in the police station. I don't want to cause any agitation elsewhere but I've explained to them that all I did was to translate the instructions on a pot of salve. However, there is some confusion and Father Kerrigan has invoked something called the Comstock laws. I wouldn't want you to trouble *anyone else*, but would be grateful if you, dear Guardian, could come and persuade them to let me out of this place as soon as possible.

Your little Melisande

'Damn you, Adam,' said the Colonel in a choked voice. 'This is your doing! How dare you get her involved in such matters? You and Miss Minton with your fine, high-flown ideas! And now Mel – with the concert tomorrow, for God's sake! – is taking the punishment for you!'

'Not a moment longer than it needs for me to take her place, I assure you!' said Adam, his face white with fury.

'Hold hard,' said Tom mildly. 'I don't think you've quite understood –'

'What is there to understand?' demanded Adam, his voice cracking with emotion. 'She's locked up in that filthy jail for something I should never have asked her to do.'

'That's one thing we are agreed on,' said the Colonel huskily, dropping the letter as he sank his head in his hands.

Tom picked up the piece of paper. 'But you are jumping to the wrong conclusions here,' he said, stepping between Adam and the door. 'Don't you see, she –' ·

'Dammit, Tom!' exploded Adam. 'There's no time for talking! Get out of my way!'

'Not until you've read this again. Look –'

'I'm warning you, Tom!' said Adam dangerously, his hands clenching at his sides.

'Damn you, Adam, will you shut up and listen!' yelled Tom. 'She's done her best to pull all your chestnuts out of the fire for you, and if you go charging in there like – like a bull in a china shop, you'll wreck it all: for you, for Harriet, maybe for Mel too!' He turned to George for support. 'Think,

George!' he pleaded. 'Isn't there something very odd about this letter? When did Mel ever call herself 'little Melisande', for God's sake? When did she ever call you 'Guardian' for that matter? And all that underscoring – more like Michaela Jennings's breathless style, wouldn't you agree?'

'It is very odd,' conceded the Colonel. 'But the strain of the situation –'

'Strain? My –' He took a deep breath and swallowed the expletive. 'It's as clear as the nose on your face if you just stop to think about it,' he said. 'When is her birthday, George?'

'What the hell has that to do with anything?' demanded Adam.

'Next week,' said George. 'Beatrice was most upset when she realised we would not be here for her coming of age. We – By God!' he exclaimed.

'At last,' sighed Tom. 'She's *under-age*, George. Guardian. Little Melisande. She's handing it to you on a plate. They've taken a young lady – as far as the world is concerned, a gently brought up young lady from a family prominent in Society – and locked her up in a jail, not even bothered to inform her guardian of it. What would Society have to say about that, eh? Your friend Judge Stanisforth, for example, whose son was dancing with her only last week at the Hutchinsons' ball?'

'But it doesn't alter the fact that the law is on their side,' said Adam. 'Giving advice on birth control is illegal.'

'But you don't give advice on birth control, do you?'

'No. We are always very careful about that.'

'That's what Mel has said, isn't it? And it's what we must stick to. All she did was to translate the instructions on – well, you know the wording you use.'

'Salve. Prescribed for irritation of the internal passages.'

'Well, I don't think we'll have to worry too much about that,' said Tom hastily, aware that George was becoming a little hot under the collar. 'Mark my words, if we hit them hard enough with false arrest, detaining a minor without informing her family, they'll be only too glad to let her go with the minimum of fuss.'

'Then what are we waiting for?' demanded Adam.

'What do you mean 'we'?' said Tom. 'You are keeping as far away from it all as possible. Mel has gone to a great deal of trouble to keep you and the dispensary out of this. And, by God, that's the way it's going to stay!'

'Miss Stevens,' said the sergeant, leaning against the bars and passing his hand over his tired eyes, 'if you could just answer me questions, we could all get some sleep.'

'Miss Voronzhey. And I have answered your question,' she said briskly. 'You asked me if that is my handwriting. I confirm that it is. As requested by one of the women who live in Harbourside, I translated the instructions on a bottle from the chemist.'

'Which woman?'

'I have no idea. I have translated instructions on a variety of bottles and jars of pills, medicines and salves for a variety of people who speak no English.'

He ran his hand despairingly through his hair. 'Miss Stevens, you promised me you'd cooperate.'

'I have done so,' she said coolly.

'You promised me you'd write out a statement and –'

'I have mislaid the paper you left.' She looked vaguely around the cell, as if she expected to see it under the wooden shelf that served as a bed. 'If you care to bring me some more . . . But I cannot really tell you any more than I have already done. And now I am very tired and thoroughly bored with this cell. I have a concert tomorrow at City Hall, so, if you please, either charge me or let me go home.'

He laughed, a barking, contemptuous sound. 'A concert tomorrow at City Hall? Holy Mother! And I'm the President of the United States!'

There was an outburst of arguing at the door to the outer office. She looked up and to her delight saw Tom and Uncle George shouldering their way through past the guard with the police captain in their wake, bleating feebly about 'information laid' and 'reasonable cause'.

George Randall pulled himself up to his full height, moustaches bristling, the shades of centuries of British imperial armies lining up behind him. 'I don't want to hear any more excuses, sir!' he boomed. 'You may save them for all the others you have to convince. Such as the City Councillors. Yes, sir, the City Councillors! You would be better employed working out how you can explain to them that the City Hall Midsummer Subscription Concert is one soloist short because you've taken to locking up pianists on charges you're not even sure exist, solely on the word of some religious bigot who has a quarrel with the Eden County Education Board! Work out how you can explain to the Principal of the College that you have locked up his star pupil – a minor to boot! – for the crime of translation! Work out how you can explain to Judge Stanisforth why the young lady he's giving a dinner for next week has spent a night shut up with thieves and murderers in the City Jail!'

The captain cracked. 'Get her out!' he said to Maloney, poised with his notebook and a stub of pencil at the bars of cell number twenty-three.

The door swung open and Mel flew out of the cell and into their welcoming arms.

'Oh, I thought I'd never get out of there!' she exclaimed. 'I was so frightened. I –'

'Hush, Mel,' said Tom firmly. 'Time enough for that when we get you home.'

'Take her home and welcome,' called the drunk in the nearby cell as they passed by, the officer obsequiously opening doors for them and stressing that the arrest was an unfortunate misunderstanding and nothing – absolutely nothing – to do with him. 'At least a body will be able to get some sleep around here without that lunatic bustin' into song!'

They bustled her quickly out into the waiting carriage and Sam turned the horses homeward.

'Uncle George, you were magnificent!' she exclaimed. 'That poor man didn't know what had hit him!'

'It was touch and go till then,' said Tom.

'Never mind all that,' said Uncle George. 'Are you all right, child? I've been so worried!'

'I'm fine now,' she said. She knew she could not tell him – or anyone – about those dreadful minutes when panic had almost overtaken her; even to think about it made her start to shake again. She had to put it out of her mind, at least for the next few days. When the concert was over, and the wedding, then she would deal with it. Not now.

435

'I'm fine,' she repeated. 'It all just seems like a bad dream. I scarcely know whether to laugh or cry!'

'A good meal, a bath and bed is what you need,' said Tom. 'I can see you don't really want to talk about it, but just tell me one thing. What was all that about singing?'

'Oh, that was so they wouldn't realise I was talking to Feodor,' she said.

'Feodor?'

'One of the boys from Harbourside. He works at the stables behind the police station and he'd seen them bring me in. I'd been wracking my brains to think how to get in touch with you – they wouldn't let me send a letter, you see, in case I wanted to 'alert my accomplices'. So when Feodor appeared at the window – he brought one of the horses across and stood on its back! – I started singing my instructions to him. In Russian, of course. Told him I'd try to write a letter, told him where to take it. Then all I had to do was get hold of some paper. So I told them I'd write out a statement if only they'd leave me in peace. And I wrote the letter and threw it out to Feodor.'

Back at the house Adam was pacing the floor in Tom's study. As he heard their footsteps on the porch he shot out of the room and opened the door before Matilda was half way up the stairs.

'Thank God!' he exclaimed, dashing forward to grasp her hands in his. 'Mel, you little fool! Whatever possessed you to go rushing in like that? You should have told them it was nothing to do with you. Do you think I would have let you go to prison in my place? I –'

The touch of his hands on hers was the last straw and the tears she had been fighting back welled up in her eyes.

'I am sorry if I deprived you of a chance at martyrdom,' she said, snatching her hands away swiftly, 'but this seemed like the better way.' She crossed to the door. 'Now, if you'll excuse me I'm very tired.'

'Mel, that wasn't what I meant at all. I just wanted to thank you for –'

'There's no need, Doctor Kingsley,' she said coldly. 'I didn't do it for you. I did it for Mrs Vaasanen and the women of Harbourside.'

436

They left her to sleep through the morning and she rose refreshed, determined to put the previous day's experience out of her mind. The concert was more important than anything else: she might never again have such a wonderful opportunity and she would *not* permit anything else to over shadow it.

There was the final fitting for the bridesmaid's dress to distract her mind until luncheon was served, and at two o'clock Gilles came to take her to the final rehearsal.

'He's terribly nervous,' said Amy to her mother, as Melisande fetched her wrap. 'Can't sit down for two minutes together. I hope he doesn't affect her too. After yesterday –'

But Beatrice was unperturbed as she waved them off. 'Mark my words,' she said to her daughter, 'if I know Mel, she'll forget her own nervousness in trying to calm him down.'

By the time they reached City Hall, she had not only calmed Gilles down, but had succeeded in making him smile once more. Mr James was waiting for them at the door and ushered them in. With Mr Paur they ran through the programme – and how different it was playing on a stage, on a grand piano, and with a full orchestra! – timing the items and the intervals and rehearsing the little duet Madame Giotto assured them they would need for the expected encore.

Paur was a hard taskmaster and he had told them from the start that he was not prepared to make any allowances for the fact that they were only students, but at last even he was satisfied and the orchestra packed up their instruments and filed out of the hall.

Beatrice was waiting anxiously for her return. 'Did it go well, my dear?' she asked.

'Yes. Mr Paur seemed to be satisfied.'

'Then why the long face?'

She shrugged. 'Oh – nothing. It doesn't matter.'

'Clearly it does.'

'It's just that – I thought Adam was – that he would –'

'We were all disappointed when he declined the invitation to join our party. But he's a grown man, my dear. We cannot force him to come.'

'I know. And I know I shouldn't care. It's just that, without him, none of this would have happened. I just – I thought he'd have wanted to see it through.'

'All the other people who love you will be there,' said Beatrice softly. 'We all want to share in your special evening. Now, off with you and rest. I'll waken you in plenty of time.'

'I'm far too excited to sleep,' protested Mel, suppressing a yawn with some difficulty. Beatrice just smiled.

By seven o'clock she was at the City Hall, exquisitely dressed from the top of her neat coiffure to the toes of her dainty golden slippers. She stood with Gilles in the wings watching the orchestra setting up the music, listening to the audience coming in, buying programmes, taking their seats, chatting to one another. As the murmur of the crowd swelled, so did the excitement that coursed through her. There was no fear now, just a swift surge of energy that made her eager to go out on to the stage and get on with it.

Madame Giotto came to take a peep at the numbers, declared herself satisfied and returned to her dressing room, her opulent robe of gold satin billowing behind her. The more nervous Gilles became, the more frantically he flirted with Mel, but she was on another plane and scarcely noticed it.

From where they stood they could see the corner of the circle and just before the doors closed, Melisande saw out of the corner of her eye someone apparently trying to attract her attention. She shaded her eyes and squinted past the stage lights until she finally made out Tadeusz and Agnete sitting in the front row! Behind them she thought she could make out the looming bulk of Mrs Lenkowa – but surely she must be mistaken! Mrs Lenkowa at a City Hall concert? As the lights came up on the orchestra she could have sworn she saw a familiar figure behind them, running his fingers through his hair, but she knew it must have been just another illusion.

Emil Paur stopped briefly to wish them good luck, then strode on stage to take his bow, followed by Nahan Franko.

She looked at Gilles and saw the blood drain from his face.

'I can't do it!' he said in panic.

'Of course you can,' said Mel, and with a boldness that surprised her, she gave him a swift hug, kissed him on the cheek and pushed him gently through the curtains.

He took a deep breath then, head high, stepped forward to take his bow. A brief pause, then Paur raised his baton,

438

brought in the orchestra and Gilles came in confidently on cue.

Mel crept away to the second dressing room and picked up her music. After a few moments she laid it aside again. She already knew it as thoroughly as anyone – including, she thought with a rueful smile, Peter Ilyich Tchaikovsky himself. She lay back on the chaise longue, closed her eyes and tried to relax.

It seemed only a few moments later that Gilles finished with the familiar flourish to rapturous applause and Madame Giotto was on stage, pouring her golden voice into the night air.

Immediately after the interval, Madame Giotto sang the last of her sentimental ballads and then Emil Paur came to lead Melisande on to the stage. She shook hands with the leader of the orchestra, curtsied gracefully and took her seat at the piano, arranging her skirts around her so that she was not restricted.

As the conductor took his place, she closed her eyes briefly to compose herself. 'For you, Maman. For you, Papa,' she murmured. She looked up, caught sight of Paur, baton raised, awaiting her signal, and felt an absurd desire to giggle at the thought of the power she held. Sternly she pulled herself together. For you too, Peter Ilyich, she thought irreverently. Then she nodded to the conductor and the three resounding arpeggios from the brass ushered in the performance of her life.

The first movement she played with controlled passion, her fingers flying over the keys, matching the flourishes and the great swoops of emotion to the dramatic outpourings of the orchestra until they reached the climax of the soloist's skill and the last liquid notes of the first movement fell into an appreciative silence. All thought of nervousness had long since been left behind and as her fingers sped over the keys she was at one with the music. The whole world had shrunk to encompass only her and the music, and she was no longer aware where she finished and the music began. Time seemed suspended. All too soon she was playing her final notes, and the orchestra brought the concerto to a close.

The applause was deafening, but Melisande was rooted to her seat. If the conductor had not come to her side, she thought she would have stayed there for ever. He led her to the front of the stage to take her bow. She tried to look up at the circle but her eyes were brimming and she could see nothing but the haloes round the stage lamps.

The applause went on and on. The audience, most of whom had taken out their subscription to the Midsummer Concert simply because of its prominence on the social calendar, had not expected to hear such excellent playing from two students. And to see the mystery girl who had taken Society by storm appear on stage was an added bonus.

It seemed as though the applause would never stop. At last she turned to the wings and called Gilles on to the stage. He tuned his violin, the conductor tapped his baton on his desk, and they played the little duet they had planned for their encore. When the applause continued, Madame Giotto joined them and they accompanied her rendition of a simple Italian ballad that had been all the rage that year.

And then, as they took their last bow together Melisande saw Karoly and Tadeusz coming down the aisle with bouquets in their arms. Oh heavens, she thought. Whose idea was this? Will they know what to do? How to behave? She glanced up at the balcony where she had first seen Tadeusz and her heart skipped a beat as she saw Adam looking down, straight into her eyes. Then she had to turn away as Karoly bowed over her hand and laid the bouquet in her arms and when she looked up again Adam was gone.

In the little room behind the stage George and Beatrice were waiting for her with Gilles and his parents.

'You must be exhausted!' exclaimed Beatrice with ready sympathy. 'All those encores!'

'Exhausted? Me?' Mel laughed exuberantly as Gilles's father handed her a brimming glass of champagne. 'I could run a race, fight an army!' she exclaimed.

'I don't think we need champagne,' grinned Gilles, putting his arm around her shoulder. 'We're drunk already – on applause! And imagine – Emil Paur wants us to repeat the concert with him and Madame Giotto! In New York!'

When they returned to the little villa on Hamilton, they were rather taken aback by the number of people in Amy's drawing room. Most of them claimed to have called in on the way back from the concert to bring Beatrice good wishes for the morrow, but she told Amy she was under no illusion. 'They are all here to have another look at Mel!'

She was passed from one to another, to receive congratulations and exclamations over her hidden talents. The few impertinent questions were parried by Amy or Tom. Behind her she heard someone say: 'My dear, she's engaged to young Trensham. I had it from his mother.'

'Nonsense. You saw her with de Villeneuve. There's a match if ever there was one.'

'Take no notice, my dear,' said Mrs Rosenberg, patting her on the arm as she flushed. 'Always they sharpen their tongues on someone. I must tell you how much I enjoyed the concert this evening. And the Rabbi too.'

'Rabbi Benjamin? He was there?' She glowed with pleasure.

'Imagine – the Rabbi in my box!' She shook her head, grey curls shaking loose from her elaborate coiffure. 'The times I've tried to interest him in a charity function! 'Put the cost of my dinner in the poor box,' he says. And then yesterday he tells me, Mrs Rosenberg, he says, there's an exception to any rule and if you were to invite me to join you at the Midsummer Concert, I'd be grateful.' She nodded over Mel's shoulder. 'And here's that nice young doctor come to bring you a drink. No one deserves it better.'

She turned to find Adam standing at her elbow with a glass of champagne.

'It is a long time since I enjoyed a concert so much, Miss Voronzhey,' he said, bowing formally over her hand as Mrs Rosenberg moved on to the next knot of people.

'I didn't think you would come,' she blurted out before she could stop herself.

He raised his eyebrows. 'I wouldn't have missed it for anything,' he said frankly. 'Nor would your youthful admirers.'

'So you brought them!' she exclaimed. 'Tadeusz and Agnete and Karoly . . .'

'And Tadeusz's parents. And Mrs Lenkowa and a few of your other helpers. And Anna and Helga and Feodor.'

'Heavens! How did you manage to keep them quiet?'

441

'It wasn't too difficult. They were a little overawed by the occasion at first and I told them all to watch me and applaud when I did. The only difficulty was when I wanted two boys to present the bouquets. They all wanted to volunteer. We drew short straws in the end – but some of the language!' He leaned towards her and spoke softly in her ear. 'I haven't heard anything so bad since a maid I once had: her vocabulary was even wider – not that she knew what any of it meant, of course!'

She blushed, tinglingly aware of the sound of his voice and the fresh smell of him, and the effect that he had on her.

'Adam! What are you saying to make Miss Voronzhey blush so!' Amelia tucked her hand into her arm. 'There's someone who'd like to meet you, Mel. You mustn't monopolise her, Adam,' she said over her shoulder. 'After all, you will have her at Springs House for the summer.'

'I can't!' she whispered hoarsely. Summer at Springs House! Summer parties, the Harvest Ball – how could she bear it? 'Really, Mrs Kingsley, I – I just couldn't! And I am expected at the Hardings . . .'

'Mrs Harding and I have agreed that you should be with us for your coming of age.'

'I know you mean to be kind, but Adam doesn't want me there. Please . . . don't you see? I –'

But Amelia was introducing her to the Spenneys, an elderly couple, and the moment to protest was gone. And so, she saw, looking over the Spenneys' heads, was Adam.

The wedding ceremony was fixed for the afternoon. The Kingsleys were staying at George's house and the two parties did not plan to meet until they reached the church.

'I may not be a blushing maid,' said Beatrice with a self-deprecating smile, 'but I still hold to the old customs, and I don't plan to tempt fate!'

Tom, as the oldest male in the family, had offered to stand as bride's sponsor and give his mother-in-law away, a prospect he found richly humorous and joked about all day. As the time approached, there was a great deal of hurrying and scurrying and worrying. The dressmaker came to oversee the dressing, the florist arranged the bouquets of roses and lilies and they were almost ready in time.

Radiant in a robe of amber silk which brought a delightful bloom to her cheeks, the bride set off in the first carriage with Tom, followed by the two matrons of honour and the bridesmaid.

George's customary air of command had deserted him in his hour of need. By the time James Kingsley had found the groom's hat for the fourth time, discovered his kid gloves on the hall table and his buttonhole in the dining room, he had decided to set off directly for the church before the groom lost his nerve entirely. Now, as George glanced anxiously over his shoulder for the sixth time, he was not so convinced of the wisdom of the action.

'Are you sure you have the ring, James?' he demanded.

'In my waistcoat pocket,' said his friend patiently. He gave his friend an encouraging grin and his eyes widened. 'George, for Heaven's sake!' he exclaimed. 'You've still got your first ring on! Put it on the other hand!'

But the ring had not been moved for years and the congregation was treated to the interesting spectacle of the best man apparently trying to wrench the groom's hand off.

'Whatever are you doing, James?' hissed Amelia. 'Everyone's looking!'

By this time the minister had noticed the confusion and trotted down the altar steps. After a brief conference he hurried them into the vestry, whence they emerged, George breathless but ringless, just as the bridal party arrived at the church porch.

From that moment the ceremony went without a hitch. As Tom handed Beatrice to the front of the altar steps, Mel took her bouquet. She had protested that one of Beatrice's own daughters should perform this service for her, but by tradition it was the role of the bridesmaid, rather than the matrons of honour.

After the blessing was pronounced, Mel took James Kingley's arm and they followed the happy couple into the vestry where they signed the register.

Thirty-six guests sat down to an impressive wedding feast at the Colonel's house, the Bennetts' villa being too small for such numbers to dine and lacking a room suitable for the dancing that was planned for later on. The Colonel had chosen the menu with great care, but Melisande had little appetite and could only toy with her food.

She played her part in the social exchanges, but did so automatically, chatting inconsequentially to Max and John Wintour, one on either side, without really knowing what either she or they were saying. It was almost as if she wasn't really there. She told herself that it was the inevitable reaction to all the recent excitement. Jail, concert, offer of a career and a wedding in the space of a few days was really too much for anyone to cope with. The adulation and attention after the concert had been very enjoyable, she had to admit. Still – she gave herself a mental shake – one could not expect that kind of thing every day.

And if you're this low spirited at a wedding, she berated herself, how ever do you think you are going to cope when you return to the mundane world of Harbourside, Melisande Voronzhey? Pull yourself together!

She looked up to find Adam regarding her gravely from the other side of the table. She dropped her eyes swiftly back to her plate. She didn't see Amelia Kingsley watching Adam watching her.

The champagne flowed freely and by the time they came to the speeches, several of the guests were already quite on the go. As Tom rose to his feet to propose a toast to the newlyweds, several of the gentlemen had to be helped to their feet.

The groom responded with a touchingly gruff little speech. 'I intend to make my dear wife as happy as is possible for one as set in his ways as I am,' he said, smiling fondly at Beatrice. 'And since I have acquired a ready-made family in Bella and Amy and their husbands, and Melisande, I rather think there will be plenty of people around to make sure that I do.' With that he proposed a toast to the bridesmaid and matrons and gratefully subsided.

The double doors that divided the saloon from the drawing room were flung open after the wedding feast for an informal ball. Mel was a little flustered to discover that she was expected to partner James Kingsley opening the dancing.

'But of course, my dear,' said Amelia. 'The bride and groom, the best man and the bridesmaid.'

'You're a joy to dance with,' said Adam's father as he whirled her off the floor at the end of the dance, almost into the arms of Adam and Amelia who were standing side by side. 'It must be the musical training that has given you such an excellent sense of rhythm. But you should be dancing with someone younger and a little more energetic than I,' he said with a smile, looking deliberately at Adam, who frowned but said nothing.

Mel had not eaten much, but she had drunk all the toasts. The wine had completely gone to her head, otherwise she might have had the sense to keep quiet.

'You are mistaken, sir,' she said in an icy voice. 'It is infinitely more pleasurable to dance with you than with a younger man who does nothing but scowl at one.'

Adam's eyes narrowed angrily. 'Very well,' he said through gritted teeth. 'If that's what you all want . . .'

As the music started up again he grabbed Melisande roughly by the wrist and pulled her towards him, and his arm grasped her slender waist like a vice, crushing her body against his in a manner that caused eyes to widen and tongues to start wagging. Sweeping on to the floor, his eyes glittering with suppressed fury, he whirled her into the dance.

'James, that was not well done!' Amelia laid her hand on his arm. 'He was trying so hard not to look at her.'

'Oh, dammit, Amelia,' he said wryly. 'I would so like him to be happy – and he's making such a mull of it! Why must he be so stiff-necked and proud?'

'Because he's his father's son,' came the soft reply.

For Melisande the dance was taking on all the qualities of a nightmare. She could not bring herself to look at Adam, but she could feel his burning gaze on her as he whirled her dizzyingly around the floor. If he did not slow down, she was going to fall, she was sure of it. All that champagne had gone straight to her head and the room was spinning round madly, the music and the voices funnelling into a maelstrom of noise. Although his grip was painful, it was all that was keeping her upright.

At last she risked a glance up at him through her lashes. He was looking down at her, a white line around his mouth and his eyes hard and glittering; the surge of emotion that washed

445

over her as their eyes met was the last straw. She began to tremble. She was sure she was about to faint.

She missed a step and he tightened his grip.

She winced. 'You are hurting my arm, Doctor Kingsley,' she gasped, enunciating the words with difficulty.

'You wanted to hurl yourself into my arms,' he ground out. 'Now you will just have to put up with it! Not quite what you expected, is it?'

'I wanted to –? I would not have approached you for the world!' she protested furiously. 'It was your father who –'

'Oh, you have twisted him around your little finger, have you not?' he snarled, seeking in his pain for the most hurtful words to say to her. 'You need not think you can do the same to me!'

'I did not twist anyone –'

'Oh, no? You twisted him the way you twisted them all. Max, Clive Trensham, de Villeneuve. A whole chain of conquests who –'

It was too much. With a sudden movement she succeeded in pulling away from him. 'I think you have said enough, Doctor Kingsley,' she said in a low, vibrant voice. 'I will relieve you of the burden of my presence.'

She turned and rushed upstairs, leaving him white with fury on the edge of the dance.

Everyone tried to carry on as though nothing had happened, but as Beatrice said with a sigh, they'd provided enough to keep the gossips in clover for the rest of the summer.

Adam turned his back on the dancing, doing his duty instead by a number of elderly ladies who were sufficiently deaf or short-sighted not to know what was going on. He kept half an eye on the stairs, but Mel did not come down again until it was time for Beatrice and George to leave.

'Be good for James and Amelia,' Beatrice said as she gave Mel a quick hug. 'It won't be for long. Try not to quarrel with –'

'Quarrel?' she said in a brittle voice. 'I assure you I have far better things to do.' She forced a smile to her face. 'Stop fretting, Aunt Beatrice. I'll behave myself, I promise. Off you go now or you'll miss your train. Uncle George is beginning to look harassed. That's the third time he's had his watch out!'

The bride and groom descended the steps to the waiting carriage, the guests throwing handfuls of rice and orange blossom petals over them. As George handed his bride proudly into the carriage, she turned on the step and tossed her bouquet straight into Melisande's arms.

Everyone was quite understanding when Mel fled in tears: George and Beatrice gone, Amy and Tom off to Albany tomorrow with John and Bella, the strain of the concert. . . . Everyone was very understanding, but Amelia had seen the raw emotion in her face as she turned away.

She found her eventually in Beatrice's dressing room, standing in front of the dressing table and trying, without much success, to repair the ravages with a lace edged handkerchief.

'So silly,' she sniffed. 'They'll be back soon. And they are so happy . . .' Her voice trailed away as she struggled frantically to tuck in the stray ends of her wayward hair.

'But it isn't Beatrice and George, is it?' said Mrs Kingsley quietly.

Melisande's hands froze.

'It's Adam who has driven you up here in such disarray.'

Melisande lost herself in a sea of denials and retractions, none of which impressed Amelia in the least.

'I have been watching you for some time,' she went on calmly. 'And all this talk of Mr Trensham or young Gilles is as much hot air as talk of Adam and Sophia Patterson. He doesn't love her any more than you love either of them. You love Adam, do you not?'

'Even if I did,' she said miserably, 'he does not love me. At least . . . I don't know who he loves . . . or if he loves anyone. I thought once – but that was when – when I was just a nameless orphan.' She forced a watery smile. 'Imagine: a respected doctor and a nameless waif. And that was before I knew who he really was – who his family were. Once I met you and the Duke and realised . . . I knew then there was no hope. I thought I had resigned myself to it. Then the letters . . . I wasn't nameless any more. I was someone! But he still doesn't want me. I'm still not good enough.' She rubbed her eyes, oblivious to their redness.

447

'But in spite of it all, you still love him?'

'I have tried so hard not to,' she said brokenly. 'But – I can't help it. I even told him it – it didn't matter if he couldn't marry me.' The handkerchief tore as she twisted it in agitation.

'Child, you didn't!' said Amelia in great distress.

'I've shocked you,' she whispered. 'Hardly surprising. I – I rather shocked myself.'

'My dear!' Amelia drew her across to the chaise longue. 'I want you to listen carefully to me. There is something very important that I have to tell you.' She looked at Melisande. 'Are you listening?'

Melisande looked up at her, her green eyes wide and glistening with tears. She nodded.

'Adam is not my son. I wish he were, for I love him as my own.'

Mel's jaw dropped.

'James and I have never been able to have any children of our own.'

'Then he – the Duke – he was married before?' said Mel, finding her tongue at last.

'It's not as simple as that.' Amelia took a deep breath and seemed to brace herself. 'My father was a very selfish man,' she began, 'and although I had been engaged to James for almost a year when my mother died, Father kept finding reasons to put off the wedding. First there was the year's mourning, then he needed me to look after him and the house. I was very biddable then.' Her eyes clouded and she seemed to be looking back into the past, seeing the young girl she had been. 'James loved me and I loved him, but I was too young to see what the delay was doing to us. He - he went to stay with friends in Scotland, and then one day he arrived at our house and insisted we set a date there and then. Which we did. I did not know then the reason. Later he told me that while he was in Scotland, being young and frustrated with the long engagement, he became –' she bit her lip – 'he became involved with a young lady. It was the realisation of the damage the waiting was doing to us that made him insist we delay no longer.'

She paused, Melisande held her breath, waiting to hear the rest of the tale.

'For seven years we were very happy together, then one day a letter came from out of the blue. The young lady, from whom he had heard nothing since the visit to Scotland, wrote. There was a child, a son.'

'Adam?'

'Yes. There was no doubt he was James's son. He was devastated that she had never told him. But now she wished to marry, and the prospective husband did not want Adam.' She sighed. 'James took his responsibilities very seriously and eventually Adam made his home with.us. I – I loved him from the time we met. He was such a sunny natured child, so full of fun, but gradually, inevitably, the realities of the situation came home to him. People can be so cruel.' She bit her lip. 'I wanted to adopt him; sadly his mother would never consent. But to me he is the son I never had – and that is why I hate to see him so unhappy. You understand now, my dear, it is his birth which is the obstacle, not yours.'

'But he would have married Sophia Patterson –'

'I take leave to doubt that. If that had been serious, he could have married her any time these last two years. But he didn't, did he?'

'No. But he didn't want me either,' she said in a small voice.

'I think he felt he could not offer you a tarnished name.'

'*That* for his tarnished name!' said Mel, snapping her fingers in a most unladylike gesture.

The small gilt clock on the mantelpiece struck the hour. 'I shall have to go and make my farewells to the guests,' said Amelia. 'Would you like to stay up here until we are ready to leave? I can say you are indisposed.'

'Please. I don't think I can face them all right now.'

'Splash your face with cold water, my dear. Always works.' She turned in the doorway. 'Don't think too badly of James, will you?' she said softly. 'He has tried all his life to make up for the one mistake of his youth. And it is not all to be placed to his account: Adam's mother and my father and I, we all played our parts.'

'How could I blame him?' she asked simply. 'I would have behaved the same way if Adam had not been stronger than me.'

The guests were thinning out and Amelia was kept busy for a while helping Amy with her duties as hostess.

James Kingsley appeared at her side and she tucked her arm in his, smiling tenderly up at him.

'You told her?' he asked anxiously.

'Yes. Now for the next step.' She scanned the room for Adam and found him by the French windows that led on to the piazza, talking to Harriet Minton. 'I feel like a general planning a campaign!' she said with a conspiratorial smile.

She crossed the room to talk to them. 'It is so warm in here,' she observed after a moment. Her hand went to her wrist. 'Adam,' she said artlessly, 'I have left my fan upstairs in Beatrice's dressing room. My reticule too.'

'You must have them now?' he said, a trifle ungraciously.

'If it isn't too much trouble?'

He recollected himself. 'No trouble at all, Amelia.'

He ran lightly up the stairs and opened the door of the dressing room, running his hands through his hair as he surveyed the chaos left by the departing bride. The connecting door opened and Melisande stood in the doorway, silhouetted against the light in the inner room.

'I beg your pardon,' he said stiffly. 'Amelia said she left her fan and reticule here.'

'Oh.'

'But I can't see them.'

'No.' She stepped through the doorway and when he saw her pale, tear-streaked face, it took all his resolution not to cross to her side.

'Adam . . .'

'Yes?' His voice was taut.

'I – Amelia was talking to me.'

'Was she?' He tried to keep his voice casual, but his eyes seemed to burn into her.

'SShe told me . . .' Lord, this was difficult. And he was not making matters any easier, standing there staring at her. 'She told me about your father – and your mother.' There, it was said!

He turned sharply away from her. 'She should not have done that!'

'I'm glad that she did.' Melisande moved round the room until she could see his face once more. 'Because –' Could she say it? She *had* to say it. 'I'm glad there was some other reason

450

– however foolish – why you thought you could not marry me. It wasn't just that you – didn't love me.'

'It isn't a foolish reason!' Again he turned away, his face in shadow. 'You have your name now. Your honourable name. Why should you want to change it for my tarnished one?'

'Because I love you.'

'But I'm a bastard.' His back stiffened. 'You made your contempt for bastards clear enough.'

'What?'

'At the interview,' he said, turning to her, eyes as hard as flint. 'You pointed out that not everyone in an Orphanage was a *bastard.*' He deliberately emphasised the word.

'Adam, I never meant . . . Don't you see? It makes no difference to me who is or who isn't. I was just hanging on to my one shred of certainty about myself, that's all. But it's not important.' She moved closer to him. 'Remember, Adam, it was you who taught me that what matters is what you do with your life, not who your parents are, or were.' She swallowed hard. 'To me you're Adam Kingsley, a fine man who cares about others less fortunate than himself. Don't care for them and not care for me, Adam,' she pleaded in a broken voice. 'I need your care too. Please don't shut me out again. I don't think I can bear it.'

He turned to face her, holding himself from her with an effort.

'I never wanted to shut you out,' he said, and it was as if the words were wrenched out of him. 'But – well, that's in the past, isn't it? Everything's going to change now. You'll be going to New York with Paur and –' He shrugged and turned away to the window. 'My life's not my own, Mel,' he said, his voice cracking. 'I have so many ties here and –'

'– and you can't leave Edensville.' She chuckled. 'Adam, I never thought you would!'

He turned back to her sharply. 'Then, how?' he said with a frown.

She rose and crossed to his side. She wanted to reach out and touch him, and wound her fingers in the folds of her dress to stop herself. 'I've no desire to live in New York, Adam,' she said. 'Like you, I've got ties here. Even if –' She blinked rapidly. 'Even if you don't want me, Adam, I wouldn't turn

451

my back on the school, the children. And all my friends are here. I've already told Emil Paur that. I'm meeting him tomorrow and we're going to plan our concerts, some here, some in Albany and some in New York. I'm very excited about it all. Especially the visit to New York. But it *will* only be a visit – Edensville is where I shall come back to.' She lifted her head and looked into his hard grey eyes. 'Or Eden Springs,' she whispered. 'I'd like that even better.'

'Think hard before you commit yourself, Mel,' he said huskily. 'It's not just for now – think what will happen when my father dies: all the gossip, everyone wondering why I don't inherit the title. And if eventually you wanted children – it might matter to them.'

'No.' She smiled. 'They would see it as I do – an irrelevance to our life here in America.' She stepped forward until she was only inches from him. 'They would see only what I see – that I love you.'

His hand came up to wipe away the teardrops sparkling on her eyelashes. He ran his hand slowly down her face and looked at her for a long moment. Then his iron control cracked and he swept her into his arms, crushing her close to him; he bent his head to hers and their lips met with all the pent-up and frustrated passion of the past year.

Her soft mouth parted and he kissed her eagerly, his fingers caressing the bare skin of her shoulders and arousing the most delicious sensations in her. She returned his fierce embrace and as she put her arms round him, her hands slipped beneath his jacket and he groaned against her mouth as she ran her fingers down his back. Before she was well aware that they had moved, they were both lying on the chaise longue.

He felt they could lie there forever, exploring one another, but when, after a moment, they parted, gasping for breath, he became aware that she was no longer relaxed in his embrace.

'Mel?' he said softly. 'What is it?' He dropped his hands from her shoulders. 'Mel? I didn't mean to frighten you,' he said anxiously. 'It's all right,' he reassured her, forcing himself to draw away from her. 'I've no more desire than you to go too far: the last thing in the world I want . . .'

'Adam, it isn't that,' she said breathlessly.

'We'll go up to Niagara tomorrow and tell George and Beatrice, get their permission,' he reassured her.

'Adam, stop!' she said, pressing her hand over his mouth. 'It isn't that. I – It's just that – are you quite sure, Adam? I don't want you to feel I've forced you to –'

He took her hand in his and drew it down. 'I've no objection whatsoever to you forcing me to do anything,' he said with a grin. 'It isn't many men who have the felicity of a proposal from the woman they love.'

'You didn't think very highly of my first proposal,' she objected.

'I think you got the two proposals in the wrong order,' he said wryly. 'You'll understand I'm a little sensitive on that point.'

'You are sure?'

He loosened his cravat. 'If I haven't convinced you yet that I love you,' he said, his voice thick with longing, 'that I've loved you for longer than you can imagine, then I'm just going to have to convince you a little harder.'

His arms tightened around her waist and as his lips moved over the soft skin below her ear, scattering kisses on her throat and her bare shoulders, Melisande cast all doubts to the wind and gave herself up to the delicious sensations his mouth was arousing in her.

He had no idea how much time had passed since he had come upstairs. They seemed to have been on the chaise longue for ever – and yet not long enough. His shirt tail had slipped out of his cummerbund and the feel of her urgent body beneath his and her hands on his bare skin was more than he could handle. With a stifled groan he drew reluctantly away from her.

'You realise that you are taking unfair advantage of me?' he said huskily when he was at a safe distance from her.

'Advantage?' She sat up reluctantly, a dreamy expression on her face.

His lips twitched. 'I don't forget that you've seen me stripped of all the appurtenances of civilisation,' he chuckled. 'Whereas I –'

'Ohh!' she exclaimed, her face flushing up to her ears. 'How could you remind me of that! I don't think I have ever been so embarrassed . . .'

'It gets that out of the way, doesn't it?' he said. 'Next time won't be so bad. Unless I take on a fit of the vapours at the sight of *you*,' he teased. Then the laughter died out of his face. 'Mel, I meant what I said about Niagara,' he said, taking her hand in his. 'I can't wait much longer.'

'Nor I,' she said, slightly shocked at her own boldness. 'You know, Mrs Chobley was right,' she mused.

'What?' He looked at her in some amusement. 'I don't at all see where Mrs Chobley comes into this!'

'She said I'd understand it all 'when I had my own feller'. And she's right. I do.'

'Oh, Mel, my darling! I'm going to have to kiss you again!'

He was half kneeling on the floor, half pressed against her; she had forgotten everything else; she was drowning in the sensations that washed over her at his touch. And then the door opened.

'I wonder what Adam did with my bag?' said Amelia, then her voice trailed away as she saw the couple entwined on the chaise longue.

'Ah! Amelia!' Adam's voice came out in a strangled croak as he rose hastily. 'I – er – I didn't do anything with your bag. I never did find it. I was – ah – distracted.' He tried heroically not to look at Melisande, but when a stifled giggle came from the sofa, he blushed and ran his fingers through his hair.

Amelia looked fondly at the two of them. 'May I take it that all is now settled between you?' she asked. 'All the nonsense to be forgotten?'

'Yes,' he said, reaching out his hand to Melisande.

'You have asked her to marry you at last?' demanded James.

'Not exactly, Father,' said Adam. 'Mel asked me first!'

'Good heavens!' said Adam's father, his eyebrows disappearing into the lock of hair that flopped over his forehead. 'Mel asked you? Well! But – so long as you've sorted it out at last, I'm happy for both of you.'

'I'm sure you have a great deal of wasted time to make up for,' said Amelia saucily. 'Come, James, we shall have to look for my bag another time.'

'What? You mean you actually did leave it up here?' demanded Adam. 'It wasn't just a ploy to throw us together?'

'Oh yes, it's here somewhere,' she said, grinning round the door. 'I always like to do things thoroughly.'

'Amazing woman!' said Adam as the door closed behind them. Then his smile changed and a new, more disturbing light came into his grey eyes. 'Mel?'

'Adam?'

'One more kiss, my love – and then I had better take you back to Amy.'

'You are going back to Eden Springs?'

'Only to pack a case,' he said, sweeping her into his arms. 'Then I'm off to find a special licence – and the time of the next train to Niagara.'

You have been reading a novel published by Piatkus Books. We hope you have enjoyed it and that you would like to read more of our titles. Please ask for them in your local library or bookshop.

If you would like to be put on our mailing list to receive details of new publications, please send a large stamped addressed envelope (UK only) to:

Piatkus Books: 5 Windmill Street
London W1P 1HF

PIATKUS

The sign of a good book